THE
Amorous
Adventures
OF CHARLIE
MEYER

ALSO BY
ARTHUR D. HITTNER

FICTION

Artist, Soldier, Lover, Muse

Four-Finger Singer and His Late Wife, Kate

The Caroline Paintings

NON-FICTION

Honus Wagner:
The Life of Baseball's 'Flying Dutchman'

At the Threshold of Brilliance:
The Brief but Splendid Career of Harold J. Rabinovitz

Cross-Country Chronicles:
Road Trips Through the Art and Soul of America

THE Amorous Adventures OF CHARLIE MEYER

A Novel of the Sixties

ARTHUR D. HITTNER

Apple Ridge Press
Oro Valley, AZ

ISBN 978-0-9989810-8-6 (epub)
ISBN 978-0-9989810-9-3 (print)

Cover Design by Pure Fusion Media
Formatting by Polgarus Studio

Preface

I, like all baby boomers, grew up in a less enlightened age—socially, that is. It was an age of all-male colleges, frat boy pranks, and homophobia. Feminism, the coltish ancestor of the #MeToo movement, was beginning to have an impact, but had miles to go. It was the age of Vietnam: an era of political awareness, student empowerment, and the quest for personal enlightenment (albeit frequently pharmaceutically induced).

Like the protagonist you're about to meet, I attended a public high school in suburban New Jersey and a college on a New Hampshire hill. Some of the events described in this novel were loosely—and I emphasize *loosely*—inspired by true events (truth is always stranger than fiction, though in today's world we struggle to distinguish the two) and take place in similar settings. While the narrator of this rambunctious saga isn't me, I (and most of my peers, if they're honest) shared his anxieties, insecurities, and cluelessness about the world we were poised to enter.

This was the first novel I wrote. While three have been published since, I struggled mightily to decide if this should belatedly join them. Not because it's not as good (I'll let you be the judge of that), but because it's the story of a naïve, kindhearted, sophomoric college kid obsessed with sex and blindsided by love. It'll embarrass my children and grandchildren, but it is who we were.

A note to sharp-eyed readers of my other novels: you'll find some familiar scenes and settings (in particular, Chapters Sixty-Six and Sixty-Seven appear in highly modified form in my last novel, ***The Caroline Paintings***). Having relegated this novel to my personal literary junkyard, convinced I'd never publish it, I scavenged it for parts. The variances, however, may prove amusing.

You've been forewarned. Enjoy the ride!

To Gary, Larry, Walter and Tim,
for your input, patience and guidance;
to the late Glenn Glesmann
(the real life Blake Benton)
in memory of your friendship
and to Peggy,
for being there, serendipitously, at my own graduation
—and ever since

CHAPTER ONE

Awkward Beginnings

I was six years old, yet I remember it vividly. It was a sweltering afternoon in the summer of '55. Humidity glued my sweaty bottom to the wooden bench of our picnic table like a toasted marshmallow to a graham cracker. I can still hear the clamor of barking dogs, the drone of a neighbor's lawnmower, the rumble of traffic clattering down our busy street. The aroma of freshly cut grass wafted across a backyard littered with the detritus of childhood: a mangled old tricycle, a rusted red fire engine, an abandoned sandbox sprouting foot-tall weeds.

Susie Sadowski sat beside me on that fateful afternoon, clad in a flowered T-shirt and crimson red shorts. Sweet, six and suitably pig-tailed, she was, I suppose, my very first *girl*friend, not that the more consequential distinctions between the sexes were plain to me at the time. But she paid me little heed that day, engrossed instead in the adventures of *Curious George.* With my elbows propped on the table and my head cradled in the sticky palms of my hands, I stared lethargically into space ... until—like a bull in a bullring—my eyes were drawn to those crimson red shorts.

Prodded by the volatile convergence of boredom and curiosity, I casually slipped my little left hand down the front of those crimson red shorts. Susie grunted in mild annoyance, brushing me off with a flick of her wrist like a pesky gnat. Had I stopped there, it might have been nothing more than a harmless childhood gaffe. But I didn't, and with my next foray, all hell broke loose.

Lounging on wicker chairs on the porch above us, our mothers exchanged recipes while sipping cocktails and nibbling Ritz crackers. Neither noticed my initial indiscretion. But my second sortie into Susie's shorts was bolder. Irritated, Susie swatted more vigorously as my hand continued its stubborn descent. And this time, our mothers watched—aghast—from unobstructed, front-row seats.

"Jesus Christ!" shrieked Susie's mom, her face as crimson as her daughter's shorts. She sprung to her feet like a bobcat, sending the platter of crackers crashing to the floor as she turned accusatorially toward my mother. "Your kid's a PERVERT!" Amid the crackle of crunching crackers, Susie's mom bolted from the porch, flinging her chair against the railing as she leapt down the stairs to defend Susie's honor.

"What in God's name are you *doing*, Charlie!" my mother implored, spilling her gin-and-tonic and posing what was, under the circumstances, a perfectly reasonable question.

Alarmed by the panic in our mothers' voices, Susie and I burst into stereophonic sobs. I yanked my wayward hand from Susie's shorts just as her mom prepared to pounce. Susie bounded into her mother's arms, her face etched with terror. I, frightened and dumbfounded, tore away as fast as my little legs would propel me, bawling in bewilderment: "Susie's got no pee-pee! Susie's got no pee-pee!"

And so, with the recognition of certain anatomical disparities between males and females, my sexual education had begun.

Though oblivious to the conventions of social propriety, I was just an ordinary kid growing up in an ordinary neighborhood in mid-century America. I lived with my parents, Richard and Lydia Meyer, in a modest, six-room house in the little bedroom community of New Liberty, one of the freshly-paved, tree-lined townships popping up like acne along the suburban frontier of northern New Jersey.

My parents had served their time in nearby New York City: Dad grew up in a Jewish enclave on Jerome Avenue in the Bronx and Mom hailed from an Italian neighborhood in Brooklyn. They met in Manhattan when Dad had hair.

An accountant by trade and disposition, Dad was short and stocky, endowed with generally unremarkable looks but for a dimpled chin; dark, bushy eyebrows that arched over his muddy brown eyes like a hedgerow; and a prominent nose that hooked downward like a falcon's beak. He audited the books of the fashionable women's clothing store on the Upper East Side where my mother worked as a sales clerk. Though gray-haired and pear-shaped through most of my memory, early photos of my mother reveal a petite and shapely young woman with jet-black hair, ebony eyes, and a pleasing smile. A steamy, whirlwind romance ensued and they married in a hastily conceived Roman Catholic ceremony just four months later. It wasn't the only thing hastily conceived.

I was born on January 5th of 1949, mere weeks after the shotgun wedding. It wasn't until my mid-teens that I did the math, probably because Richard and Lydia assiduously clung to the self-proclaimed myth that they'd married a year earlier. I'd never thought to challenge this presumption. The truth cut me like a buzz saw one afternoon during my high school years when I happened across a crumpled marriage license buried in a dusty box of old family records while scouring the basement for Dad's cleverly concealed cache of *Playboy* magazines. "What the f—?" I blurted out, flaunting my burgeoning vocabulary.

My untimely intrusion into their lives explains a great deal. It explains my maternal grandparents' antipathy toward my father. My mother always referred him by his full given name, Richard. But my grandparents addressed him as "the Dick" (as in "Where's the Dick?") or simply "Dick" (as in "he's a Dick"), with a perverse flourish I'd never previously understood. I mistook it for a term of endearment.

It also explains, perhaps, Dad's ambivalence toward me. The very date of my birth, five days into the new year, was a source of profound irritation. I was two weeks late. Had I arrived on time, I'd have been a lucrative dependent on my parents' 1948 income tax return. For Dad, squandering a deduction was the fiscal equivalent of barfing at a Rotary Club luncheon.

As if to show contempt for their dissipated deduction, my parents saddled me with the moniker Charles Ulysses Meyer. Nothing wrong with Charles, or "Charlie" for short—but *Ulysses*? It was a byproduct, I suspect, of Dad's penchant for racy literature; had I been female, I'd have probably been Candy or Lolita. And Richard clearly gave no thought to the nasty acronym derived from my initials: CUM. This inconveniently overlooked detail was a source of some embarrassment early in my life; it also explained why I never had anything monogrammed later.

Dad ran the family like an impetuous dictator: quick on the draw but lax on the forethought. If the numbers crunched, he plowed ahead. It didn't take him long, for example, to commit to purchasing the home my family would occupy for the next fifty years. I can imagine the scenario:

"It's the perfect house," he'd have declared to my mother upon entering the foyer of the tiny, brand-new split-level on a quiet dirt road in the middle of New Liberty. *Perfect, perhaps, for a family of midgets.* Aware that the town taxed homeowners on the basis of square footage, Richard decided that extra space would simply enrich the town's coffers to the detriment of his own. So the house he chose was as snug as an A-cup bra on a DD bust. To my mother's dismay, the kitchen was spartan. "Where's the dishwasher?" she might have inquired. "I'm looking at her," Dad would have countered with a withering look calculated to end the discussion. "We'll get a fucking mortgage and buy the goddamn house," he'd have announced with his trademark vulgarity.

But for the Great Crotch Incident with Susie Sadowski, my childhood was relatively uneventful. The only exception was an encounter with an unleashed Rottweiler (or was it a Chihuahua?) as I skipped home from school like Little Red Riding Hood on a cold winter day. An extremely small child, it wouldn't have taken a very large dog to frighten the piss out of me. And it did. The trickle of tears that rolled down my cheeks was a prelude to the river of warm liquid descending my pant leg as I stood there frozen with fear. The dog barked and lunged at me, tugging the mitten from my right hand and prancing away haughtily like the class bully with his victim's lunch. My response was clever: "WAAAAAAAAH! WAAAAAAAAH!" Although my aversion to dogs continues, my bladder control has improved.

At the age of nine or ten, my mother dragged me, kicking and screaming, to Sunday school at the local Presbyterian church. "Why me?" I cried, dressed in an itchy pair of wool pants I'd long ago outgrown, and a sky blue woolen sport jacket with yellow pinstripes and one-inch lapels. Each step I took in those impossibly tight pants brought me one step closer to castration. I looked like a scrawny blue goat with a clip-on bow tie. "Why doesn't Dad have to go?" I asked my mother in a voice an octave above my then-prevailing soprano.

"Your father's busy," she lied. In fact, the foray into religion represented an awkward and ill-fated compromise. My mother, a non-practicing Catholic, believed that I warranted a spiritual education, while my father, a Jew-in-name-only, proclaimed all organized religion "a crock of shit."

The religious classes were a disaster. According to the pastor, acknowledging that non-believers would rot in hell was a corollary of one's acceptance of the tenets of the faith. When I returned from one of the pastor's lectures and confronted my father with his hellish fate, he turned beet red and erupted at my mother:

"What's this crap you're feeding my son, Lydia? I'LL PUT A SHOVEL UP THAT DAMN PASTOR'S ASS IF HE LAYS ANY MORE OF THAT FUCKING GARBAGE ON MY FUCKING KID!" Dad then launched into what would become a familiar diatribe on religious bullshit while my mother burst into tears. The experiment in religion was over.

My tenure as the exclusive apple of my mother's eye (and bane of my father's existence) ended with the arrival of my brother, Herman Arthur Meyer (whose initials spelling "HAM" were only slightly more felicitous than my own), in December of 1953, when I was almost five. As Mom cradled our new addition like a Fabergé egg, I glared at him with the disdain of a rejected suitor.

My infantile jealousy quickly evolved into juvenile cruelty. Paying forward, perhaps, Dad's lack of affection, I was never shy in exploiting Hermie's gullibility. When he was three (and I, about eight), I'd lure him downstairs to the large utility sink into which the washing machine drained. When the rinse cycle reached its peak, the torture began.

"Hermie," I'd say, "I'm gonna throw you down the drain!" The implausibility of his chubby toddler-body passing through a two-inch drain never occurred to him.

"No, Charlie, *please don't!*" he'd screech, his eyes brimming with tears. And then the dam would break: "WAAAAAAAAH! WAAAAAAAAH!"

My sniveling brother would seek respite from Mom, who'd dutifully report me to Dad. In the beginning, my taunting would earn me a half-hearted whack or two, but over time I suspect that Hermie's continuing gullibility annoyed my father even more than my cruelty.

I was about nine when I first became aware of the misfortune of my initials. Fat Freddie Halloran, a supremely slovenly schoolmate with a beer-drinker's gut, a twisted mind, and a precociousness in sexual matters bordering on deviance, arrived at the clever conclusion that my initials formed a slang word referring to a white, sticky substance emanating from the penis during sex. Eons behind in my own sexual education, I was blind to his prurient delight. Seeking wisdom, I foolishly referred the matter to my father.

"Dad," I asked meekly, "what's cum?"

"*What* did you say?" he muttered, recoiling as if sucker-punched.

"Fat Freddie was teasing me at school. Said my initials spell a dirty word," I said with angelic innocence. I suspect it was also a revelation to my father.

"Uh, well . . ." Dad sputtered. "Cum is something that comes out of your penis sometimes when you're older." Brilliant explanation.

"You mean like pee?"

"Lydia, is dinner ready yet?"

That truncated discussion prompted the next day's fiasco. I still played occasionally with Susie, the unfortunate victim of the Great Crotch Incident three years earlier. Believing that I'd advanced my understanding of the riddles of the penis, I asked Susie's mother if I might cum in her toilet. This was only moments after informing little Susie that I had to go so badly I was about to cum in my pants. Susie's mom was livid.

"Get the hell out of my house!" she screamed, dragging me out the back door by my collar as I struggled to comprehend the nature of my infraction. I never saw Susie again.

My naïveté was put to the test once more a year or so later by our regular babysitter. Betty was a tall, voluptuous sixteen-year-old with a boyfriend named Carl. I suspected that Betty was at least a nine on the ten-scale for hot teenage girls, and I found myself increasingly fascinated by such things. My parents forbade visits by boyfriends during Betty's babysitting sessions. On more than one occasion, however, I could've sworn I'd heard Carl's voice in the living room while I lay in bed. I said nothing to my parents, fearful they'd dismiss Betty, saddling Hermie and me with a mustachioed old battle-axe in her stead.

One night when my parents were out, I heard heavy breathing and rhythmic moaning emanating from the living room. There was also that disquieting sound (*thwack!*) of sweaty flesh as it peeled itself repeatedly from the surface of the clear plastic slipcovers which enveloped our living room furniture. I arose from my bed and crept to the top of the stairs to investigate.

I gasped as I glimpsed Carl on the couch, bare-assed on top of Betty, plugging our stark-naked babysitter relentlessly from behind with his erect and seemingly gargantuan penis.

"Aaahhh, aaahhh, AAAHHH!" sweaty Betty panted as she blissfully absorbed his rapid thrusts, her arms and legs sticking to the couch like bubble gum to the sole of a shoe.

"*Thwack! Thwack!*" the couch squealed as the couple wriggled in unison over its indestructible plastic surface.

While relieved that my gasp was insufficiently audible to alert the writhing couple to my presence, I was bewildered by what I'd witnessed. Carl's creative use of his penis was a new concept to me, and Betty's apparent pleasure in being pounded so indefatigably was mystifying.

Though my head was throbbing as I tried to make sense of what I'd seen, I crept quietly back to bed. For months—maybe even years—the revelations of those few moments stuck in my mind as firmly as Carl's penis in Betty's behind.

CHAPTER TWO

The Great Guy-Wire Incident

In addition to my enduring mental images of Sweaty Betty's Big Bang, I was obsessed in those early years with anything and everything relating to baseball.

My father's Bronx heritage connected us both to his boyhood team, the New York Yankees. By the time I was six, I'd spent hours camped in front of our cranky DuMont television, peering at the grainy black-and-white Yankee telecasts that flickered across its meager fifteen-inch screen. I was charmed by the mellifluous voice of Mel Allen, the Yankees' genteel announcer, whose colorful descriptions of the heroic feats of Yogi and the Mick were legendary. "That ball is going, going, gone! How about that!" he'd declare in his trademark Alabama drawl. Had Dad approved, I'd have gulped a six-pack of the golden-hued Ballantine Ale that Mel promoted so vigorously during each broadcast. *There's a game today, they're set to play and when you hear the umpire say "Play Ball!"... you know it's time for ... baseball and Ballantine, baseball and Ballantine ...* Whatever the reason, the game of baseball grabbed me by the balls, both figuratively and literally (as will soon become apparent), and never let go.

I was ten years old in the summer of '59 when Dad sponsored my first Little League team, naming it for his accounting firm, Meyer & Company. Seeking a team nickname suitably consistent with the community's colonial pretensions, he anointed us the "Town Criers." It was yet another example of my father's penchant for acting first and thinking later. The moniker was contracted by our mocking opponents to the "Meyer's Criers," a woefully embarrassing name for an underachieving collection of immature kids prone to tearful displays of frustration.

The sartorial splendor of the Meyer's Criers left much to be desired. Dad got a bargain on a batch of baseball uniforms. Unfortunately, they were all extra large. Most of us were barely visible under the deluge of fabric. As a consequence, the team more closely resembled a chapter of the Ku Klux Klan than a collection of ballplayers. To make matters worse, every uniform bore the same unlucky "13" on the back.

"How will they tell us apart?" I asked my father.

"What difference does it make," he said. "You all stink."

My teammates were a motley bunch, with more talent for expectoration than for baseball. Our catcher, Fat Freddie Halloran, the juvenile expert in cum, had also managed to perfect the Saliva Spew, a loathsome skill involving the discharge of a colossal flood of saliva over home plate each time he came to bat (he found it too challenging to propel the spit through the iron rungs of his catcher's mask without drenching himself). The Saliva Spew was more than a demonstration of vulgar virtuosity—it was also the team's most productive line of defense. The puddles of noxious fluid at home plate were an effective deterrent to scoring: opposing players were tagged out repeatedly when they refused to slide into the swamp that Fat Freddie had nurtured.

Our opening day starting pitcher was my good friend Nathaniel "Pukey" Greenburg. Pitching made him nauseous. A gangly beanpole of a kid who'd yet to grow into his body, he earned his nickname by projectile vomiting before almost every inning, turning the dugout into a veritable mine field. He walked the first six batters he faced that day before becoming more economical and hitting the next two, necessitating brief delays while the whimpering victims were delicately extricated from the cesspool at home plate. While I, too, failed to distinguish myself that afternoon, I managed some pretty impressive foul tips in the course of three consecutive whiffs. It was the harbinger of a dismal season: the 1959 Meyer's Criers scored five runs—all year—en route to a perfect record of no wins and eighteen defeats.

Parent-organized activities like Little League were the exception rather than the rule. We kids engineered our own activities, established our own rules, and applied them on a commonsense basis with a minimum of rancor.

Stickball, a variant of baseball, was our game of choice. Only two players were necessary, though more could be accommodated as circumstances required. The equipment requirements were minimal: a sawed-off broomstick and a firm, pink rubber ball. The balls we favored were made by Spalding, the sporting goods company, and could be purchased at the local 5- & 10-cents store for about a quarter apiece. Referred to colloquially as "Spaldeens" (with the accent on the second syllable), the balls were hurled by the pitcher to a batter who stood to either side of a strike-zone box inscribed in chalk against a concrete wall.

Our ballparks were makeshift and ground rules were unique to each. We mostly played in a large open space between buildings within an old, dilapidated garden apartment complex a few blocks from home. We dubbed it The

Ghetto. The pitcher's mound was an island of hard, bare ground in a sea of crabgrass punctuated by dandelions. The wall we utilized was the side of a garage.

There's no baserunning in stickball. Anything hit by the batter and caught cleanly by the pitcher (whether on the ground or in the air) was an out. An apartment building formed a natural right and center field barrier while a crumbling garage bounded the field on the left. Balls hitting the sides of the buildings on a fly were doubles; triples if they hit the sagging roof and homers if they cleared it. Broken windows, albeit rare, were the batter's responsibility, though on the occasions they occurred, we fled The Ghetto at the speed of a Sandy Koufax fastball.

Pukey Greenburg and I were frequent combatants at The Ghetto. Once he outgrew his vomiting phase, he matured into a pretty fair athlete. Like virtually everyone my age, Pukey was much bigger than I, but what I lacked in size I made up for with a fierce determination bordering on recklessness. Pukey usually came out on top in our hotly contested ballgames, but I did pull off at least one notable victory—at an enduring cost.

The Ghetto had its idiosyncrasies, the most vexing of which was an exposed guy wire, a taut steel cable running at a forty-five-degree angle from a ground anchor to the telephone pole it helped to support. We each knew full well that the wire was there and routinely managed to avoid it. But one day, with an imaginary runner on third and two outs in the ninth inning in a game I led by one run, Pukey hit a dying quail of a pop-up in the direction of the guy wire. I sprinted after it like a bat out of hell, giving absolutely no thought to my personal welfare. I broadsided the guy wire with my groin as I miraculously snatched the Spaldeen from the air during the last split second of its descent, bouncing off that steel cable as if it were a trampoline and shooting backward with the same force with which I hit it. The high-pitched shriek I emitted was a hybrid between a blood-curdling howl of agony and a roar of victory, for inasmuch as I nearly castrated myself and eliminated generations of future Meyers, *I caught the fucking ball!* This fact was of limited comfort, however, as I doubled over in pain, clutching my wounded crotch like a beloved teddy bear as tears welled in my eyes while Pukey convulsed in hysterical laughter.

For weeks afterward, I monitored my penis daily for signs of atrophy, hoping that the huge red welt would disappear. Though it pulsated for weeks, I was too embarrassed to utter a word to my parents about the incident, though it was all I could do to walk normally. Masturbation was impossible for what seemed like ages. And while the welt eventually disappeared, restoring hopes of the sex life I was just beginning to imagine, my collision with the guy wire would impact me in a highly unusual manner in the years to come. It would be only one in a long line of genital calamities and equipment malfunctions that would befall me on the rocky road to manhood.

CHAPTER THREE

The Romaire Derriere

I entered high school as a puny, timid seventh-grader, like a guppy at SeaWorld. New Liberty had yet to open a middle school, so students were cast from the genial embrace of grade school into the menacing maelstrom of New Liberty High. I was a mere snack to the letter-jacketed jocks roaming its vast, locker-lined hallways like vultures in search of prey.

"Hey fuckface, whatcha doin' in my hallway?" bellowed a senior with arms the size of tree trunks as I scurried to my very first class. As he glared at me with feigned rage, a winsome blonde came to my rescue.

"Leave the little bastard alone, Meat," she said to him with a look of casual annoyance. "It's the kid's first day—give 'im a break!"

The blonde was Rita McCauley, a junior, captain of the cheerleading squad, and the most beautiful girl I'd ever seen outside of a *Playboy* centerfold. I fell instantly in love. She wasn't too tall (I always dismissed tall women, even from my fantasies), had perfectly chiseled (even slightly muscular) legs, a pleasingly narrow waist, and cleavage you could nest in. Most of all, she was down-to-earth *sweet*, unlike the majority of her prickly cheerleading cohorts. I remained infatuated with Rita until, according to rumor, she ran off after graduation to live with some struggling actor in New York City. Though I'd never spoken a single word to her, her brief intercession on my behalf was enough to nurture for years a fantasy world in which, by a myriad of means, I won her over, we married, had four kids, a cat, daily sex, and sixteen grandchildren.

The blow of Rita's departure was softened by the arrival of Miss Jeanine Romaire, a pulchritudinous English teacher of French descent who joined the faculty at the start of my freshman year. I use the adjective *pulchritudinous* for three reasons: first, she included it in her first vocabulary list; second, it means "having great physical beauty"—which describes her precisely; and third, to prove I actually learned something in her class in spite of my endless leering and drooling. Petite, lean, and dark-haired, she favored pencil-thin black skirts and lacy white blouses. Miss Romaire's derriere was like the convergence of two Spaldeens, each firm and perfectly rounded. Few of us could concentrate on anything else.

Though perpetually the focus of male attention, she handled it with aplomb. She was well aware of her effect on immature high school boys. She may have even known of the vulgar suggestions involving her private parts that an anonymous admirer had etched indelibly upon the boys' room wall. Despite it all, Miss Romaire was as cool as Lauren Bacall (*You know how to whistle, don't you? You just put your lips together . . . and blow*).

Her ability to rise above the fray made her a formidable target for "Fast Eddie" Wilson, a fiendishly clever but loutish freshman whose obsession with Miss Romaire's derriere was exceeded only by his compulsion to puncture her legendary cool. His opportunity arose with Shakespeare's *Midsummer Night's Dream*. In Act V, Scene 1, stand-ins for the star-crossed lovers Thisbe and Pyramus converse through a hole in the wall separating the properties of their respective parents who are bitter rivals. Sitting on the edge of her desk, her sleek legs crossed in seeming defiance of the constraints of her impossibly taut skirt, Miss Romaire recited four lines directed by Thisbe to her lover Pyramus:

> *O Wall, full often hast thou heard my moans,*
> *For parting my fair Pyramus and me!*
> *My cherry lips have often kissed thy stones,*
> *Thy stones with lime and hair knit up in thee.*

Whether or not the Bard intended these lines to be sexually suggestive, they aroused Fast Eddie. Encouraged by his equally immature peers, he dared Miss Romaire to expound upon the *moans* and *cherry lips* that *kissed thy stones* with *hair knit up in thee.*

"Your curiosity is commendable," Miss Romaire said with a look of bemusement. She demurely uncrossed her legs, arose from the desk, and sashayed in the direction of her smirking inquisitor. "Give it some of your patented deep thought, Eddie, and prepare me a 500-word essay on the subject for tomorrow's class."

Fast Eddie slumped into his seat like the victim of a shootout in a TV western, pondering whether he had the stones to write an essay on Shakespearean oral sex practices. Then, to the utter delight of the class, the indomitable Miss Romaire threw down the gauntlet—in verse:

> *We'll be able to tell*
> *In those five hundred words*
> *If you're endowed with stones*
> *Or a pair of turds.*

It was turds, apparently, as the essay never materialized. The lascivious lout had indeed lost out to the Great Derriere; there was nary a peep from the juvenile creep for the rest of the year.

By my freshman year, I was—like most other boys my age—obsessed with girls, but with an unfortunate emphasis on the unattainable. That made virtually all of them fodder for fantasy. Few were short enough or sufficiently deranged to harbor an interest in a nerdy pipsqueak like me. My mother bristled at my lack of self-confidence. "You're as cute as a bug, Charlie," she was wont to say, though I hardly thought it qualified as a compliment. Though I was fortunate not to have inherited the hooked nose or hedgerow eyebrows of my father, I did manage to secure his most appealing attribute, a dimpled chin. Too bad it was obscured by a faceful of zits.

Though "attainable" girls sent signals my way, I was impervious to their entreaties. Karen Kaplan was certainly short enough. Four inches shorter than I, she'd also skipped a couple of grades, failed to sprout breasts, and was far more linear than curvaceous. For some reason, Karen fixated on me and sought to make headway. It was like trying to coax a rock to rumba.

"*The Birds* is opening this weekend," she informed me one day as we filed into class.

"Uh huh," I grunted, ignorant of Alfred Hitchcock and indifferent to Karen's apparent fascination with the incipient aviary invasion of the local movie house.

"Wanna go?"

"Nah," I said.

"How about *Come Blow Your Horn* . . . with Frank Sinatra?"

"Hate Sinatra," I said, taking my seat, while she fumed. She pursed her lips, blinked slowly, and stared at me with a mixture of pity and contempt.

"Or maybe the film about you," she said.

"About me?"

"Yeah, *Come Blow it Out Your Ass*, you jerk-off," she said, loud enough for the class to hear, before stalking away in disgust.

Funny thing is that when she matured physically, Karen morphed into a smart, shapely young lady. I would have given my left testicle to take her out in those later years but she, in apparent retaliation for my earlier slights, studiously ignored me.

The advanced academic classes dominating my high school curriculum were populated mostly by Jewish kids, many of whom embraced me as a half-breed or, as Pukey put it, a *half-Hebe* or *semi-Semite*. Those classes were decimated during the Jewish holidays. The only ones attending were me, a Pakistani kid, two Asian girls, and Bertram O'Connor, an Irish kid who figured his presence was the result of a clerical error. I tried to convince my father that I was a half-Jew and, at the very least, should be allowed to take off half of the Jewish holidays.

"You wouldn't know Chanukkah from a yarmulke," he said. "Shut the fuck up and go to school!"

In the spring of freshman year, Pukey goaded me into joining him for freshman baseball tryouts. Against my better judgment, I capitulated. While he became a stalwart, I barely survived the final cut. And while he shagged flies in the outfield, I became intimately acquainted with that splinter-laden slab of pine that served as the dugout bench.

The New Liberty High School athletic teams were known as

the *Labradors*, the *Labs*, or—to the wise guys in school—the *Labia*. At first, I had no idea what that meant. I looked it up in a dictionary. It defined the word by reference to vulvas, which I thought were Swedish cars. I then made the mistake, yet again, of asking my Dad:

"Dad, what's a *labia*?"

"Are you fucking kidding me?"

My first real date came near the end of sophomore year, a double date arranged by Pukey and his girlfriend, Barbara. Barbara's best friend was Sharon Hettleman, a motor-mouthed brunette with ample breasts whom I knew only vaguely. I knew, however, of her tarnished reputation. She was one of those girls reputed to "put out" for guys. While such notoriety was sometimes justified by a preponderance of mean-spirited anecdotal evidence (however circulated), on other occasions it was an undeserved badge of dishonor resulting from a soured relationship or a craven attempt by an insecure male to win peer admiration for his imaginary sexual conquests. But high school kids are rarely discriminating, and I, being a basic jerk, assumed (and embraced) the worst. And worse than that, so did Pukey, whose primary objective was to get me laid.

We met at Wimpy's, a local hamburger joint. It was the kind of place where Richie and Fonzie would shoot the breeze in *Happy Days*. *The House of the Rising Sun* was wailing from the jukebox when we sauntered in. We grabbed a booth against the back wall, under a fading photo of James Dean.

After introductions, the conversation turned quickly to varsity sports. Naturally, Pukey's baseball exploits received the lion's share of the attention. When Sharon asked, I conceded I'd been on the team. But I cringed when Pukey made an oblique reference to the "unfortunate injury" that ended my career.

"God, Charlie, what happened?" she asked, chomping on her bacon double cheeseburger like a beaver gnawing a log. Her voice had the cadence of a machine gun volley. Before I could deflect the question, Pukey launched into an unflattering narrative of my most distressing baseball misadventure since the Great Guy-Wire Incident.

"Well," he began with a mischievous grin, "the half-Hebe was knocked senseless by the cup in Tank's jockstrap." He burst into delirious laughter.

"Seriously?" asked Sharon, nibbling on a french fry, while I blushed in anticipation of my inevitable humiliation.

"I'm not shitting you!" Pukey said. "Coach makes the little runt play third base ... and when some buttface hits a towering pop-up between home and first, Charlie and Tank collide," he said, chortling, his account peppered with raucous slurps from his king-sized chocolate shake. Tank was the nickname of Jason Tarver, a six-foot-four-inch senior catcher who was built like a tank and doubly dangerous when clad in heavy catcher's gear (which included, of course, a protective cup constructed of rock-hard plastic). "Charlie face-butts Tank's cup, knocking Charlie on his fuckin' ass, while Tank catches the pop-up like Charlie's invisible."

I kicked Pukey under the table as everyone broke into laughter. The story was true. I quit the baseball team soon after that episode, which had left me lightheaded for a week. Today, they'd have treated me for a concussion, but then it was merely a source of school-wide amusement. How I'd managed to endure so many crotch-related calamities to that point in my life is beyond me.

I elected to change the subject. "So ... uh ... Sharon, tell me more about yourself," I said, drowning my embarrassment in my chocolate malt. But what I *really* wanted to ask was this: *Sharon, did you really suck off your old boyfriend's cock in the back of a schoolbus last spring like Pukey told me?* To which she would have responded (in my twisted mind): *No, it was actually last winter. Shall I slither under the table and show you how?*

Sharon answered my *actual* question with a ten-minute monologue on her favorite recording artist (Herman's Hermits—*ugh!*), favorite sports team (the last place Mets— *what a loser!*), favorite TV shows (*The Man from U.N.C.L.E* and *Gomer Pyle, U.S.M.C.*—*do I detect an alphabet fetish?*), favorite flavor (rocky road—*who eats gravel?*), and favorite color (blue—*who fucking cares, Sharon?*). But despite my indifference to her favorite things (except, perhaps, for her alleged back-of-the-bus shenanigans), Sharon was pleasant, reasonably attractive, acne-free, modestly intelligent, and (as previously noted) well-endowed. So when our evening drew to a close, I turned up the charm, scoring a limp handshake along with her telephone number.

Two weeks later (Pukey had advised me not to appear overly eager), I called Sharon and asked her out. To my shock, she accepted. And before I knew it, we were an item for the balance of sophomore year and into the following summer.

As my interest grew, I gradually discounted the questionable reputation that I'd attributed to Sharon before that first date. But the bad girl image festered in my subconscious, as I found myself picturing the (probably apocryphal) schoolbus blowjob with increasing frequency as the summer progressed.

The turning point in our relationship occurred one late summer evening in her family's basement rec room. Sharon and I sat together on the big, modular couch watching the legendary TV spies Napoleon Solo and Illya Kuryakin outsmart the vicious agents of T.H.R.U.S.H. as they clumsily plotted to subjugate the world on *The Man from U.N.C.L.E.* At the height of an improbable motorboat chase and to the accompaniment of a cacophony of gunshots and explosions, we plunged well beyond the theretofore intuitively established barriers of intimacy and mutually ventured into those dangerous sub-equatorial regions. This was a risky endeavor: her parents were just upstairs and her mother was not beyond an unannounced visit to the rec room to conduct reconnaissance in the guise of offering refreshments.

As my left hand (the same one which had so briefly explored the nether regions of six-year-old Susie Sadowski nearly a decade earlier) worked its way with some difficulty into Sharon's snug, denim hip-huggers and descended haltingly toward her crotch, I conjured up Shakespeare's dicey reference to "the hair knit up in thee." That, in turn, evoked a fleeting image of Miss Romaire's derriere. Meanwhile, Sharon rather skillfully unzipped my jeans and confidently slipped her hand into my bulging tightie-whities. What she found, however, perplexed her mightily: *it was hard—but wait! It was none too straight!*

"Your cock's fucking *crooked!*" Sharon yelped in astonishment, just as the basement door flew open and her mother appeared at the top of the stairs bearing a tray of sweet-smelling, freshly-baked, chocolate chip cookies and a couple glasses of Coke.

"Refreshments!" she announced as she started down the steps, and "Oh, my Lord!!!" seconds later when she spied me feverishly prying my arm from her daughter's crotch as if trapped in a broken vending machine.

"Mom!" shrieked Sharon, wriggling free of my arm though stubbornly refusing to release her death-grip on my cock until it exploded in her grasp just as the tray flew from her horrified mother's fingertips like an incomplete forward pass. "You fucking CAME!" Sharon growled, glaring at me incredulously, while her mother screamed and the tray careened off the wall raining Coca-Cola onto our heads. Ice cubes and shards of broken glass clattered across the basement floor while cookies rolled in all directions like an advancing infantry.

I instantly jettisoned any pretense of courage. I tore up the basement stairs, two steps at a time, with my heart rumbling like a jackhammer. Not only had I discharged my load indiscreetly, but I had deduced two important things: first, that Sharon Hettleman had indubitably been in guys' pants before (and that her bad rep, long since dismissed, was likely legitimate) and, way worse, *my penis was preposterously CROOKED! I was a fucking freak!*

If the truth be told, I'd always been anxious about my penis, especially in the wake of the Great Guy-Wire Incident. I was younger then, and had little baseline evidence regarding normalcy. When, after my penis healed, I was finally able to have a painless erection, I thanked God that the stickball maiming hadn't interfered with my genital function. But what I didn't realize then was that the guy-wire mashing had damaged my dick, that its healing produced scar tissue, and that the scar tissue would soon alter my peter's posture, leaving it crooked at the very instant when it should have stood at attention. I assumed, naively, that phallic contortion was just another milepost on the road to sexual maturity. Now that I knew better, I faced a fearsome future as a full-fledged phallic freak.

CHAPTER FOUR

Big-Boned, Big Boner

S haron and I didn't speak again that summer, and I haven't a clue how she pacified her traumatized mother. Pukey, as luck would have it, was away at summer camp until nearly Labor Day. So I was free to torment myself in private over the horrific events of that dismally memorable evening and to begin to adjust to a life with a crooked cock.

When school resumed in the fall (my junior year), it was as if nothing had happened. Sharon and I continued to enforce our mutually imposed silence, but without tension or animosity. Sharon was too shocked, disgusted, or proud to further sully her reputation by telling tales of Charlie's Crooked Cock. Pukey, on the other hand, had found a new love at summer camp and was oblivious to everything else. So I remained on my own, which was probably just as well.

I sorely missed the comfort of having a girlfriend, but the Rec Room Debacle rendered me gun-shy. I was a sexual loser: the hairy triangle had become my Bermuda Triangle. Between The Great Crotch Incident and the Rec Room Debacle, I was convinced that the crotch of every young female concealed a trip wire that summoned her mother.

I screwed up the courage to date several times over the

ensuing year, but couldn't contemplate a second date. A second date could lead to a relationship, a relationship could lead to sex, and sex would spell disaster.

By senior year, I'd grown accustomed to my self-imposed chastity. I focused instead on my studies. My grades soared. Admission to a good college was now a legitimate expectation.

It was during the second half of my senior year that I began to notice Rachel Gunther. More accurately, I noticed the attention she paid to me. We had been classmates for years, shared many of the same courses, and were generally friendly, but there had never been any romantic spark. Physically, Rachel was only marginally appealing. She was, as they say euphemistically, "big boned," had severe facial features, and was two inches taller, twenty pounds heavier, and a whole lot stronger than I. She was redheaded, slightly pigeon-toed, and thoroughly self-absorbed. On the other hand, she was smart, had *massive* breasts, and her own car, a bright red 1965 Chevy Malibu convertible with an aggressive V-8 engine, red interior, and a white retractable roof. In the same way in which dog owners resemble their dogs, the aggressive Malibu (which I dubbed "Big Red") was the anthropomorphic version of Rachel, only better looking.

Above all, as I'd quickly come to recognize, Rachel was exceedingly clever and fiendishly manipulative. She wouldn't hesitate to utilize any available means to achieve her desired ends. I was a deer in her crosshairs.

Rachel claimed to date college boys regularly, though I uncovered no evidence to support her contention. It was part, I suspect, of the worldly and experienced self-image she so carefully cultivated. What I did know, however, was that none of her alleged college boyfriends had offered to take her to our senior prom, and Rachel was fiercely determined to attend.

Her intentions were transparent from the start. She'd targeted me as her ticket to the prom and had only to inveigle an invitation. But her scheme harbored advantages for me. I had little interest in a serious relationship and I, too, could attend the prom without the stress of romancing the perfect partner. And if casual petting proved a part of the bargain, I could be more than content venturing into the mountainous terrain above her waist, avoiding her trip-wire and my tragically twisted tent-pole.

As I let Rachel spin her web, I felt like an actor in a Shakespearean comedy (which, of course, reminded me yet again of Miss Romaire and her derriere). I decided to let her sweat it out, feigning interest but not chomping at the bit. Her Chevy Malibu came in particularly handy for movies, burgers, even personal errands. If I was falling in love, it was with Big Red.

It was two months to prom night and I'd yet to pop the question. I saw no need to rush. Besides, who was I to be taken for granted? But I knew that if she wooed me too hard, adult situations might arise. I'd made it this far without public revelation of my sexual deformity and wanted nothing more than to preserve my grisly secret. So I walked the proverbial tightrope between showing too much interest and too little. Either way, physical contact was inevitable.

A month before the prom (which she babbled about incessantly), we attended a movie. I tolerated her handholding and smooching. We returned to the Malibu after the show. Rachel did the driving—Big Red was *her* car and *she* was in control. Rather than drive me home, she steered Big Red off the main road and onto the dirt path that led to the reservoir at the western end of town.

"Where are we going?" I inquired with growing alarm.

"Don't get your panties in a bunch," she said, employing her favorite palliative phrase. "I wanna show you something."

I began to panic. What body part was she planning to show me? What would I be obliged to reveal in return?

I became increasingly apprehensive as Big Red penetrated the forested path to the edge of the reservoir. Finally, Rachel pulled the car into a clearing by the water. She turned off the ignition and headlights. Big Red's mighty V-8 engine sputtered as if to warn me. Slowly, Rachel unbuttoned her blouse, removed it, and tossed it behind us. Not content to wait for me, she reached back and unhooked her bra. Her *mountainous terrain* tumbled forth like an avalanche as she flung her bra carelessly into Big Red's plush back seat.

"Since you're so slow on the uptake, dickhead, I decided to give you a preview of prom night," she announced. "If your head wasn't so far up your ass, you'd recognize these as the best pair of tits in New Liberty." It was as if I'd been thrust at the bust of the overinflated heroine of the cult classic *Attack of the 50 Foot Woman*.

So that was her plan. Tempt me with your tits, give me a sample, and dangle the rest, so to speak, as a prom night party favor.

My first reaction was to bury my face in that mountainous place and just hide. Yet despite my ambivalence, I could feel the blood rushing into my deviant dick. I feared becoming the hero of the *Attack of the 50 Foot Penis*. As long as Rachel remained trapped behind the wheel, I felt reasonably safe. With my head buried tightly in her cleavage, I maneuvered myself so as to corner her in the driver's seat while shielding my rapidly swelling lap from detection. But Rachel would not be contained: her powerful arms shoved me back across Big

Red's wide bench seat as she shimmied out from behind the wheel. When she not so subtly placed her hand on the bulge in my trousers, I shuddered.

"What the fuck are you doing?" I muttered with alarm.

"Do you really have to ask?"

I had to make a quick choice: employ evasive action or go on the offensive. I chose the latter, hoping to distract her. I reached beneath her skirt and fumbled for a route to the forbidden triangle. My right hand breached the top of her panties and turned south, plowing through *the hair knit up in thee.* Suddenly, the thrust of that Shakespearean phrase became all too apparent, as my hand became entangled in Rachel's prodigious bush like a hiker lost in the forest. I'd need a crowbar and a compass to get out.

"What the fuck are *you* doing?" she asked me.

While I struggled to free my hand from its pubic imprisonment, Rachel continued to torment me, massaging that bulge like a baker kneading a ball of dough and crushing my scrotum as if she were mashing potatoes. I was nearly ready to erupt when she lurched toward my pants zipper and began to tug. But just as I was on the verge of exposure and certain humiliation, a siren wailed, a red light flashed, and my beleaguered pecker exploded, thoroughly saturating my pants. A car door slammed and a flashlight flared, shining first through the back windshield and then the driver's side window.

Rachel was in utter disarray as the officer trained his light on the scene. I, though soggy (a fact unbeknownst to fair Rachel), was at least fully clothed.

"There is a God!" I whispered to myself as the policeman motioned Rachel to roll down her window. Unlike Rachel, I had a chance to escape unexposed.

"Fuck!" Rachel muttered as she scrambled to quell the chaos consuming her torso. As I dislodged my face from her cleavage and my hand from her bush, Rachel threw her arms over her bare chest in a colossally hopeless effort to preserve her dignity.

"You lovebirds know this is restricted property?" the officer snickered with the look of a lottery winner. "Run along now before I decide to run you in."

"Yes sir!" we clamored in unison.

For the first time I can recall, Rachel was speechless. She clumsily retrieved her blouse, turned on the ignition, and steered Big Red in the direction of home. Neither of us uttered a syllable until she dropped me off.

"Not a word to anyone, fuckface!" she said as I opened the passenger-side door and exited the car. I took my sweet time, reveling in her humiliation.

"Don't get your panties in a bunch," I replied with a smirk.

CHAPTER FIVE

A Day at the Beach

Rattled by her indecent exposure episode with the local police, Rachel decided that the less said about the incident, the better. But she was irked that I'd yet to invite her to the prom, now just a few weeks away. She resolved to confront the matter the very next morning.

"Okay, dickhead, are you taking me to the fucking prom or not?" she demanded, casting off all pretenses of grace and guile.

"Thought you'd be going with one of your college boyfriends," I answered facetiously.

"Fuck you," she said. "We going?"

"Fuck *you*," I said. "Sure."

Now that I was committed, our relationship took on a different complexion. There was no more wooing or pursuing. Instead, Rachel promulgated a "to do" list detailing my errands and social obligations in advance of the prom.

One of these was Senior Beach Day, a trip made by prom couples to the Jersey shore on one of the last, meaningless school days of our rapidly concluding senior year. When I mentioned it to my parents, my father was unrelenting.

"No one plays hooky on my watch, kid. You go to school, not some frickin' beach!"

I'd have gladly used Dad's proclamation as an excuse, but I knew it wouldn't fly with my peers, much less with Lady Rachel. So on the appointed day, with my parents none the wiser, I stuffed my gym bag with a towel and swimsuit and strolled to the bus stop where Big Red sat idling. After taking down her top (Big Red's, that is), Rachel headed south on the Garden State Parkway toward the shore. It was a cloudless day with temperatures bound for the nineties.

We reached the beach in late morning. At a greasy clam shack, we gorged on fried clams, french fries, and shakes, cleansing our palates with contraband beer. It was the first of many mistakes I would make that day. I'd also forgotten the sunscreen.

By mid-afternoon, the blazing sun had turned my skin the color of Big Red. It hurt to move or speak. Chills and nausea rolled over me like the incoming tide. Rachel was unfazed. She'd noticed other couples covering up with blankets, ostensibly to shield themselves from the sun, but more pointedly to serve as camouflage for extracurricular activities. Not to be outdone, she unfurled a large blanket over the two of us, crawled underneath and immediately unhinged her top (not Big Red's). Staring at me as if I were an idiot, she broadcast an unmistakable "come hither, jackass" alert. Then she lunged for my swim trunks.

By this point, I was out of it. I was nauseated, sunburned, dizzy, drunk, and delirious. I don't remember much of what followed, but according to witnesses, I unleashed a blood-curdling wail of agony before blowing lunch in noxious waves on Rachel's chest. Mortified, she sprang up reflexively, exposing her vomit-laden breasts to a bevy of stunned classmates, while struggling mightily to pry my hand from her dangerously sagging bathing suit bottom.

I was too far gone to feel any embarrassment, at least at the time, but Rachel was incensed beyond words. In a matter of weeks, she'd exposed herself to both the New Liberty police force and the Class of '67. She hosed herself off and made a beeline for Big Red, burning rubber as they fled the parking lot without me.

I don't recall how I got home that day, or how I managed to explain my condition to my parents (a school chemistry experiment gone awry?), but after that fiasco I never saw Rachel again. When I called the next day to apologize, she invited me to deposit our prom tickets where the hot summer sun never shone. While I wouldn't miss Rachel, I was devastated by the loss of Big Red.

Senior Beach Day was the final indignity in an inglorious high school career. Despite countless social and sexual disasters, I'd managed to maintain the ugly secret of my warped wiener. Since my grades rose in inverse proportion to my plummeting social prestige (and in direct proportion to the curvature of my cock), I was accepted by Roberts College, a small, geographically isolated but highly regarded all-male school in Trumbull, New Hampshire. But before I could begin that next chapter, I'd have to endure yet another New Liberty summer.

CHAPTER SIX

Dancing Doughnuts

I f my senior year in high school ended ignominiously, the summer that followed was transformative.

My father made it clear that my loafing days were over. I was expected to contribute to the cost of my college education. "So you better fuckin' get yourself a summer job," Dad said. Two of my father's clients hired summer help. One was an electrical contractor working on a construction job in New York City and the other a mom-and-pop grocery store in New Liberty. The former job would require that I get up early, take a bus into the city, and work as an electrician's "helper" at the site of a forty-story Manhattan skyscraper then under construction. I could blow off the fortieth floor and plunge to my death. The latter job was part-time and involved shelving groceries, manning the cash register, and delivering orders to local patrons. I could sleep late and the commute was five minutes. This was a no-brainer.

"I'll take the grocery store job," I told my father.

"You'll take both jobs, you lazy bastard," Dad said. "You think my parents paid my way through college while I slept late every morning? You think college is cheap? Got a scholarship in your back pocket that you failed to mention?"

I was like baseball manager aggrieved by an umpire's bad

call. Keep complaining and I'd get my butt kicked out of the game. So I shut my mouth and contemplated a summer at hard labor.

I started my career as a construction grunt on a hot, humid morning in early July. I arose at 5 A.M. (for the first time in my entire life), scarfed down a bowl of soggy Cheerios, and sleepwalked the half-mile to the bus stop for the commute to Manhattan. From the George Washington Bridge Bus Station, I descended into the netherworld of the New York City subway system. A throng of sweaty bodies jostled me on a grimy platform with the ambience and aroma of a gas station restroom. I scrupulously guarded my wallet, my watch, and my manhood. A rush of fetid air and an ear-splitting screech announced the arrival of the "A" train, a graffiti-laden metallic hunk resembling an exploded can of alphabet soup. The subway ride was like a colonoscopy, a steamy, smelly journey through the rectum of Manhattan.

With considerable difficulty, I bulled my way out of the crowded train at Columbus Circle, in accordance with my father's directions, and walked the two blocks to the address he'd given me. Eventually, I located the foreman for the electrical contracting company for which I'd be working.

"Whaddya want, kid?" the foreman said gruffly as I entered his makeshift office on the ground floor of the forty-story steel skeleton that aspired to become a skyscraper. Older and grayer than I'd expected, he was sipping coffee from a paper cup while seated behind a desk fashioned from a pair of sawhorses and a hollow-core door.

"Uh . . . I'm Charlie Meyer," I said. "I'm supposed to be working as an electrician's helper?"

The foreman glanced at me casually, his eyebrows arching

as he sized me up. "*You?*" he said, noting my underwhelming physique. "You'll prob'ly blow off the fortieth floor!" *My worst fears confirmed.* He gauged my attire: jeans, a polo shirt and sneakers. "Does this look like a goddamn playground?" He opened a brown paper bag, extracted a jelly doughnut, and took a hearty bite. "Buy yourself some work boots . . . get rid of that candy-ass shirt . . . and get your ass back here in the morning ready to work!" he said, shooing me from his office.

Things worked out better the following morning. The foreman surveyed me (now properly attired), issued an ill-fitting hard hat, and dispatched me to the thirty-seventh floor to assist Ben Goldman.

Construction jobsites in the late Sixties were all-male affairs and, as I couldn't help but notice, X-rated. Plywood boards, employed as temporary walls, served as canvases for creative but lewd artistic expressions. Punched-out knotholes became gaping vaginas around which clever "artists" drew spread-eagled females in various states of submission. Male genitalia also popped up with regularity (so to speak), though none were as crooked as mine.

Ben Goldman was genial, short and stocky, about sixty years old, with a heavy Bronx accent. He was happy to have a "go-fer" like me at his beck-and-call. I dispensed tools and supplies like an operating room nurse. We began on the thirty-seventh floor, working our way down as the summer progressed. At this stage in the building's construction, each floor was little more than an unenclosed concrete slab, fully exposed to the elements, a barren, windswept ridge perched high above the canyons of New York.

It was immediately clear that my fear of plunging to my death from the fortieth floor of the building was unwarranted.

I'd plunge from the thirty-seventh.

A significant part of Ben's job was to lay wire at ceiling level along the perimeter of each floor. This he would do from atop a six-foot ladder placed about two feet from the building's edge. Ben had no issue with heights—but I did.

From the very first day, I was petrified by my proximity to oblivion. I would cower and shake when obliged to approach Ben's edge-hugging ladder. Ben, of course, found my anxiety amusing. "You won't feel nothin' when you land," he said, "and the flight'll be amazing!"

It was on the thirtieth floor that my life almost ended. The morning was hot and hazy, the languid air rank with a malodorous mixture of vehicle exhaust and rotting garbage. Below us, cab horns blared like angry geese and sirens wailed like spoiled children. I'd just returned from Stein's Deli with Ben's coffee and a glazed doughnut for each of us.

Ben was pulling wire along the eastern perimeter of the building as I approached. As had become my habit, I crept ever more deliberately as I neared the edge. Four feet from the brink, I tripped on a wayward bolt imbedded in the concrete floor. My brief life flashed before my eyes as I stumbled forward, jettisoning the coffee and doughnuts in a desperate attempt to avert a thirty-story descent. A split second later, I found myself sprawled, face down, on the concrete slab, my eyes hovering over the precipice, watching in utter horror as our glazed doughnuts danced through the sky on their thirty-story journey to annihilation. I haven't eaten a doughnut since.

My part-time work at the grocer would be a calming antidote to the terror of my day job—or so I thought. Roth's Corner Grocery was a throwback. It was little more than a hole-in-the-wall, run by the same couple, Monte and Edna Roth, for over forty years. Mr. Roth was a prodigious nose on legs, with barely a hint of a torso, arms, mouth, and eyes; his wife was a swirl of white cotton candy on a stick.

The prices at Roth's were higher than the supermarket chains, but its clientele was fiercely loyal. Some had been customers since the Depression. The Roths were the only shopkeepers willing to sell on credit during those difficult times. Loyalty had its rewards, and the business survived the onslaught of supermarkets and convenience stores. Unlike their larger counterparts, the Roths knew their customers by name and still delivered groceries to those too busy or infirm to shop in person.

I worked at Roth's about fourteen hours a week: four hours each on Tuesday and Thursday evenings, when most of the week's deliveries were made, and six hours on Saturday, when much of the restocking was done. I particularly liked doing the deliveries. Customers tipped generously, neatly supplementing my modest hourly wage.

The job was not without its challenges ... even on the first day.

By now a licensed driver, I'd driven only our family's '56 Mercury Phaeton. The Phaeton was a tank—hulking but powerful, with an automatic transmission. We were a one-car family: Dad figured that if Mom needed the car she could drive him to work, and if I needed a car, too bad. As a consequence, I walked to work at the grocery store and was obliged to use the Roths' clunky '58 Rambler station wagon for deliveries. But it was a manual transmission, and I'd never driven one.

"Piece of cake," Mr. Roth assured me. "A quick lesson and you'll be on your way."

I gamely joined him for my lesson in driving a stick shift (a not-so-subtle reminder, in my supremely oversensitive state, of the proper penile posture). Mr. Roth explained and demonstrated the basic concepts. Then I took the wheel and circled the block, accompanied by crunching and groaning sounds from the gearbox, Mr. Roth, or both. When I completed my circuit, he pronounced me ready and helped me load the car with groceries. Was he in collusion with my father, planning to exterminate me before college could drain the family resources? Was this the back-up plan, when the effort to blow me off the New York skyscraper had failed to achieve its dastardly end?

I set off on my delivery route, dreading every step on the clutch and tug of the stick. At first, I stalled at each stoplight and stop sign, sheepishly waving traffic by as I struggled to tame the reluctant Rambler. But by the end of the day, I'd achieved a modicum of competence. All that remained was my final delivery: a house on a hill. I drove up, parked at the top of the hill, and dropped off my last box of groceries. I returned to the Rambler and started the car. My mind went blank. I panicked. The car stalled, then rolled backwards as I furiously clutched, braked, and yanked at the gearshift. The Rambler groaned like a moose in heat, the gears grinding in agony, as the car slipped further and further down the incline. I pictured doughnuts sailing into oblivion.

Somehow, by the grace of God, I managed to engage the emergency brake, impeding my descent as the car pirouetted and plowed tail-first into a massive oak. Miraculously, I emerged unscathed. The Rambler, however, was smashed like a Halloween pumpkin.

Devastated at the damage I'd wrought on my very first day on the job, I returned to the site of my last delivery and phoned Mr. Roth. As I wrestled for the words to describe what I'd done, he erupted into paroxysms of nasal laughter.

"Good riddance to that old piece of shit!" he cried out in ecstasy. "With the insurance check for that old clunker, I can buy a *real* car!"

Charlie Meyer had dodged another bullet. Without even waiting for the insurance money, the Roths bought themselves a brand new Pontiac station wagon *with an automatic transmission.* We were back in business.

CHAPTER SEVEN

Nude Descending a Staircase

M ost of my deliveries for Roth's Corner Grocery were to elderly widows, ancient couples, and the occasional widower, all of whom were grateful for my weekly appearance and assistance in unloading and shelving their groceries. But two of my customers were particularly noteworthy for radically different reasons.

My first outing in the Roths' new Pontiac was also my introduction to the inimitable Mrs. Perkins. When Mr. and Mrs. Roth went through the roster of the evening's deliveries, they chortled when they came to her name. I sensed a private joke that they preferred to keep between them at my expense.

While wary, I was thoroughly unprepared for what I encountered upon my initial visit to the ramshackle home of Mrs. Ethel Perkins. She was a plucky old coot in her eighties with an incongruously ribald sense of humor, a love of drama, and a fertile imagination. In short, she was fucking crazy.

The Perkins house was in the oldest part of New Liberty. Ramshackle, in fact, was too kind a description. The paint was peeling, the garage nearly collapsed, and the place was teeming with cats, both inside and out.

Climbing the crumbling porch, I heard shouting inside. An

elderly woman (Mrs. Perkins, it turns out) hurled obscenities at "Harold," whom I eventually deduced was her *deceased* husband. "Harold" responded in kind, in a marginally deeper inflection that sounded suspiciously like Mrs. Perkins. When I rang the bell, Mrs. Perkins appeared, clad in only a well-worn negligee.

"Ahhh, you must be the radio repairman," she said, my boxful of groceries notwithstanding. "Come right on in."

At a loss for words, I entered the dark, creepy foyer. The stench of cat was pervasive. Hurdling several felines, I followed her to the living room. She motioned toward the radio, a dusty relic from the Thirties.

"No, no, Mrs. Perkins, I'm Charlie from... uh... Roth's Corner Grocery... with your weekly delivery."

She stared at me uncomprehendingly, whirled toward the stairwell, and addressed her dead husband. "HAROLD! Get your fat ass down here. Tell this young gentleman what's wrong with the radio!" She turned to me: "Gotta fix it in time for Mr. Roosevelt's radio address... we never miss a fireside chat!"

She then excused herself, bade me to wait at the bottom of the stairs, and climbed slowly to the second floor. A black cat hissed in the corner; two others tore through the room as if fired from bazookas. Moments later I heard, in what now was painfully obvious to me as Mrs. Perkins's voice impersonating dearly departed Harold: "Nothin's wrong with the radio, Ethel. This young gentleman is just here with the groceries. Have him put 'em in the kitchen and come back to bed, Love-Muffin, before I lose my erection!"

Mrs. Perkins tramped back down the steps. As my eyes adjusted to the dim light, I glimpsed a sight that would haunt me forever: the crazy old lady was now completely and utterly naked! I was simultaneously stunned, nauseated, and speechless.

Looking straight at me, now apparently perceiving *me* as her amorous husband, she bellowed: "You get those pants off *now*, Poopsie-Woopsie . . . and get your big fat prick into the bedroom THIS MINUTE!"

I recoiled when she lunged at me, scattering countless felines as I flopped backward onto the living room couch. My landing produced a mushroom cloud of cat hair that spread across the room like nuclear fallout.

To my eternal relief, as if summoned by a whistle audible only to her, Mrs. Perkins did an about-face, bare-assed, and climbed slowly back upstairs, ostensibly to await a ravishing by me in the role of Harold. Horrified, I bolted to the kitchen, deposited the box of groceries on the kitchen table, and made a beeline for the exit.

Despite my terrifying introduction to Mrs. Perkins, I adjusted to the challenges of my weekly visits to her wacky world. Harold was a recurring character and it behooved me to play along with the lunacy—to a point. In time, I knew what to expect and learned how to handle the unexpected. I came to believe that Mrs. Perkins was less wacko than she appeared, that most of her antics were deliberate, and that she was a born actress with a penchant for performance. She delighted at shocking the uninitiated. Unfortunately, she was also appallingly horny and an avowed exhibitionist, dicey qualities in an octogenarian.

CHAPTER EIGHT

Catherine

It was a stormy Thursday evening when I first met Catherine O'Meara. Massive raindrops pummeled the windshield as I maneuvered the Roths' shiny, new Pontiac to the top of her driveway. I parked, opened the tailgate, and hoisted the box containing her grocery order up the steps to her front door. Soaking wet, I rang the doorbell. No one answered. Delivery night absences were rare; customers generally called if they planned to be away. As I turned to leave, Mrs. O'Meara opened the door. She was clad in a white terrycloth robe; her hair was wrapped in a towel.

"I'm *so* sorry," she apologized as I stood on her doorstep like a drenched puppy. "I was just leaving the shower when you rang. Please come in."

I'd expected yet another octogenarian, but Mrs. O'Meara was anything but. She was young—in her early to mid-thirties—and remarkably attractive. Her loose-fitting robe failed to camouflage her perfect figure. Errant strands of blond hair poked through the edge of her turban. Her eyes were a striking delft blue. I followed her as she led me through the hallway and into the kitchen.

"Put the groceries on the counter over there," she said, "while I get you a towel to dry off."

"Thanks, Mrs. O'Meara, but you don't have to . . ."

Her kitchen was clean and orderly. An empty can of Campbell's Tomato Bisque sat on the counter. The aroma of simmering soup filled the room.

"So you're the new delivery boy," she said when she returned with a large blue bath towel. I nodded in affirmation. Somehow, I resented the reference to "boy," though I undoubtedly looked considerably younger than my eighteen years.

"I'm Charles," I told her, abandoning "Charlie" in an effort to feign maturity.

"I'm Catherine," she countered, shaking my hand.

The plush texture of the towel on my scalp and face caused me to fixate on her terrycloth robe and her smooth, pale skin. She inquired about my work for the Roths. I explained that it was a part-time summer job preceding my freshman year at Roberts College.

"Excellent school," she said. "Your parents must be proud of you."

Dad could give a shit, I thought. "Yes, of course," I said. "Can I help you with the groceries?"

"I'm fine," she assured me.

I turned to leave. Like most home delivery customers, Catherine paid for her groceries monthly on credit, so there was no need to act as cashier. She led me out, dipping into her purse to extract a particularly generous tip.

"That's *way* too much," I said, hoping she wouldn't reconsider.

"I'm sure you can use the money for school," she said with a smile as I opened the front door. She offered to lend me an umbrella, but I was already too wet for it to matter. I walked out the door and was swallowed again by the storm.

Catherine was charming and beautiful. Yet I couldn't help

feeling there was something awry. My next visit would heighten the mystery.

I looked forward to the following Thursday evening. I rearranged the order of my deliveries so that Catherine would be my last stop. If the opportunity to linger presented itself, I wanted the freedom to stay.

It was nearly seven o'clock when I arrived at her house. She was dressed this time, wearing a loose-fitting yellow blouse and flattering white shorts. I couldn't help but notice a feature I'd missed on my initial visit: a long, deep scar that ran horizontally across the top of her forehead. Obscured by the turban on my first visit, it was plainly visible now. I stared briefly, catching myself before she noticed.

"You're a bit drier this time," she said with a grin.

As she led me through the living room and toward the kitchen, I spied a studio photograph on the fireplace mantel. Catherine appeared in the right background of the picture, smiling. To her right stood a handsome man in his thirties. In the foreground was a beautiful little boy, perhaps three or four. It was unmistakably a family portrait. Flanking the photo were several casual snapshots featuring one or more of the trio appearing in the formal photograph.

The pieces were coming together. The scar, the eerie silence in the household, the strong whiff of loneliness.

"Don't let me interrupt your dinner," I said when I saw that her meal, a fragrant chicken, vegetable and rice sauté, had already been set on the kitchen table.

"Not at all. Have you eaten?"

"Not yet, but—" I had barely begun to make polite excuses when she beckoned me to sit down and join her.

"I rarely have company. Join me . . . please . . . there's more than enough to share." I suppressed my elation.

Catherine peppered me with questions as we ate, eliciting the dull outline of my life to date. While I touched briefly on my unsatisfying social life, I steered clear of the sexual calamities and gruesome deformities that had torpedoed it. Just being in her presence was oddly comforting. She was complimentary and encouraging.

It was after nine o'clock when I left. I thanked her profusely for dinner.

Thinking back over the evening, I was haunted by the realization that we'd shared only the details of my life. Catherine had revealed little about herself. She had a college degree but worked as a receptionist for a local doctor. That was all I knew. She was well versed in the art of deflecting attention from herself. Though she took pains to hide it, her sadness and loneliness were palpable.

CHAPTER NINE

The Confession

I'm not sure what compelled me to pierce the veil that Catherine invoked as a shield from her past. Though we barely knew each other, she'd breached my own defenses with ease. I wanted to know as much about her as she knew about me.

As the summer progressed, we spent nearly every Thursday evening together. She fed me as well as my ego. We talked of everything . . . but her.

I resolved at last to tread delicately into that forbidden territory. I addressed her tentatively, steeling myself against retreat. "Catherine," I said, "you've barely told me anything about yourself."

She turned suddenly silent, pursing her lips. "Let's call it a night," she replied, crushing me. I tried desperately to backtrack, but to no avail. I hated myself for prying, cursing myself for threatening our friendship, enigmatic as it may have been.

"It's okay, Charles, really," she said. "I'm just tired. I'll see you next week."

I was crestfallen as I left her house that night. I'd always found a way to sabotage my relationships. In the past, it had been my sexual cataclysms, insecurities, and general ineptitude. Those blunders cost me transient attachments with immature girls. My friendship with Catherine meant so much more.

I was anxious when I arrived at Catherine's doorstep on the following Thursday. When she opened the door, her eyes were swollen and red.

"Are you okay?" I asked her as I hoisted her box of groceries over the threshold.

"It's nothing, Charles," she insisted, absent her usual welcoming smile. "I'm fine. Really."

As I followed her through the living room and into the kitchen, I noticed the family portrait was missing from its familiar perch on the mantel. It rested instead on the coffee table by the sofa, embroiled in a sea of wadded tissues.

I put the groceries on the kitchen table; there was no sign she'd eaten or was preparing to do so. Then she turned to me, tears gathering in the corners of her eyes. Without thinking, I reached out to embrace her. To my surprise, she wrapped her arms around me, laid her head on my shoulder, and openly wept. I acted on instinct, gently stroking her soft, blond hair while holding her tightly. Gradually, she composed herself, releasing her grip.

"Can I get you a beer?" she asked, though she'd never before offered me anything stronger than a Coke.

"I'd love one."

She fetched a can of Rheingold for each of us and sat down at her usual place at the kitchen table. I joined her. She hesitated for a few seconds, staring at her unopened beer. "Grief is like quicksand," she said, gently wiping away the remnants of her tears. "The more you struggle, the deeper you sink."

I reached across the table, grasping her left hand, waiting

patiently as she mustered the courage to elaborate. Finally, she lifted her head and prepared, at last, to unburden herself.

"It was three years ago today: July 13th, 1964," she said. "An absolutely beautiful morning. John and I piled Matthew into the car and we headed out to Long Beach Island, our favorite spot on the Jersey shore. Matthew had just turned four."

Catherine inhaled deeply, and then a smile lit up her face. "He was *so* incredibly cute—running around on the beach, dancing in and out of the waves, laughing. We built a sand castle. I'll never forget the look of shock and disappointment on his little face when a wave came along and swept it away.

"It'd been a glorious day," she recalled, "but then thick black clouds began to creep in." Her smile evaporated. "So we picked up our things, hopped in the car, and headed home.

"We were on the Parkway near Asbury Park when the rain began. In no time, it was coming down in sheets. Deafening thunder, violent lightning. Windshield wipers couldn't keep up. Couldn't see more than a few feet ahead." She fiddled absent-mindedly with her beer.

"We headed down into an underpass. We didn't realize, at first, that it was flooding... and then..." She stopped momentarily, fortified herself with a slug of her Rheingold, then proceeded. "John hit the brake, but instead of slowing down, we hydroplaned.

"We sideswiped the concrete wall of the underpass, then spun back onto the roadway, splashing through at least a foot of water. We were okay—somehow—until a second or two later when this big, black pickup plows into the driver's side of the car... like a freight train. I'll never forget that horrific sound—crunching steel, shattering glass. And Matthew— terrified—screeching '*Mommy! Mommy!*'

"I looked at John. He'd absorbed all of the impact. His chest was . . ." Catherine paused, patting her eyes with a tissue. "He was bleeding profusely, moaning softly. And then . . . those awful gurgling sounds . . ." Her voice cracked with raw emotion. "With his last ounce of strength . . . he whispered . . . '*I love you both*' . . . Four simple, beautiful words: '*I love you both*.'" Catherine broke down as she repeated her husband's final utterance.

"He let out this long, low breath . . . and I knew he was gone. I was paralyzed with fear. I tried and tried but I couldn't get free of my seat belt, so I just sat there wailing. My face was covered in blood." Again she paused, catching her breath and settling herself with a long sip of beer. Her grief escaped slowly but surely, like air from a punctured tire.

"Matthew was belted into his little car seat behind John. I suddenly realized he was no longer screaming. I panicked. And then I blacked out. I never reached him," she said, tears pouring down faster than she could wipe them away. "Next thing I remember was the flashing lights. Emergency vehicles. Scores of them . . . a paramedic reaching into the car, trying to stanch the flow of blood from the gash on my forehead." She traced the line of her scar with her index finger.

"For a moment I was lost; I didn't know where I was, what had happened. Then I saw John's body beside me and it all came rushing back. But where was Matthew? The car seat was empty. I was hysterical. '*Where's Matthew! Where's my little boy!*'"

I didn't know what to say. Although violent sobs now punctuated her frightful narrative, she was fiercely determined to press on. She took another reinforcing sip of beer while mine sat virtually untouched before me. Liquid was welling up in my eyes as she continued, a bit more calmly now.

"Matthew had already been evacuated to the hospital at

Asbury Park. That's all they'd tell me. They looked me over, peppered me with questions—checked for internal injuries. I don't know if I was even able to respond. I was in shock. They opened the passenger side door and lifted me onto a gurney.

"They rushed me to the hospital where they'd taken Matthew. He was in surgery, a nurse told me when we arrived in the E.R. They assured me he was in the best of hands."

Catherine sighed audibly.

"Matthew died on the operating table," she said simply, straining once again to contain her tears.

Catherine and I sat quietly for several minutes, her moist blue eyes fixed on the tabletop, mine focused on hers. She took a long, last draw on her Rheingold and returned the empty can to the table.

I wanted to say how sorry I was, but I sensed that she craved neither sorrow nor pity. Instead I got up, walked around to where she sat, and clasped my arms gently around her neck from behind. She kissed my arm; I felt the warmth of her tears. I held her like that for a long while. Neither of us spoke.

"Shall I keep you company a while longer?" I finally asked her, breaking an extended silence.

"No, Charles," she said, squeezing my hand, "but thank you . . . for being here. I haven't talked about this . . . for a very long time."

She marshaled the energy to get up. It was my signal to leave, so I hugged her again and bade her goodbye.

"See you next week," she said as she closed the front door behind me.

Catherine's catharsis was an extraordinary event. She was a remarkable woman tormented by a horrific moment that had unalterably changed her life. For almost three years she'd lived stoically, mourning her husband and child and nurturing her survivor's guilt. I wanted so badly to help her escape the prison of her heartache.

Catherine's outpouring had a curious effect on me. I felt older, more mature, in her presence. I was touched that she had chosen to confide in me, trusting me, an eighteen-year-old misfit, with her heart and soul. Perhaps there was more to me than I had dared to imagine.

CHAPTER TEN

Transformation

The summer of '67 was winding down. Juggling two jobs, I had little time for myself. I didn't see friends, didn't date, and had virtually no social life. My Thursday nights at Catherine's were all that sustained me.

Catherine and I drew even closer after the Great Catharsis. Released from the paralyzing shroud over her sorrowful past, she began to contemplate a future. She talked of returning to school for a business degree. I was happy for her, but selfishly, the prospect of her leaving to pursue new opportunities distressed me.

As our conversations evolved, Catherine probed more deeply into my own conundrums. Why did I feel so ambivalent toward my parents? Did they condone (or even know of) our friendship? Why wasn't I out with some "lucky" girl rather than sharing a slapdash dinner with a much older woman? She even asked if I'd attended my prom.

My ease with Catherine gave me the courage to answer her questions honestly, even when the answers were embarrassing. I'd never seen her laugh so hard as when I recounted the saga of Senior Beach Day or the calamitous night in Sharon's basement. I admitted I was a virgin, though she doubtless knew so instinctively. But I drew the line at crooked penises and premature ejaculation. She told me about her high school and college boyfriends and even hinted at some of her own early sexual experiences.

Catherine had become my best friend and I, by default, hers. Much as I cherished our ability to discuss almost anything, I found myself increasingly conflicted.

Catherine was almost twice my age. Anything more than a platonic relationship was unfathomable. But that didn't prevent me from desiring her, even falling madly in love with her. Age aside, she was all I could ever want in a woman, and she clearly treasured my friendship. Could she be similarly conflicted about me? Was it so inconceivable? Could the passion in our hearts overrule the logic of our minds? Or was this tantamount to pondering incest with your big sister?

I imagined Catherine asking herself corresponding questions. Why was she spending so much time with a man/child half her age? Was it a badge of shame or a reflection of desperation? Could she demonstrate her affection for me, however amorphous, in any physical manner? Or was I deceiving myself even to presume such questions had entered her consciousness.

A week before I was due at college, Catherine invited me over for a farewell dinner. By then, I'd happily hung up my hard hat forever and completed my tour of duty with the Roths. I was grateful for the opportunity to spend a few last precious hours in her company.

It was clear when I arrived that the night would be memorable. She wore a fashionable short skirt in a black-and-white herringbone pattern with a black silk blouse in lieu of the much more casual attire she'd favored on my prior visits. Silver spiral earrings dangled from her earlobes and a matching, single-strand necklace intersected the delicate vertical lines of her neck. She donned make-up that accentuated her piercing blue eyes and minimized the scar on her brow. Her shimmering hair cascaded over her shoulders, flowing down her back like a curtain of silk. I couldn't take my eyes off her.

She'd pulled out all the stops. Lights were low and candles flickered like fireflies on the formal dining room table. Our prior meals had been relegated to the kitchen.

"Tonight's dinner is in your honor," she said proudly as I admired her elaborate preparations. "I made chicken *cordon bleu* with fingerling potatoes." I had no idea what that was, and the only potatoes I'd ever consumed were the size of my fist, cut into french fries, or pulverized and dehydrated into tasteless Potato Buds.

"Why all the fuss?"

"You're about to embark upon a turning point in your life," she said. She was referring, I presumed, to my leaving for college, but her comment would take on a more profound meaning as the evening progressed.

The meal was amazing. Catherine served wine, and though I didn't know a fine French wine from Ripple, I savored it with the aplomb of a connoisseur.

When we'd finished dinner and dessert (a baked Alaska, no less), we retired to the living room. I sunk into the soft couch, sated from dinner and lightheaded from the wine. Catherine sat down beside me, casting off her shoes and curling her smooth, firm legs up beneath her. She told me how much my friendship had meant to her, how my campaign to ease her grief had liberated her. She would miss our time together, she said, but it was inevitable that we both move forward with our lives.

I was both flattered and crushed. I knew that we could never sustain the intensity of our relationship as we each moved on, both emotionally and geographically. But I was ill-prepared for such an abrupt end to our time together.

As I poised to respond, Catherine drew her index finger to her lips in a gesture of silence. "I have a parting gift for you," she said, "something I hope will express my deep affection for you . . . and prove valuable as you move on with your life."

I could feel tears well up in my eyes as I confronted the reality of the end of our treasured relationship. "I'm ashamed I brought nothing for you," I said.

"You've already given me more than you will ever know." Catherine unfolded her legs and shifted closer to me, smiling ever so sweetly. It was only when she placed her hands gently on my cheeks and kissed me tenderly on the lips that I sensed what was about to occur. Then she kissed me again—more deeply this time—as she casually began to unbutton her blouse. My heart was pounding as she took me by the hand and led me up the stairs.

As my father's relatives were wont to say at Passover Seder, this night was truly unlike all others. Up to this point in my life, this was the place in the narrative when something ludicrous would occur. Susie's mom would explode in horror as I probed poor little Susie's private parts, Sharon's mother would descend the staircase just as Sharon recoiled from my crooked cock, the policeman would interrupt my exploration of Rachel's lower regions, or I'd vomit gratuitously over her naked breasts. *This night would be different.*

Catherine's gift of herself was more generous and meaningful than I could have possibly imagined. Over the next few hours, she guided me sensitively and compassionately through the rugged wasteland of my sexual anxieties. With patience and encouragement, she taught me to touch, to share, and, ultimately, to make love with every measure of my heart, my body, and my soul. And if that weren't enough, we discovered, to our mutual surprise, how the unique curvature of my penis created more friction—and actually *heightened* her pleasure. When we'd finished our lovemaking, her sparkling delft eyes smiled at me knowingly. "What you've been ashamed of all this time," she said, "is a miracle that will absolutely thrill any woman lucky enough to have you as her lover. Your so-called 'crooked cock' isn't an unseemly secret," she added with a chuckle, "it's a secret weapon."

In a single night, I was transformed from a virgin to a stud. My childhood was shed like the skin of a rattlesnake.

CHAPTER ELEVEN

Goldfish in a Barrel of Piranhas

Rather than drive me to Roberts College, Dad dropped me off at a Greyhound bus station in northern New Jersey. Comparing the cost of gas, automobile depreciation, and lodging with the price of a bus ticket, he declared the latter the preferable option. Why endure a ten-hour round-trip when a one-way ticket would suffice?

"You're missing the point, Richard," Mom said, sobbing, as I yanked my footlocker from the trunk of our car. "This is our *son* and he's going to college!"

"Do the math, Lydia. It would work out the same way even if he wasn't related," Dad said, missing the point entirely.

Perhaps he was right, though for the wrong reasons. The bus ride (seven hours, with four stops) heightened my sense of independence and gave me freedom to ponder my future. I'd never lived away from home and was thrilled to escape New Liberty. I'd sorely miss Catherine, but was secure in the knowledge that our time together had prepared me, both emotionally and physically, for the next chapter of my life.

I arrived at the bus station in Trumbull, New Hampshire, retrieved my footlocker from the bowels of the bus, and caught a cab to campus (Dad, incidentally, had neglected to include the cab fare in his calculations). Arriving at my assigned dormitory (Rowley Hall), I claimed my key and located room 107, a surprisingly spacious single on the first floor.

"Don't pop a hernia your first day on campus. Let me give you a hand." Those were the first words uttered to me by Izzy Matz, a fellow freshman destined to become my best friend, as he helped me maneuver my footlocker down the hallway and into my room. Izzy was a Bostonian with an insatiable love for the Red Sox and the mournful ballads of Leonard Cohen. His dorm room, two floors above mine, was a shrine to the singer/songwriter whose morose, gravelly voice spewed interminably from his stereo.

Izzy and I had much in common: a shared love of baseball, and pasts steeped in social anxiety and sexual frustration. In many ways, he was worse off than I—he'd had no Catherine to transform him. And unlike me, Izzy was a virgin. Gangly, bespectacled, and hampered by a nerdy demeanor and unpolished social skills, he seemed a good bet to remain one for a while. Or so I thought.

Roberts College had a long tradition as an all-male bastion of higher education and social dysfunction. The only coeds on campus were a hundred or so female exchange students, many of whom gravitated to Roberts to participate in its renowned art programs. The male/female student ratio was a whopping fifteen-to-one. Freshmen had even longer odds, as all of the visiting coeds were upperclassmen.

To mitigate the odds, the college staged freshman "mixers," importing busloads of unwitting female students from nearby colleges for evenings of dancing, debauchery, or both. It was like releasing goldfish into a barrel of piranhas.

Izzy and I resolved to hunt goldfish. The buses were still unloading the unsuspecting prey when we arrived at the student union for the season's first mixer. As hordes of Roberts freshmen lay in wait, scores of women poured into the fray, promptly second-guessing the wisdom of their plunge into the pond.

There's a science to attending a mixer. The horny male, or *piranha*, formulates a strategy based on his evaluation of three factors. The first, or *Pulchritudinous Factor*, is simple: how good-looking does a young lady, or *goldfish*, have to be to warrant your time and effort? With a high *Pulchritudinous Factor*, you require nothing less than a goddess; those with a low *Pulchritudinous Factor* are content with little more than a pair of breasts—any size will do and they don't have to match. Second is the *Confidence Index*, which, roughly speaking, is the product derived by multiplying one's level of confidence (or desperation) by his subjective evaluation of his own appeal. Finally, there's the *Grass is Greener/Ass Gets Leaner* conundrum, the tension between early versus deferred action. If you pounce too soon (i.e., before all the *goldfish* are released into the pond), you run the risk of missing out on something better; if you wait too long (i.e., after the *piranhas* have devoured most of the *goldfish*), you could emerge with nothing at all. If you wait, you're of the *Grass is Greener* persuasion; if you pounce, you favor the *Ass Gets Leaner* philosophy.

With his low *Confidence Index*, Izzy set the *Pulchritude* bar low while opting for the *Ass Gets Leaner* philosophy encouraging early action. When a rather plain-looking young woman attracted no immediate takers, he sidled over and asked her to dance, leaving me to fend for myself.

Thanks to Catherine, I had a loftier *Confidence Index* and set my *Pulchritude* bar substantially higher. Uninspired by the early pickings, I played the *Grass is Greener* card, waiting until most of the evening's imports had filed in and most of the *piranhas* had fed. It was a risky tactic, though there was always the chance that a *piranha's* early prey might be spit back as unsuitable or escape the *piranha's* grasp and flop back into the pond. My patience was rewarded when an attractive blonde strolled in and passed unscathed through the dwindling gauntlet of ogling males. Her hair was a bit over-teased and her mascara unduly generous, but what the heck. I asked her to dance.

The band was deafening, making conversation nearly impossible.

"Hi, I'm Charlie," I screamed into her ear as if talking to a near-deaf grandparent.

"Hi, Cholly!" she said before inaudibly muttering her name.

"Charlie," I said, correcting her.

"Got it—Cholly!"

Pretty as she was, it was a discouraging start. I decided to try another tack.

"Where . . . are . . . you . . . from?" I hollered at the top of my lungs, carefully pronouncing each word in an effort to pierce through the din.

"Brooklyn, New Yawk!" she bellowed, and now I understood. "Cholly" was Brooklynese for "Charlie." New York accents repulsed me, and hers was particularly grating. It was like talking to a Mafioso. As my enthusiasm waned, another guy sensed an opening and performed *the snake*, a maneuver I'd witness on many occasions over my college career. *The snake* was a guileless attempt by a guy with a high *Confidence Index* (or alcohol level) to intercept (or *snake*) a woman from a guy with a lower *Confidence Index*. This time I was relieved to be an enabler.

Izzy, meanwhile, was still dancing with his original partner. They were clearly enjoying themselves. By now, the pairings had been completed and only the wallflowers remained. Deflated, I made my way through the exit, across the green, and back to the refuge of Rowley Hall.

Back at the dorm, I resolved to assuage my disappointment by writing a letter to Catherine. It'd been six weeks since our magical night together. I missed her comfort and company. But aside from the lame thank you notes that my mother had forced me to write to relatives in appreciation for holiday or birthday gifts ("Dear Grandma. Thanks for the neat pajamas. I wear them all the time. Love, Charlie"), I'd never written a letter in my life.

I toiled into the early morning hours on my Epistle to Catherine. I longed to convey my feelings of loneliness, without sounding needy or immature. I couldn't reveal how much I still pined for her, but wanted her to know that I cared for and missed her. I wrote of my new friend Izzy and my futile night at the mixer. I signed it "Your dear friend always" instead of "Love." I feared the latter might sound misguided or pitiful, even if it more accurately reflected my feelings.

Izzy wore a shit-eating grin when we met in the dorm the next morning. "Charlie . . . my . . . *man*!" he chirped, sounding like a refugee from the beat generation.

"Sounds like someone had a good evening."

"Fuck yeah!" he gushed, his eyes dancing. "Her name's Leah. She's from Mountain View Junior College. Grew up near Boston. Can recite the Red Sox starting lineup. Digs Leonard Cohen. What's not to love?"

"Sounds like a recipe for mutual boredom," I said, but I was happy for him.

"And Charlie," he said, still aglow. "She's agreed to come up for Homecoming Weekend!"

CHAPTER TWELVE

All the Way With LBJ?

"**D**ate weekends" were among the more problematic idiosyncrasies of life at an all-male school. Absent a ready supply of women, guys imported out-of-town dates. Homecoming, the year's first big date weekend, revolved around Roberts' football rivalry with Rutherford College. Why anyone would glorify a ten-year streak of embarrassing gridiron slaughters as a rivalry was baffling to me, but it did serve as a ready excuse for drunken celebration.

The fact that even Izzy was able to secure a date for Homecoming depressed me. He offered to have Leah arrange a blind date, but I was justifiably hesitant. A blind date could prove devastating in the first five minutes, and unless you were one of the assholes (of which there were many) willing to "ditch" your date on Friday night, you'd be locked into an excruciating three-day weekend with a girl you reviled (or who reviled you). It was an even worse bet for the date, of course, risking abandonment in a strange town in the company of a couple thousand horny drunks.

Wishing I could invite Catherine (who hadn't responded to my letter in over three weeks), but recognizing the absurdity of the premise, I broke down and agreed to let Leah "fix me up." Challenging the logic of the *Pulchritudinous Correlation*

Principle was like toying with explosives. The maxim was straightforward: good-looking girls tend to have good-looking friends; homely girls attract homely friends. As delightful as Leah was—a fact I was able to confirm during the several subsequent visits she made to see Izzy before Homecoming— she was no Raquel Welch.

Leah arranged the particulars of my blind date. My cold comfort was her assurance that my date was "cute" and "a lot of fun," a classic example of damning with faint praise.

Our preparations for the weekend were simple but critical. First, I obtained a room for my date at Richard's House, an off- campus guesthouse operated by the college for the accommodation of out-of-town dates. As was the case with almost every building on campus, student tradition furnished a colorful nickname. Richard's House became Big Dick's, a perfectly inappropriate name for a weekend accommodation for women. But Big Dick's was ideal for blind dates, especially when expectations were as low as mine. So as not to seem overly presumptuous, Izzy secured a room for Leah as well, though he fervently hoped that she'd choose not to use it. Like many schools at the time, the college's rules of conduct (dubbed *Roberts Rules of Disorder*) included "parietals," regulations restricting overnight occupation of men's dorm rooms by women, though enforcement was virtually non-existent. Unless you announced to a campus cop at three in the morning that a naked young woman was spread-eagled on your floor, you were generally safe. Next, Izzy cajoled me into accompanying him to Alice's, a notorious, hole-in-the-wall drugstore in a back alley off Main Street. For years, Alice's had billed itself as the "store for all your weekend needs," a euphemistic phrase embracing all manner of condoms and sex toys.

I don't know why Izzy chose *me* to join him on his first trip to Alice's. It's not as if I'd been there before. Although he likely presumed otherwise after I'd told him of my last night with Catherine (save for the part about my convoluted cock), I'd never actually used a condom. But, like a precocious Boy Scout, it never hurt to be prepared.

We were not prepared, however, for the staggering range of options available at Alice's. Big ones, small ones, lubricated, unlubricated, ribbed, reservoir-tipped, even flavored condoms. I wondered (but refused to ask) if they came in special shapes for special dicks like mine. When she sensed our embarrassment and confusion, Alice came to our rescue. A short, rotund, gray-haired woman in her late sixties, Alice was a dynamo and a local legend. She was everyone's crazy aunt, the incorrigible old biddy who had the balls to tell dirty jokes in mixed company.

"How can I help you sexy gentlemen?" she asked in her scratchy but ebullient voice. Izzy motioned toward the towering rack of condoms. "Ah," Alice said, waddling out from behind the counter toward the condom display, "you need a sock for your cock!" We nodded sheepishly. "Let me guess," she continued, "you're freshmen who want to be properly sheathed when opportunity knocks. Am I right?" Again, we nodded.

"Don't lose your stiffy over all the choices, gentlemen," Alice cackled. "You don't need a Cadillac when a Ford will do. Keep it simple," she advised as she reached for a basic box of a dozen Trojans. "You'll be fine with these," she assured us. We paid for our Trojans and scurried back to the dorm.

I remained ambivalent about Homecoming. I knew how important it was to Izzy. He was infatuated with Leah and contemplating the demise of his virginity. I, on the other hand, just hoped to survive the weekend. A good time would be a bonus. And if my date was a disaster, I owed it to myself, to her, and especially to my friend Izzy, to handle the weekend with at least a modicum of grace.

Izzy met our dates when their bus arrived on Friday afternoon. It was a bitterly cold and cloudy November day; six inches of fresh snow blanketed the campus the previous evening. Still in class when the girls got in, I'd planned to meet them at the dorm after Izzy checked them into Big Dick's.

When I arrived at Rowley Hall, my heart sank like the Titanic. "Cute" she was not. She had a bulbous nose, beagle ears, and a thick black unibrow perched like a charred rainbow above her Coke-bottle glasses. She was a dead ringer for President Lyndon B. Johnson, perhaps the ugliest mug on the face of the earth! I tried to keep it together as I thrust out my hand to LBJ.

"Charlie, this is Sheila," Izzy said, oblivious to my disappointment. LBJ, smiling meekly, shook my hand with the ardor of an octogenarian.

I was totally screwed.

Izzy had procured a case of Budweiser from an accommodating senior down the hall. Maybe, I thought, with a little help from my Buds, I could get through what would surely be a daunting weekend.

At dinnertime, we walked across campus to LaRouche Dining Hall (a.k.a. "The Douche"), a cavernous, cafeteria-style eatery with generally passable food. It was common practice to obtain guest passes to The Douche for one's weekend dates. Not only was it cheap and convenient, but it afforded the more fortunate of our classmates a chance to flaunt their trophy dates. It was not unusual to witness an upperclassman escorting a voluptuous nymph into The Douche to the accompaniment of envious applause. Conversely, jeers and catcalls might herald a less propitious pairing. As I entered, I tried to remain just far enough behind my date to avoid attribution, and was relieved when our arrival provoked no audible reaction.

It was painfully obvious to me that LBJ was as socially inept as I'd been in my pre-Catherine days. Given my quandary, I was of three minds: one part of me had empathy for her plight; another wanted to hide all weekend in the library with the dateless nerds. The third part felt guilty for what the second part thought.

The four of us spent the first portion of Friday evening in my dorm room. The alcohol was the perfect salve for my sorrows. While Izzy and Leah became increasingly amorous, I labored to eke out even a rudimentary conversation with LBJ.

"So, how do you find Mountain View Junior College?"

"Right up route 5."

"No, I mean do you *like* it?"

"Old road. Lot of potholes."

"Ugh," I muttered under my breath, not sure how much more I could possibly take. To my credit (and detriment), I felt compelled to make the most of the evening and to act like a gentleman. To my horror, the kindness I rendered was misconstrued. With Izzy and Leah pawing each other in the corner of my dorm room, I needed a quick change of venue lest LBJ turn frisky.

"Let's give Leah and Izzy some time to themselves," I proposed. I remembered the football pep rally and bonfire then taking place on the college green. I grabbed a six-pack with one hand and her clammy palm in the other and dragged Sheila off to the green.

Seeking fortification, I chugged a beer on the way. Seeking to impress me, she chugged two.

"Who's playing tomorrow?" LBJ asked me, though "Beat Rutherford!" signs were plastered everywhere.

"Rutherford College."

"Against who?"

"Roberts . . . of course."

"Oh."

A massive bonfire rose from the center of the green. The blaze spread quickly through a prodigious pile of railroad ties stacked one upon another as if constructed by some giant Gulliver with mutant Lincoln Logs. The intense heat of the conflagration was a welcome counterpoint to the chill of the evening. Students snuggled with their dates, hypnotized by the dancing flames. LBJ squeezed my hand and laid her head on my shoulder. The quicksand (to use Catherine's metaphor) was getting deeper.

By now, I'd had enough. LBJ was turning amorous. Thanks to the Buds, her shyness and inhibitions were dissipating. I had to extricate myself from this morass as quickly as possible. No way was I going all the way with LBJ. Lacking any other viable alternative, I resolved to ditch my date—with dignity.

For the typical Roberts slimeball, ditching your date was easy: take her someplace public and disappear. She'd get the message. It was a tempting plan, and we were already in a public place. Unfortunately, it was not a plan I could embrace. I needed a kinder, gentler approach. I quickly devised an alternative strategy.

Operation Time Warp was as simple as it was preposterous. First, I'd have to assure that Izzy and Leah had vacated my room. Then, I'd need to get LBJ drunk enough to lose track of time, but sober enough to walk with me back to her lodging at Big Dick's.

Finally, I'd need to persuade her that it was at least two in the morning, the time by which dates were required to vacate the dorms under the parietal rules, affording me an excuse to abort the date without a mutually embarrassing rejection. She didn't need to know that we all ignored parietals.

Fearing we'd prematurely exhaust our six-pack, I reached for an empty and pretended to chug it while LBJ guzzled yet another fresh can.

It was barely eight o'clock. I'd have to trick LBJ into believing it was six hours later. As the alcohol worked its magic, I suggested we return to the dorm. She was more than eager to comply.

Fortunately, my room was as empty as the six-pack. When LBJ excused herself to pee, I set my devious plan in motion. I snatched the clock on my desk and advanced it six hours, resetting my watch to match. All that remained was to doctor her wristwatch.

I switched on the stereo and turned down the lights. Having relieved her bursting bladder of nearly a six-pack of Bud, LBJ staggered back into the room, careening onto a chair.

"C'mon, let's dance!" I commanded.

"I dunno," she said, initially resistant. The beer had taken its toll. I yanked her up like a rag doll. We danced to *End of the Night* by The Doors. The title was eerily apt. As she leaned against my shoulder like a lumpy sack of potatoes, I brushed my hand across her wrist in an effort to locate the latch on her watch. It was like trying to unhook a bra. I failed miserably.

When the music stopped, we collapsed onto the bed. The 'come hither' look she flashed set off frantic alarms in my head. When she leaned over to kiss me, I took evasive action. I clumsily grabbed her wrist. "Ouch!" I muttered nonsensically. "Your watch is sharp!"

"My watch . . . is what?"

Somehow, my bizarre comment produced the desired effect. Rather than debate the validity of my bogus complaint, she simply removed her watch and set it down on the bed. She was too drunk or distracted to take note of the time.

Before she could resume her advances, I excused myself for the bathroom, surreptitiously pocketing her watch on the way. I reset it to match my own.

Upon my return, I nonchalantly dropped the watch to the floor. "Your watch fell onto the floor," I said cleverly as I reached down chivalrously to retrieve it.

"But it was just—"

I glanced conspicuously at the time. "Oh my God! It's after two o'clock!" I exclaimed. "I've got to get you out of here!"

"Whaaat? It can't be!" she said, staring at her watch in disbelief. "My watch is wrong."

"No, Sheila, check the clock on the desk! And look—my watch says 2:10. See? I've got to get you back to Big Dick's!"

LBJ glazed over as I explained the universally scorned parietal rules. Disappointed, harried, and three sheets to the wind, she collected her things. We took the roundabout route to Big Dick's to avoid the library clock tower, and I whisked her quickly past the overhead clock in the guesthouse vestibule when we arrived. Under my watchful eye, she teetered up the stairs and into her room. Relieved, I excused myself for the night. *I was free!*

When I returned to the dorm at a little past nine, Izzy accosted me in the hallway. His face was ashen.

"What's wrong?"

"Leah *freaked out!* When I reached for a condom she screamed bloody murder . . . like I was going to rape her! Then she gets up and *jumps out my fricking window!*"

This was not good, especially since Izzy's room was on the third floor.

"Where is she now?"

"No idea! I ran out after her but she just vanished! Grabbed her clothes, left her coat and shoes. Just fricking jumped, goddammit!" Izzy's face was bright red, his eyes bulging.

"Did she say anything? Did she give you any warning?"

"No! We'd been fooling around for a while. She seemed to want to go further . . . then, *poof!* She lets out this scream, opens the window, and jumps like a fucking paratrooper!"

It suddenly dawned on me that Izzy was the new Charlie. Until Catherine, it had been me who, on the precipice of ecstasy, suffered one classic mood-wrecking, relationship-rending indignity after another: intruding mothers, leering police officers, a severe case of sun poisoning, anything to frustrate sexual momentum. Poor Izzy was the heir to my high school legacy.

On the other hand, given my unfortunate history in such matters, I felt uniquely qualified to address the crisis.

"Izzy," I said calmly, "you check out Big Dick's. Maybe she went back there. I'll look around campus."

While Izzy set out for Big Dick's, I decided to check the library. One of the few campus buildings open at that hour, it was a logical sanctuary on a football weekend. But before I got there, I heard muffled sobs emanating from the portico of the college chapel next door. The porch was dark. Mounting the granite stairs to investigate, I glimpsed a shadowy figure huddled in a corner.

"Leah?"

"Go away!"

"Leah, it's Charlie."

Leah was shivering, coatless, in the cold New Hampshire night. I took off my parka and draped it around her shoulders. She was weeping uncontrollably, gasping for air between sobs.

"Are you hurt?"

"I'm fine! Just leave me alone!"

"You have to get out of the cold. I know a quiet place in the library we can go to warm up."

She recoiled when I reached for her. Though her blouse and skirt were (thankfully) present and accounted for, she was disheveled and shoeless. With a little coaxing, she finally arose. She resisted my efforts to carry her, insisting on trudging the fifty or so yards to the library on her own. The dateless nerds populating the library's front rooms stared in bewilderment as I escorted a trembling, barefoot woman into the bowels of the building.

When we reached the basement, I led Leah to a small, private study room behind the stacks. Her feet were freezing, dirty, and bleeding. I ran to a men's room and emerged with paper towels doused in warm water to help her clean up, then used my hands to warm her feet. By now, her sobbing had abated. Her breathing steadied as she gradually regained her composure.

"What happened, Leah?"

"It wasn't Izzy's fault," she said, confirming my suspicion that her action emanated from a deeper place. She sighed. "I'm . . . very fond of Izzy . . . and I . . . I wanted to . . ." Her voice trailed off, though I knew what she meant.

"You should consider a career as a stunt woman," I joked in an oblique reference to her third floor leap, trying to cut the tension. She allowed herself the hint of a smile.

"I feel awful, Charlie," she said. "I don't know what possessed me to . . . I'm *so* sorry." Fortunately, she related, a snow bank had cushioned her fall. I resorted to small talk in an effort to calm her. She then turned deadly serious.

"When I was thirteen," Leah began, stroking her cheeks nervously while staring at the floor, "my... uncle..." She shuddered, her eyes downcast, her voice wavering. She struggled to utter the words. "He *raped* me!" A flood of tears accompanied her shocking revelation. She paused, summoning the resolve to proceed. "I was too frightened and ashamed to tell my parents," she said, her hands shaking. "I didn't think... they'd believe me." Leah looked up at me plaintively. "I can't believe I'm telling you this," she said, her cheeks soiled with tears. "I've buried it for so long!"

I reached out and grasped her hands. She squeezed them like a frightened child. Slowly, she composed herself. Her uncle, she explained, had used a condom. Izzy, of course, couldn't possibly have known of the association between the basic prophylactic device and her childhood trauma.

"I've never told *anyone* about this," she confided, wiping her tears, "but now I have to deal with it" she said haltingly, "for myself and for Izzy."

I didn't know how to respond. I was privy to a hideous secret that she'd harbored for a third of her life. *Psychology I* hadn't prepared me for this.

"I won't say anything to Izzy," I told her. "That's for you to do when and if you're ready. But you need to understand that he's nuts about you... and he won't be able to comprehend tonight's events without some perspective."

"You're right," Leah replied. She shifted uncomfortably in her chair, "but I can't face Izzy tonight." Her teeth were still chattering from her exposure to the cold. "Until this evening, I had no idea how much I'd repressed that episode... how much it haunted me." Leah looked me in the eye, and then leaned forward, kissing me softly on the cheek. "Thank you," she said.

"For what?"

"Just . . . thank you."

"Don't mention it," I said. "Wait right here while I go back to the dorm, find your shoes and coat, get you a pair of socks. Then I'll walk you to the guesthouse or we'll call you a cab. Will you be okay here alone for a few minutes?"

"Yes . . . thanks," she whispered as I left.

Izzy was waiting anxiously outside my room when I returned to the dorm.

"She's not at—"

"I found her. She's a little shaken up, but okay."

"Thank God!" he said, emitting a massive sigh of relief. "Where is she?"

"She's at the library," I told him, "but I think it would be best if I took her back to her room. I need to bring her shoes and coat. Do you have a pair of socks she can borrow?"

"Uh, sure, I—"

"She's too embarrassed to face you tonight. This wasn't your fault, Izzy; she made that clear to me."

It seemed cruel to leave Izzy without a more adequate explanation, but I owed it to Leah to let her decide what to say and when to say it. Izzy wasn't happy with me, but there was little I could do. I retrieved Leah's shoes and coat, grabbed a pair of socks, and ran back to the library. Leah declined the offer of a cab and allowed me to escort her to her lodgings. Fortunately, she was too engrossed in her own problems to inquire about LBJ. I hoped and prayed that we wouldn't encounter her at Big Dick's. Fortunately, we didn't.

The girls met us at Rowley Hall late Saturday morning. Leah had revealed her breakdown to LBJ, as well as its genesis, and was now prepared to address it with Izzy. As Leah and Izzy conversed behind closed doors, LBJ and I were left to pick up the pieces.

LBJ stared right through me. "I know you deceived me last night," she said, her eyes narrowing. "It all fell into place this morning when Leah told me what happened to her. The timelines didn't mesh. You couldn't have been with me at the same damn time you were with her. And, of course, the clock in my room didn't quite match my watch, though I was too blitzed to notice 'til this morning."

I struggled in vain for an appropriate response. "I'm sorry, I—"

"Never mind," she snapped. "I get it: you weren't that into me. It's okay." Her mouth tightened. "You were devious," she said with a scowl, "but not cruel. And according to Leah, you were an angel to her, so you can't be a total ass." I'd dodged another bullet. "There's a bus back to Mountain View in an hour," she said. "It's much better that way; we won't need to go through the motions."

I didn't protest. "I'm sorry," was all I could manage. I walked her to the bus station, thanked her for coming, and offered yet another feckless apology.

Izzy was a new man after his conversation with Leah. Her revelations shocked him as much as they had me, but he no longer felt responsible for Leah's frightening reaction.

As she prepared to head off to the football game with Izzy, Leah pulled me aside.

"Sheila told me about last night. I want you to know that as bizarre as that was, I understand why you did it. You could have just abandoned her . . . but you didn't."

As I started to speak, she stopped me. "I'm equally to

blame," she said. "Sheila's my friend. I felt sorry for her. I wanted her to have a chance to meet someone nice. Izzy thinks the world of you, but I didn't know you well enough when I set you up with Sheila," she said. "It was a bad match. I'm sorry." Izzy motioned for her to catch up with him. "Be right there!" she called out before turning back to me. "You're a really good guy, Charlie, and I'll always be grateful to you for helping me through a very rough night."

I was touched by Leah's kind words and pleased that Izzy had found such a good woman so soon. I also felt just a little less guilty about Operation Time Warp. Though I'd be spending Saturday night of Homecoming in the depths of the library, I'd had more excitement in one eventful night than most classmates would experience during their entire college careers. I was confident that things could only get better. Until, of course, they got worse.

CHAPTER THIRTEEN

Catherine and The Nun

I checked my mailbox daily in the weeks that followed, hoping for a letter from Catherine. Two months had passed. I was puzzled and hurt. I tried to phone several times, but the phone rang on and on, always unanswered. I thought I'd drop by during Thanksgiving break, but my plans changed when Izzy invited me to join him with his family in Boston for the holiday.

One morning in early December, I received an envelope addressed to me in a delicate feminine hand, with a San Francisco postmark but no return address. I tore open the envelope. It was from Catherine.

> *Dearest Charles,*
>
> *I'm so sorry it's taken me this long to write to you. As you'll see from the postmark, I've left New Liberty and moved to San Francisco. Your letter took ages to reach me (no thanks to the Post Office) and I've been very busy between making the move and finding work.*
>
> *I've got a sister here, and she's been gracious enough to allow me to stay with her while I look for a place of my own. I was also able to find a temporary job in a doctor's office nearby.*

I'm returning to school—at the University of San Francisco. I'll begin working toward my business degree when the new semester starts in January. I've wanted to do this for years and finally got up the courage. I credit you for that.

I put my house on the market in September, not long after you left. I knew it was time to move on. I'd spent the last three years of my life mourning the loss of my family. I was in a rut, but I didn't recognize the depths of my paralysis until you wandered into my life. You helped me understand how I'd stagnated, and reopened my heart and mind to fresh possibilities. At the same time, I hope I've helped you appreciate what a magnificent person you are and the wealth of opportunities that lie within your grasp.

I very much miss our impromptu dinners and delightful conversations. I loved your sweet letter and the sentiments you expressed. Loneliness is almost always the uninvited guest that accompanies you as you start a new life. But neither of us is totally alone: I've got my sister and you've got your pal Izzy.

I wanted to tell you of my decision in person, but I didn't know when or if I'd see you again, or how you'd react. I hope you won't be sore with me over having to find out this way.

It may seem cruel of me to omit a return address. Our friendship came at the perfect time for each of us. Each learned much from the other, and each encouraged the other to move on. We *must* move on, Charles. We can never improve upon what we had and meant to each other. Nor should we try.

I'll always cherish your friendship. I know you'll

become the best young man you can be, and that you'll
find a woman better (and younger!) than I with whom
to share your life (and your "secret weapon"!). Don't be
impatient; your time will come.

Love always,
Catherine

I had all I could do to contain my tears, but I knew that
Catherine was right.

It was tough to return to New Liberty for Christmas knowing
that Catherine was gone. I drove past her house, though I can't
explain why. A "SOLD" sticker covered the real estate sign
impaled into the front yard like a toothpick into a cheese cube.
It seemed so final and irretrievable.

Christmas break at home was like a prison sentence, except
that the food was worse. Whenever Dad grew weary of Mom's
middling mealtime repertoire (construction-grade meat loaf;
lamb chops as rubbery as the soles of my Keds), he'd hand me
a ten-spot and send me out for a take-out pizza or Chinese food
(or, in his politically incorrect vernacular, a "Dago Pie" or
"Chink Chow"). It was on one such errand, a trip to Fong Hu
Chinese Restaurant (which even its Asian patrons referred to
as *Fuck You*), that I bumped into Annie.

Annie Christiansen had been my classmate until junior year
in high school, when her parents transferred her to an all-girls'
Catholic academy. Invariably characterized as "perky" and
"innocent," she was the epitome of the girl-next-door. She'd
always been pretty (shapely body, naturally blond hair, sweet
smile, clear blue eyes), but now, at eighteen, she'd filled out
exquisitely and was a veritable paragon of pulchritude.

Despite her appeal, Annie Christiansen had always seemed

out of bounds. Her family was notoriously religious. And while several of my high school classmates harbored crushes, she politely declined all entreaties. Her faith and indifference to dating had earned her the unflattering nickname "The Nun."

"It's been a long time, Annie," I said when she joined me on the take-out line. I muttered something feeble about how wonderful she looked. She accepted the compliment with grace, noting that I'd grown several inches since our paths last crossed during sophomore year. She told me she was attending St. Augustine's College, a small New Hampshire school just an hour from Roberts.

"When do you go back?" I reached across the counter to exchange my ten-dollar bill for a brown paper bag—a welcome reprieve from the brick-like meat loaf threatening to emerge from the oven when Dad abruptly pronounced it "Chink Night."

"A week from Friday," she replied. "Can't wait . . . hanging with the parents is the pits."

Like the robust odor of my grease-stained bag of moo shu chicken, I thought. "I can relate," I said.

Annie retrieved her order, an equally pungent package of moo goo gai pan. As we turned to leave, I reached out and touched her arm. "Annie, why don't we meet up for a movie before you go back to school? It'll give us a chance to catch up."

She hesitated briefly, then smiled. "Sure, why not?"

I picked up Annie the following Wednesday night at her parents' house. I'd met them several times when we were young, and they purported, at least, to remember me. They were solicitous enough, but I couldn't shake the sense that they were vetting me. I apparently passed the test, and Annie was entrusted into my care for the evening.

I took her to see *Bonnie & Clyde* with Warren Beatty and Faye Dunaway. We topped off the night with dessert at Wimpy's. Although she intrigued me that evening, I treated her more like a friend than a date.

Later, when I dropped her off, I couldn't help but notice her parents stationed at the front window, nervously awaiting her return. So I hugged her (you don't kiss a nun, do you?) and made some vague reference to seeing her again soon.

CHAPTER FOURTEEN

Pull Up Your Panties and Cover Your Titties

When I chose to attend Roberts, I vastly underestimated my tolerance for winter. It was brutal. On my way to breakfast at The Douche one January morning, the hairs in my nostrils froze. It was thirty-six below zero. Once snow arrived in force by mid-November, it was a constant presence. Drifts as high as eight feet lined the frozen walkways along the college green.

It was a skier's heaven, but freezing my butt off while strapped to a pair of bed slats held no appeal for me. Apart from skiing and studying, the only attraction of winter at Roberts was the tradition of Winter Carnival.

Winter Carnival had evolved over the years from an idyllic weekend to a three-day bacchanal and orgy. Beer was to partying undergrads like vodka to Russians. It took a confident and courageous woman to accept an invitation to that February weekend on the campus of Roberts College.

After the Homecoming debacle, I knew I wouldn't entertain a blind date. When Izzy and Leah offered to fix me up ("I've got someone great for you this time, Charlie," she promised), I politely but firmly declined. A weekend in the library would easily trump another blind date.

I did have another option. I could invite Annie the Nun. Would she even consider submitting to three days with me in this snow-saturated sanctum of debauchery? Would her parents approve? What the heck, I figured, she can only say no.

It took twenty minutes of phone calls to wend my way through St. Augustine's gauntlet of secrecy to uncover the number for Annie's dorm. I'd shoveled an entire roll of quarters into the pay phone before I finally managed to reach her.

"Charlie! How'd you get my number?" She sounded more curious than defensive.

"I know a guy at the C.I.A."

"So what can I do for you?"

"You can be my date for Winter Carnival." Annie laughed out loud, a discouraging sign. I plowed on nonetheless. "I'm serious, Annie. It's our big winter weekend. I'd like you to come."

She responded with the enthusiasm of an undertaker. "I don't know, Charlie," she sighed. "Can I think it over?"

"Of course," I said, promising to call her back the next evening.

I resolved to give it my very best shot. I'd call a florist and send her a bouquet in the morning. I'd include a clever card. Engaging Izzy to help me compose the perfect poetic lines (and employing a six-pack of Bud for inspiration), we came up with this:

> *Do me the honor of being my date*
> *And Carnival weekend will surely be great!*

We got less corny but more raunchy as the Budweiser kicked in:

Because you're religious and truly devout
I'll try to assure no one grosses you out.
But if you're offended by my little ditties
Then pull up your panties and cover your titties
'Cause accepting my invite would make you a fool
Since Carnival weekend's a bitch at this school!

Upon further reflection, we thought it best to abandon the final six lines.

When I dialed Annie the next evening, I knew at once that I had broken through. "The flowers were *beautiful*!" she crowed. "The card, too. Okay, I'll come down for Carnival! But only . . ." and here was the caveat, "on the understanding that we're *just friends.*"

"Great!" I said, pleased more by her acceptance than her caveat. "It'll be an adventure!" I promised. And it was.

CHAPTER FIFTEEN

The Nun Cometh

I had no illusions about my date for Winter Carnival. Annie would be great company, but there was little chance of anything more. We were merely old friends. I got that. *At least I thought I did.* She was beautiful, sweet, and as pure as the blanket of snow that choked the Roberts campus on that Winter Carnival weekend in February of '68. Her school, St. Augustine's, was an all-women's Catholic school, a veritable nunnery. My first Winter Carnival would be a *look but don't touch* kind of affair. I could live with that. *At least I thought I could.*

I met Annie's bus at the station on Friday afternoon. I nearly keeled over when I saw her step off. She was even more striking than I'd remembered. Her hair was longer than I recalled and the smile she flashed when she spied me was mesmerizing.

Annie made the trip in the company of Maria Landers, an attractive St. Augustine's junior who was Annie's sorority 'big sister,' a kind of mentor to the younger pledge. Maria was a tall, slim, and leggy brunette, with a closely cropped, boyish haircut that made her look like Mia Farrow. It was obvious that the two had become close friends. I also sensed that Maria's attendance at Winter Carnival was a persuasive factor (along with my flowers and corny poetry) in Annie's decision to accept my invitation.

Since Maria's date was in class, I grabbed both their overnight bags and walked the girls to their weekend accommodations at Big Dick's. As they checked in at the front desk, I had flashbacks of Homecoming Weekend, dragging a plastered presidential look-alike past the same desk, hoping she'd fail to register the time on the lobby clock. This would be a much better weekend. *At least I thought it would.*

Maria went on to her room. I walked Annie to hers. After dropping off her luggage, I noticed that the lock on her door didn't catch properly. We reported it to the desk clerk on the way out.

I gave Annie a tour of the campus en route to my dorm. The heavy cover of fresh snow imparted an eerie silence to the college green. The trees were cloaked in a sheath of white, like a dusting of confectioners' sugar. The snow-covered buildings glistened in the winter sun like a row of vanilla cupcakes in a bakery display case. A monumental ice sculpture of a satyr towered over the center of the green, setting a provocative tone for the weekend.

Izzy and Leah were already sipping makeshift cocktails when we reached Rowley Hall. After the introductions, Izzy pulled me aside.

"Shit, Charlie, she's drop dead gorgeous!" He patted me on the back in mock congratulation.

"Hottest nun in America."

"You know what they say about Catholic girls . . ."

I didn't, but it didn't matter. The weekend was off and running.

Izzy and I took Leah and Annie to dinner at The Douche. *Big mistake.* As we headed toward the cafeteria-style counter, scattered clapping erupted like gunshots. The applause multiplied, then swelled to a full-blown standing ovation. I took a peek around the hall, looking for whatever hot date might have provoked this boorish display. It took only a moment to conclude (to my concurrent thrill and horror) that the cheering was directed at Annie (and, by attribution, me).

Annie didn't immediately comprehend the significance of the commotion. When it dawned on her, she was mortified. I, on the other hand, ran the gamut of emotions: from empathy for Annie's embarrassment to euphoria for the acknowledgment of my impeccable taste and good fortune in securing such a fetching Carnival date. Rarely were such kudos bestowed upon mere freshmen!

Annie turned beet-red. Leah, by now thoroughly familiar with the primitive manners at Roberts, sprung into action to contain the situation. "They're a bunch of animals," she told Annie, grasping her arm in reassurance. "Don't let them get to you. Just fill your tray with food and follow us to the back of the dining hall. Don't even glance at the bastards." Leah's intercession was timely and her advice on the mark. I was ashamed of myself for the part of me that basked in that vulgar adulation.

Annie was subdued throughout dinner. Later, she asked me pointedly: "Is that the way Roberts men generally treat women?"

"No," I lied, "it's not always like that. But it wouldn't have happened if you weren't so stunningly beautiful." Sure, blame her. Yet the backhanded compliment seemed to defuse her irritation.

"Never mind. I survived," she said, smiling humorlessly.

The snow crunched underfoot as we walked across the green back to my room.

"I really didn't think your parents would approve of your being here," I said. "Do they know?"

· "They don't know *what* they want," Annie said dismissively. "They're overly protective, as you couldn't help but notice during Christmas break. But at the same time they're worried that I didn't date enough in high school; that I'll become a pathetic old spinster. So I mentioned this weekend . . . just to get them off my back."

"And their reaction?"

"Dad has you pegged as Jewish, so you're not marriageable, but he thinks you're a 'nice boy' anyway. And Mom was all for it. But she gave me an interminable lecture about what drunken guys at college can do to poor innocent girls like me. . . . How would she even know? Anyway, they both think I'm way more naïve than I actually am." Had I fallen into the same trap?

Izzy had again procured the requisite alcoholic provisions for the weekend, but had something unexpected in reserve. "Thirty-two bucks an ounce," he boasted as he yanked a glassine bag from his jeans pocket. "Best weed on campus!"

I glanced at Annie to gauge her reaction. Reading my mind, she smiled approvingly. Izzy lit a joint and passed it around. Annie inhaled like she'd done it before. Izzy ratcheted up the stereo; even Leonard Cohen sounded good. We acted like assholes. It was fun.

Leah and Izzy took their leave around midnight. Perhaps this would be their night. Izzy told me that Leah was making progress in conquering her sexual phobias and predicted that the loss of his virginity was "just around the fuckin' corner." He'd targeted this weekend. I gave him a knowing wink as he led Leah back to his room.

Left to our own devices, Annie and I spent the rest of the

evening dancing, talking, and laughing under the spell of Izzy's weed. I'd meticulously respected the boundaries she'd imposed. It took a heroic effort, however, to restrain my growing urge to *pull down her panties and uncover her titties* (to bastardize our poetic artistry).

It was well past one o'clock when I walked Annie back to Big Dick's. Outside the front door, she thanked me for a "really neat evening." Feeling my self-control waning, I ventured an innocent kiss. She returned it grudgingly. I declined to press my luck and bade her good night.

When I ran into Izzy the next morning, he was grinning from ear to ear, flashing the "thumbs-up" sign.

"Got laid! Boinked! Pounded the pussy! Did the nasty! Hid the sausage! Popped my cherry!" he announced in rapid-fire fashion.

"Congrats, you old fucker!" I said. "Was she okay with it?"

"No problems this time. Locked the window in advance," he deadpanned. "How about you?"

"Just a measly kiss."

"Too bad," Izzy said. "But you're a campus hero, Charlie. No one's got a hotter date. And nobody needs to know that she won't put out."

Izzy was right. At least three acquaintances stopped to congratulate me that morning as I made my way to Big Dick's to collect Annie. I wasn't sure how to react. Offer a sly grin? Stick out my tongue and pant? Should I say "thanks" or "fuck you"? One asshole asked if I was really serious about my girlfriend and if not, could he have Annie's number? "Fuck you!" I said.

Saturday was dominated by campus activities—an afternoon basketball game, a Simon & Garfunkel concert that night. Paul

Simon's lyrics were magical, though brimming with yearning and regret. As I glanced at Annie standing beside me that evening, rocking gently with the music, her honey blond hair silhouetted against the stage lights, I felt my resolve weakening. I listened with longing as Art Garfunkel crooned the concluding quatrain of *For Emily, Whenever I May Find Her:*

> *And when I awoke and felt you warm and near,*
> *I kissed your honey hair with my grateful tears.*
> *Oh I love you, girl.*
> *Oh, I love you.*

Way more elegant, I conceded, than *pull up your panties and cover your titties.*

Though I savored every second with Annie, her caveat weighed on me like a holiday fruitcake. It took virtually every ounce of self-restraint I could summon to keep myself in check. I really liked this girl. This "friend" shit was getting old.

When I returned her to Big Dick's on Saturday night, I resolved to be somewhat bolder. This time I kissed her less tentatively. She returned the kiss a little less grudgingly, but she chose not to linger, quickly excusing herself to head upstairs. *Foiled again!*

I mulled it over as I trudged along the snowy path back to the dorm. What were my options? Should I be patient, build on our friendship, and hope for an eventual breakthrough? Should I admit defeat and cut my losses? Should I auction her phone number to the highest bidder? Or was there some missing piece to the puzzle I hadn't yet grasped?

The next day, Sunday, would prove a climactic day—in every sense of the word—in my relationship with Annie Christiansen.

Attendance at Sunday morning church services was part of Annie's weekend agenda. She'd made it clear that she didn't mind going alone, and I was more than happy to oblige her by sleeping in. We'd meet up at Big Dick's after her return from mass.

Izzy, high on his second consecutive night of "pounding the pussy," had some early morning advice for me: "Be a *mensch*," he said (whatever that meant), "and take her to church. Show up early at Big Dick's. Tell her you'd like to accompany her. It'll be a pleasant surprise. She'll love you for it. What have you got to lose?"

Despite the anti-religious fervor I'd inherited from my father, I had to agree that I'd nothing to lose. Fortunately, my mother had slipped a jacket and tie into my footlocker when we packed for Roberts in the fall. I put them on, feeling silly and uncomfortable. But with my parka covering them, no one would notice.

I reached Big Dick's at about eight. I strolled through the lobby and climbed the stairs to Annie's room. I knocked. No answer. I was sure I'd heard laughter and squealing inside.

I knocked again, louder this time, while the racket inside persisted. Finally, I heard Annie shout "I'm coming!" So I waited. If I didn't know better, I'd have guessed that Annie wasn't alone. What could be going on in there? Again, I heard Annie's voice, much more forcefully this time: "I'm coming! I'm *coming!*" Or was it "Come in! Come in!"?

As no one came to the door, I deduced she'd shouted "Come in!" I turned the doorknob. The bozos at Big Dick's hadn't repaired the lock, so the door gave way easily when I pushed forward. What I witnessed at that moment is forever etched in my psyche.

Annie was splayed across the bed, stark naked, as her

"friend" Maria, head buried in Annie's crotch, elicited moans of delight from her "little sister." Her hands gripped Maria's temples firmly but tenderly. Annie arched her back, writhing euphorically as Maria devoured her. So engrossed were they in their ecstasy that they didn't even notice my entrance.

"I'm COMING!!!!!" screeched Annie once again. She really meant it this time, as she convulsed in waves of utter rapture.

It was probably my gasp (followed by a hearty "WHAT THE FUCK!") that finally alerted the girls to my presence. Annie leapt up in panic, covering herself with a sheet, while Maria emitted a barely audible "Oh, shit!" as she calmly emerged from between Annie's legs. *Pull up your panties and cover your titties!*

"What are you *doing* here, Charlie!" Annie blurted out in a mixture of embarrassment and anger. I didn't know whether to run or hold my ground. I was aghast. I held my ground.

"I thought I'd surprise you and take you to church!" I stammered.

"Looks like we're all surprised," Maria quipped as she coolly donned a robe.

My shock gave way to epiphany. Suddenly, I knew why Annie didn't date guys in high school. Guys thought her religious devotion precluded her dating, but religion was merely her cover. After all, diddling with Maria had surely trumped churchgoing on this particular Sunday morning.

> *Annie's no nun,*
> *She's a les-bi-an!*

Annie's lesbianism was her deep, dark secret (except, of course, to Maria). Obviously, her parents didn't know. And even if they'd suspected, a Winter Carnival date with good old

Charlie at a school notorious for horniness was another perfect cover. I wondered if Maria really had a date at Roberts. Was this just a lesbians' getaway, safer perhaps than a rendezvous in a dorm room at St. Augustine's?

"I'll see you after 'church'," I said in disgust as I stomped out the door. Annie didn't run after me—she wasn't exactly dressed for it. Anyway, what could she possibly say? I'd caught her *in flagrante delicto*—red-handed—her panties down and her titties uncovered. *Res ipsa loquitur*: the facts spoke for themselves.

Like most guys at the time, I was blissfully ignorant about homosexuality. We'd joke about it, of course, displaying the sensitivity of two-by-fours, while at another level, perhaps, masking our own sexual insecurities. And lesbianism was even more inscrutable, if somewhat less offensive or threatening. But all of this was largely academic—I had no personal experience with homosexuality, largely because most homosexuals remained in the closet, afraid of the disapprobation of their friends, neighbors, and (especially) their families. So, when I left Big Dick's that morning, I was unable to process the discordant thoughts bombarding my mind. I was shocked and devastated. I also felt betrayed. Yet certain things were newly apparent. Even though I strained to comprehend her sexual preferences, I understood Annie's dilemma, her motives, and the ambivalence she must have felt toward me. I didn't quite know what to do next, so I walked aimlessly around campus feeling sorry for myself until I was too cold to walk any further.

Annie was waiting for me when I returned to the dorm. She stood outside my door, still bundled in her full-length gray winter coat.

"I thought you weren't coming back," she said as I unlocked my room, still shivering from the cold. I didn't respond. We walked in and sat down. She spoke softly but firmly: "I'm sorry ... and totally embarrassed ... by what you saw this morning. I can't justify it to you. I'd understand if you never chose to speak to me again." She hesitated when I failed to jump in, fearing that I'd already determined to shut her out. "I've known since the eighth grade that I was attracted to women," she said. "My family doesn't know ... and I'd like to keep it that way."

"I won't spill the beans," I said scornfully.

"I didn't say that to beg for your silence," she clarified, "though I'd much appreciate it. I just wanted you to understand my predicament." She took a deep breath. "Only three people have ever known: two former lovers and Maria. It's been more difficult than you can possibly imagine to pretend that I'm straight—to live a lie—every day of my life."

"Annie, you don't have to go into this—"

"I do, Charlie. I do. I know you're hurt and feel used, but that's not how it is. It was so nice spending time with you during Christmas break, and I really enjoyed your company this weekend. Except for this morning, I'm glad I came."

You came, all right, I wanted to say in my twisted, despondent state, but thought better of it.

"I'm ashamed that you caught me like that, but I'm no longer ashamed to be gay." She unbuttoned her coat. "I was afraid and ashamed throughout high school. I prayed to be 'normal' ... but nothing changed. The Catholic Church doesn't condone homosexuality, so I abandoned much of my faith. We are who we are, Charlie, whether we like it or not."

Annie's words were heartfelt, even eloquent. As my sense of anger and betrayal gradually abated, I began to feel some empathy for her, difficult as it may have been at that moment. I finally gathered the courage to speak.

"I can't say I fully understand, Annie... at least at this particular moment. But I appreciate how hard this must be. And I feel sorry for you in that respect," I said.

"I don't want your pity," she said without rancor. "I want you to forgive me, but only for pretending to be someone I'm not. I want you to accept me as I am. You are the only guy in the world who truly knows me now," she said. "You liked the girl you thought I was. Can you like the girl I really am?"

That, indeed, was the question.

CHAPTER SIXTEEN

Annie's Not Your Nun

I thought a great deal about Annie over the next several days. How could I not? I said nothing to Izzy—or to anyone else—about what I'd witnessed. Izzy assumed my dejection related merely to Annie's failure to respond to my affection. He had no idea how much more complicated it was.

After several days of contemplation, I decided I was ready to talk with Annie again. When she picked up the dormitory hall phone she was cautious. She could be easily overheard, she said. Could we get together and talk more privately?

St. Augustine's was about an hour north by bus. I offered to come up to see her that Saturday.

Annie met me at the bus station. After exchanging greetings, we walked to an off-campus restaurant, choosing a quiet table in the back. I launched the conversation.

"I've been thinking a lot over the past few days. The shock has finally worn off," I said as I absent-mindedly perused the menu. "I think I can talk more rationally now. I have a lot of questions."

"I'll answer them as best I can."

"Why did you agree to be my date in the first place?" I asked her pointedly.

"You were rather insistent," she said. "I didn't want to mislead you. I tried to be clear we were friends, nothing more."

"Didn't you know how much I cared for you? That I'd want to break through whatever barriers you'd set for me?"

"I worried about that," she admitted. "I *wanted* to spend the weekend with you. I thought I could control matters well enough to avoid any consequences. I was obviously wrong about that, and I'm truly sorry I hurt you." A waiter sauntered by. We waved him off.

"What about Maria? Did she really have a date? Or were you simply arranging a lovers' tryst at my expense?"

Annie pursed her lips. "Maria had a date. She's bisexual—sexually attracted to both women and men. Her date may or may not have known of her preferences, but that's her business. I don't ask."

"Are you in love with Maria?"

"No," she said definitively. "She's older and much more sophisticated than I am . . . more of a mentor than a lover. She's helped me to better understand my feelings and urges. She's given me confidence in myself, helped me to accept myself for who I am."

Everything Annie had said thus far made sense. Yet there was more I needed to know.

"I've never been in this position, Annie. I haven't been exposed to homosexuality. There's a lot I don't fully understand." I paused for a sip of water. "Can I ask you some even more personal questions?"

Annie looked me in the eye and leaned forward. "When I told you that you are one of only four people on this Earth who know my secret, I hoped I could confide in you without your judging me. So sure, fire away."

"How did you know—" The waiter returned. We each took

a perfunctory glance at the menu, ordered quickly, and shooed him away.

"How did you know you were gay?"

"I was always more comfortable around girls," she explained. "Guys are more aggressive. I knew I attracted guys . . . and some of them I liked . . . but none of them interested me in a sexual way." Annie brushed back a wayward strand of hair. "In my junior year, I had a crush on one of my female classmates. She sensed it and approached me one day after class. 'Do you like girls?' she asked. I didn't know whether to answer honestly. I took the chance and said yes. That was the turning point. She was my first lover." She paused, her sparkling blue eyes fixing on mine. "Does that help?"

Actually, it did. But I still wanted one more answer to a question I was reluctant to ask. Our waiter came by with our Cokes, giving me the moment I needed to overcome my hesitancy.

"You explained that Maria was bisexual," I said. "Could you be bisexual, too?"

Annie exhaled deeply. "A fair question," she said, "but I'm not sure there's an easy answer. I probably just don't know yet. I know that . . . to this point . . . no guy has attracted me sexually like the women I've been involved with. Beyond that, I can't really say for sure."

I sighed. "A week ago I thought of you as a super-religious innocent, this naïve China doll. But it feels as if I'm the one who's naïve."

Annie grimaced at my 'China doll' reference. "I was trapped in that other persona—the 'Nun' thing. I knew they called me that," she said with a smirk. "I was losing my religion all the while I was struggling with my sexual identity. But being 'the Nun' protected me. Kept me from awkward situations. Helped me preserve my secret while I sorted things out."

"What are you doing at a Catholic college?" I asked.

"It suited my parents. It seemed a small price to pay to maintain my cover."

I made my final inquiry gingerly. "Is there a way we can be friends? Could we ever be more than friends?"

"I'd cherish your friendship," she said, "but I thought after last weekend that I'd surely lost you. You can certainly tell from what you witnessed that I'm not that China doll you talked about . . . and I'm well past naïve." We both took sips of our Cokes. "But to answer your question is hard. Friends can be lovers, I suppose . . . physically . . . but I can't have you fall *in love* with me if I can't return your affection. That wouldn't be fair to you. I'd just hurt you all over again." Her answer left some room for hope, but whether that was a good thing was eminently debatable.

"I'm grateful for your honesty," I said, "and especially your trust." Her eyes fixed warmly upon mine. "I won't betray it, Annie, and I want very much to remain your friend."

"I'd welcome that. And I want you to know how good it feels to share this with someone, especially you."

"Would you come back to Roberts if I asked you?"

She smiled. "Only if you think you can handle it." It was a considerable caveat. Neither of us said anything for a few moments. Annie tilted her head and smiled. "Actually, as I think about it," she mused, "it might be fun to pretend, as long as we recognize that we're role-playing."

I gave her a quizzical look.

"I can help you become the 'big man on campus' that I think you'd like to be," she said confidently. "I can pretend to bask in the glow of the bullshit applause at The Douche—I know you call it that, by the way," she chuckled, pausing as the waiter delivered our burgers. She sampled a french fry before continuing. "We can smooch in public. I can make every guy envy you. It might be fun," she laughed. "But really, Charlie, I should only be your back-up date. If someone else comes into your life, she—or maybe *he*," she giggled, "should take priority."

Over the coming months I would think often about our conversation. Whether I could handle the reality of what she'd told me remained an open question.

CHAPTER SEVENTEEN

The Steel Prick

Freshman year at Roberts had been anything but uneventful. I'd endured a Homecoming debacle with the female incarnation of President Johnson; rescued the briefly loopy, third-floor-leaping Leah; and waltzed through a whacked-out Winter Carnival weekend with a nearly-nun-turned-lesbian. This was *not* the freshman year I'd envisaged. Buoyed by the confidence imparted by my sexual education crash course with Catherine and our mutual discovery of the magical power of my crooked member, I'd set out in search of a normal social life featuring a legitimate relationship with a real, *heterosexual* girl. And maybe I'd even get laid, like my good friend Izzy and virtually everyone else at Roberts, it seemed. Instead, my freshman year had been just another series of frustrations and calamities, each more absurd than the last. By this point, I was more than ready to escape for the relative calm of a summer in New Liberty.

Through one of my Government professors, I secured a summer internship with one of his former students, the city manager of Havenhurst, New Jersey, a small city not far from New Liberty. The city manager was Robert C. Johnson, Jr., a strapping six-footer whose dark-rimmed glasses, well-chiseled features, and overall good looks reminded me of Superman's alter ego, Clark Kent. But where Superman was the *Man of Steel*, Johnson was the *Steel Prick*.

"Call me Bobby!" he roared, brutally squeezing my hand while escorting me into his well-appointed office on my first day. "Glad to have you with us," he said. "It's going to be an interesting summer." He was certainly right about that.

There was a disingenuousness to Bobby Johnson. His studious effort to project an image of urban sophistication was a harsh repudiation of his rural Midwestern upbringing. He was also *way* too slick. As I'd later learn, Bobby was an Iowa farm boy who'd leveraged a Roberts College scholarship to help him escape the agrarian life embraced by his parents and grandparents before him. His abandonment of his rural roots was complicated only by the fact that he'd impregnated, then reluctantly married, his high school sweetheart Paula, a classic farmer's daughter with no appetite for the fast life coveted by her overbearing husband. Bobby refused to allow Paula's indifference to temper his ambition; he was determined to parlay his position as one of the country's up-and-coming city managers into bigger and better things—regardless of the consequences.

As would soon become evident, pretty young women were Bobby's kryptonite. Office scuttlebutt had it that his previous assistant, a married female, had resigned suddenly when her husband discovered she'd been plunking her boss. In the hands of a clever practitioner, sexual harassment in the late Sixties was more an art form than a peril. And Bobby was an accomplished artist.

Bobby's new assistant was Bunny Davis, a dimwitted but exceedingly attractive young woman who'd recently graduated from a middling college with a major in urban studies and a minor in professorial seduction. Bunny had few administrative skills. As a consequence, I was saddled with a boatload of menial tasks. Nearly every afternoon, however, I was given an assignment designed to dispatch me from the office.

"Charlie!" Bobby would shout from his wood-paneled office across the hall from my cubicle. "Go see the Fire Chief. Get a list of his equipment needs for next year's budget." Never mind that the budgeting process for the next fiscal year wouldn't begin for months. When I'd make the required inquiry of the fire chief, he'd chuckle and shoo me away. By then it would be nearly five o'clock, so I'd just head home for the day without returning to the office. That fulfilled Bobby's objective—he and Bunny would be free of prying eyes.

After a week of such wild goose chases, I resolved to confirm my suspicions, reentering my cubicle on the pretense of retrieving a file. It was almost six o'clock. The office appeared empty. But as I approached Bobby's closed door, I heard a rhythmic rumbling accompanied by a refrain of increasingly urgent moaning.

Amused and intrigued, I arrived early the next morning. While Bunny's belongings lay on her desk, she (judging from the cacophony of sighs and pants) was lying on Bobby's desk absorbing another vigorous thumping. Chalk it up as No. 2.

I came to take pride in my running fornication census. I'd routinely make a conspicuous exit each afternoon as I walked by Bunny's desk for the elevator, then return ten minutes later (on the pretense of forgetting something) to tally another plunking for the census. Co-workers would keep watch during lunch hour and alert me whenever Bunny would vanish into Bobby's den of iniquity. By mid-summer, my official count was up to nineteen.

Discretion was not Bobby's forte. Like a privileged athlete, he considered himself immune to public disapprobation. So infatuated was Bunny with Bobby that she was oblivious to everything and everyone else. Before long, the entire staff was wise to their serial trysting and I was acknowledged as the official scorekeeper. I used my tear-away paper calendar as a tally board, displaying on my desktop the up-to-date monthly Copulation Count. Pools sprung up with running odds predicting the number of quickies likely to be recorded during the coming week.

The low point occurred one morning in late July when, after Bunny's exit from Bobby's lair (hair tussled, skirt on backward), I attended a meeting in Bobby's office with a bevy of councilmen. I was appalled when I noticed (then tried futilely to ignore) a nasty puddle of a telltale sticky substance oozing slowly over the edge of Bobby's desk.

One day in early August the trysts ceased. Had the Steel Prick gone flaccid? Did Bobby and Bunny have a falling out?

Curiously, at about the same time, I began to endure reamings of a different sort from the Steel Prick. On a nearly daily basis, Bobby would emerge from his office and scold me publicly over some imagined inadequacy in my work. I was surprised that he'd any idea what I was doing in the first place. Bunny, for her part, was unusually curt with me, no longer breezily witless as had been her style.

Initially, I was at a loss to explain their radically changed behavior. But then it came to me: there was a snitch in our midst. Someone had informed Bobby of both the transparency of his infidelities and my involvement in mocking him by tallying his coital conquests. I was vulnerable, but determined to hang on for the summer's few remaining weeks—if for no other reason than to collect my remaining paychecks.

Though the tally for August remained frozen at zero, I was

convinced that Bunny and Bobby were banging, just not at the office. I decided it was my civic duty to investigate. I covertly secured Bunny's address from her personnel file. That night, after both she and Bobby had departed for the evening, I drove by her apartment. As anticipated, Bobby's sleek red Porsche was parked out in front.

Later that week, Bobby's wife Paula made an unannounced visit to the office. To my surprise, she hadn't come to see Bobby. She'd come to see me.

Paula Johnson was pretty, though perhaps a tad overweight, with the pallid countenance of a woman whose self-esteem had endured constant bruising. We'd met several times previously when she'd dropped by the office to see Bobby. But on this day, there was anger in her eyes and a wrathful determination in her voice.

"Charlie," she said, a forced smile on her face, "is there someplace we can talk—privately?" I managed a weak nod as I led her to an empty conference room. I was apprehensive. She was calm and brutally direct.

"I know all about my husband's philandering," she said, putting me at ease after we'd seated ourselves in the high-backed leather chairs and shut the heavy wooden door. "It's not the first time and it won't be the last. He's a shameless bastard who should have his prick cut off." Harsh, perhaps, but I certainly understood her sentiment. "He doesn't know it yet, but divorce papers are being drawn up as we speak. Our marriage is over." Then she turned, raised her head, and looked me straight in the eye: "It's all about vengeance now," she seethed.

"Uh, Mrs. Johnson, I—"

"Call me Paula, please."

"Why come to me, Paula?"

"Because I hear you're particularly clever and have as little respect for Bobby as I do," she said. "My sources also tell me that you'd been keeping score . . . in a manner of speaking . . . and that some bootlicker spilled the beans on you to my husband. And I also hear that you've been paying a price for your irreverence."

I was heartened both by her knowledge and belligerence. I'd felt sorry for her, assuming she'd been shamelessly duped and blissfully unaware all summer. That was apparently not the case. She was now fighting back. I liked that. But I knew that Paula had not sought me out simply to refute her naiveté or vent her anger.

"I don't know what I can possibly do, Paula," I said, still trying to assess where the conversation was heading.

"Look, Charlie, it's as simple as this: I see you as a potential ally to help me settle the score. He's preyed on you. So it occurred to me that you might enjoy a measure of revenge as well. I want to embarrass him like he's embarrassed me; publicly reveal him for the jackass he is."

"How?"

"That's where I thought you might be helpful. You're clearly resourceful. And given your current situation, I doubt you have much to lose," she concluded, quite accurately. "Just give it some thought." She stood up to leave. "No obligation. Your involvement, if any, will remain our little secret. And if you're the least bit uncomfortable with any role in this, I'll understand completely."

I replayed our discussion repeatedly in my mind throughout the day. It evoked a range of emotions: I was embarrassed that I had been so involved with mocking Bobby's infidelities and had done so behind his back, astonished at having been approached by Paula with such a bizarre request, and sorely tempted by the opportunity to exact my own revenge by devising a plan to expose Bobby's audacious infidelity. I should have simply demurred and let Paula work out her own issues, unjustifiably victimized as she might have been. But Bobby had been an asshole from the day I met him and richly deserved his comeuppance. And Paula was right: I had little to lose. It was my crooked prick against Bobby's steel one. Game on!

After ruminating over the problem for several days, I decided to seek a sounding board. I'd seen Annie several times over the summer, and our friendship had only grown stronger. Given our curious history together, I felt I could comfortably discuss anything with her. She would also bring an entirely different perspective to the matter.

"I have no idea how you get yourself into such ridiculous situations," she said after hearing my story. She was right, of course. Outrageous circumstances had become my stock-in-trade. "You know you should just walk away from this," she said, "but you won't. You need closure and you think you're on the moral high ground. So, no matter how hard I try to dissuade you, you're going to do this." She was right. "The trick is to keep from embarrassing yourself more than you embarrass this idiot Johnson." Right again.

We proposed and rejected one scheme after another. Tape recording a tryst would provide incontrovertible evidence, but it was no longer a viable option. Tape recorders were bulky and with all copulation having moved off-campus, there was no way to plant one in Bunny's apartment without committing a felony. The suggestions became increasingly absurd.

"I've got a crazy idea," Annie said. "You can't help but remember my friend Maria," she began. I rolled my eyes and she smiled. "Well, anyway," she said, "Maria is a theater major and lives in southern Connecticut."

"That's nice."

"How's this: what if Maria and I masquerade as prostitutes who've both been impregnated by your boss during a *ménage a trois*. We go to his office together and demand 'hush money' payments we claim he promised us. We do this in earshot of this Bunny character and she'll probably freak out!"

"How in God's name do you come up with shit like that?" This stuff was coming from a girl I once believed was inches from a nunnery. Yet it had potential. It was almost too absurd not to be credible, and we hadn't come up with anything better. If Annie and Maria could pull this off, it would be both hilarious and duly embarrassing to the Steel Prick.

Over the next week, Annie secured Maria's cooperation (she was amused and always primed for a challenge) and I ran the plan by Paula Johnson. Paula was dubious (as well she should have been) but saw little downside and gave her blessing. She suggested we plan it for the following Thursday morning when the Steel Prick typically scheduled a weekly update with city councilmen. All the better to have a receptive audience, she reasoned.

On the appointed day, I picked up Annie and Maria at Annie's house where Maria had spent the preceding night, first in the company of Annie's unsuspecting parents and then, presumably, in Annie's bed. I cringed at the thought and was jealous of Maria's good fortune.

I pulled my car over at a secluded spot on the side of the road to allow the two women to strap small pillows to their abdomens and change into maternity dresses that Maria had found in a thrift shop. Watching them surreptitiously in the rearview mirror as they changed unabashedly in the back seat gave me shivers. They painted themselves with heavy eyeliner and candy apple red lipstick. They giggled like little girls pretending to be adults, though in this case they were actually impersonating floozies. They tested out dialogue, employing their trashiest faux New Jersey accents. When they pronounced themselves ready, I drove the rest of the way to the office, dropping them off at a coffee (or was that *cawfee*?) shop down the block to kill the hour or so before their performance was slated to begin.

"Break a leg!" I implored them.

At precisely 10:15 that morning, while the councilmen were meeting with Bobby, two trashy pregnant ladies strode purposefully into Havenhurst City Hall. They attracted the desired attention as they marched up to Bunny's desk like angry guard dogs.

"Can I *help* you?" asked Bunny, taken aback by their aggressive demeanor.

"Damned straight you can!" bellowed Maria. "Where's that perve widda wanderin' peckah?"

Staff members had begun to make their way toward the commotion.

"I'm sorry, ladies! You can't come in here like this and rudely interrupt city business!" said Bunny.

"Was that creep on city bis'ness when he lured us into his fuckin' t'reesome and knocked us *both* up the same fuckin' night?" screamed Annie, laying on a nearly impenetrable accent as a crowd gathered around Bunny's desk, taking it all in. "That fucka owes us! Let me at 'im!" Annie's trash-talking sexpot act was making me crookedly hard.

Annie whisked past Bunny and lunged for the door to Bobby's office. She twisted the knob and the door flew open.

"There you are, you fuckhead!" she squealed. "So where's that fuckin' hush money you promised us, you shit?"

As the councilmen turned in astonishment, Maria took her cue: "Johnson, you jerkoff, you ain't gonna have your way wit' us and wawk away like ain't nothin's happened. Pay up, asshole!"

"What in God's name is going on here, Bobby?" demanded Councilman Rodgers.

"I have no idea who these women are!" Bobby protested, springing from his desk. "Call the cops and get these bitches the hell out of here!"

I watched Bunny as the color drained from her face. Rather than call the police, she bolted from the room in tears.

"We get the dough by the end of the week or we'll fuckin' sue your sorry ass!" Maria hollered at the top of her lungs. "And keep it in your pants from now on, you prick!"

Their performance complete, Annie and Maria strutted out like a pair of peacocks. At least twenty sets of eyes trained on them as they departed. Bunny was nowhere to be found.

"I haven't any idea who the hell these two women are!" Bobby insisted to anyone who would listen. The councilmen had already walked out of the meeting, shaking their heads in disbelief.

I quickly left the building and headed for the street where I found Annie and Maria grinning ear-to-ear. I walked up to Annie and planted a big kiss on her lips.

"How about me?" purred Maria, a wide smile on her painted face. I kissed her too.

Bunny never did return to work. Bobby tried, but failed, to convince anyone of his ignorance of the entire matter. Paula Johnson obtained her divorce with a generous property settlement and relocated with her son to Iowa. To express her appreciation, she presented me a gift certificate to Sympatico, the best Italian restaurant in the state. No one ever connected me to the city hall drama. Bobby somehow kept his job (the good old boys still had each other's backs) but his next assistant was an immensely overweight and decidedly unappealing sixty-year-old guy.

Not surprisingly, I didn't get a recommendation for my effort that summer and, to my knowledge, no other Roberts College student ever graced Havenhurst City Hall as an intern again.

CHAPTER EIGHTEEN

Bursting Bubbles

Spending the summer with my parents was a nightmare. Shortly after my last visit at spring break, Dad had converted my bedroom into a den. Nobody (not even my brother, Hermie) had bothered to warn me. I felt like an intruder in my own home. My "stuff," such as it was, was packed away in boxes in the attic.

"You're not a kid anymore," Dad said when he detected a hint of disappointment on my face. "Did you think we'd preserve it as a shrine to our first-born, the college boy?" Mom just shrugged, confirming by her expression that it was my father's idea and she'd had nothing to do with it. I slept in the basement.

As whacked-out as my Havenhurst internship had been, at least it kept me out of the house. That freedom was made possible by my use of the extra car that my parents had recently acquired. They bought it while my father was stripping my old bedroom of all evidence of my prior occupation. Though she never admitted it, I always suspected that the additional car was my mother's idea, a kind of peace offering to assuage her guilt over my cold-hearted displacement.

Despite my long hours away from home interviewing fire chiefs and counting coital encounters, I still couldn't evade my parents' persistent meddling.

"You need to meet a nice girl, Charlie," my mother would repeat on an almost daily basis.

"I'm fine, Ma," I'd respond on an almost daily basis.

"What about that nice local girl, Annie, that you see every now and then," she asked me once.

She's a lesbian, Mom, I wanted to answer, but thought better of it. Not only would that have required a good deal of delicate explanation, but it would have also blown Annie's cover once my mother broadcast the news throughout northern New Jersey. "She's just a friend, Mom."

A few weeks later, another conversation came out of the blue:

"Your Aunt Harriet's good friend has a daughter," Mom said.

"That's nice, Ma."

"Harriet says she's a real beauty and doesn't have a boyfriend at the moment."

"That's nice, Ma."

"Her name is Miriam and Harriet told her all about you. She'll set you up."

"Ma!" I exploded. "Who told Aunt Harriet to do that?"

"It was *her* idea. I think you should meet this Miriam—it will do you good." Go on a blind date with someone your *maiden aunt* set you up with? Are you kidding me?

"No way, Mom," I said, just as my father entered the room.

"My sister's gone out of her way to do you a favor," he barked. "You'll go and meet Miriam, goddammit, and you'll have a fucking good time!"

What began as a suggestion had morphed into a nonnegotiable demand. There was little use in resisting; I couldn't possibly change the outcome. I'd go out with Miriam, find her revolting, and never see her again.

"Fine! I'll go out with her!"

My Aunt Harriet was a spinster, older than my father but way more Jewish. Unlike Dad, who had pegged all religion as bullshit, Harriet was active in the local synagogue and had many friends there. Beryl Levy, Miriam's mother, was one of her closest. Within a day of my grudging surrender, Harriet and Beryl had set a time and date for my meeting with Miriam. I felt like I'd been ambushed by a Yenta. They'd probably already arranged a wedding date and were just now working on the guest list and meal selections.

I drove to Miriam's parents' house and rang the bell at the appointed hour. Beryl Levy, a fat, gray-haired, matronly woman opened the door. Shit, I thought, please don't let Miriam look like this!

"So, hello! You must be Challie!" she said, inviting me in. Her accent was grating New Jersey with classic Yiddish overtones.

"Charlie," I corrected her politely.

"Norman!" Beryl called out to her equally rotund husband. "Come meet Harriet's nephew, Challie!"

I shook Norman's chunky right hand and surveyed my surroundings. Vases, religious paintings, and tchotchkes filled the room. It looked like a funeral parlor. A pungent odor wafted in from the kitchen. I recognized it immediately as the stench of stuffed cabbage, the dish my paternal grandmother would invariably prepare for us when we visited her apartment in the Bronx. I despised stuffed cabbage.

"Sit! Sit!" said Norman, directing me toward the living room couch. Preserved in its clear plastic slipcover, the couch was a relic. The displacement of air when I sat produced an unwelcome farting sound, like a whoopee cushion. I glanced at the Levys as if to assert my innocence. I wondered how much longer it would be before another rotund member of the Levy family would materialize and be introduced as my date (or, God forbid, my future wife).

After what seemed like an eternity, Miriam Levy sauntered into the living room trailed by a large black poodle. She was mercifully trim and noticeably busty (Miriam, not the poodle). Her demeanor was nonchalant and aloof. Her short skirt betrayed unusually chunky legs but her face (or what I could see of it) was pleasing. She wore a big bouffant hairstyle and a truckload of makeup. Could have been much, much worse, I persuaded myself.

As I stood up to introduce myself, the hairy creature lunged and began to dry hump my left leg (the poodle, not Miriam).

"He likes you," Miriam said, grinning.

"Uh... I'm not particularly fond of dogs," I said as I struggled to shake the little bastard off my leg with no assistance from Miriam or her parents.

After I managed to break free from the drooling, humping mongrel, Miriam and I headed to the car. Ensconced in the passenger seat, Miriam fished a large wad of bubblegum from her suitcase-sized pocketbook.

"Gum?" she offered.

"No thanks," I said. She unwrapped a generous hunk of bright pink gum and stuffed it into her mouth.

"College boy, huh?" she said, smacking away at her resinous mouthful.

"Yeah. Just finished my freshman year at Roberts College in New Hampshire."

"Joisey schools not good enough for ya?" She blew and burst her first of a night's worth of bubbles.

"Just wanted to get away from home, I guess."

"And did ya?"

"Did I what?"

"Get away from home?"

"Uh, *yeah*," I said. "Like I said, I'm going to school in New Hampshire."

"Huh," she muttered. "Nice country."

"It's a state."

"You're a funny guy," she said as another bubble exploded from her mouth, spreading its residue across the bridge of her nose. With her thumb and forefinger, she deftly retrieved the blasted shards, reformed them into a neat wad, and shoved it back into her mouth.

The dismal tone of the evening having now been set, I had only to endure Miriam's company for another hour or so over dinner in the restaurant the matchmakers had selected for us. It was little more than a glorified Jewish delicatessen with table service. I was out of my element. The waitress, eighty if she was a day, waddled to the table.

"What can I get yas?"

I had no idea. I just knew enough to stay away from tongue and gefilte fish. "A brisket sandwich?" I wondered aloud, perusing the menu as if written in Hebrew.

"One brisket sandwich," she repeated. "And how about you, missy?"

"I'll have the stuffed cabbage." Naturally.

Somehow, I survived the meal. The conversation, what there was of it, was hardly scintillating. A hairdresser-in-training, Miriam got animated only when describing her favorite hairdos: bouffants, beehives, buns, hairdos for short hair, hairdos for long hair, hairdos for damn poodles. To my relief, she passed on dessert (gefilte fish sorbet?) and opted instead for another wad of bubble gum. At least I think it was another wad. I could barely contain my zeal at the prospect of taking her home.

"You're kinda cute, Challie," she said to me after I pulled into her driveway and walked her to the front porch. "And, ya know, tonight wasn't a total waste. At least we get our parents off our backs for a while." She amplified her observation with a knowing smile and one last massive explosion of bubble gum before mercifully disappearing through the front door.

CHAPTER NINETEEN

The Five Axioms of Sexual Wisdom

Miriam was right. Our unproductive evening together did in fact keep my parents at bay, at least for a while. Although there were no more attempts to set me up with daughters of friends of aunts or the like, there would be one last parental intrusion to endure that summer.

A week or so after Annie and Maria's Oscar-worthy performance at Havenhurst City Hall as two-thirds of a dastardly *ménage a trois*, I invited Annie out to a celebratory dinner at Sympatico, an elegant dining experience made possible by the generous gift certificate bestowed on me by the wildly appreciative Paula Johnson. I made the mistake of casually disclosing my plans to my parents. You didn't take just any girl to Sympatico, they calculated, especially as they assumed it was on my dime. Sympatico was a big deal. Therefore, my parents concluded, this "friendship" with Annie must be something serious. Once again, since there was no way I would be willing to explain to them the actual circumstances justifying this extravagant "date" (much less my relationship with Annie), I decided to let them believe what they wished.

Shortly before I'd have to leave to pick up Annie, my father approached me with an uncharacteristically earnest look on his face. "It's time we had a little talk, son," he said. "Come join me in The Den." There were two *firsts* within those two simple sentences. The first was the use of the word *son* to address me. It was either "Charlie" or "Little Bastard," but never *son.* Secondly, it was the first time I'd been allowed into "The Den" (formerly known as my bedroom) since I'd discovered its transformation three months earlier. The Den had become the exclusive sanctuary of my father, a place where not even Mom was welcome. This *is* serious, I thought.

Dad sat down in his favorite chair and beckoned me to pull up a seat. Thus far, he hadn't said another word. He carefully selected a pipe from his pipe rack, opened a pouch of tobacco, and casually filled the bowl. It took an eternity to light the damn thing. When he'd finally managed to produce a paltry plume of putrid smoke, he turned and cleared his throat.

"Son," he said pensively, "it's time we had a talk about the birds and bees."

My jaw went slack. What the fuck! Richard Meyer, nicknamed "The Dick" by my maternal grandparents in recognition of his premature impregnation of my mother, was offering *me* advice on sex? I'd venture to say that I could enlighten *him* infinitely more, based on my own outlandish experiences to date, than he could educate me based on his premarital *faux pas* and his years of re-reading *Candy, Lolita, Ulysses,* and *Lady Chatterley's Lover.* But it was clear there was no escape, so I girded myself for the onslaught of sexual wisdom from the Oracle of New Liberty.

"All you need to know about sex, son, can be summarized in five simple axioms," he proclaimed, as if plucking the insight of the ages from the ether. This would be the Meyer family equivalent of Moses' revelation of the Ten Commandments, albeit five short. I yearned for a strong drink.

"**Axiom No. 1**," he said soberly, "is the following:
Don't stick your dick where it doesn't belong."

OK, Dad, I thought, thanks a lot for that precious insight. I suppose you shouldn't stick it into an electrical outlet, but how, wise Oracle, do you decide where it *does* belong? But before I could address the Oracle for clarification, he'd moved on to **Axiom No. 2**:

"***Don't sow your wild oats in fertilized fields.***"

This one made sense, I think, but only if you changed "fertilized" to "fertile." Or was he actually advising me to keep clear of pregnant women?

"Did you mean *fertile* fields?" I asked.

"Don't be a wiseass," he snapped, so I backed off and waited for his delivery of **Axiom No. 3**:

"***A bird in the hand is worth two in a bush***," he pronounced, glancing at the ceiling as if summoning the remaining two axioms. This one was prone to a variety of interpretations. It depended on what he meant by a *bird* or a *bush* and, once you divined that, whether he meant two *birds* in a bush or two *hands* in a bush. I decided to defer any further analysis as I sensed that **Axiom No. 4** was about to tumble from the Oracle's golden tongue:

"***I never met a condom I could trust.***"

First off, how does one meet a condom? Go to a condom bar? And what was the corollary here? *Therefore, don't use a condom*? Really?

After a long and painful silence, the Oracle's lip began to quiver. **Axiom No. 5** was about to spring forth:

"***Don't drink the water***," he proclaimed. This one was especially unfathomable and possibly disgusting so I let it go, realizing I had to get going to pick up Annie for our dinner at Sympatico.

Annie was in hysterics as I revealed to her my father's Five Axioms of Sexual Wisdom while we chatted over plates of lasagna. Her parents, she admitted, had never broached the subject with her. She was eternally grateful for that, she said, particularly in light of her sexual orientation. She'd continued successfully to maintain her cover but her parents, like my own, had begun to infer more from our relationship than was justified.

"I'm not sure how to keep them from believing we're romantically involved," she said, "but at the same time, it's easier to say nothing than to explain the truth or invent some bullshit story that will someday explode in my face."

That turn of phrase brought back memories of Miriam Levy, an experience I had also shared with Annie to her great amusement.

"If I convince them otherwise, they'll be all over my case," Annie said. "They'll try to set me up with some poor guy who'll be blissfully unaware that he's dating a lesbian."

Those words hit close to home. "Maybe I can set you up with Miriam," I joked.

She laughed, but then her expression turned serious. "I've got a favor to ask."

"Anything, Annie."

"I suspect you've noticed my parents peeking out from behind the drapes each time you drop me off?"

"Actually, yes," I admitted. Who could miss it?

"Maybe it's unfair of me to ask this of you, but would you be willing to try your own hand at some acting when you drop me off tonight?"

"What did you have in mind?"

"Perhaps a convincingly passionate kiss to satisfy their curiosity and keep them in check?"

It wouldn't be acting at all.

When I pulled up her driveway that night, I let myself go. Annie's parents, as anticipated, were lying in wait, peering out from behind the lace curtains lining the living room window. They had a full view from the driveway to the porch. Wise to our audience, I opened the passenger door and walked Annie to the front porch. There, under the harsh glare of the porch light, I gave Annie the warmest, most passionate kiss I could muster. It was no act. When Annie responded in kind, I wanted so badly to believe that at least some part of her reaction was equally genuine. Our performances complete, I squeezed her hand and walked breathlessly back to my car.

The summer was finally over. To my dismay, I realized that I was in the very same place I'd been when the summer began—crazy in love with a lesbian.

CHAPTER TWENTY

Nude Descending into Uranus

M odern art was a mystery to me. That's one reason I decided to take Professor Wilbur's survey course on *The History of Modern Art* (HoMA, for short) during the fall term of my sophomore year. The presence of a dozen coed exchange students was the other.

Since HoMA was the first art course I'd taken since my crayon days, I took it pass/fail. Even if I didn't fathom any of it, I was sure I could memorize enough to squeak by my final exam.

HoMA was taught by John Wilbur, a pony-tailed string bean of a man who was a dynamic instructor and a nationally recognized art historian. Students adored his courses—more than a hundred had enrolled in HoMA—but I fancied myself a particularly tough nut to crack. Almost immediately, I was flummoxed by the hideous examples of "art" which spewed forth from his slide carousel. Unfortunately, with but one exception, the coeds were no better.

That one exception was Colette Davis, a sophomore exchange student from Smith College. According to rumor, she hailed from a wealthy San Francisco family and was among the "flower children" participating in the legendary 1967 Haight-Ashbury Summer of Love. Colette dressed in a manner befitting her bohemian tendencies: peasant skirts, tie-dyed shirts, and a ubiquitous strand of love beads. On the first day of class, I made it a point to grab the seat beside her in the rear of the spacious lecture hall.

The course began with selections from the Armory Show, the 1913 New York exhibition that introduced *avant-garde* European art to a bemused American audience. First up was the notorious *Nude Descending a Staircase (No. 2)* by Marcel Duchamp, a painting that *The New York Times* famously ridiculed as akin to "an explosion in a shingle factory." It depicted a fragmented figure (reputedly a female nude) descending a stairway, the splintering planes tracing her downward motion. It reminded me of crazy old Ethel Perkins descending the staircase of her dilapidated New Liberty home in her freakishly wrinkled birthday suit.

"One of my favorites," Colette whispered, referring to the Duchamp, not Crazy Ethel.

Professor Wilbur flashed a slide of another Duchampian masterpiece, this one entitled *Fountain.* Must be some kind of joke, I thought. *It was nothing more than a urinal!* No joke, the Professor assured us. It was nothing *less* than a major benchmark in the history of modern art. According to Wilbur, this was one of Duchamp's "Readymades," unadorned ordinary objects masquerading as art.

"Are you kidding me?" I grumbled, louder than necessary. Colette grinned. Was she equally outraged or mocking me?

I'll admit I knew nothing about art, modern or otherwise. It wasn't as if Richard and Lydia Meyer had ever taken little Charlie to an art museum. So here I was, an art neophyte, face-to-face, as it were, with a urinal. Not just any urinal, but *the world's most famous urinal* about which, according to Professor Wilbur, reams had been written and doctorates earned.

"And for your assignment," he said as the class wound down, "I'd like you to consider the artworks I've shown you today and submit your own analysis to me by Friday."

I spent two fruitless days contemplating Duchamp's shattered *Nude* and his preposterous urinal. I felt like an idiot. I had no idea how to attack the professor's assignment. I became anxious each time I peed. Then, on Thursday afternoon, I had a classic "What-the-Fuck" epiphany: I'd give the old professor some of his own medicine.

I began by purchasing the current *Playboy* and a *National Geographic* from the college bookstore. In the *Playboy* was a rare photo of a strolling nude (rare because *Playboy* nudes are typically splayed in reclining positions as if pleading for imminent ravishment). From *National Geographic*, I snipped a large color shot of a random planet. Utilizing my fourth grade collage skills, I pasted the planet on the bottom of a sheet of typing paper and the nude above it, tilting her slightly downward. With a Magic Marker, I drew a primitive stairway linking the two. Finally, I fashioned a label from yellow construction paper on which I inscribed the planet's name, "URANUS." I pasted the label beneath the planet.

Voila! I'd created *Nude Descending into Uranus*, by Charlie Meyer.

Though perversely proud of my creation, I had reservations about handing it in. At ten percent of the grade, it probably didn't matter. To mitigate the risk of embarrassment, I chose to submit it anonymously.

Professor Wilbur revved up his projector at the start of class on the following Tuesday. I winced when he showed his first slide: *Nude Descending into Uranus*, by Anonymous. The class burst into irrepressible laughter. Colette squealed in delight. I cringed, covering my eyes.

"One of you submitted *this* in response to last week's assignment on Marcel Duchamp," the Professor said without derision or rancor. "He, or perhaps she," he corrected himself, "neglected to sign it, which is a shame," he said.

Beads of perspiration peppered my forehead.

"Anything can be art," the Professor said. "It can be beautiful, emotional, novel, humorous. It can be pre-existing, like Duchamp's *Fountain*, or satirical, like *Nude Descending into Uranus*," he continued.

Professor Wilbur glanced conspicuously at his classroom seating chart, then gazed toward the rear of the lecture hall where I sat slumped in my chair. I bolted upright in terror when he called my name.

"Tell us, Mr. Meyer, is this art, and if so, why?" This couldn't be random. The Professor had deduced, by process of elimination, that I was Anonymous. I wouldn't be for long. "Please stand up, Mr. Meyer," he instructed me from the podium, heightening my impending humiliation.

"Uh . . ." I stammered, summoning the fortitude to respond. "It's . . . um . . . it's no less art than . . . Duchamp's work," I declared with false bravado. "Not so much for its aesthetic appeal," I blathered on, gaining momentum, "but because when considered in the context of what we discussed last week, it evokes reaction and promotes discourse." What was this bullshit I was spouting? Or had I somehow just unconsciously stumbled, like some Alice through a rabbit hole, upon the true meaning of modern art?

"Well stated, Mr. Meyer," the Professor commended me. "Now would you like to come down here and sign your work so I can give you the 'A' you deserve?" Professor Wilbur flashed a big grin as my classmates, Colette included, broke into raucous applause.

CHAPTER TWENTY-ONE

The Deer and the
Two-Hundred-Pound Eggplant

"I absolutely love *Uranus*," Colette Davis gushed as we rose to leave the lecture hall. Anyone overhearing that comment out of context would have cringed.

"Yours isn't bad either," I said, still basking in the glow of my improbable classroom triumph. She winced, but playfully.

"I'm Colette Davis, by the way."

"Charlie Meyer, though I suspect you know that already."

Colette's charm and appeal were undiminished by her offbeat manner and dress. Her eyes, liberally flecked with a kaleidoscope of hues, defied color categorization. Her soft, round cheeks were delightfully freckled and her lips tilted gently upward at the corners of her mouth. She wore her dark brown hair in a long, loosely-braided ponytail.

I parlayed our unconventional introduction into a rendezvous at the Student Union.

"I like that you took a risk by thinking outside the box," Colette told me as she sipped a cup of herbal tea.

"When it comes to art, Colette, I don't know my ass from my elbow."

"Or Uranus from a urinal," she said with a grin. "Still, I

thought you were very creative, even if you can't draw worth shit." Colette sprouted dimples when she smiled. I found her bright, witty, and exceedingly charming. Though from radically different backgrounds, different coasts, and with nothing ostensibly in common, we seemed to be proving the adage that opposites attract.

A studio art major, Colette was passionate about modern art and an ardent disciple of Professor Wilbur. She took my ignorance of art as a personal challenge. "What are you doing at about ten on Saturday morning, Charlie?" she asked.

"Waking next to you after a wild night of sex?"

She dismissed my impertinence with a fleeting grin. "I thought I might take you on a tour of your college art gallery."

"I'd like that," I told her, elated at the opportunity to spend more time together.

"And Charlie?"

"Yes?"

"About that wild night of sex?"

"Yes?" I asked hopefully.

"I wouldn't bet Uranus on it."

By week's end I was a campus sensation. *Nude Descending into Uranus* was reproduced on the front page of *Roberts Rules*, the campus newspaper, together with a photo of, and interview with, its befuddled creator. Coeds stopped me on campus to chat about art. I felt like the character Peter Sellers would play about a decade later in the movie *Being There*, a simple-minded nobody whose naïve pronouncements are misconstrued as profundity.

Izzy, who was my new roommate for sophomore year, was astounded at my celebrity. "You date a blond bombshell like Annie, create acclaimed artwork by accident... and now you're the plaything of the cutest coed on campus," he said. "How the hell do you do it?"

"Appearances can be deceiving," I said. "*You* get laid almost every weekend. How many times have I been laid? Here's a hint: it's more than never and less than twice." But with my implausible newfound fame, that seemed destined to change.

Several days following my guided tour of the Roberts Art Gallery (the RAG to the *cognoscenti*), Colette invited me to her off-campus apartment for dinner. Presuming it would be just the two of us, I dug into my desk drawer for the package of condoms which had been collecting dust since Izzy and I did our Homecoming shopping at Alice's the previous year. Were they still functional, or had they turned as dry and brittle as my sex life? I thought of my father's Fourth Axiom: *I never met a condom I could trust.*

A generously proportioned young woman answered the door when I arrived at Colette's apartment. She was clad in an unflattering, loosely-fitting muumuu.

"You must be Charlie—I saw your picture in the paper. I'm Molly, Colette's roommate." This was distressing. I tried to camouflage my disappointment over the presence of an interloper.

"Colette's in the kitchen preparing dinner," Molly said as she escorted me in. I detected the aroma of tomato sauce mingling with the scent of fresh brownies.

"I'll be right there," Colette shouted as I took a seat in the living room beneath a large abstract painting. I noticed that the table had been set for three. Bummer.

Colette emerged from the kitchen with a bottle of rosé wine and three glasses, filled each halfway, and joined us in the living room. She wore a colorful peasant blouse, her trademark love beads, and bell-bottom jeans that hugged her shapely rear like shrink-wrap.

Why the fuck is your roommate here, Colette? I longed to shout. *I brought a pocketful of Trojans with me!* Instead, I asked her about the abstract canvas behind me.

"Yes, it's my work," she replied with obvious pride. It consisted of large splotches of purple interspersed with slashes of brown and viscous drippings of blood red.

"Uh . . . what do you call it?"

"It's untitled." The inclination of modern artists to abstain from titling their artworks had struck me during our tour of the RAG. It seemed to me a pretentious affectation.

"I don't get this 'untitled' shit, Colette. Why not give the observer a clue?"

"That would compromise his experience in viewing the artwork," she replied, "prevent him from applying all of his powers of observation and imagination untethered by suggestion." *What the fuck, Colette?* Recognizing that her response had activated my bullshit meter, she tried a different tack. "What would you title it?"

I carefully considered the canvas. "How about *Collision Between Deer and a Two-Hundred-Pound Eggplant?*" Colette and Molly both cracked up.

"See, you've proven my point," Colette said. "You saw something in my painting that I would never have dreamed was there. And that's cool." I supposed she had a point, but I remained skeptical.

The wine had begun to take the edge off my disappointment over Molly's presence. We sat down to a dinner of spaghetti and *not*-meatballs made from tofu. The tofu balls looked like my *National Geographic* photo of Uranus. They were equally unappetizing.

Molly had been Colette's roommate as a freshman at Smith College. She'd come to Roberts to take courses in English literature. Judging from their mode of dress and the hippie paraphernalia that filled the apartment, Molly and Colette were cut from the same cloth, though Molly required considerably more fabric.

For dessert, we feasted on Colette's brownies. Tofu-free, they were luscious. It wasn't until I'd scarfed down three that the girls revealed that the brownies had been liberally laced with hashish. That explained the goofy smile on my face and the accelerating tilt of the room. I could almost feel the horror of the two hundred pound eggplant as the deer approached and impact became inevitable. I had no idea how much of this stuff I could tolerate before entirely losing my grip, but suspected I had already exceeded my threshold.

My recollection of the balance of that night is spotty, but some of those "spots" are indelibly fixed in my memory. I recall the girls undressing. I recall sitting naked, legs crossed, on the living room floor. I remember two pairs of hands exploring two sets of breasts, kissing Colette, kissing Molly, and Molly kissing Colette. I remember screaming, at the top of my lungs: "WHY ARE THEY ALWAYS LESBIANS?!"

Through waves of disorientation, I remember caressing "the hair knit up in" two Bermuda triangles and anxiously reciting the perplexing words of my father's third axiom, "a bird in the hand is worth two in a bush!" And I recall exclamations of pleasure as two pairs of hands delicately outlined the exaggerated curvature of my penis.

Finally, I remember Molly and Colette engaged in vigorous lovemaking as I sat beside them on the floor, almost in tears, fumbling with my Trojans and repeating, over and over, "I never met a condom I could trust!"

The rest of the night remains a blank. I suspect I had intercourse, as I'd polished off a half-dozen condoms, trusty or otherwise. I just don't remember how or with whom. But I do remember my expression of horror when Molly encouraged me to play the *Nude* and descend into *her* anus. "Axiom No. 1!" I shrieked. "Don't stick your dick where it doesn't belong!"

I don't know how I got back to the dorm that night. When I awoke in the morning, miraculously in my own bed, I remained dazed and confused. Izzy said I'd staggered in at four o'clock screaming, repeatedly, "Dad was right!"

I was too embarrassed to ask Colette what actually happened that evening. I resolved, however, to stop eating brownies (Axiom No. 6?) and eschew further encounters with flower children (and lesbians!).

CHAPTER TWENTY-TWO

Pierogis and Barracudas

Fall fraternity "rush" took place on three consecutive evenings at each of the twenty fraternity houses that dominated the social (more accurately, *anti*-social) life at Roberts College. On those three nights, juniors and seniors who typically acted like drunken Neanderthals donned jackets, ties, and their most obsequious smiles in an effort to recruit clueless sophomores. The greater the fraternity's social cachet, the more relaxed the recruiting process and the harder to obtain bids. The lower a house stood on the campus totem pole, the more desperate its brothers for new members.

Izzy had decided he didn't need to pay for a couple dozen new friends and elected not to rush. I, on the other hand, needed some kind of spark to jolt me out of my ludicrous attraction to lesbians.

I decided to rush at least two fraternities, using a process of elimination to select my targets. After eliminating the boozer abodes, the jock houses, and the stoner societies, just two options remained: Delta Upsilon Delta and Psi Phi.

Delta Upsilon Delta ("DUD") was a tough sell. The brothers were mostly geography majors (who took geography after sixth grade?) and outing club members (a group for outdoorsmen, they assured me, not fools intent on unmasking homosexuals). Frank Sinatra was crooning on the house stereo—reason enough to flee.

Departing DUDsville, I hiked across campus to Psi Phi (playfully referred to in print as "SciFi"). The SciFi House was about as far as you could get from fraternity row. A row of commercial buildings shielded it from Main Street like linemen defending an aging quarterback. The house, a once-imposing Georgian with a listing portico and crumbling cupola, seemed on the verge of collapse.

Instead of Sinatra, *The Twilight Zone* theme song played in an endless loop on the House's prodigious sound system. The brothers were mostly pre-law or pre-med—as opposed to pre-unemployed like the geography majors at DUD.

What SciFi lacked in structural stability and social cachet, it more than made up for in affability. These guys had to be friendly, since few rushees managed to find their way this far afield. Whether I'd wowed them with my sparkling personality, my recent campus celebrity, or my willingness to pay dues, I quickly received a bid and elected to become a brother.

I was one of a dozen members of the SciFi pledge class. Pledge term, from mid-October to early December, was the traditional period of indoctrination for pledges. It began with "sink night," a ceremony in which pledges affirmed their commitment to imminent brotherhood. It ended with "hell night," during which we submitted to various degrading pranks to demonstrate our worthiness—or confirm our stupidity.

Despite some mild "hazing" of pledges by their brothers-to-be, SciFi recognized it could ill afford to risk the loss of prospective members by alienating them with demeaning stunts. The college's limited tolerance for such activities also

contributed to the low-key tenor of the pledge term. "Hell
night," therefore, was relatively tame, involving little more
than shutting a dozen pledges into an unventilated room with
twelve pitchers of beer, a dozen foul-smelling pierogi cigars,
and a mop. Our instructions were to smoke the cigars,
consume the beer, and mop up the resulting vomit. I managed
to endure the experience with my guts intact.

To celebrate our initiation, SciFi engaged a band to perform at
a houseparty planned for Saturday night of the weekend
before Christmas break. Eager to impress, I phoned my
favorite lesbian.

"So, Annie," I said when she picked up the phone, "remember
your foolish offer last spring?"

"Offer? What offer?" She was obviously playing it coy.

"The image-inflation special," I said. "You offered to pose as
my non-lesbian date to impress the shit out of my classmates,"
I reminded her.

Annie sighed. "Did I *really*?"

"Well, I—"

"I'm kidding!" she laughed. "But which *me* do you want?
Knocked-up Annie, the Havenhurst harlot . . . or your sweet
little China doll, Annie the Nun?"

"What if we split the difference?"

"I'll see what I can do . . ."

Annie arrived on the Saturday afternoon bus. Although she'd
never attended a fraternity party, Maria had provided a
thorough and graphic briefing on what to expect. I was
confident that we'd "ace" *House Parties I*.

The band was setting up when we arrived. From the Tube
Room, repository of the only House television, came shouts of

"Sue! Sue! Fucking Sue!" What sounded like a pep talk among members of an ambulance-chasing law firm was actually a futile attempt to deter the House canine, a *male* dog named Sue, from dry-humping the legs of the brothers arrayed on the Tube Room couch. Meanwhile, in the kitchen, several brothers were hard at work preparing Orange Blossoms, a nasty concoction of cheap gin, orange juice, and orange sherbet blended together in a large (virgin) plastic garbage can and stirred vigorously with a hockey stick.

Annie's entrance brought a halt to all activity. Even Sue quit his humping. Jaws dropped and eyes popped. Wearing a fashionably short black skirt and a white, form-hugging sweater, Annie was dazzling. Like a kid with a hot new toy, I basked in my brothers' envy.

What I hadn't anticipated were the shameless efforts by a handful of covetous brothers, to the obvious consternation of their dates, to sidle up to Annie and make small talk. This was the first step in the *snake,* that dastardly date-poaching ploy seen at my first freshman mixer. Wise to their agenda, Annie politely rebuffed each intrusion. To further taunt her thwarted suitors, she bestowed an occasional kiss or hug, just to underscore her loyalty to me. I couldn't have asked for more (and yes, of course, I tumbled even further into the quicksand of Annie-adoration).

To this point, it had been a terrific evening. The band was brilliant. A true nun would have blanched at Annie's seductive dance moves. But she saved her most memorable move for last.

By about eleven o'clock, the Orange Blossoms had taken their toll. It was now garbage time—the part of the evening when the drunks plied their mischief before mercifully collapsing into unconsciousness. The most notorious of the

House louts was Rich Bell, known pejoratively as Slick Dick. His date having long ago abandoned him in disgust, he was plotting an encore of the most offensive ploy in his arsenal of boorishness, the *barracuda.* The stunt consisted of maneuvering undetected behind a shapely female and, when the opportunity presented itself, sinking his teeth into her derriere. He'd bagged at least two victims already.

"Keep an eye on that asshole," I cautioned Annie, pointing out Slick Dick as he crept behind another guy's date on the Blue Room dance floor.

"I got it," she said confidently, adding "Maria briefed me on the *barracuda.*" Maria never ceased to amaze me.

When, inevitably, Slick Dick staggered in our direction, I reiterated my warning. For Slick Dick, Annie would be the prize of the night. She danced on, fully cognizant of the looming danger. Her perfect butt in his sights, Slick Dick slithered behind Annie, coiled like a cobra, and poised to strike.

"Watch out!" I shrieked over the roar of the band.

As Slick Dick lunged toward her bottom, Annie whirled, flexed her knee, and slammed her foot into Slick Dick's groin. An absolute *balls*eye. The move would've impressed Bruce Lee.

While Slick Dick lay on the floor, doubled-over and grimacing in pain, Annie and I departed the Blue Room to a chorus of cheers.

CHAPTER TWENTY-THREE

Flophouse Heaven

Spring break is a rite of passage. In my case, it was more like a voyage into oblivion.

Blake Benton, a sophomore fraternity brother, floated the idea in a drunken stupor one evening in the Tube Room. An avid sailor and consummate chick-magnet, Blake thought it would be a blast to charter a sailboat in Ft. Lauderdale for spring break. He figured that hot coeds would be more inclined to party on a sailboat than in some sleazy hotel room. We'd cruise along the canals of the Intracoastal Waterway and venture out to sea around Miami. That Blake could induce his indulgent divorced father to foot the bill made his proposal all the more tempting.

Three of us, all sophomores and equally inebriated at the time, weighed in on the plan.

"Out-*fucking*-rageous idea!" proclaimed Russell Herzog, a.k.a. "Tractor," a huge, muscular, Kansas farm boy and defensive lineman whose presence at Roberts was as close as he'd been to the sea.

"Sign me up!" Benny Romero chimed in with equal enthusiasm. Benny was a pre-med from Phoenix for whom a backyard swimming pool qualified as a large body of water.

"I'm not so sure about this," I whined, thinking of Gilligan's

Island and the ill-fated "three-hour tour." But when I remembered the shapely castaways on the *S.S. Minnow* (the libidinous Ginger and sweet Mary Ann), I warmed to the idea. "What the heck," I said. "Count me in."

Except for Blake, none of us had ever sailed before. I couldn't even swim.

With my parents under the carefully cultivated impression that I was in Massachusetts with Izzy for spring break, I found myself barreling down the Atlantic coast in the back seat of Blake's '68 Ford Fairlane. We'd decided to make the thirty-hour drive without a break, rotating drivers regularly.

In 1969, Interstate 95 was incomplete. In parts of South Carolina, we were obliged to navigate two-lane highways littered with speed traps where enterprising state troopers routinely ambushed unsuspecting spring breakers. Oblivious to the risks, we were waved over almost immediately by a beefy state trooper who ordered us out of our car. That our vehicle bore New York plates and transported four teens were not points in our favor.

"Long way from home, eh boys?" the trooper bellowed in his heavy Southern drawl. He was puffy-faced and sported a gut that bespoke an abundance of doughnuts. "What y'all doin' here in *my* state?" he said imperiously.

"On a joyride, sir, dropping acid while surveying the doughnut consumption habits of your state troopers," I muttered under my breath, obviously insensitive to the potential for the kind of creepy rural experience which would soon characterize the plot of the movie *Deliverance*.

"*What* did you say?" the officer barked at me.

"Uh, nothing, sir," I replied like a choirboy. After a brief pause, he returned to the script.

"You know you boys was doin' forty in a thirty-five zone?"

"Sorry, officer," Blake said. "Didn't know we were going that fast."

"Gonna have to write y'all up," the portly patrolman proclaimed. "It'll cost you fifty bucks plus court costs. 'Course we'll need to hold all four of you boys in the tank overnight 'til your hearing tomorrow mornin'," the tubby trooper told us. As the anticipated wails of protest rose among us, the officer added a well-rehearsed qualifier.

"Now, now, boys, don't get all whiny on me. You seem like nice fellas . . . so there just might be another way," he said. "How 'bout you just pay me that fifty now . . . in cash . . . and I'll go ahead and tear up this here little ticket and let y'all go on your way."

We looked at each other in resignation. The cop was more crooked than my dick. But our anxiety over the prospect of a night in a rural Southern jail cell easily trumped our sense of moral indignation. So we delved into our wallets and assembled the ransom.

"Now that probably makes more sense, fellas," the treacherous trooper said as he pocketed the cash and walked away. "Y'all come back, now!"

We crawled through the rest of South Carolina and parts of Georgia, driving like little old ladies, until we crossed the Florida border. While Blake, Benny, and Tractor napped in rotation, I couldn't sleep. As dawn broke over the Sunshine State, I was slumped in the back seat, unshaven, bleary-eyed, and looking remarkably like the character Ratso Rizzo (played by Dustin Hoffman) on the bus to Miami at the end of *Midnight Cowboy*.

Blake was driving as we approached Ft. Lauderdale. A pair of hitchhikers caught his eye. He slowed for a closer look, then slammed on the brakes.

"What the fuck, Blake?" Benny protested, lurching forward along with the rest of us. "We've got no space as it is!"

Blake was no idiot. The hitchhikers were ravishing females in skimpy cut-offs and revealing tank tops. We found a way to squeeze them in, ever more grateful for the lack of space.

Beth Danvers was a voluptuous brunette, about five-foot-eight, with dazzling green eyes and shoulder-length hair. Her hitchhiking companion, Lisa Long, was an inch or so taller and a tad thinner, with blue eyes and long, stringy, blond hair. They were spring-breaking seniors thumbing to Florida from Delaware State. Wasting no time, Blake invited them to join our incompetent crew. With no plans or lodgings and a limited budget, they were more than delighted at the prospect of bunking on a sailboat with a quartet of equally enthusiastic guys—even if we were only sophomores.

We collected the sailboat at a marina in Ft. Lauderdale. Aptly named *Wet Dreams*, it was a twenty-eight-footer sleeping four comfortably and six creatively. Blake, assuming the mantle of captain, ordered his crew to seek out "provisions," a nautical term for alcohol. What the ladies lacked in seafaring skills they made up for in other ways, such as their capacity, as twenty-one-year-olds, to legally purchase all of the beer and wine we'd require. As a bonus, their backpacks were bursting with weed. The provisions stowed, Blake flipped on the motor and steered us south on the Intracoastal Waterway.

After dinner at a waterside restaurant, we secured a mooring for the night. Thus far, our trip bore the promise of an idyllic spring break: warm breezes, unlimited alcohol, and our very own Ginger and Mary Ann. But I could sense a perilous competition developing for the attention of the outnumbered women. As a social experiment, I worried we'd hit the proverbial reef.

It was well into morning when we retired for bed on that first night. Blake and Tractor slept in the forward cabin while Benny and I shared the larger main cabin with the girls, who slept on the floor.

We spent the next day exploring the territory along the Intracoastal Waterway. The ladies tortured us in their bikinis.

Beth and Lisa knew full well their effect on us. Flirtatious babble, leering, flexing, even drooling—they'd endured it all. They knew that if they paired off with two of us, there'd be hard feelings on the part of the others, and if they didn't, the frustration would be exasperating for everyone. So later that night, after we'd eaten some dinner, swigged a few beers, and smoked a few joints, Beth engaged Lisa on the bow for a private, all-girls' summit on the matter. When they returned, Beth took the floor.

"You guys have been sweet allowing us to share your boat," Beth said. "We truly appreciate it," she added, "but we also know that you're here to have fun . . . and maybe even get laid once or twice." We looked at each other with trepidation, anticipating our incipient abandonment.

"But we're not clueless, guys," Lisa said. "We're feeling the tension."

"So here's our proposition," Beth continued. "Lisa and I will pair off with two of you tonight," she said, "and the other two tomorrow. And so on . . . as long as everyone's happy with the arrangement."

Trepidation gave way to astonishment. We were either victims of an early April Fools' Day gag or grand prizewinners of the Spring Break Jackpot.

Lisa laid down the ground rules. "We'll draw straws for tonight. You don't have to participate if you don't want to," she acknowledged, "but this way, we don't have to sleep on the floor anymore. We can all relax and have fun. Whaddya say?"

It was a perfectly logical—if highly improbable—solution. A no-brainer for the ages. Within nanoseconds, we'd all signed on to their so-called "LEON Plan" (a Lay Every Other Night) and eagerly awaited the results of the first drawing.

Blake and Tractor drew the short straws for the first night. Since they'd slept in the forward cabin the previous evening, the girls simply joined them there while Benny and I set our sights on tomorrow.

The next day was slated for our deep-sea excursion into the waters off Miami. It was a cloudless morning. The sea air was invigorating. Our route required us to "tack," or make frequent shifts in direction, to most efficiently exploit the wind at our sails. When performing this maneuver, Blake would holler "Coming about!" to alert us to the imminent shift of the sail, so we wouldn't be broadsided by the bottom rail, or boom. Though he'd never been on a sailboat, Tractor proved a quick study and competent first mate upon whom Blake could rely in executing sailing maneuvers. The rest of us were content to simply dive for cover each time Blake barked out his warning.

Three hours into our voyage, dark clouds emerged to our south. I felt a growing unease, recalling Catherine's description of the menacing skies that augured her tragedy. Before long, rain was pelting us from a ninety-degree angle. *Wet Dreams* bobbed in the suddenly turbulent waters like a rubber ducky in a bathtub. While Blake maintained his cool and Tractor gallantly assisted in guiding the boat toward the safety of shore, Benny, Beth, Lisa, and I cowered in the cabin like terrified toddlers. Visions of Gilligan's Island flashed through my mind as my stomach churned. Soon, I was blowing lunch, breakfast, and yesterday's dinner over alternate sides of the boat. I wanted to die. Beth and Lisa administered to me as best they could until Lisa herself unleashed a sequence of vomiting unrivaled until the release of *The Exorcist.*

A few minutes later, as quickly as it had struck, the storm subsided and the seas (unlike my stomach) began to calm. After what seemed like an eternity, we sighted the shoreline south of Miami and motored in.

Lisa and I couldn't get off the boat quickly enough. I don't recall ever feeling worse. While the others secured the boat and disembarked for a bite to eat, Lisa and I staggered ashore, still reeling from our ordeal. We agreed that we'd both need a night off the boat to tame our gyrating stomachs.

We found ourselves in a seedy part of Miami with few lodging options. We were not in a shopping mood. Any hotel with a bed that didn't rock in the waves would do. We brought a change of clothes from the boat and lurched into the first hotel we found.

A balding sleazeball in a sweat-stained tank top manned the front desk of The Blue Pelican. Peeling paint was the lobby decorating motif.

"Hourly or daily," he said, not bothering to look up.

"Pardon me?"

"Ten an hour, thirty a night. Clean sheets, cash up front."

This seemed ominous, but when I paused to consult Lisa, her vacant look told me all I needed to know. I dug three tens from my quickly thinning wallet and slapped them on the counter.

"Big spender!" the clerk croaked facetiously. "Sign the

damn book," he said. As he retrieved the key, I inscribed the ledger *Fred and Wilma Flintstone*.

"Yabba dabba doo," the clerk mimicked.

Our tiny room had all the amenities of a prison cell: a flimsy double bed, allegedly clean (though prominently stained) sheets, a tattered chair, and a broken floor lamp with a torn lampshade. The frosted-glass window was sealed shut. A bare bulb hanging precariously from the center of the ceiling constituted the only functional lighting and a small, portable fan provided the ventilation. The *en suite* bathroom consisted of a discolored sink, a stained toilet, and a cracked tub. It wasn't the Ritz. On the other hand, there were no rolling waves.

"I see they upgraded us," I said. Lisa managed a weak smile before collapsing onto the bed. We were both asleep within minutes.

Lisa was stirring when I awoke. The frosted glass window admitted no natural light. I wasn't sure if it was day or night. I checked my watch. It was almost noon. My stomach was no longer churning and the pounding in my head had subsided. I was starving.

I watched Lisa as she began to stir. The color had returned to her cheeks. Though fully clothed when she'd fallen asleep, she'd shed all but her panties at some point during the sweltering night.

Lisa caught me staring at her from across the bed. She smiled, extended her arms, and drew me close. We kissed. That was the aperitif. The entrée followed. And once again, as it had done for Catherine, my marvelously mangled member delivered the dessert course—a convulsive climax the likes of which Lisa had never before experienced—or so she alleged. We had indeed been upgraded at The Blue Pelican. We were in Flophouse Heaven.

CHAPTER TWENTY-FOUR

Billy Ray and the Bandana Man

I t was after one by the time Lisa and I showered, changed, and escaped The Blue Pelican. When we reached the marina, the sailboat was gone. The manager handed us a note Blake had left for us:

Hey, lovebirds. Waited til noon. Scored six tickets to a Chambers Brothers concert at Lockhart Park in Ft. Lauderdale. Hitch a ride and meet us at gate at 6 P.M.
Blake

Our sexual appetites sated, we addressed our empty stomachs at the nearest greasy spoon. A well-worn waitress, her mascara as thick as charcoal briquettes, served us slimy burgers and oily fries. Our gullets lubricated, we headed toward the old highway to Ft. Lauderdale. It was a mile hike through shabby neighborhoods far from the spring break grid.

The old highway was elevated, with no shoulders to accommodate hitchhikers. We'd have to catch a ride at the base of the entry ramp. A half-hour passed without success. Running short on time, we tried the old bait-and-switch: Lisa thumbed while I remained invisible. Soon, a battered red pickup pulled up. I emerged casually from the shadows as the passenger door swung open. A burly, thirtyish guy in torn jeans and a tattered tank top hopped out, motioning Lisa into the middle of the front seat and relegating me to the jump seat behind. A dirty red bandana hung loosely from his sinewy neck. The scruffy, pony-tailed driver was shirtless, a bulky strand of heavy metal chains clinging to his neck like a Doberman's collar.

"Where to, pretty lady?" asked bandana man, treating me as if I were still invisible. His drawl was pronounced.

"Ft. Lauderdale," Lisa said timidly as the men inched ominously closer.

"Well ain't it your lucky day! Headin' just that way. Reckon we can drop you off there, right Billy Ray?"

"Yep."

I quickly regretted our ill-considered decision to hitch a ride from Billy Ray and the bandana man and grew concerned for Lisa's safety—not to mention my own. As I surveyed the truck, I couldn't help but notice the two rifles secured to the gun rack on the back of the cab.

"Ever been on an alligator hunt?" bandana man asked.

They had a foolproof plan: rape us, kill us, then use us as alligator bait!

"Know what?" I said. "I just remembered that I left my backpack at the luncheonette. Would you mind just dropping us off at the next exit?" It was a lame effort at terminating this joyride before it terminated us.

"Nah, we're gonna take you right on up to the Fort," said Billy Ray, smart enough (surprisingly) to see through my transparent escape attempt and ornery enough to fully exploit my discomfort. "No need to be worried about these good ol' boys," he assured us with a sinister chuckle.

Bandana man reached beneath his seat, extracting a half-empty bottle of Jack Daniels. He took a heady swig and passed it on to Lisa. She took a short but reluctant sip in an effort to placate her cab mates. The biting odor of whiskey flooded the cab. Billy Ray snatched the bottle from Lisa and took a long, hard gulp before passing it back to bandana man.

We'll never even make it to the alligator swamp! These drunken heehaws will plow the truck through the guardrail and we'll plunge to our ignominious deaths like buffalo stampeding over a precipice.

Billy Ray flipped on the radio. Bandana man warbled along with Johnny Cash as he sang the inane lyrics of his '68 recording, *I've Been Flushed from the Bathroom of Your Heart.* Our redneck hosts were entranced by the music like cobras in the thrall of a snake charmer.

The risk associated with hurtling over pockmarked highways at eighty miles an hour with a drunken driver is that you might fucking die. Or, if you were particularly lucky, you'd simply reach your destination faster than anticipated with your heart in your throat. Fortunately, it was our lucky day. When Billy Ray swerved into the breakdown lane and announced, "This be the Fort, y'all!" Lisa and I jumped from the cab faster than we'd rolled off the sailboat the night before.

"Not fun," Lisa said, emitting a generous sigh of relief as the pickup drove off. "Not fun at all."

"I wasn't worried," I teased her. "But if they'd tried to rape you, I swear I would have flattened them with one of the rifles on the gun rack behind me."

"*Gun rack?* They had rifles?"

"Yeah, but it really didn't matter," I said. "They could have strangled us with their bare hands."

Unwilling to press our luck by thumbing another ride, Lisa and I caught a cab to the concert in time to meet Blake, Benny, Tractor, and Beth.

"You guys have fun?" Benny asked.

"Words don't begin to describe it," I said, my heart lodged in my throat like a chicken bone.

CHAPTER TWENTY-FIVE

Hometown Heterosexual Hero

The balance of our spring break excursion was considerably less traumatic. Overall, we had a blast. I got laid three times. And not a single lesbian was involved, so far as I could tell.

To assuage my guilt at deceiving my parents about my trip to Ft. Lauderdale, I decided to call them upon my return and lie some more. Phone calls with my parents were a necessary evil, a chance for Mom to catch up and Dad to vent. Unfortunately, my father picked up the phone and the conversation proceeded in predictably ludicrous fashion.

"Hi, Dad. Where's Ma?"

"She's on the crapper, kid. What's up? Don't tell me you need money again."

"No, Dad. Just calling to say hello."

"Well, hello, then," he said before screaming offline to my mother. *"Lydia! Get off that thing and pick up. It's your son, the college boy!* OK, your mother just picked up."

"Hello, dear," Mom purred. "How was your spring break in Massachusetts?"

"I had a wonderful spring break, Ma," I said, choosing my words like a lawyer.

"So what did you do?"

I spewed my guts out sailing, got nearly killed by a pair of whiskey-imbibing, gun-toting rednecks, and got laid three times. "Nothing much," I said.

"Well, we're glad you had a good time, Charlie. We missed you. And how's Annie?"

"She's fine, Ma," I sighed, "though I haven't seen her lately."

"You schtupping her yet?" my father interjected with his customary lack of tact.

"Richard!" Mom protested, on cue.

"No, I'm not schtupping Annie, but if I ever do, I'll remember all five axioms, Dad."

"What's he talking about, Richard?"

"Never mind, dear."

"So, Charlie, how's school?" Mom asked.

"School's fine, Ma."

"How's your accounting course?" my father asked, knowing full well I wasn't taking one and never would.

"Dad, I told you I'm not taking an accounting course," I said before blowing it with unnecessary elucidation. "I'm taking a religion course, one on the twentieth century American novel, and a couple in art history."

"Jesus! I'm actually paying to fill your damn head with biblical bullshit and pornography? And how do you think you're gonna get a decent job with courses in goddamn art history?" Dad's last question was a legitimate one—one I'd asked myself as well before further indulging my newly discovered penchant for the subject.

"Uh, Dad . . . I've actually applied for a summer internship at the Clark Art Institute in Williamstown through my art instructor, Professor Wilbur."

"That sounds exciting," my mother said before Dad launched into his final volley, like the climax in a fireworks display.

"I didn't raise my kid to turn into some pansy prancing around an art gallery hanging candy-ass pictures! Or maybe you're already a pansy. Is that why you're not schtupping Annie?"

"Now calm down, Richard," my mother pleaded. "Your son's not a pansy, are you dear?"

"No, Ma, I'm not a pansy," I assured her. "I have to go now. Nice talking with you guys," I lied again before mercifully hanging up.

A couple days later, I was on the receiving end of a phone call from Annie. As I'd told my parents during their inquisition on the subject, I hadn't seen her for a while, though not for lack of interest. While we'd talked several times since the fall, I'd been hesitant to resurrect the emotional tumult that routinely accompanied our encounters. After the usual pleasantries, Annie made a strange announcement:

"I need a man," she said.

"Now there's an interesting development."

She laughed. "No, Charlie, I need a *male* date for my sorority's annual Spring Fling thing in a couple weeks."

"How poetic."

"I need you to be my Hometown Heterosexual Hero," she said. "Everyone has a date for this event, and I'd like to keep up appearances."

"Well, I owe you one. Your shot to the nuts of Slick Dick at last spring's houseparty is now SciFi legend."

"You can look at it that way if you like, Charlie, but I'd also love to see you again. I've missed you."

"Do I need to be wary of some sorority sister pulling off the *barracuda* on me?"

"I promise . . . no one will bite your ass."

"Not even you?"

She let that one pass. "I'll get you set up in a room at the St. Augustine Inn for that night, my treat," she said, "and you can ride up here with Maria's boyfriend from Roberts . . . he's got a car. So, can I count on you?"

"You can always count on me," I said with a hint of resignation.

"Thanks, Charlie. See you in a couple of weeks," she said before hanging up.

As always, I was ambivalent about seeing Annie. She excited me—in every possible way—but it was maddeningly frustrating to rein in my fervor for a girlfriend who just happened to be an avowed lesbian. My spring break liaisons had been pleasant and uncomplicated. The vacation from complication had been a welcome change. Now I risked ratcheting up the emotional anguish once again.

I met Maria's boyfriend on the Roberts campus and we drove together to St. Augustine's. I had no idea whether he knew of his girlfriend's bisexuality, but was certain I shouldn't inquire. I wondered whether it was better knowing and enduring the kind of turmoil I felt or remaining blissfully ignorant.

We arrived on campus and set out for Annie's sorority house. She greeted me with a bright smile and a warm hug. I could already feel my defenses melting away.

"Thanks for doing this for me," she said. "You look great."

"And you're looking pretty decent yourself," I said in heroic understatement. Her tight jeans were torturing me.

With a couple of hours left before the event, there was just enough time to register at the inn and change for the party.

Annie's "Spring Fling thing," as she called it, represented a complete turning of the tables. It was not only disconcerting, but also a rude awakening. Instead of men judging their fraternity brothers' dates, women were mentally ticking off the various attributes and detriments of their sorority sisters' escorts. I felt like a piece of meat. Was I prime rib or rump roast? Now I understood how Annie must have felt when she endured that raucous welcome last winter at The Douche. Not that the reaction I elicited was in any way comparable: to be fair, I'd rank it halfway between subdued and non-existent. Did her sisters consider the strikingly beautiful Annie to be slumming it with a short, "cute" guy like me? Would she have been content dating Charlie Meyer had she been heterosexually inclined? These questions obsessed me as I shuffled around the dance floor with the prettiest girl on it.

Annie doubtless sensed my discomfort but had her own script to follow. She showered me with seemingly gratuitous kisses and hugs in a well-choreographed effort to feign heterosexuality. Where I once pined for such demonstrations of affection from Annie, these attentions felt achingly hollow. Was it my self-consciousness, my weariness with the relationship's complications, or the essential futility of my attraction to Annie? I diligently discharged my assigned role in spite of my considerable misgivings.

When the party ended, Annie offered to walk me back to my room. I told her it wasn't necessary, but she insisted. We said little to each other on the way.

"Can I come upstairs with you for awhile?" she asked when we reached the inn.

"Sure, if you'd like to."

Upon entering the room, she sat down beside me on the bed. She asked me what was wrong. "Something's obviously bugging you, Charlie."

I sighed. "I'm just not sure I can do this anymore."

"Do what?"

"Pretend—no, I'll be more precise . . . pretend I'm pretending."

"I don't understand," she said.

"I think you do. I'm *pretending* to your friends that we're a loving couple . . . and I'm *pretending* to you it's just an act. Yet through all of that bullshit, Annie, I want something more between us . . . something more than friendship."

Annie said nothing, though I could see tears beginning to form in the corners of her eyes. This couldn't have come as a revelation to her.

"Your public signs of affection tonight . . . they just stung, Annie . . . because they weren't real," I said, my voice cracking. "You were role-playing." I bit my lip, trying to contain my emotions. "I just . . . can't . . . do this anymore."

Annie was fending off tears. Prior to this moment, she'd always seemed in total control. I felt guilty, but relieved, at long last, at having fully and honestly expressed my feelings. I had no idea what to expect next, though what happened was virtually unimaginable.

Annie turned to me, placed her hands gently on my cheeks, and kissed me like she had that night on her front porch, deeply and passionately. Only this time there was no audience to play to. She slowly unbuttoned her blouse while I sat there, dumbfounded. A stray tear trickled down each of her cheeks. Then she sighed deeply, as if to acknowledge that she'd passed a point of no return. And she had.

Though neither of us spoke a single word, there was nothing remotely tentative about our lovemaking that night. It was as if she knew instinctively that it had been inevitable, and she had finally found the strength to accept it. And it was everything I could have hoped it would be: breathtaking, rapturous, tender, and warm.

When it was over, Annie embraced me tightly. She smiled sweetly, but her thoughts remained shrouded in silence. *Was this love or an elaborate goodbye?*

"Annie, what did we just do?"

"Really?" she said, instantly regaining her composure.

"You know what I mean."

She hesitated before speaking, searching for the appropriate words. "That was not *pretend*, Charlie," she said emphatically. "I do love you."

I was by now well beyond the boundaries of my comprehension. Before I could respond, she quietly got up and began to dress.

"I think I should go," she said softly. "I don't care to analyze this now. Let's meet downstairs for breakfast tomorrow at nine. We can talk about it then."

CHAPTER TWENTY-SIX

The Morning After

I barely slept that night. I had just experienced my most poignant sexual encounter since that transformative night with Catherine and yet, for the life of me, I couldn't divine its meaning, particularly to Annie.

Annie arrived at the inn's dining room promptly at nine. I was already seated at a quiet corner table. She looked cheerful—a good sign.

"I'm starving!" she said in lieu of a greeting, temporarily deflecting my anxiety. She *had* been starving, judging from the size of the order she placed. Finally, I couldn't take the tension anymore.

"What happened last night?"

She took a sip of her coffee. "Did you really think I'd have all the answers?"

"How about one or two . . . at least to start?"

"Okay. First of all, I meant what I said." She looked me in the eye. "I do love you. And, for the record . . . just in case you were wondering," she said, "you were my first."

It was a dubious distinction, I suppose, with a range of possible implications, but far more pleasing than not. I realized then that in our wide-ranging discussions about her sexuality, I'd never asked her if she'd been with a man—I simply presumed she hadn't.

"So how do I compare with Maria?" I asked mischievously.

"Shut up!" She grinned. "You *do* have a crooked penis, though."

"Long story," I said, "for another time . . . Is Maria's straight?"

"Maria's anything *but* straight."

"So, Annie," I asked, turning serious again, "why did you do it?"

"Because, at that moment, I wanted to make love to you." It was music to my ears. Then I asked the question that continued to plague me.

"Are you now officially bisexual?"

"I don't know . . . maybe," she said, "but it's not as if a bell rang . . . like in *It's A Wonderful Life*."

"How do you know? Who could hear bells over the sounds of the earth shaking?"

"Who said the earth shook?" We both laughed.

"Be that as it may, where exactly does this leave us?"

"Who knows? Maybe I am bisexual . . . or maybe last night was simply an aberration." It felt as if everything had changed, and yet nothing had changed.

Annie paused for another sip of coffee. "From my perspective, there are suddenly new possibilities," she conceded, "and from yours . . ." She took a moment to collect her thoughts. "You might see last night as having leveled the playing field a little." She grasped my hand over the tabletop. "Does that make any sense to you?"

"I think so," I answered tentatively, though I would have much preferred an epiphany.

"Good. Let's eat breakfast."

CHAPTER TWENTY-SEVEN

Summer of Sixty-Nine

I t was late May when I received word from the Clark Art Institute. I'd been chosen for one of two college internship positions for the summer of '69. My father was thrilled for me.

"Screw that, Charlie," he said.

"Dad, it pays well and includes meals and lodging."

"Fine," he conceded when he realized I had no need of a family stipend. "Just watch for the pansies."

My father's disapproval notwithstanding, art history had progressed from curiosity to passion to declared major. I was a hayseed in the world of art, but perhaps it was this absence of preconceived notions that made the subject so appealing to me. There was no right or wrong. My emperor with no clothes was your genius—and vice versa. Roberts was nationally known for its art and art history programs, and Professor Wilbur was its rock star. For some reason, he'd perceived in me a spark he could fan into a flame. He'd encouraged me to apply for the Clark internship and his glowing recommendation was undoubtedly pivotal in my acceptance.

The Clark is a venerable art museum nestled in the rolling hills of Williamstown in the northwestern corner of Massachusetts. Its majestic white marble edifice overflows with celebrated French Impressionists including Renoir, Degas, Manet, Monet, and Pissarro, as well as a legion of American masters from Homer to Sargent.

The internship program was a first class affair. Interns were housed in Wilson Manor, an imposing Victorian estate a short walk from the museum grounds. I had a spacious private room and friendly hosts who furnished two meals a day. A room down the hall was reserved for the second intern who had yet to arrive when I'd first settled in.

After an exploratory stroll through town, I climbed the ornate staircase to my room on the second floor of the Manor. I noticed activity in the room down the hall and knocked on the open door. A trim, petite young woman turned and smiled, beckoning me in. "*Bonjour,*" she chirped in delectable French. "You must be the other internee," she said, revealing a prominent accent and a delightfully fractured command of English.

"Guilty as charged," I said, hesitant to correct her reference to me as an inmate. "Charlie Meyer," I announced, shaking her small, delicate hand.

"I am Brigitte Lemaire," she said, accenting the last syllable of each name. Her short, dark hair was elegantly trimmed and her large brown eyes were inviting. She had a small, pert nose and a luminous, toothy smile.

The resemblance was uncanny: Brigitte Lemaire was the second coming of the legendary Miss Jeanine Romaire, the teacher whose lacy white blouses, pencil-thin black skirts, and exquisite derriere had tantalized my entire high school. The confluence of erotic high school memories and burgeoning sexual fantasies left me breathless.

Dinner at Wilson Manor took place precisely at seven o'clock. Brigitte and I took our places along with our host and hostess, George and Carla Wilson, the fourth generation of Wilsons to occupy the Manor.

Our first meal together gave us all a chance to get acquainted. George, a retired Colonel, had served with distinction in both World War II and the Korean Conflict. His wife, Carla, had been a successful painter and close friend of the late Francine Clark, one of the primary benefactors of the museum.

Brigitte's parents lived in a grand Parisian home adorned by a distinguished art collection. Her father was a banker, her mother a respected art historian. Brigitte had just completed her sophomore year at Montreal's McGill University, one of the most prestigious schools in Canada. Her special interest, she said, was late nineteenth and early twentieth century French painting, a field in which the Clark was particularly well endowed.

By comparison, my own resume was underwhelming. I had meddling parents and a crooked dick. I came from fucking New Jersey. I was in love with a lesbian who just might be bisexual. My principal triumph in the field of art was my *Nude Descending into Uranus.* Except for my Roberts College pedigree, I had precious little to offer. To avoid embarrassment, I deflected the conversation to the accomplishments of our hosts.

Dinner had been deflating. Like a bubble rudely exploded by the gum-chomping Miriam Levy, my own balloon had suddenly burst. My chances with Brigitte Lemaire were as much fantasy as my juvenile longings for her doppelganger, Miss Romaire. My summer was off to an inauspicious start.

CHAPTER TWENTY-EIGHT

Subterranean Spring

Brigitte and I reported to work at the Clark after breakfast the next morning. We were greeted warmly by the Director and introduced to Myron Wheems, a gaunt, gray-haired gentleman in his late sixties who directed the internship program. Wheems, himself a renowned specialist in French Impressionism, took an immediate shine to Brigitte. After a tour and orientation, he led us into his office.

"I've assignments for each of you that I trust you'll find exhilarating," he said, wheezing like an ancient canine. I'd a sneaking suspicion that Brigitte was in line for the plum assignment.

"Brigitte, given your interest in French Impressionism, I'd like you to work with me on a catalogue the museum will be publishing on nineteenth and early twentieth century French painting at the Clark," Wheems said. Bingo, I thought. The dirty old man gets to work with the nubile young chick while they mutually wax poetic on all things French for the next three months. Okay, what's he got up his sleeve for me?

"Charles . . ."

"That's Charlie, Mr. Wheems."

"Charlie, then," he said disdainfully. "Your job will be to assemble provenance, exhibition history, and other relevant information relating to a fine collection of American paintings owned by Mrs. Doris Darlington. Mrs. Darlington, who's quite elderly, lives in Lenox, just south of here. Her collection is a promised bequest to the museum and . . . to put it delicately . . . we'd like to gather as much information as possible before her demise."

So Wheemsie here gets to drool over Brigitte while I'm shuffled off the reservation to make nice with some superannuated matron on her last legs.

I requisitioned a museum vehicle for the trip to Lenox the following morning. Though refreshingly pastoral, the drive down winding Route 7 was a forty-five minute haul.

The Darlington Estate was situated on an isolated road a mile from the center of Lenox. Approached by a long, winding driveway and sheltered by a row of tall oaks, the imposing brick residence had been built in the Colonial revival style during the Depression. Money was evident here.

I parked the car and rang the bell. A housekeeper, later introduced to me as Luisa, answered the door and escorted me inside.

"Mrs. Darlington has been expecting you," she said as she led me through the entry, past a magnificent double staircase, and into a stately library with oak-paneled walls, coffered ceilings, and an abundance of world-class art. There, in an oversized leather wing chair, sat a handsome woman well into her eighties. She was attired in a richly embroidered brocade dressing gown, her thick gray hair tied neatly into a loose ponytail. Her bearing was elegant, her features patrician: sharp nose, thin lips and dark, intelligent eyes. A dimple was revealed in her easy smile.

"Mrs. Darlington, this is Mr. Meyer from the museum," Luisa announced.

"Ah, Mr. Meyer, welcome to my humble home," she said with a playful grin, offering me her hand.

"Honored to meet you, Mrs. Darlington."

"We're not formal here. Please call me Doris. And what shall I call you?"

"Charlie, Mrs. Darlington—uh, Doris."

Doris directed me to a matching wing chair to her left while Luisa plied me with a tall glass of lemonade.

"Now then, tell me something about yourself, Charlie."

Doris was a breath of fresh air. Somehow, over the next half-hour, she managed to glean from me a willing recitation of the highlights (and several lowlights) of the life of Charlie Meyer. She was fully engaged throughout, peppering me with perceptive questions and eliciting details I'd neglected to relate. She broke into hearty laughter when I described how I'd first become interested in art following my creation of *Nude Descending into Uranus.*

"You know, Charlie, I recall vividly my own reaction to Duchamp's *Nude Descending the Staircase* when I attended the Armory Show in New York back in '13. While almost everyone else considered it scandalous, I was intrigued." She paused for a sip of tea. "In fact, I met Marcel at a party in Greenwich Village just before the end of the war. It was shortly after he made a *splash* with his urinal," she said, launching into laughter over her purposeful pun. "He was such a rascal! But I was brazen. I told him I thought the urinal was . . . well . . . what we would now call sexist. And you know what he did? He extracted my address from the hostess and appeared on my doorstep a few days later with an enormous carton. I invited him in and watched with intense curiosity as he opened the box. Guess what I found inside."

"I have no idea," I said, eagerly awaiting the story's climax.

"A bidet! Signed by the artist! 'I call this *Subterranean Spring*,' he said proudly. 'This isn't Paris,' he went on to say. 'It wasn't easy to find a bidet in New York City!'"

I laughed. "What became of *Subterranean Spring*?"

"It's here! My husband didn't approve," she said with a sly smile, "so it was relegated to the cellar where it remains to this day."

When I felt bold enough to embrace the role of interrogator, Doris regaled me with more fascinating stories of her eventful life. Born in 1885, Doris had a privileged background.

"I was burdened by wealth at the outset," she said. "My father and grandfather were tycoons. Railroads, steel, pharmaceuticals—anything they touched turned to gold." She patted her forehead gently with a handkerchief. "But it didn't suit me to be a rich man's daughter, to be 'introduced' to society at a silly debutante ball. So I rebelled. I ran off and married a big, burly prizefighter in '03. I was barely eighteen. It didn't last a year," she recalled, her memory sharp as a tack. "So I worked my way back and forth across the country for a couple of years, working in saloons, dance halls, theaters, even mining camps. You see," she said, pointing at a framed photographic portrait of a tall, shapely, dark-haired young woman on the mantelpiece, "I was a pretty attractive young lass in my day. I found stimulating work and interesting company wherever I went."

Doris's tales were riveting. I asked her about an intriguing photograph depicting her and what appeared to be a young Franklin Delano Roosevelt.

"Ah, yes," Doris said, a smile spreading from her lips. "I had a bit of an affair with dear Franklin for about six months back in '08. He'd been married to Eleanor for about three years and was working for a Wall Street law firm when we met. I'd pretty much finished sowing my wild oats and was back in New York working as a legal secretary at the same firm. While he respected and admired his young wife, I don't think he had the ardor for her that was necessary for a productive marriage. She wasn't particularly attractive, and Franklin had a wandering eye. Franklin and I had some wonderful times together ... and I don't think Eleanor ever caught on ... but our affair was destined to failure," she sighed. "Franklin was an ambitious man and I was an inconvenient complication."

"When did Mr. Darlington—I presume there was a Mr. Darlington at some point—come into the picture?"

"Donald Darlington was a dashing banker, a member of the very same upper class from which I'd fled. But he was charming, intelligent, generous, and good in bed," she said with a devilish grin. "Donald just swept me off my feet. We married in 1920. He passed away in '54, but not before earning his own fortune on Wall Street, building this marvelous house, and, with my active participation, creating this fabulous collection of art."

Before I realized it, Doris and I had been talking for hours. I could see that she was growing tired.

"I'm afraid all of this reminiscing has worn me out. What great memories, though!" she laughed. "You're a wonderful listener ... and a very attractive young man. If I were your age, we'd be together in bed right now!" she said with relish. "But at this age, I'm afraid I simply need a nap. So, if you don't mind terribly, can we pick up again tomorrow, same time, same place? I'll introduce you to my paintings—they're like old friends, you know—and you can meet my granddaughter who'll be arriving tonight. I think you'll like her," she said.

"Of course. It was a pleasure talking with you, Doris," I said. "I look forward to tomorrow."

I helped Doris as she grabbed her cane and gingerly arose from her chair. I bade her goodbye and headed back north, picturing old Wheems expelling gasps of stale breath while leaning lasciviously over Brigitte's delicate shoulder, now thoroughly convinced that the plum assignment was mine.

CHAPTER TWENTY-NINE

Dirty Old Homme

I ran into Brigitte on the stairway as we came down for dinner that night. She was clearly despondent.

"How was your day at the museum?"

"It was *loathsome*," she said. Even the word *loathsome* sounded sexy when filtered through Brigitte's endearing accent.

"How so?"

"Myron Wheems is a dirty old *homme!*" she said categorically. "Constantly he paws on me, hovers on me. It is *absolument insupportable!*" she insisted, challenging my comprehension.

"Did you say anything to him?"

"How can I?" she said in frustration. "If I do, he shall discharge me from my catalogue assignment, no? I fear he shall banish me to the bottom-most floor where I shall spend the rest of the summer—how do you say it—twiddling my pinkies!"

"What you need is some leverage. I may have an idea," I said cryptically.

The following day was brutally hot. I arrived on schedule at the Darlington Estate and found Doris waiting for me in her favorite armchair.

"Today, I'll take you on a tour of the collection," she said. "Then I'll show you where we keep our files so you can delve right in."

As I awaited the tour, I noticed movement beside the large swimming pool just outside the sliding doors that opened to the backyard. A striking, bikini-clad figure basked in the hot sun, perched on a lounge chair beside the pool.

Doris noticed my understandable distraction. "That lovely creature is my granddaughter, Julianna," she said proudly. "I'll introduce you two later," she promised. "If you don't mind, Luisa will fix a nice lunch for you and Julianna by the pool."

"Won't you be joining us?"

"I'm sorry to say that I'm due for a visit to one of my legion of physicians. George, our caretaker, will drive me there after you and I complete our tour."

Doris arose slowly and with difficulty. When she'd secured her balance, the tour began in the library with a large, nighttime portrayal of three cowboys enjoying a modest prairie dinner as they sat around a campfire. Behind them, the firelight illuminated a battered wagon piled high with animal pelts. Stars sparkled in the night sky above.

"This marvelous painting is by Frederic Remington," she said. "He painted it in 1905. Remington's night scenes are among his most desirable. It had been in the collection of a railroad man whom Donald knew in Oklahoma. When the Depression hit, fine paintings became suddenly available at very reasonable prices. Donald and I fared comparatively well in those years, despite the hard times. We didn't hesitate to take advantage of opportunities as they presented themselves."

"Were you living here when you acquired this?"

"No," she said, "we didn't build this monstrosity until the mid-Thirties. We bought the Remington while we lived on a ranch we owned for a short while near Oklahoma City where Donald had business interests at the time. Donald called it the Triple-D ranch, presumably for Donald and Doris Darlington. I always told my friends that it was named for my bra size!" Doris cracked me up.

The tour proceeded in this heady fashion for some time. Doris was energized by the pleasant memories associated with so many of the works in her collection. The Remington was merely the tip of the iceberg. There were majestic western landscapes by Thomas Moran, Frederic Church, and Albert Bierstadt; a mesmerizing painting by Maynard Dixon of white, puffy clouds above a jagged mountain range; rugged Maine seascapes by Winslow Homer and figural works by William Merritt Chase, Childe Hassam, Frank Benson, and John Sloan. But those were only the classics acquired during her husband's lifetime. After his death, Doris indulged her more contemporary tastes, acquiring representative works by such artists as John Marin, Jasper Johns, Andrew Wyeth, Willem and Elaine de Kooning, Roy Lichtenstein, Clyfford Still, Robert Motherwell, and Robert Rauschenberg. She had purchased many of the later works directly from the artists during studio visits in New York and nurtured friendships with many of them. In all, there were more than sixty canvases and works on paper in the collection destined for the Clark.

When we finished the tour, we returned to the library where Doris unveiled her files on the collection and explained their organization. From this point on, I would be free to come and go as I wished, consulting files and examining paintings as I deemed necessary. Her agenda for the day having been fulfilled, Doris graciously withdrew to attend to the demands of her health and directed me outside to meet Julianna.

"Charlie Meyer," I said, introducing myself to Julianna moments after she emerged, dripping wet, from a dip in the pool, like a mermaid in a Pre-Raphaelite painting.

"Nice to meet you, Charlie Meyer. I'm Julianna Darlington."
She flashed an easy smile as she gently patted herself dry with
a beach towel.

Julianna possessed the same richly flowing dark brown hair
and curvaceous figure that stood out in the old photographs of
her grandmother. But her lips were fuller, more glamorous,
and her eyes even darker, the color of rich espresso. Her nose
was strong and straight, and when she smiled, I detected
ample evidence of the Darlington dimple. She wore a sleek,
mocha-colored bikini that nearly matched the rich tan hue of
her glistening skin while accentuating the cleavage wrought
by full, firm breasts.

"Are you visiting with your parents?" I asked her.

"Mom and Dad are travelling in Europe," she said as she sat
on a lounge chair, "so they shipped me here for a couple of
weeks with Gram."

"Your grandmother's an incredible lady."

"She's a real pistol, isn't she? Her health's fragile these
days . . . so my time with her is precious . . . but it can get a little
dull just sitting by the pool all day."

I was beginning to see Doris's hand in this private luncheon
arrangement. Julianna, it appeared, was equally cognizant of
her grandmother's intentions. Who was I to complain? I
needed to be certain, however, that I wasn't dealing with an
overdeveloped fifteen-year-old.

"So, Julianna, are you in college?"

She laughed. "Checking to see if I'm jailbait?"

"Something like that," I conceded.

"You're safe," she assured me with an endearing grin. "I
graduated from high school in Scarsdale this spring. I start at
Mt. Holyoke College in the fall." I smiled, brushing my hand
across my brow in mock relief.

As a native of New Jersey, I knew of Scarsdale, New York, and its tony reputation. Though our hometowns were geographically close, they were worlds apart both economically and culturally.

Indulging ourselves on the sumptuous poolside lunch prepared by Luisa, we discussed our contrasting upbringings, our parents (she considered hers equally bizarre though in different ways), my two years at Roberts, and her expectations and apprehensions about college life. I couldn't help but wonder at the irony of a guy like me, barely two years removed from a life of social incompetence in a two-bit Jersey suburb, inhaling a lobster-laden salad with the gorgeous granddaughter of a wealthy dowager on an elegant Berkshire estate. Incongruous as it might have been, I felt strangely at ease. Julianna was as open and engaging as her grandmother.

It was difficult to drag myself away, but I felt obliged to return to the library after our lunch to begin my work compiling dossiers on the artworks comprising Doris's intended bequest. I couldn't help but cast an occasional admiring glance at Julianna as I worked. By mid-afternoon, I bade Julianna and Luisa goodbye and returned to Williamstown.

Brigitte was unusually quiet at dinner that night. After we'd finished and headed to our respective rooms, I asked her what was wrong.

"Wheems!" she said before slamming shut the door to her room.

CHAPTER THIRTY

Our Scheme to Ream Wheems

I went right to work when I arrived at Doris's house the next morning. She was not in her usual wing chair and Julianna was not about. I grew concerned.

I was relieved when Doris and Julianna jauntily strolled in a couple of hours later. They'd been out shopping, Julianna reported, as she restored her grandmother to her favorite perch in the library. Julianna then retired to her room to don her bikini and collect some poolside reading material.

Once Julianna was ensconced in her lounge chair by the pool, I rose from the desk and strolled over to speak with Doris. I'd debated the propriety of approaching her on the two matters on my mind. As it turned out, my hesitancy was unwarranted.

"Good morning, Doris."

Doris peered at me over her reading glasses, lowering her copy of *The New York Times*. "How are you today, Charlie? Are you finding your way through the files?"

"Everything's great," I assured her. "The files are impeccably organized and full of useful information. But I wonder if I can talk to you about a couple of personal matters."

"I'd be honored if you would." She beckoned me to sit down in the wing chair beside her.

"Well, first," I began cautiously, "I wanted to ask if it would be okay with you if I invited Julianna out for dinner and a movie."

"Hah!" Doris laughed heartily. "Why do you think I introduced you? I'm sure she'd be delighted! Now what else is on your mind, Charlie?"

I was more diffident regarding my second request. I felt I might be treading well beyond the boundaries of propriety.

"Doris, do you know Myron Wheems at the Clark?"

"Of course I do. Why do you ask?" Doris carefully folded her newspaper and placed it on a side table. She took off her glasses.

I proceeded to tell her about Brigitte and Wheems aggressive behavior. I also explained Brigitte's fear of being reassigned from her dream job if she registered a complaint. Doris became visibly agitated. I hoped it was not at my temerity in raising the issue. "That's outrageous!" she growled. "We'll address this *immediately*." She pointed toward a nearby telephone, instructed me to retrieve it, then dialed.

"Myron Wheems, please. This is Doris Darlington." After a brief delay, Wheems picked up. Though I was privy to only one side of the conversation, the tenor was readily apparent.

"Myron, how would you feel if I withdrew my bequest to the Clark to protest some highly improper behavior on your part?" I sensed befuddlement on the other end of the line.

"Well, Myron, I have it on excellent authority that you have been inappropriately intrusive with a delightful young intern named Brigitte Lemaire," she said firmly.

"I don't give a damn what you think or whether she's complained to you, Myron... and it is none of your business how I know." Doris pursed her lips. "I have three demands," she said. "First, you will *absolutely* cease any and all activity which might seem even remotely inappropriate where Miss Lemaire is concerned ... second, you will apologize to her *immediately* for your misbehavior ... and third, you will *not in any manner* deprive Miss Lemaire of the opportunity to continue on her current assignment at the Clark. You will offer her your full cooperation, expertise, and guidance on that project ... in lieu of your roving hands! Is that understood?

"Good, then. Goodbye, Myron." Doris slammed the phone back onto its cradle. She then smiled and looked at me. "Problem solved."

"Pretty impressive," I said. I was truly in awe of this amazing woman. "I can't thank you enough. Brigitte will be immensely grateful."

"What good is pull if you can't use it?" she said. "Now why don't you go outside and ask my granddaughter to dinner?"

I did as I was told. I asked Julianna to join me for dinner and a movie on the following night. She eagerly accepted. Life was grand.

CHAPTER THIRTY-ONE

Belle de Jour

B rigitte was buoyant at dinner that evening. Since Wheems's
depravity made for inappropriate table conversation, she
buttonholed me afterward, gazing at me curiously.

"Today, something . . . *magnifique* . . . did happen," she said,
searching my eyes for signs of involvement. "Mr. Wheems—he
apologizes to me! He says he is very sorry and he will not
debauch me further!"

"That's great news," I said, amused, as always, by her choice
of words. I couldn't restrain a sly smile. With a glint in her eye,
she strode right up to me, kissing me firmly on the lips. "*Merci*!"
she purred. "How did you do it?"

"A friend with influence," I said.

Brigitte was more grateful than I could have imagined. Shortly
after leaving her in the hallway, she knocked on my door.

"There is a *film français* at the cinema in the town tonight. I
would like for you to accompany me as my . . . how do you
say . . . treat?"

Presuming she was referring to a French movie, I gladly
accepted her invitation, though I'd never seen a French movie
I even remotely understood—even with subtitles. They all
ended randomly, as if someone had accidentally tripped the

plug on the projector, leaving me clueless. But French movies were often sensuous. That part I usually understood.

The movie, *Belle de Jour,* starred Catherine Deneuve as a beautiful French housewife who carried on a secret life as a high-class prostitute. I *adored* Catherine Deneuve. I'd drool at her recitation of the French national anthem. Trouble was, she looked remarkably like my lovely lesbian-sometime-lover, Annie. So here I was, with a French bombshell attending a French film featuring another French bombshell who reminded me of my lesbian lover.

"You have, how do you say, a *crunch* on Mademoiselle Deneuve?" Brigitte observed as we filed out of the theater after the show.

"A *crush*, yes, absolutely . . . she's a very beautiful woman." Had she caught me drooling during the movie?

"*Très sexy*," she said, eyeing me lustfully. I had a growing suspicion that Brigitte took my obsession with Catherine Deneuve as a personal challenge.

We returned to our lodgings after midnight. Time to call it an evening. Or so I thought. I accompanied Brigitte to her door. As I turned to return to my room, she clutched my arm and yanked me into her lair where she attacked me like a dog in heat. She ripped open my shirt, scattering buttons across the floor like loose change. My pants slid to my ankles. She shoved me onto her bed. Brigitte was nearly on top of me as I foraged through my wallet in pursuit of a condom. My crooked dick intrigued her but failed to slow her assault. But alas, it rendered its magic. When she climaxed she came in waves like the French Foreign Legion.

And that was only the initial assault. Brigitte was a veritable nymphomaniac. She'd wait patiently for my erection's resurrection and then pounce again. And again. Not that she wasn't alluring—as amply evidenced by my repeatedly resurgent dick—but my efforts to keep pace with her ravenous appetite put me at serious risk of dick-annihilation.

After her third orgasm, Brigitte looked at me as if I were some prodigy. "Your penis, it is *très spécial*, no? *C'est magnifique!*" Who could have ever imagined, after all the nights I lay in bed dreading my life with a crooked cock, that instead of fearing revulsion, I'd worry about wearing it out?

Brigitte was the realization of my high school fantasy. It was like making simultaneous love to Miss Romaire (with her taut *derriere*), Catherine Deneuve (whom I *loove*) and the equally exquisite Brigitte Lemaire (why did so many French names rhyme with *derriere*?)! It was a virtual foursome, a *ménage à quatre!*

My man-parts sore and my sleep sorely compromised, I had all I could do to extract myself from Brigitte's bed the next morning. Are all French women this voracious? Or was it the allure of my serendipitously skewed phallus? She was still asleep when I collected my tattered clothes (along with a few buttons) and returned to my room. I was as exhausted as she was insatiable.

I was halfway through breakfast when I remembered my date with Julianna. Could I summon the stamina? I considered postponing it. A postponement would disappoint both Julianna *and* Doris. I hadn't the heart to do that. And perhaps, I rationalized, it was better to detach myself from Brigitte's hypnotic orbit for at least one night, just to catch my breath.

I was listless by the time I reached Lenox. Bleary-eyed, I greeted both Julianna and her grandmother as I repaired to my corner of the library to resume my work.

"You look pallid, Charlie," Doris said. "Are you well?"

"I'm fine, thanks . . . just didn't sleep too well last night."

When Julianna dropped by later in the morning, I was barely functional.

"Looking forward to this evening," she said.

"Me too." I smiled, though I was dead tired and ached all over. My dick hadn't been this sore since I nearly severed it on that guy wire. I hadn't a clue how to combat a sexual hangover since I'd never experienced one. How would I face our impending date, much less enjoy it?

Later that morning, I had a brainstorm. I found Julianna in her usual spot by the pool.

"I have to return to the museum for a meeting," I fibbed, "but I'll be back to pick you up by six."

"No problem," she said. "See you then!"

I abandoned my papers and jumped into the car. It was almost noon. I drove along Route 7 until I found a clearing at the side of the road. I pulled over, rolled into the back seat, and went to sleep.

The blare of a truck's horn stirred me to consciousness. It was almost 5:30. Five hours of sleep did the trick. I was myself again. I returned to the driver's seat, pulled onto Route 7, and drove back to the Darlington Estate. On the way, I stopped in Lenox to make a last-minute dinner reservation and check the movie schedule.

Two movies were playing: *Hello Dolly!* with Barbra Streisand and, implausibly, *Belle de Jour*! Watching *Belle de Jour* two nights in a row was sure to fuck me up. But the choice between the snouty Streisand and the sultry Deneuve was a no-brainer.

Julianna was ready when I arrived. She wore a low-cut top and tantalizingly tight jeans. Her attire was a welcome contrast to my rumpled shirt and slacks, victims of my five-hour snooze. Doris, playing the grandmother hen, was there to see us off.

"You look like you slept in those clothes," Julianna said perceptively. I offered some lame excuse and returned the non-compliment.

"You, on the other hand, look ravishing," I told her.

We engaged in a wide-ranging conversation over dinner in a little French bistro. We talked about books (her poolside reading included *Portnoy's Complaint* and *Slaughterhouse-Five*), tastes in music (she was partial to The Beatles and Motown while I preferred Simon & Garfunkel) and ambitions (she hoped to travel the world, I hoped to make it out of the northeast corridor). The more we talked, the further Brigitte receded from my consciousness. That was, of course, until the opening scenes of *Belle de Jour*.

All at once, my weary brain was swamped with provocative images. Catherine Deneuve as the seductive prostitute; Annie, her doppelganger, making love to me at the inn; Brigitte playing the insatiable nymph; Miss Romaire's exquisite derriere; and now, this alluring young woman beside me. I was suffering from a severe case of sexual and emotional overload. I was taut as a guy wire.

When Julianna snuggled up to me and squeezed my hand I nearly exploded. *Anxiety attack!* I summarily excused myself and retreated to the men's room. I splashed my face with cold water. My heart was pounding. I broke out in a cold sweat, on the verge of passing out. I shut myself into a stall and sat there, trying to tame my emotions. After about five minutes, I willed myself up, threw some more water on my face, and returned to my seat in the theater.

Julianna flashed a look of concern. "Are you okay?"

"Must have been something I ate," I alleged. "I'll be fine in a few minutes."

I'd regained control by the time we left the theater. I asked Julianna if she'd enjoyed the movie.

"I did," she said. "But I can tell you've got a crush on Deneuve." She gave me a seductive wink.

Not again!

When we approached the driveway to the estate, Julianna urged me to pull over. We were well clear of the house, shielded from view by a row of tall oaks. I stopped the car, dreading a relapse, angry with myself for wearing a button-front shirt.

The evening was beautiful, the black sky rampant with stars. Julianna slid over and kissed me. In contrast to Brigitte's relentless assault just hours before, Julianna was passionate and gentle.

Suddenly, I knew I couldn't go on. There were more than enough reasons why. First, I was an emotional wreck, in love or infatuated with too many women at once. Second, though her considerable physical attributes belied her youth, Julianna was barely beyond high school. Third, I was afraid I'd relapse into the hyperventilating hulk I'd become for a few brief moments in the theater rest room, unable to control my emotions. And fourth and fifth, my prick was sore and I had exhausted my entire supply of condoms with Brigitte.

"Let's stop here, at least for tonight," I said haltingly. I could tell she was taken aback. I struggled for the right words, a magic sentence that would buy me a reprieve without offending her.

"Julianna," I stammered, reaching for her hand and grasping it firmly, "it wouldn't be fair to mislead you. I'm involved in other relationships. And I'm confused." She gazed at me in bewilderment. I stroked her cheek. "I don't know what to say except that I adore you and I don't want to sabotage our relationship."

Julianna was silent for an unusually long time. She, too, didn't want to say anything she'd regret or reveal her intense disappointment at my awkward rebuff. I wondered if I'd made the wrong decision, undermining a nascent relationship that had at least as much promise as any of my other inscrutable alliances.

"Okay, we'll call it a night." Her voice was tinged with chagrin. She sighed deeply, withdrawing her hand. "I'll see you tomorrow."

I restarted the car, pulled up to the house, walked her to the door. Silence prevailed.

I drove back to Williamstown in a stupor.

CHAPTER THIRTY-TWO

Grandmother Knows Best

The weekend offered a welcome respite, that much better for the fact that Brigitte had returned to Montreal to visit family and friends. I enjoyed a measure of peace, free from the distraction of women. Imagine me, the guy with the crooked cock, inundated by female attention. Catherine would have been proud.

The awkward conclusion of my evening with Julianna haunted me. Was I protecting her or shielding myself? While I pondered that conundrum, I had to attend to another pressing matter: I'd run out of condoms.

Curious as to how and where I'd finally managed to exhaust the dozen condoms I bought at Alice's drug store in the fall of my freshman year, I took a brief mental survey. For starters, I recall half the box missing after my drug-induced threesome with Colette and Molly. No clue if I'd used them, lost them or ate them, but they were gone the next morning. I'd had three unforgettable encounters during spring break. That accounted for nine. I finished the box with Brigitte. What about Annie?

Though I couldn't completely reconcile the numbers, I knew it was time to reload. A visit to the local drugstore did the trick. It was smoother than my initial condom-procurement expedition with Izzy. With my newfound confidence, I chose the 36-count box. What a stud!

Sunday evening brought my troubles again to the fore. Brigitte, whom I'd last seen lying marvelously naked beside me on Friday morning, was due back shortly, and tomorrow, I'd have to face both Julianna and Doris.

I decided to duck Brigitte, if at all possible, until Monday night, preferring to focus on the repair of my relationship with Julianna. Another wild night of sex with Brigitte would hardly prepare me for a delicate conversation with Julianna the next morning.

My plan was going smoothly through Monday morning. I'd heard Brigitte arrive late the previous night but made no effort to greet her. I skipped breakfast to assure the successful completion of Operation French Bombshell Evasion. I hadn't a clue what I'd say to Julianna.

When I arrived at the Darlington Estate, Luisa informed me that Julianna was out. I wasn't sure if that was good news or bad. Doris, however, was waiting for me in the library when I entered.

"Sit down, Charlie," she beckoned me solemnly.

"Sure, Doris, what's up?" My jaunty response was scant camouflage for my growing sense of dread.

"Though we've known each other briefly, you feel almost like a part of my family," she said, freaking me out a bit. "And, of course, you know by now how much I adore my granddaughter . . ."

"Of course." I shifted uneasily in my chair.

"Julianna's not been herself since you went out together on Friday night. She denies that anything's wrong and won't confide in me. That, alone, is highly unusual." Doris rubbed her eyes thoughtfully. "I think she went out this morning solely to avoid facing you."

The somber look on my face confirmed her assumption that something was amiss between Julianna and me.

"I really don't have any business prying into your affairs, and I won't be offended if you politely ask me to mind my own business. But if I can help in any way . . ."

While it might have been inappropriate at some level (particularly given the involvement of her own granddaughter in the matter), Doris's attempt at mediation was, at least to me, a welcome intervention. I recognized her familial conflict of interest, but I really had no one else to talk to. Was I going to call Dad for relationship advice? *Just keep it in your pants, kid, and you won't get into trouble*, I could hear him bluster, although doing just that on Friday night with Julianna seemed to have prompted much of the problem. And besides, none of his axioms was even remotely applicable.

"If I explain it to you, I'm afraid I'll badly tarnish your image of me," I said.

"I doubt that, Charlie, but it's solely up to you."

I hesitated. How could I explain my multiple, screwed-up relationships without sounding shallow, stupid or vain? Would I be violating a sacred trust with Annie to reveal the root of my problems with her? Doris was patient with me as I sifted through my options. Yes, I would sound shallow, stupid and vain, and yes, I would technically breach my commitment to Annie. But in the end, Doris was probably the only person in the world who could help me sort it all out.

"Sit tight, Doris," I said as I prepared to launch into my tortured story, "this is not going to be pretty."

I told her first about Annie: my early infatuation with Annie the Nun, my shocking discovery of her sexual preference and the concomitant revelation of her true persona, my hopeless love for an avowed lesbian, and the equally surprising night at the St. Augustine Inn that scrambled our entire relationship. I related the story of Brigitte: her victimization by Myron Wheems and how Doris's own intervention and Brigitte's gratitude unleashed a sexual rampage that laid waste to my mind and body just hours before my date with Julianna. Finally, I described my great fondness for Julianna, my concerns about her youth, and my hesitation to further complicate my life by complicating hers with my affection and confusion.

Doris listened intently, more amused than horrified. "A remarkable saga," she said at last. "Yet there's nothing in that freakish narrative to render you blameworthy. To the contrary," she said, grinning, "you're the victim of your own charm."

I was relieved. I was not, in her estimation, a deviant or miscreant. That much was good. But where did I go from here?

"I'll tell you what I'd suggest, but feel free to take it with a grain of salt. This is merely the advice of one old lady who has seen much worse in her time than what you've just described.

"First, you're in love with Annie. That's not something you come by easily. But until she can sort out her sexual needs and identity and commit to you unconditionally, you shouldn't commit your heart to her either.

"Second, as to Brigitte, there's nothing wrong with a good roll in the sack . . . God knows I've been there . . . but reading between the lines, I'm doubtful that your physical relationship with Brigitte will ripen into anything more meaningful. You are both very different—you're probably little more than convenient sexual partners. I'd say enjoy it . . . but don't let it poison more promising relationships."

Doris's perception was uncanny and her logic unassailable.

"And as for my lovely granddaughter . . ." She lowered her voice almost conspiratorially. "She likes you very much and, from what you tell me, that feeling is mutual. Yes, she's young . . . but Darlington blood matures quickly. She's anything but naïve. She's beautiful and she's clever." Doris reached across and touched my arm. "But the truth is, Charlie, that you barely know her. Give the relationship some time to develop. Tell her you'd like to pursue her, but at a more deliberate pace. Clear up the current confusion, if you can, and suggest that she consider spending a weekend with you back at school this fall. If, by that time, you both have interest in each other, you can see what develops."

"You have a gift," I said. "You should charge by the hour."

She laughed. "I've got all the money I need. Relationships are the true currency of life."

I thanked Doris profusely for her attention and advice. Before I could return to my work, she asked if it would be okay if she had a brief chat with Julianna about some of what we had just discussed.

"If you can manage to strip out all of the homosexual and heterosexual sex, that would be most welcome," I said with a grin.

"Not much left," she chuckled, "but I'll try."

My session with Doris was liberating. That night, I invited Brigitte out for coffee. I learned that, among the people she visited in Montreal, was a boyfriend, Marcel. She was, she conceded, sometimes a bit too amorous, but she had enjoyed our encounter and (despite the existence of Marcel) looked forward to an occasional reprise. It was, as Stephen Stills would describe it a year or so later, a "love the one you're with" kind of thing, and it was okay with her if it was okay with me. It was indeed. Suffice it to say that I would make more than a dent into my newly restored supply of condoms to satisfy our mutual urgings over the balance of the summer.

Doris, as usual, worked her magic with Julianna that same evening. When I saw Julianna the next morning, she immediately came by to talk. She apologized for her reaction and said that she now better understood my hesitancy on Friday night. We went out together a couple more times before she ended her two-week visit with her grandmother, keeping things mostly (but not entirely) platonic. We promised to write each other, and she hinted that she'd welcome an invitation to visit me at Roberts in the fall.

Annie, however, was a whole other story.

CHAPTER THIRTY-THREE

Fertilized Fields

Brigitte and I were getting down and dirty on a Sunday afternoon in late July when Mrs. Wilson knocked at my door.

"A call for you downstairs, Charlie."

"Be right there, Mrs. Wilson!" Brigitte giggled as I hunted for my clothes. "I'm coming!" I shouted.

"Not any more," she chirped.

My shirt was inside-out as I descended the stairs to the telephone in the hall below.

"Charlie?" whispered a familiar voice as I picked up the phone.

"Annie! How good to hear your voice!" Annie and I had exchanged several long, newsy letters over the summer and had spoken once or twice, but I hadn't seen her since our unforgettable encounter at the St. Augustine Inn.

"You, too," she said, almost mournfully.

"Is something wrong?"

"We need to talk."

"What's up?"

"This would be much better in person. I could come out next weekend..." "Of course," I said, the concern bleeding through my voice.

"There's a Greyhound from Grand Central to Lenox arriving at two o'clock next Saturday. Can you meet me there?"

"Sure, Annie. See you then."

Just when our relationship had begun to show promise, something was awry. An array of potential issues ran through my mind. Had she reconsidered her brief fling with bisexuality and elected to stay with the all-girls' team? Had she been outed and subsequently ostracized by friends and family? Was she ill? Was it her family? Maria? Had she fallen in love with someone else—male, female, transsexual? The possibilities were endless. I was a nervous wreck all week as I anxiously anticipated her arrival.

I borrowed a car from the Wilsons and drove to Lenox on Saturday afternoon. It was a nearly perfect mid-summer's day. Cumulous clouds floated like cotton puffs against a pure blue sky. The little Berkshire town was clogged with tourists, many there to attend the weekend performances at the Tanglewood Music Festival. I spotted Annie carrying a small valise at the bus stop near the town square. She looked tired and pale. I thought I detected a touch of sadness in her eyes. Her greeting lacked its customary animation.

"Did you get anything to eat?" I asked her.

"Just an apple on the bus," she said. "I could use a bite."

It was mid-afternoon and the lunchtime crowds had thinned. I took her bag and we strode into the closest restaurant. I ordered a coffee for myself and a sandwich for her. She hadn't said much, and when I glanced into her eyes I saw them tearing over.

"What is it?"

"I'm pregnant."

Her words floated in the air like a dark cloud before

penetrating my consciousness with a thud. I stared at her blankly, unable to speak. It took me a few moments to connect her condition to our night at the St. Augustine Inn. Our lovemaking had been so unexpected that I hadn't the wherewithal to even consider the need for protection; nor had she. What were we thinking?

I wasn't going to insult Annie by asking her the obvious question. I knew I'd been the only one. I thought of my father's second fractured axiom: *Don't sow your wild oats in fertilized fields.* And—adjusting for the apparent malapropism—I'd done just that.

"I guess we weren't thinking too clearly that night," I said, stating the obvious.

"I guess not," she said, wiping the tears from her eyes.

"Annie, I don't know what to say . . ."

"Let's start with an understanding: we both bear equal responsibility for this. Agreed?"

"Of course." I reached across the table for her hand. "How long have you known?"

"I began to suspect about a month ago when I didn't get my period. I confirmed it two weeks ago."

"Why didn't you call me?"

"I didn't know how to tell you."

I'm not sure how I maintained my calm. Perhaps it was Annie's equanimity.

"Any thoughts . . . about what you want to do?"

"What *we* want to do."

"Right. What we want to—"

"No, Charlie. Not yet." There was tension in her voice.

"Did you tell your parents?"

"No, although they've noticed the weight I've put on. But it's the last thing they'd suspect of their innocent darling daughter."

"Does . . . does Maria know?"

"Nobody knows . . . but you, Charlie." She gently rubbed her temples. "But telling you . . . is an enormous relief."

I, on the other hand, had been suddenly plunged into a parallel universe in which I could be a husband, a father—or a co-conspirator.

"What about counseling. Have you talked to anyone?"

"No."

"Perhaps we should." I was trying to be constructive but Annie was unreceptive.

"This is for *us* to work out," she shot back, much to my dismay.

When she'd finished her sandwich, she rose from the table. The four or five pounds of extra weight did nothing to detract from her beauty, but the anguish in her eyes broke my heart. I paid the bill and walked her out. Once outside, I took her in my arms and hugged her like there was no tomorrow.

Back at the Manor, I introduced Annie to the Wilsons and to Brigitte, whom I had forewarned of Annie's visit. Annie and Brigitte clicked immediately. I wondered what each would have thought if they'd known the details of my relationship with the other. We had enough to worry about as it was.

In anticipation of Annie's visit, I'd bought tickets to a play at the Williamstown Theatre Festival. Annie was reluctant, but humored me by attending. While it improved her mood, I found it impossible to concentrate on the performance. Later, in my room, we spent an emotional night in each other's arms, chaste, and on occasion, in tears.

Annie slept better than I did. My mind wandered as the reality of her pregnancy settled in. I thought back about my life just twenty-four hours earlier. Except for my anxiety about

Annie's visit, I was truly happy—carefree as a toddler at play. But that image was now suffused—*pregnant*, to use a more relevant term—with an entirely different meaning. I lifted my head and peered at Annie, asleep beside me, her hair splayed across her pillow, her remarkable beauty masking the turmoil—and the *child*—growing inside of her. I wanted so badly to make everything right, to relieve her burden as well as my own. Yet I felt helpless, like a rat in a maze. Our mutual fear of saying the wrong thing had already hampered our fledgling efforts to address our options. But as I tossed and turned, I realized that no one was better equipped than Doris to guide us through that maze. All I needed to do was to convince Annie to allow her to try.

I broached the matter indirectly as Annie and I shared breakfast the next morning. "Since you're here, there's someone I'd very much like you to meet," I told her. I'd written Annie about Doris earlier in the summer. I wrote of how close I'd become to her and how much she meant to me. "You'd like her, Annie."

Annie was hardly in the mood for a social visit with an ancient dowager who had tickled my fancy. But I begged her indulgence and she finally relented. And as much as it embarrassed me to burden Doris with yet another personal catastrophe, I knew she represented the best chance we had to break the impasse that had settled uneasily upon us. I neglected to inform Annie of the true purpose of our visit.

As I'd expected, Doris leapt at the opportunity to meet Annie and graciously invited us to join her for lunch.

Annie was astounded by the opulence of the Darlington Estate. Her eyes lit up like a ten-year-old on her first trip to Disneyland. Luisa led us through the library and out the sliding doors that opened to the bright backyard where Doris awaited us. Bedecked in a long blue dress with playful white polka dots, she sat in a wicker chair at a canopied table by the pool. A wide-brimmed hat provided cover from the hot sun.

"And you must be Annie," Doris said cordially as we entered the shaded patio. "Charlie's told me so much about you ... Please, grab a chair and join me." The table had been set for three. At each place was an elegant plate of Caesar salad with grilled chicken and asparagus accompanied by hearty slices of freshly baked bread and a large glass of mint-laced iced tea.

Although I hadn't informed her of our quandary during my brief telephone conversation that morning, Doris could read me like a book. She sensed when I was in trouble—it seemed an all-too-common occurrence—and she had probably already figured out why.

In spite of her initial reticence, Annie warmed quickly to Doris. Before she was even halfway through her elegant salad, Annie had been gently coaxed into divulging much of her biography, omitting, of course, the chapters relevant to our present quandary. I persuaded Doris, in turn, to share with Annie some of her own favorite anecdotes, including the tale of Duchamp's whimsical bidet.

When the moment was right, Doris boldly ventured forth to address the elephant in the room. "When Charlie called me, he told me only that he wanted me to meet you and, of course, I was delighted for the opportunity," she told Annie. Doris then reached out to touch my arm. "But at this point, I think I know Charlie better than he knows himself ... I can't help feeling that something is deeply troubling you both. And if my instincts are correct, I'd like to help ... if I can."

Annie sensed an ambush. She glared at me. "What's going on here?"

"Annie, *please*." I reached out for her hand; she yielded it grudgingly. "We're in trouble, Annie. I trust Doris implicitly. Please give her a chance to help us . . . *please*."

Annie yanked her hand from my grasp. "What have you told her?" she asked me accusatorially. I realized then that I needed to come completely clean with Annie so that any discussion that followed would be frank and open.

"Absolutely nothing about what you told me yesterday," I said. "But some weeks ago, at a time when I was very confused and troubled about a number of things—including my relationship with you—I sought Doris's advice . . . I felt a need at that time to explain our relationship . . . including your sexual orientation. Doris helped me to sort things out." I didn't want to get into any further details—such as Julianna and Brigitte—and I was relieved when Annie didn't inquire. But a look of betrayal flashed across her face.

"Look, Annie," I said, my voice rising in frustration, "I'm truly sorry that I breached your trust. Doris will keep your secret . . . I've told no one else . . . I swear it."

Annie was justifiably angry, but there was much more at stake now. Doris seized the moment.

"I apologize in advance if my intuition is off base, Annie, but are you pregnant?" No words were required to confirm her suspicion.

It was suddenly clear to both of us that the time had come to sort through our predicament instead of simply bemoaning our fate. When I squeezed her hand, I felt Annie's resistance finally melting away. I sensed now that Annie understood why I held Doris in such high esteem. I think she also understood that what Doris already knew about her could only be helpful in formulating any advice she might be able to offer us. Doris took the bull by the horns.

"Have you discussed your options?"

"Not yet," I said. "We're still struggling with the reality of the situation."

"I understand," she said before turning to Annie. "Can I ask you a few personal questions?"

Annie nodded tentatively.

"Let's start with your religious background . . ."

Any ambivalence Annie still harbored quickly succumbed to the sheer force of Doris's presence. Annie fortified herself with a long swig of her iced tea before glancing my way for reassurance and encouragement. "Go ahead, Annie," I said. So she did.

She told Doris about her Catholic roots. "Charlie used to call me 'The Nun,'" Annie recalled with a smile, the first real smile I'd seen since her arrival the previous day. "But I can't be at peace," she said, her smile evaporating, "with a religion that treats me as an abomination."

"Of course," Doris said. She thought a moment and posed a follow-up question. "To what degree does what remains of your religious belief system . . . let's call it your moral compass . . . affect your decision?"

"Abortion involves the termination of a life," Annie said. "No small matter."

"Is that an *absolute bar* to the abortion option," Doris asked her, "or a fact to weigh in the balance?"

"I presume what you're asking is whether I could live with myself if I chose to have an abortion." Annie took another sip of iced tea as she pondered her response. "I believe so . . . but it's too early to be sure."

"And what about you, Charlie. Does abortion present a moral dilemma for you?"

"Not as much as it does for Annie," I admitted.

Doris turned back to Annie. "If you chose to go forward with your pregnancy, would you feel compelled to raise your child?"

"I'm not cut out at this time in my life to be a single mother," Annie said, looking at me as she continued, "and I don't care to drag Charlie into a lifetime relationship built on a mutually foolish mistake."

Doris shifted her gaze from Annie to me. "Charlie, how would you feel about marrying Annie if she were *not* carrying your child?" Doris asked. It was an emotionally loaded question. After a moment of hesitation, I trained my eyes on Annie as I answered.

"Some day, if Annie loved me as I love her, and *if* Annie could be entirely comfortable in a heterosexual relationship . . . with no regret about abandoning her gay identity or lifestyle . . . then I would treasure a life with Annie."

Annie met my proclamation of love with a look of utter exasperation. "I'm no more resolved in my sexuality now than I was when we created this child, Charlie," she snapped. "Your answer was peppered with 'ifs' that are not and may not be easily or quickly resolved." Her response stung me, but didn't surprise me.

Doris brought her hands together in contemplation. "What I'm hearing from you both, I think, is a realization that there's no assurance now, or likely in the near future, that you can both commit to the kind of unqualified relationship that Charlie has described. Is that fair?"

"Yes," Annie responded firmly. I nodded with a tinge of resignation.

"If marriage and your mutual raising of the child is not an option, then we need to look harder at the questions of adoption and abortion," Doris said. A bank of clouds had settled overhead prompting Doris to lean forward and remove her hat. Instead of her customary ponytail, she unleashed a surprisingly thick, flowing mane of gray hair. "Annie, let me ask you this . . . is abortion so abhorrent to you as to compel you to carry this child to term, with all of the physical and emotional disruptions and complications attendant upon that commitment?"

"If I could do it *without* disruptions and complications, I'd answer yes. But my life is already more complicated than I'd ever imagined," Annie said. "Carrying a baby to term would be difficult, and I refuse to accept that obligation as a penance for allowing ourselves to get into this predicament."

Doris then urged us to address the abortion alternative. "Are you troubled by the illegality of abortion?"

"Of course," Annie acknowledged. "There are risks with sleazy, backroom procedures . . ."

Doris looked hard at both of us. Annie had done the heavy lifting, parsing through her religious, moral, and pragmatic principles in response to Doris's perceptive inquiries. I had little to add once the prospect of marriage slipped quietly off the table.

"If I could arrange for a capable, qualified physician to perform an abortion under proper clinical conditions, would you feel differently?" While that question was directed to both of us, I felt it was Annie's to answer.

"You can arrange that?" she asked.

"I believe that I can," Doris replied. I didn't see a need to press her for details. I knew her well enough to recognize that her connections were enviable, though it surprised me to learn that they straddled the line of the law.

Annie looked at me, seeking, I think, my blessing.

"It probably makes the most sense," I said to her, "but only if you think you can live with it."

"I'll have regrets," Annie said, "whatever I do."

"Aren't you putting yourself at risk by involving yourself in this?" I asked Doris.

"I'm a feisty eighty-five-year-old. What can they do to me?"

"Then I think that's the road we should take," Annie said with finality.

I nodded in a combination of relief and assent, but my elation was tempered by the realization that we hadn't discussed the cost.

"Any idea what this might cost?" I asked Doris.

"No, but we can work that out later," she said dismissively, assuring there would be no further discussion on that topic. "Okay, then . . . If you're sure about this, I'll make the necessary inquiries and contact Charlie when I have something definitive to report."

"Doris . . . you're an angel," Annie said gratefully.

"I'm not sure that's the proper metaphor under the circumstances," Doris said, "but I'm pleased to be able to help."

CHAPTER THIRTY-FOUR

The Triple-Breasted Mama

Three days later I received my instructions from Doris. Annie, having returned to New Liberty, would meet me that Thursday in New York City at the Park Avenue apartment of Doris's old and trusted friends, Dr. and Mrs. Longworthy. Dr. Longworthy, a retired obstetrician, had arranged for a former colleague to perform the procedure. Annie and I would be welcome to stay with the Longworthys for as long as necessary. Prepayment, Doris advised me, was a *fait accompli*; reimbursement would be deferred until later, she decreed.

I hitched a ride from Williamstown to the bus station in Pittsfield on Thursday morning. While well-to-do New Yorkers commuted to and from their summer Berkshire "cottages" in their air-conditioned Cadillacs and Jaguars, the underclass traveled with less aplomb. The bus ride was positively Dickensian. Thirty or so less fortunate souls (myself included) took their seats in a grimy, fossilized bus. The vast majority of the windows were inoperable and the heat was oppressive. The bus reeked of diesel fuel.

My fellow passengers included service workers from the Berkshire resorts, wrinkled pensioners, and a smattering of young people of little means and fewer prospects. I took an aisle seat beside a tall, gaunt, white-haired old man. Behind me sat a haggard man in his thirties, clad in a tattered Army jacket despite the stifling heat. A morose gentleman in his late fifties or early sixties occupied the seat in front of me. Across the aisle sat a frantic teenaged couple, each of them cradling a tiny infant while they fumbled clumsily with bottles, diapers, and assorted baby-related paraphernalia.

The presence of the young couple and their newborn twins unleashed emotions I'd managed until now to restrain. I was travelling to New York on a dubious mission. What if Annie had decided instead to keep the child, to accept my offer of marriage? The thought unsettled me. And what if, on the eve of the scheduled procedure, she loses her nerve, abruptly aborting the abortion?

The heat and humidity intensified as the bus pressed on. The molten air was permeated by the acrid smell of diesel. I began to feel woozy. My head started to spin, first gently, then more rapidly. Suddenly, on the verge of unconsciousness, I felt myself slowly ascending into the ether. My slumping body appeared lifeless below me. Beside me hovered my snowy-haired seatmate like a ghost, his eyes vacant, his mouth agape. I'd tumbled headlong into a fractured version of Dickens' *A Christmas Carol*, a reluctant Ebenezer Scrooge in the spell of my very own Ghost of Christmas Future. In July! How messed up was that?

The white-haired apparition pointed grimly toward the young couple across the aisle. The infants wailed uncontrollably. "Shut THE FUCK UP!" the harried father cried out repeatedly as the twins continued to shriek. He suddenly looked up at me. I shuddered. It was as if I were looking in a mirror. *His face was my face*! It was *me* screaming shamelessly at those poor, helpless twins!

To pacify her progeny, the mother reached down to unbutton her blouse, unleashing *three* prodigious, milk-swollen breasts! Her inconsolable infants flew to her outermost nipples, sucking voraciously. As they devoured her bosom, the besieged mother cast her sad blue eyes upward until they fixed on mine. I knew at once that those eyes were Annie's—and her face was Annie's! In an instant, I felt myself hurtling downward, my mouth clamping greedily on the unclaimed nipple of the beleaguered woman's middle breast like a jumper cable on a balky car battery. The twins released their ravenous grip on their mother's breasts, staring at me ferociously. The first child's face morphed into that of Annie, while her twin bore my countenance! They raised their tiny arms in jealous anger and lunged at me furiously, scratching my cheek and banishing me from their mother's bosom.

"What *is* this?" I heard myself shriek at the white-haired apparition. "Why are you showing me these hideous things?"

There was no response, though I could feel myself drawing away from that horrifying hallucination as the cadaverous figure pointed me toward the morose man seated before us. He was sobbing. When he turned and stared at me, I perceived my features on his grief-stricken face.

"We killed them!" he howled. "We killed them!"

"Killed whom?" I heard myself ask.

"We murdered the twins!" he cried yet again, tears streaming from his eyes—*my eyes*—in torrents.

I, too, began to weep. I'd had enough of these ethereal escapades. But the Ghost of Christmas Future had one more revelation in store. He motioned me toward the Vietnam veteran.

"No more, please!" I beseeched the phantom. My protests went unheeded. I trained my eyes on the unfortunate vet in the tattered Army jacket as I hovered over him. I recoiled in horror when he turned toward me. His face, like the others, was mine, but the top of his head had been blown away. His eyes were empty sockets. His right leg was a bleeding stump, severed above the knee. Suddenly, he raised an M-16 semiautomatic rifle, pointed it at my head and began to squeeze the trigger.

"NO! NO! NO!" I bawled. "DON'T SHOOT! NO!"

I felt the gentle hand of my elderly seatmate on my shoulder, coaxing me back to consciousness.

"Are you all right, young man?" he asked with a look of genuine concern. "You must have been lost in a whale of a nightmare," he said.

"I . . . I guess so," I answered, trying to gather my wits about me. I was drenched in perspiration and embarrassed by my outburst. My eyes were brimming with tears.

"Here," said the elderly gentleman, handing me a handkerchief. "Your cheek is bleeding."

CHAPTER THIRTY-FIVE

The Dastardly Deed is Done

The bus made a scheduled stop about an hour north of New York City. I hurried out for some fresh air. I knew, of course, that my out-of-body experience had been merely a dream, my troubled subconscious playing tricks on me. It had to have been the stifling heat, the biting odor of the diesel fuel. Yet I couldn't shake the nagging sense that it had been more vivid, more real, than any nightmare I'd ever endured. And unlike the hallucinations visited upon Ebenezer Scrooge, I felt powerless to avert the horrible fates foretold by my own implausible phantom.

I was drained when we finally reached the bus terminal at Times Square and Forty-Second Street. I took the "F" train to Lexington and Sixty-Third, then walked the couple of blocks to my destination. I survived a perfunctory grilling by the doorman and proceeded to the twelfth-floor apartment where Mrs. Longworthy welcomed me. Aristocratic in bearing and sumptuously attired, she seemed perfectly suited to her Park Avenue address. She appeared to be of the same vintage as Doris.

"Hello, Charlie," she said, extending her hand to me. "Annie's already arrived. She's in the guest room unpacking."

The Longworthys' large pre-war apartment was elegant but comfortable. European antique furniture complemented their extensive collection of old world ceramics. My eye was drawn to a large painting adorning the wall over the living room sofa.

"Picasso. A bullfight scene from 1934," Mrs. Longworthy explained. I stared at it, mesmerized, until Annie appeared.

"Charlie, you look and smell awful."

"The bus had no air conditioning . . . and the windows didn't open. The diesel exhaust was a bonus," I said. I neglected to mention apparitions, three-breasted women, or blown-away vets.

It was nearly dinnertime. A lavish meal was in the offing, like a last cigarette before a date with the firing squad. I suggested that dinner might be infinitely more pleasant if I'd the benefit of a shower and a change of clothes.

"Great idea," said Annie.

Dr. Longworthy joined us for dinner. A tall, distinguished man in his eighties with a well-trimmed goatee, he was a cross between Don Quixote and my Ghost of Christmas Future.

The connection between Doris and Mrs. Longworthy was readily apparent. They were cast from the same mold.

"I met Doris just before the First World War." Mrs. Longworthy paused as a uniformed maid emerged from the kitchen to serve the first course. "Thank you, Gloria," she said as a delectable salad was placed before her.

"We were rebels, Doris and I," she said proudly. "And a bit naughty, too!" She laughed. "I'm afraid we ran around with married men and—"

"And," her husband announced with a flourish, "I was *one* of them!" His laugh was hearty but shrill, like the caw of a crow.

"I was struggling to build my practice. My marriage had been an abject failure." He paused to pour himself some wine. "Elizabeth breathed the life back into me," he said, glancing lovingly at his wife. "I divorced, we married, and the rest is history . . ." It seemed unreasonably simple, if somewhat scandalous, particularly for the era.

"Doris is very enamored of both of you," Mrs. Longworthy said, "and she's a woman of impeccable taste."

"A remarkable lady," Annie said. "And you and Dr. Longworthy are so kind and generous . . . we can't thank you enough." I enthusiastically concurred.

"We've made unconventional choices in our own lives," Dr. Longworthy said, "so we don't judge others. And for Doris, we'd do anything."

The love fest was over. When dinner had drawn to a close, it was time to reveal the plans for our criminal conspiracy.

"Dr. Epstein is a former colleague of mine . . . a fine doctor," Dr. Longworthy assured us. "He'll perform the procedure in his office before it opens for the day. He's here on Park . . . six blocks north . . . a short walk. You'll need to be there by seven o'clock sharp." He directed the rest of his explanation to Annie. "A nurse will take your history and prepare you for the procedure. It'll be quick and virtually painless. You'll remain in the office for observation until Dr. Epstein is satisfied that there are no complications." He paused. "Do either of you have any questions?"

We glanced at each other and shook our heads.

"Annie, we'd like you to remain with us at least through tomorrow night. Can you do that?" Annie nodded.

"All right, then, both of you should get some sleep."

We returned to our room, finally alone.

"You okay, Annie?"

"Fine."

"It's not too late to change your mind."

"My mind is made up," she said curtly.

"What did you tell your parents?"

"That I was visiting you in Williamstown. They suspect nothing."

After a few moments of silence, Annie said: "I can scrape up a couple thousand to repay Doris . . . money my grandmother left me."

"I should pay for this," I said.

"Don't pull that chivalrous bullshit on me!" she snapped. "We did this together, we'll share the responsibility in the same manner." I deserved that.

"I'll take it up with Doris when I see her in Lenox." I didn't reveal that I'd be hard pressed to raise even half that much.

Annie and I traversed the six blocks to Dr. Epstein's office the next morning in relative silence. Only the doctor and his nurse were present when we arrived. The nurse escorted Annie into an examination room, leaving me alone in the waiting room.

The wait seemed eternal. I heard nothing and no one came or went until the office formally opened at nine o'clock. Finally, the nurse emerged and led me back to where Annie lay on an examination table in a makeshift recovery room. She was still slightly groggy from the local anesthetic. The tears in her eyes brought tears to my own. I held her hand as she wept softly for several moments before calming herself.

"We're done here, Charlie," she said. I wasn't quite sure what she meant. Before I could respond, Dr. Epstein came into the room, asked Annie some follow-up questions, imparted some instructions, and declared her fit to leave. We departed as silently as we'd arrived.

Annie went immediately to bed after the cab dropped us off at the apartment, leaving me to continue my vigil in the company of our hosts. Dr. Longworthy checked on her regularly.

"She's fine," he said. "It is a difficult time for her. She's sleeping now . . . more for emotional solace than for any physical reasons," he explained. "I'm afraid she just wants to be left alone for a while." Though it pained me to do so, I respected her wishes, even going so far as to spend the night alone in the Longworthys' third bedroom.

After a night of fitful sleep, I reentered the guest room on Saturday morning. Annie was awake, though not yet dressed.

"How are you feeling?"

"I'll be okay," she said. Her tone was dismissive.

"Can I get you anything?"

She didn't respond at first. A few moments later, she confirmed my worst fears.

"I don't think we should see each other for a while."

"But Annie—"

"Please, Charlie. I need some time and space. Can't you understand that?"

I hesitated, then capitulated.

"I can try." It was impossible to mask my hurt.

"Thanks, Charlie. I'm staying here for one more night," she said, "but I'd prefer if you'd go back to Williamstown today."

"Uh . . . sure, if that's what you really want." I was crestfallen.

As I prepared to leave, she spoke to me one last time.

"Charlie," she said mournfully, "they were twins."

CHAPTER THIRTY-SIX

Piddler on the Roof

The bus ride to Massachusetts was worse than the sweltering ride to New York. Not because of the bus—this one was air-conditioned—but because of my profound sense of emptiness after Annie's rejection.

As my internship drew to a close, I descended into a deep, dark funk. Unlike Picasso, whose despair gave rise to the creativity now celebrated as his "Blue Period," my own Blue Period was a pageant of debauchery and degradation. I banged Brigitte until I could hardly walk. She couldn't help but feel my misery.

"You are down in a dump, Charlie, no?" she said to me in her near-miss English.

"Down in *the dumps*," I said. "Yes, I suppose so."

"Your *très* beautiful Annie?"

"*Oui*," I responded, exhausting my French vocabulary.

"Do you wish to talk about it?"

"No," I said, ending the conversation.

Doris couldn't help but notice my deteriorating mood. While I'd thanked her repeatedly for all she had done for us, I was uncharacteristically distant. She left me alone for a while, hoping I'd snap out of it.

After watching me mope for a week, she summoned me to

the library for a chat. I unburdened myself completely, recounting our experiences and Annie's reaction. Doris was sympathetic, but not even she could mitigate the pain.

"Let her be," she advised. "Any attempt to intrude will only make things worse." She was right, of course, but I'd waded too far into my quagmire of despair to turn back now. My Blue Period had begun to consume me.

It was hard to bid Doris adieu. She'd been my mentor, my shrink, and above all, my dear friend. My work would provide the basis for a definitive catalogue of her collection when it eventually debuted at the Clark. I would write her often in the months that followed.

Saying *au revoir* to Brigitte was easier. I'd catch up on my sleep and save a fortune on condoms.

I moved into the SciFi House for my junior year. My roommate was Tractor, the jumbo Midwestern farm boy and defensive lineman who'd been Blake's most reliable crewman on our Spring Break frolic. It felt strange abandoning Izzy, but for most juniors, moving to one's fraternity house was standard operating procedure. Though the accommodations were decidedly substandard, they included free-flowing alcohol, a prerequisite for my plunge into despondency. My Blue Period sprouted like a noxious weed.

I elected to go totally blue. I painted our room midnight blue, bought a matching blue bedspread, hung ugly blue curtains. I binged on blues singers Billie Holiday and Etta James as well as Muddy Waters and B.B. King. I listened *ad nauseam* to recordings of Elvis's *Blue Suede Shoes*, Roy Orbison's *Blue Bayou* and the French orchestral *Love is Blue*. I even played the sappy *Blue on Blue* by Bobby Vinton, mostly as penance. I ate blue cheese and blueberry muffins and wore blue jeans. I attended anti-war rallies, becoming increasingly vocal in my opposition to the Vietnam War. My hair lengthened and my beard grew out. I resisted the urge to dye them blue.

While Tractor considered my behavior aberrant, he took my idiosyncrasies in stride. Parked mostly on the gridiron or in the library, he barely noticed the havoc I'd wreaked on our room. We used it sparingly anyway, to afford privacy for date weekends or as a refuge for study. We slept in a common top-floor "bunk room," huddled under electric blankets cranked up to combat the freezing air that infiltrated the drafty cupola.

Alienation and lethargy were the hallmarks of my Blue Period. I thoroughly ignored Izzy. I drank and smoked pot, mostly alone. I lost interest in my courses. In a few short months, I'd transformed from a popular guy juggling relationships with three gorgeous women to a classic Roberts degenerate with a waning interest in the opposite sex.

I reached my nadir on our first home football weekend in early October. I'd toyed with the notion of inviting Julianna, but thought better of it, recognizing that my fragile emotional state could subvert our fledgling relationship. Instead, I descended the stairs into the fraternity's taproom. I poured myself a beer . . . then another . . . and another.

Four hours later, I found myself perched on the SciFi roof. I'd climbed through a dormer window and staggered across the unstable surface to the tilting front portico. Despite my fear of heights, I sat on its edge, overlooking the front porch. The House hosted a band for the night. While everyone else had a date, I roosted forty feet up feeling sorry for myself.

Unsurprisingly, the roof was devoid of a bathroom. When my bladder threatened to burst from the dregs of a dozen beers, I stood up unsteadily, zipped down my fly, and unleashed a torrent of urine onto a cluster of partiers on the porch below. At that, my brothers resolved to take action, alarmed as much by my precarious predicament as by the shower I'd rained on their dates. It was Tractor who pulled me to safety, sweeping me off the roof like an opposition quarterback, and depositing me safely into the bunk room for the night.

Leah, as always, was Izzy's date for the weekend. Unaware of my rooftop escapade, they came by the fraternity house, unannounced, to visit on Saturday afternoon. Izzy, though stung by my apparent abandonment, harbored the hope that we could rekindle our lagging friendship.

Tractor intercepted them on their way to my room.

"You don't want to go in there," he said.

"Why not?" Izzy asked.

"He's blitzed again."

"*Again?*"

"Pretty much a daily routine," Tractor informed them. To demonstrate the depths of my depravity, he described my performance in Piddler on the Roof.

Stunned by these revelations, Leah and Izzy marched to my room and rapped on the door. I lurched to the door and opened it, if only to stop the infernal pounding. The disapproval that registered on their faces was commensurate with the dissipation on mine. Izzy dragged Leah from the room to spare us all further embarrassment.

Rather than let things fester, Izzy resolved to act.

I emerged from my stupor in time to grab dinner alone at The Douche. Upon my return to the House, Izzy and Leah accosted me. "Follow us," they demanded, herding me up to my room.

"You need fucking help, Charlie." Izzy spoke sternly, like a parent berating his toddler, but with a decidedly more colorful vocabulary. "You're fucked up beyond comprehension."

I didn't deny it, but said nothing. Leah assumed the mantle of the "good cop." "You were there for me when I needed you," she said. "I laid some serious shit on you that night, and you came through for me. Now tell us what this is about and give us a chance to help you."

I resisted the urge for a beer. I couldn't sink any lower and I had grown weary of blue. So I let the floodgates open. I revealed Annie's pregnancy, the abortion, and her subsequent rejection.

"Jesus, Charlie, it's a wonder you didn't kill yourself!" Izzy blurted out. Leah responded with a *what-the-fuck* smack on the back of his head.

"You need to snap out of this," she implored me.

Fortunately, they had a plan. "You'll stay with us at the dorm tonight and spend the day with us tomorrow," Izzy commanded. "You need to get out of this place for a while."

I felt guilty intruding on their weekend, but I knew they were right. I had to escape the keg and the weed and all of the blue shit that had come to define my life. And I needed to get over Annie. So I spent that night and the following day with my friends. It was a timely intervention and a welcome reprieve from my doldrums.

On Monday morning, I met with Professor Wilbur, now my faculty adviser. His secretary had summoned me the previous Friday. I feared the worst.

"I think you know why I called you here," he said, his ponytail wagging as he spoke. I didn't.

"You were my most promising student last year," he said, "and the reports on your internship at the Clark were spectacular." So far so good. "But you're a completely different person this fall."

A grunt was the most I could summon in response.

The Professor was undeterred. "Your essay on Picasso's Blue Period was nothing more than a sheet of blue paper," he said. It rang a bell, but I didn't recall handing it in.

"A witty play on Rothko's color emotion?" It was my best shot, given my lack of ammunition.

"You scored last fall with *Nude Descending into Uranus*, but what's clever the first time is merely lazy and derivative the next."

"Fair point," I conceded.

"I know you well enough to recognize something's wrong."

I decided to drop the wise-ass façade and come clean. "I'm sorry, Professor," I said, "I've had . . . uh . . . some personal problems."

"Can I help?"

I appreciated his concern but declined his offer. "I've been in a major league funk for the last month, but I think I've turned the corner," I assured him.

"I'll give you another chance," he proposed. "Submit to me a proper paper on Picasso's Blue Period by the end of the week. And remember," he said, "Picasso's Blue Period was followed by his Rose Period. Brighter," he said, "and more cheerful. Perhaps you can emulate him."

I was ready to heed my wakeup call. My transformation began at the hardware store where I scored a can of high-gloss, blood red paint. Instead of simply obliterating the blue on my walls, I let my inspiration run amok. Rothko would have been proud.

I discarded the blue bedspread and tore down the blue curtains. I deep-sixed Billie Holiday, Etta James, Muddy Waters and B.B. King. I trashed my recordings of *Blue Suede Shoes, Blue Bayou,* and *Love is Blue*. I saved the worst for last, shattering Bobby Vinton's *Blue on Blue* to smithereens. I kept the beard, my long hair, and the blue jeans.

By the time Tractor returned from football practice, the conversion was complete. He entered the room and smiled.

"Welcome back, bro!"

I spent the rest of the week rectifying my Picasso fiasco. I submitted a thoughtful, well-researched, and meticulously documented thirty-page paper to Professor Wilbur. I'd painted the cover page red. "Rothko Red," I'd scribbled on a note clipped to the cover. "They were out of Picasso Rose."

CHAPTER THIRTY-SEVEN

Cinderella

I debated making the call. I hadn't seen Julianna since June. I'd been too preoccupied with pregnancies, abortions, and Blue Periods to write her the letter I'd promised. Nor had she written me. Was it possible that she'd learned of Annie's pregnancy and abortion from her grandmother? I rather doubted that: Doris had a well-developed sense of discretion. On the other hand, Julianna was her prize, her only grandchild, and what grandmother in her right mind would want her granddaughter dating a guy who'd knocked up his lesbian girlfriend?

Yet what did I have to lose? It took an hour to penetrate the formidable barriers to telephone access at Mt. Holyoke College. Julianna's was the eighth voice I'd encountered. I felt like the prince in *Cinderella*, brandishing a phone instead of a slipper.

"It's great to hear from you," she said with genuine sincerity. An encouraging sign.

"I meant to write. I'm sorry."

"Me too."

"I'd like to make it up to you with a weekend at Roberts. Are you game?"

"It depends, Charlie," she said. "How many women are you currently involved with?"

"I deserved that."

"You haven't answered my question . . ."

"Just one," I said, "Miss Julianna Darlington."

It was the right answer. Julianna accepted my invitation for Roberts' Homecoming Weekend with an enthusiasm that would have been unlikely had she known of my proclivity to impregnate college girls. The call came to an abrupt end when the pay phone devoured the last of my quarters.

It was good to be functional again. Like an alcoholic seeking redemption, I made the rounds of the House, apologizing to my brothers for my month-long bender. I made it a point to spend time with Izzy and thanked him for his efforts in bringing the tyranny of my Blue Period to an end.

As my Rose Period took root, I disciplined myself not to dwell upon Annie. It was easier said than done. While I'd resigned myself to her loss, I was concerned for her well-being. I resisted the urge to call, knowing it would reopen fresh wounds.

My first news of Annie came from a chance encounter with Maria. Strolling across the green with her date on a Saturday afternoon, she broke away briefly to greet me. She'd joined a small theater company in Concord after her graduation, she told me, and was dating a Roberts grad student.

"Are you still in touch with Annie?"

"I see her on occasion," she said, revealing little. "And how are you, Charlie?" I hesitated, unsure of how much Maria knew about the events of last summer. She immediately sensed my unease. "I know about the abortion," she said.

"How is she, Maria?"

"She had a hard time coping for a while . . . she's much better now."

"I'm glad to hear it."

"And how about you?" she repeated.

"I miss her," I said.

"For what it's worth, I don't think she's over you, either." Her boyfriend was growing impatient. "But she still associates you with a troubling chapter in her life."

"I can understand that," I said. "Would you do something for me, Maria? Would you tell her that I asked of her? I'll keep my distance . . . but it doesn't mean I don't care about her."

"Of course. Listen, it was great to see you . . . I've got to catch up with my boyfriend. Take care, Charlie." And she was gone.

CHAPTER THIRTY-EIGHT

Cuter Than a Pot-Bellied Pig

My first Homecoming date looked like LBJ. But not Julianna. Not by a long shot. Nor was she the blond, blue-eyed, wholesome girl-next-door type that Annie had appeared to be. Julianna Darlington was taller and curvier (in all the right places), with a sense of confidence and an aura of sophistication well beyond her years. She was very much a Darlington: a thoroughbred with the charm, brains, beauty, and wit possessed by her grandmother.

When I met Julianna at the bus, she wore an impeccably tailored gray herringbone overcoat with a cream-colored cashmere scarf and a gray knit hat. Bundled against the mid-November chill, she reminded me of Julie Christie in *Dr. Zhivago.* I, on the other hand, appeared in a worn black parka and a fraying ski cap, an outfit more suitable for robbing a gas station than for hosting a Darlington. My hair was shoulder-length (for the first time in my life) and my beard was full.

"That homeless look is quite becoming," she chuckled.

"Wait til you see my cardboard box," I said.

After a deep and mutually encouraging kiss, we walked briskly across campus to the fraternity house.

There was no need to stop at Big Dick's: Julianna would stay in my curtainless, Rothko-esque room at SciFi, either with (as I'd hoped) or without me. If all went as I'd imagined, the only Big Dick she'd encounter this weekend would be mine. After all, it'd been *my* idea to jam on the brakes back in Lenox. I'd restocked the condom drawer—just in case.

I showed Julianna around the house.

"It's a dump," she said, grinning.

"Thanks," I said with mock pride.

As I led her to my room, Tractor came gamboling down the stairs with his girlfriend, Mary.

"Speaking of refuse, I'd like you to meet my gargantuan roommate, Tractor, and his diminutive girlfriend, Mary."

Mary, a student at a nearby nursing school, was a delight. She was a rare combination of sweet and sassy, a perfect match for Tractor. Like Tractor, she grew up on a farm, in Ohio rather than Kansas. "A farm's a farm," Tractor was wont to say. According to Tractor, Mary was "sweeter than sorghum and cuter than a pot-bellied pig." I had no clue what sorghum was but I was certain she trumped the pig. The problem was that Tractor was at least 275 pounds and little four-foot-ten Mary would have been lucky to break a hundred with a sack of sorghum strapped to her back.

In the midst of my recent bender, I'd had the temerity to ask Tractor how he could make love to Mary given their obvious physical disparity. "Anyone driving a Tractor knows how to plow," he said. It was something my father might have said if he hadn't been raised in the Bronx.

According to Tractor, I could get shitfaced anywhere, so I'd surrendered the use of our room to Tractor and Mary for most of the fall. For that, I'd earned a weekend of virtual exclusivity. So while Julianna and I monopolized the room, Tractor would be obliged to plow elsewhere.

Julianna gasped when I unveiled my newly redecorated room.

"Not what I'd expected," she said, sniffing as she took note of my unconventional paint job. "Smells like you painted it yesterday. Were they all out of beige?"

"Not exactly," I said. "Did you notice how I channeled Rothko?"

She surveyed the walls, three of which bore large splotches of blood red splattered against the existing background of midnight blue.

"Looks like a slaughterhouse," she said.

I took her hand and led her across the room. "Let me reveal my genius . . . masterpiece by masterpiece." I began with the large red square over the bed. "This one I call *Untitled (Red Square No. 1)*."

"That's brilliant!"

"Thanks."

"No, I mean that's a brilliant red you plastered on that poor wall," she said, giggling.

Undeterred, I soldiered on, directing her to the nearly identical red splotch on the opposite wall. "This one I've dubbed *Untitled (White Square Blushing)*. Can't you just *feel* the warmth of emotion pulsating from that simmering red?"

"My cheeks are burning," she said.

"See, it's the raw emotion!"

"No, it's hot in here." She took off her overcoat. "Can I open a window?"

"Okay, go ahead . . . ridicule my genius. You'll feel foolish someday when they herald me as the next Andy Warhol."

"Or Charlie Asshole." Clever, I thought.

"And now for the *pièce de résistance*," I said, pointing to the circular red eruption across the room, "the third work in my trilogy."

"*Untitled (Your Anus)*?" she proposed, laughing.

"Actually, I like that. I was going to call it *Untitled (Your Nipple)*," I said. "But I'd need to do some hands-on research before I could etch that title in stone."

"Well, well," Julianna said, smiling broadly. "Not quite the same reticent Charlie I recall in the car outside Gram's house last summer." I inferred from her seductive look that we were about to atone for that fiasco.

She took my hand, led me toward the bed, and sat down. The sparkle in her espresso eyes left little doubt of her intentions. No dummy, I sat dutifully beside her. Slowly, she undid the top two buttons of her white silk blouse, her eyes fixed on mine, testing me, imploring me to redeem myself. And so I did—with the enthusiasm of a prospector who'd uncovered the mother lode. My nipple research revealed breasts like Goldilocks' third bowl of porridge: not too big, not too small, *just right.*

Julianna was no shrinking violet. She lowered her hands, unzipped my jeans, and discovered something else she hadn't expected. "What have we here?" she said, mildly surprised but clearly undaunted by the pronounced bend of my alert penis.

"A double-jointed joint," I said, "courtesy of a nasty encounter with a guy wire at age twelve."

"Poor thing," she muttered in mock sympathy, conducting her own research while I struggled to keep from bursting.

"You're gifted, Charlie, and I'm not talking about the Rothkos," she said after we'd finished our first round of lovemaking. "You should patent that double-jointed joint of yours."

"And have every Tom, Dick, and Harry walking around with

a crooked cock? No way. Wouldn't you rather be the luckiest girl on earth?"

"Don't know . . . that would call for additional research . . ."

We never made it to dinner.

.

CHAPTER THIRTY-NINE

Come Again?

"You know, Charlie... I tell Gram *everything*," Julianna said with a playful grin when we awakened on Saturday morning.

"That's sick," I said, convinced she was kidding. Yet it set me to thinking about how much of what Doris already knew about my summer tribulations should be revealed to Julianna—and when. I decided that now, at least, was not the time.

The conventional plan for a Homecoming Saturday would be to grab some lunch ("strap on the feedbag" in Tractor-speak) and attend the football game. We'd smuggle in some gin and get plastered while watching Roberts get the shit kicked out of it for the twelfth straight time. On defense, we'd cheer for Tractor, who'd take out his considerable frustrations by knocking the crap out of a handful of opponents as well as a teammate or two. Entertaining, perhaps, but no solace for the soul.

I had a better idea. I asked Julianna her views on the Vietnam war. I was pleasantly surprised by the passion of her response. She spoke of her dissatisfaction with the dearth of anti-war activity at her own college. "I think it's presumptuous for women to let the guys bear the brunt of responsibility for protest," she told me, "just because they're the ones putting their lives on the line." She was adamant that women should contribute more to the anti-war effort.

"Well put, J.D.," I said, impressed by her zeal. "Well, it just so happens that there's an anti-war demonstration planned for today outside Memorial Stadium . . . just before the game. Placard-carrying longhairs chanting anti-war slogans. Wanna be my date?"

"Be delighted, C.M.," she said with genuine enthusiasm. "Say, Charlie," she mused, "what's your middle name?" It was my fault for playing the initials game. I'd regret it for the rest of the weekend.

"Uh . . . yours first."

"Doris."

"Go figure."

"Your turn."

"Ulysses."

"No way!" It took a few moments, but she managed to connect the dots as my parents never had. "Wait a second," she said, stifling an embarrassed laugh. "Your initials are C-U-M? *Really*? That's outrageous! How could your parents do that to you?"

"You haven't met my parents."

"That's like pinning a 'Kick Me!' sign to your child's butt!"

Julianna was in hysterics when I described the childhood misadventures I'd experienced with little Susie and Fat Freddie Halloran as a consequence of my unfortunate initials. And for the next half hour, her stock response to whatever I said was "Cum again?" Thanks, Mom and Dad.

I dropped by Rowley Hall before the rally to introduce Julianna to Izzy and Leah. While the girls were getting acquainted, Izzy pulled me aside.

"I was going to ask how you were doing," Izzy said, "but the answer is plain. Beautiful, charming, and only a freshman? Come *on*! You're still my hero, Charlie." Then he jabbed his right index finger into my sternum. "Don't mess it all up by taking her to that rally ... rumor is there'll be a counter-protest," he said. "Could be trouble ..."

Izzy's relative indifference to the anti-war movement was a sore spot with me. "Draft lottery's next month," I reminded him. "Could send us *both* to Vietnam. Don't you think we should be *doing* something ... instead of sitting on our asses?"

"Just be careful—both of you. Please."

The protest was planned to coincide with the massive March on Washington scheduled for that afternoon. So while half a million people marched on the capital, at least two hundred students, instructors, townsfolk, and friends congregated in front of Memorial Stadium an hour before game time carrying placards (*Out of Viet Nam Now!*, *Save Our Sons*, *Nixon Sucks*), chanting slogans (*Hell no, we won't go!*) and singing John Lennon's melodic plea for peace (*All we are saying ... is give peace a chance*). The protest was calm and congenial, though campus police and a handful of town cops milled around just in case.

Julianna reveled in the mission, chanting and singing. She was clearly enjoying herself. I stayed close, hoping I hadn't made a mistake in persuading her to join me.

The rally garnered enthusiastic support from students and others filing into Memorial Stadium for the game. But later, after the crowd had thinned and the game had begun, a groundswell of opposition arose from a group of out-of-town rednecks and self-styled "patriots" with a less liberal bent.

"Go home you frickin' longhairs!" bellowed a horde of

hardhats bearing placards with the combative *America: Love It or Leave It* slogan. The counter-demonstration was clearly more than spontaneous, just as Izzy had warned.

In the blink of an eye, all hell broke loose. A hardhat launched a bottle, scoring a direct hit on a fellow protester. Projectiles rained down on us with abandon. Cries of alarm arose as a handful of protesters retaliated. Within moments, the affair escalated dramatically. Anti-protesters brandished their placards like machetes, striking at random targets and provoking howls of anguish. Julianna shrieked as a brick skidded across the ground in front of us.

"Let's get out of here, now!" I shouted to Julianna.

"No way!" she screamed, her ire up. "These shitheads aren't getting away with this! No . . . damn . . . way!"

I grabbed her arm, yanking her toward me. "Out of here, Julianna, *this fucking minute!*"

I hadn't gotten the words out of my mouth when some scumbag flung his protest sign in our direction. The heavy two-by-four that supported it grazed my arm before striking Julianna squarely in the chin. She went down in a heap. I reached for her in a panic as town and campus policemen burst into the crowd, snatching protesters and hardhats indiscriminately in a belated effort to quell the disturbance. I clutched Julianna's arm, dragging her away like a recalcitrant child. She was whimpering, more from shock than pain. We tore ourselves from the pack and ran as sirens wailed and ambulances rushed to the scene.

When we'd moved safely beyond the fray, I stopped, grasping her wrists, my eyes brimming with alarm. "Are you okay?" I was frantic. A trickle of blood flowed from her chin.

"I'd like to beat the *SHIT* out of that bastard!" she cried. Her spunk was intoxicating.

"Down, girl," I commanded. "Heel!" As soon as she'd caught her breath, she broke out laughing. Her mirth was infectious. I gathered her into my arms and squeezed. She was a pistol, just like her grandmother.

Fortunately, Julianna's injury was minor. Though a small cut and a nasty bruise marred her chin, she wore them like a badge of honor. She was positively beaming. While Julianna deserved a purple heart for her bravery and determination, the entire episode scared me shitless. Seeing her on the ground, bleeding, had turned my stomach.

"Okay," she said after I'd helped her clean and patch the wound back at the House, "when's our next skirmish?"

I smiled despite myself. I then felt an unmistakable stirring in my loins. Julianna, missing nothing, grabbed my hand and yanked me up the stairs to our room. "Cum again?" she said lustfully.

CHAPTER FORTY

The Tyranny of the Little Blue Capsules

"September fourteenth," announced a disembodied voice. "September fourteen," droned its counterpart, "oh-oh-one."

"April twenty-fourth." The first voice again.

"April twenty-four," came the monotone rejoinder, followed by "oh-oh-two."

So began a grimly memorable and transformative night for millions of American males as they watched or listened to the infamous draft lottery broadcast live on national television and radio on December 1, 1969.

Izzy had invited me to join him and several of my old dorm mates at Rowley Hall for a lottery "party." "Wake" would have been a more apt description. Seven of us huddled around Izzy's radio, listening to the impassive voices of robotic Selective Service officials as they extracted large blue capsules serially from a glass jar. Like fortune cookies at a Chinese restaurant, each capsule contained a slip of paper bearing a date. The date was announced grimly to an audience of hyperventilating, draft-eligible young men and posted like race results on a board bearing numbers from 1 to 366. The lower the number, the more likely you were to be inducted, shipped to Vietnam, and either killed, maimed, or reduced to a turnip. According to the announcer, those with birth dates corresponding to any of the first 120 numbers were likely to be drafted; those in the next 120 had an even chance of induction; and those above 240 were home-free. It was like a bad television game show, with millions of lives hanging in the balance.

The "party" premise was simple. Once the birth date of one of the attendees was selected, the poor bastard would guzzle a shot of whiskey, symbolic, perhaps, of the shots he'd have to dodge in Southeast Asian jungles after graduation stripped him of his educational deferment. The lottery's winners were losers and its losers were winners. When the birth date of the next lottery casualty was chosen, he and the previous victim would each down a shot, and so on until the last man's birth date was selected. By then, the first sucker would be the most thoroughly plastered, a condition befitting his fate. The winners were those who remained after the 240th date had been chosen.

The radio coverage began at eight o'clock that evening. Within minutes, we heard shrieks of anguish accompanied by the sound of beer bottles exploding against the brick wall of the floor above us, a sign that the lottery had claimed its first Rowley Hall casualty. As the night progressed, blood-curdling screams and cries of rage descended in waves across campus.

All seven of us escaped selection through the first seventy-eight dates, a considerable statistical accomplishment. But then, fittingly, the grim reaper revealed Halloween, October 31st, as the seventy-ninth date selected.

"Fuck! Fuck! Fuck! Fuck! Fuck! Fuck! Fuck! Fuck! Fuck!" screamed a junior from down the hall. The next date picked, November 9th, snared our next victim.

"Shit! Shit! Shit! Shit! Fuck! Fuck! Fuck! Fucking shit!" was the poor bastard's only marginally more creative response.

Five of us remained alive, as it were, through the first hundred selections. Then the Selective Service sycophant yanked the 101st capsule from the fucking jar:

"January fifth," he said.

"January five," repeated his mimic, "one-oh-one."

"Shit! Fuck! Shit! Fuck! Goddamn it! Fucking crap! Ball-busting motherfucker!" I howled. My proverbial number had come up. I was doomed. "Goddamn fucking shit!" I added for good measure as I downed a shot along with the two earlier victims and slumped into a corner to drink myself senseless.

Izzy went next at 175, leaving him in limbo. The recipients of the two highest numbers, winners of "get-out-of-jail-free" cards in this gruesome equivalent of Russian roulette, had already committed to the armed services as participants in the U. S. Army Reserve Officers' Training Corps (ROTC, for short), a training program for commissioned officers conducted on campus by the U.S. Army. What kind of bullshit was that?

I staggered back to SciFi where more carnage was evident. The Tube Room was in shambles. Shards of glass radiated from a gaping hole in the television screen. Tractor, whose birthday was in five days, had drawn number 10. As gentle a man as he was under ordinary circumstances, he was capable of near-homicidal violence on the gridiron or, when some Selective Service functionary sentenced him to a tour in Vietnam, in the Tube Room.

"He just snapped," Benny told me. "When they picked his date, he shot up like a howitzer. Hurled a bottle right through the screen. We had all we could do to contain him."

"Where is he now?"

"Probably in your room," Benny said, "but I'm not sure it's safe to go up there."

Drunk enough to ignore his advice, I careened upstairs and cautiously opened the door. Tractor sat on the bed, scowling.

"Hey, man," I said. "Heard you kinda lost it tonight."

"Yeah," he acknowledged, his rage largely dissipated. "I'll be paying for that damn television for the rest of the year."

"They screwed me, too," I told him. "Number 101. Heard you were 10. Guess you'll get there first and I'll meet you there later."

"I'll save you a place in my pup tent," he said.

CHAPTER FORTY-ONE

Things Are Not Always As They Seem

"**Y**ou look like a hairball some cat coughed up!" This was how my father greeted me as I stepped inside the front door of the Meyer homestead for the Christmas holidays.

"Nice to see you too, Dad."

"Why do all you kids have to look like Jesus Christ?"

"It's the dawn of the Seventies, Dad. It's how college kids look these days."

"How was your trip, dear?" Mom interjected, trying her best to deflect the conversation.

"I despise buses," I sneered.

The welcome-home exchange was just a warm-up. The fireworks came at dinner when Dad suggested I join the ROTC. Dad and I, digging in at opposite ends of the table, volleyed barbs back and forth like tennis players in a Wimbleton death match, the dinner table our virtual tennis court. Mom and Hermie sat at either side of center court, my brother's head swiveling like a windshield wiper as he gleefully followed the action while Mom cowered as the intensity steadily escalated.

"No, Dad. Not interested," I said, serving cleanly.

"You'll cut off your face in spite of your nose," he said, returning my serve with a malapropistic forehand. "You're a smart kid . . . you should go in as an officer."

"I don't plan on going in at all," I swatted back.

"You're such a fucking stupid kid!" A nasty backhand. "You've got a duty to serve your country, goddammit, that's just how it is!"

I attacked him with an overhand smash. "My duty, Dad, is to *oppose* this stupid war!"

"By joining those little pissant, communist, hippie weirdo fags burning their fucking draft cards?" A desperation shot, barely clearing the net.

"Yes, Dad," I said, trying to put him away with a vicious crosscourt missile, "that's exactly what I'm planning to do: demonstrate against the goddamn war. It's immoral. It needs to stop. Young men are dying needlessly."

"NEEDLESSLY?" he lunged, grunting, showering shards of Potato Buds onto the court from the corners of his mouth. "Do you think young men died needlessly defending your goddamn freedom against those fucking Japs and Jerries? You sissies don't know what it means to fight for fucking democracy. Where do you think you'd be now if we hadn't stood up to those slants and Nazis?"

"You never even left the country during the war, Dad," I reminded him, maintaining the pressure with a high, arcing lob.

"That's besides the point!" he blathered, barely able to retrieve my shot. "If we let the Reds take Vietnam, the dominoes fall one by one until Ho Chow Mein is running the United States of Fucking America!"

"That's Ho Chi Minh, Dad . . . and I doubt he'd be much worse than fucking Richard Nixon." A winner! Point, game, and match, Charlie Meyer.

"You ungrateful little bastard! Don't you dare disgrace your family by marching with those faggots!" His fury illuminated his face like a red neon light as he slammed the fist bearing his metaphoric racquet onto the table in disgust.

With that, I'd had all I could take. I arose from the table and stomped off to what used to be my room, forgetting momentarily that Dad had converted it into his man cave during my freshman year. "What's the damn point?" I mumbled to myself as I retraced my steps, slinking down to the basement I'd been condemned to inhabit since my bedroom hijacking. I slammed the door violently behind me, nearly tearing it from its hinges with the force of my anger.

I called Julianna in Scarsdale the next morning.

"Things suck here," I told her, recounting the donnybrook with my father over the war. "I can't even *breathe* in this house! I know you probably just got home and all . . ." I felt my frustration building as my voice trailed off. "But would you mind a little company, just so I can clear my head?"

Julianna was happy to accommodate me. I jotted down the directions and bolted from the house like The Road Runner eluding Wile E. Coyote.

It'd been over a month since Julianna and I had spent that magical and eventful weekend at Roberts. I relished the sight of her. Her parents, Beverly and Donald Jr., were gracious and welcoming, claiming they'd heard much about me from both Julianna and Doris. I was instantly envious of the seemingly normal family life that Julianna enjoyed, if you could consider life in a sixteen-room Scarsdale mansion truly normal. I felt guilty about my enmity toward my father and the helplessness of my mother, but saw little prospect for an end to the incessant battles that had become increasingly commonplace during my visits home.

"I envy you," I told Julianna. "It seems so peaceful here."

"Things are not always as they seem," she said cryptically.

I savored the Darlingtons' hospitality, but with Christmas just two days off, I felt compelled to leave them to their preparations. Julianna's willingness to listen sympathetically as I vented was comforting. By the time I said my goodbyes, my anger had nearly abated. I steeled myself for my return to the front lines.

Before departing, Julianna and I made arrangements to celebrate New Year's Eve together in Scarsdale, where I'd attend the Darlingtons' annual New Year's Eve party and spend the night. She promised an unforgettable affair.

An undeclared truce settled over the Meyer household the following week. Dad barely spoke to me while I responded in kind. Mom did the talking for all three of us, ruminating ceaselessly on scores of mundane topics, eliciting occasional grunts of recognition from Dad or me. It wasn't ideal, but it was peaceful.

Julianna's house was a beehive of activity when I arrived mid-afternoon on New Year's Eve. What I envisaged as a modest neighborhood gathering would be anything but. Three catering trucks, a florist, and a liquor store van crowded the driveway. A uniformed maid opened the door and escorted me to the den where I found Julianna perched on a plush leather recliner absorbed in Mario Puzo's *The Godfather.* Mrs. Darlington waved from the living room as she barked orders to the catering crew.

Julianna looked up at me and smiled. "You look a bit bewildered," she said. I bent down and kissed her on the cheek.

"I was expecting an intimate neighborhood party . . . not a Times Square extravaganza."

"This is Scarsdale. Nothing here is intimate... Brace yourself."

Though the party was slated for seven, the first guests were almost an hour late, embarrassed by their relative promptness. Within the next hour, the crowd swelled to more than sixty.

I was hopelessly out of my element. The rarefied atmosphere of Scarsdale was alien to me. I'd worn a jacket and tie, but they were no match for the impeccably tailored Italian-cut suits, Brooks Brothers ties, and custom-made shoes that were *de rigueur* for the bond traders, industrialists, and ad men on the Darlingtons' guest list. Even the caterers outclassed me.

The ladies split into two distinct groups. The first were the Trophy Wives, statuesque former models or secretaries under thirty-five years of age, most of them blond, representing second or subsequent marriages for older, financially successful husbands who were already on the prowl for their wives' successors. The Trophy Wives came attired in tight-fitting gowns suitable for the red carpet at the Oscars, calculated to flaunt the physical attributes that won them spousal status and would eventually earn them a comfortable alimony. The second group, the First Wives Club, were the clever survivors, older, smarter, and more resourceful than their perky-breasted counterparts, resigned to their partners' occasional dalliances, secure in their grasp on the family purse-strings (and their husbands' scrotums), and destined to become well-heeled dowagers in widowhood. The First Wives were adorned in over-the-top custom ensembles designed to camouflage their bulbous hips and sagging breasts.

In contrast to my tawdriness, Julianna looked stunning in a slinky, shimmering black gown that hugged her hips and breasts like I had at Homecoming. She outshone even the most voluptuous of the Trophy Wives.

Unlike me, Julianna's parents reveled in their accustomed milieu. Armed with cocktails, they worked the crowd from opposite ends of the room, sidling up to guests and leading with a pertinent quip or an off-color joke before moving on to the next assemblage.

Mr. Darlington basked in the aura that emanated from his beautiful daughter, missing no opportunity to flaunt this year's curvier, more mature version of J.D. to his horny male friends and business acquaintances. Julianna was a stand-in for the trophy wife he didn't have. Mrs. Darlington, though endowed with many of the same physical attributes that distinguished her daughter, had added a few inches here and a few pounds there over the years. She compensated, or so it seemed, with aggressive conversation and plenty to drink.

Sensing my discomfort amidst the aristocracy of Scarsdale, Julianna wriggled free from her father's clutches to keep me company for a while.

"I'm sorry, Charlie, you really couldn't have known what you were getting into."

"Not the Budweiser crowd from New Liberty," I said. "This is a major league spectacle."

"The real spectacle is yet to come," she said prophetically. "Remember, I warned you to brace your—." Before she could finish her sentence, one of her father's friends swooped in, snared Julianna by the arm, and dragged her off in a brazen attempt to foist her on his pimpled, overweight son. "Sorry," she mouthed, pursing her thumb and forefinger in a sign that she wouldn't be long.

Mildly dismayed, I strolled to the bar where a bow-tied bartender presided over a selection of top-shelf spirits, none of which bore the Budweiser logo. *When in Scarsdale, do as the Scarsdaleans do.* So I ordered a single-malt scotch. A short, paunchy, middle-aged man sidled up to me as I sampled a tumbler of sixteen-year-old Lagavulin. I nearly gagged—it tasted like sixteen-year-old turpentine.

"You've got great taste in Scotch . . . young man," he said, overtly restraining an oncoming belch.

"Indeed," I said with pretensions of sophistication before mangling the brand name. "There's nothing like Lagavulman," I warbled.

"Jack Carruthers," he said, introducing himself and offering me his puffy right hand. I shook it unenthusiastically. I could tell he was already sloshed.

"Our host . . . tells me . . . you're his daughter's . . . boyfriend." He punctuated his sentence with hiccups, ending it with a definitive belch.

"Guilty," I said.

"Well you're one . . . lucky . . . sonofabitch!" He chuckled lecherously.

"I am," I confessed.

"Some piece o' ass . . . that Julianna," he said. "Sure as hell wouldn't mind . . . getting my d—" I didn't allow him to finish his salacious sentence. Instead, I lifted my scotch and deposited its sixteen-year-old contents down his hairy chest before walking away. For better or worse, no one seemed to notice, and Carruthers was too shocked or plastered to object or retaliate.

Mrs. Darlington intercepted me as I retreated across the room. She offered me up like an appetizer to a pair of wrinkled matrons, charter members of the First Wives Club.

"This is Charlie Meyers," she said, pluralizing my name more out of inebriation than ignorance. "He's a friend of my daughter's," she said, discreetly minimizing our relationship. I shook each of their meaty hands as they identified themselves, serially, like game show contestants. Spying someone more important, Mrs. Darlington flitted away, leaving me in the clutches of the Witches of Scarsdale.

As the insipid conversation grew tiresome, Mr. Darlington made a welcome appearance, rescuing me from the coven.

"Charlie," he said to me.

"Mr. Darlington," I responded.

"Charlie," he repeated in monotone.

"Mr. Darlington," I countered.

"Come with me for a minute," he said, snatching me by the arm. "I want to talk to you." He led me through the crowd to the library, free of all but a handful of guests.

"I just want to say one word to you," Mr. Darlington said. I had a sudden sense of *déjà vu.* "Just one word," he repeated.

"Yes sir."

I didn't realize something was afoot until I noticed, from the corner of my eye, that several more guests had filtered into the library, staring at us. Julianna was among them.

"Are you listening?" he asked me, sensing my distraction.

"Yes I am," I said.

"*Plastics!*" he said, raising his voice so that his rapt audience could hear his line.

"Uh . . ." I mumbled haltingly, dead certain now that I had been played. When I smiled at him, he briefly lost his composure, momentarily flashing a sly grin but then quickly reverting to character.

"There's a great future in plastics," he said, poker-faced. "Think about it."

"Yes I will," I replied on cue.

"Shh . . ." Mr. Darlington whispered, lifting two fingers to his mouth. "Nuff said. That's a deal."

With that he collapsed into convulsive laughter, joined by at least a dozen spectators. Julianna was in stitches. Her father, a movie buff and practical joker, had just completed a flawless reenactment of the famous 1967 "plastics" scene from *The Graduate* between Walter Brooke (as Mr. McGuire) and Dustin Hoffman (as Benjamin Braddock, the young college grad who is seduced by Mrs. Robinson, but falls instead for her beautiful daughter), with me cast involuntarily in the role of poor Ben.

"Okay," I conceded to Mr. Darlington, "you had me 'til 'plastics'."

Mr. Darlington's admirers, obviously in on the joke, congratulated him as he exhibited a triumphant smile. Julianna, still laughing her gorgeous butt off, put her arms around me as if I'd been a willing participant rather than the butt of a practical joke.

"I told you to brace yourself," she reminded me, still grinning. I worried aloud that her mother would pick up where her father left off, luring me to her bedroom and seducing me like Mrs. Robinson. "If she does," Julianna said, laughing, "abandon the script this time!"

I told Julianna of my encounter with Jack Carruthers. "He's a lush and a pervert, but essentially harmless," she said, shaking her head. "He's had the hots for me since I was thirteen."

By the time 11:30 rolled around, we both craved a break from the drinking and boisterous revelry. In search of privacy, Julianna led me through a series of corridors to a doorway that opened on a luxurious indoor pool.

"What the . . ." I gasped. "Are you kidding me?"

"Yeah, yeah, I'm the little rich girl with toys galore. It's embarrassing," she conceded, "but also pretty awesome." She tilted her head toward the far wall. "Come on, there's a changing room in back."

As we approached the changing room, we heard muffled voices—and suspicious moans. Like a doomed protagonist in a grade B horror movie, Julianna reached for the door. I tried to stop her, recalling the agony I'd heaped upon my own head when I turned the doorknob into Annie's room that fateful Sunday morning at Big Dick's. But I was too late. Behind the open door was Mr. Darlington, his pants pooled around his ankles, his dick dripping over the splayed, partially clothed, and gently heaving body of one of the Trophy Wives.

Julianna turned blood red, the color of my pseudo-Rothkos, and slammed the door shut. It was as if she'd been smashed in the chin by another two-by-four. Before I could lift my own chin from my shoe tops, she'd bolted past the pool and up the stairs. I ran after her, chasing her through the maze of corridors, up a back stairway and into her room where she burst into tears.

At first, she was inconsolable. Her face registered the disappointment of a child disabused all at once of the legends of Santa Claus and the Tooth Fairy. It's how I must have looked when I discovered Maria devouring Annie's crotch.

I offered to hug her, uncertain whether she'd rather share her horror or wallow in it without my interference. She elected to wallow.

From downstairs we heard the countdown, in unison: "Eight, seven, six, five, four, three, two, one . . . HAPPY NEW YEAR!!!"

It was a bizarre way to end one decade and begin another. As Julianna had observed a week earlier, things are not always as they seem.

CHAPTER FORTY-TWO

The Condom Conundrum

It would be a gross understatement to describe the next morning as strained. Mrs. Darlington, hung over and barely functional, said little while Julianna and I assembled a makeshift breakfast in the kitchen. Mr. Darlington was dazed and bedraggled. An eerie silence was pierced only briefly by my limp morning greetings to Julianna's parents and their tepid rejoinders.

I was certain that Mrs. Darlington remained ignorant of her husband's infidelity. Her stupor seemed alcohol-induced. Though I knew her but slightly, I couldn't imagine her this tranquil had she known of her husband's decade-capping Trophy Wife-drilling.

As for Mr. Darlington, the less said the better. Blithely acting as if nothing had happened would have been a tasteless and provocative affront to his daughter, while dropping to his knees to beg forgiveness was not in his DNA. He'd treat it like any other business predicament, taking time to devise a multi-pronged strategy to deal with his dumbfounded daughter, her bewildered boyfriend, and his oblivious wife.

Julianna had virtually sobbed herself to sleep the previous night. She'd resisted my efforts to comfort her. She had little more to say in the morning. She sighed, shuffled into the bathroom, and robotically showered and dressed while I did the same. I was reduced to a detached observer, filled with that painfully helpless feeling I'd experienced on the day of Annie's abortion. When I finally addressed her, Julianna muttered something about "needing some time," another gruesome reminder of that last day with Annie.

After an intensely self-conscious breakfast, I bade my hosts goodbye, thanking them for their hospitality. In return, I received a listless hug from Julianna, a genial but pained "goodbye, so glad you were able to join us and hope we see you again soon" from her hung-over mother, and a peremptory farewell from her guilt-ridden dad.

Julianna called early the next morning.

"I'm so sorry for the way I acted yesterday," she said. "You didn't deserve that."

"No need to apologize."

"This time, it's me who needs to escape," she said. "I know it's presumptuous, but could you tolerate a visit from a messed-up girlfriend?"

"Which one?"

"The one who didn't so much as give you a New Year's kiss the other night."

"That still doesn't narrow it down."

"The one most likely to make up for it today."

"Oh... *that* one." While I longed to see her again, I wondered how savvy and sophisticated Julianna would react to the circus she'd encounter at the Meyer homestead. "Sure, come on down," I said recklessly. "Why don't you stay for dinner? You can leave in the morning." It was an impulsive response without forethought—something my father would have done. The Meyer dinner table was a combat zone. I'd also no inkling of how my antediluvian parents would approach the sleeping arrangements.

"I look forward to meeting your parents."

"Bring a flak jacket."

My mother was thrilled and intrigued by the prospect of hosting a visit from Julianna. It was an unprecedented event. Never before had I invited a girl into my fucked-up home. And for good reason. I knew I could count on Mom, but Dad was the ultimate loose cannon.

I warned Hermie of my girlfriend's impending arrival. He broke into raucous laughter. "You're screwed," he said.

Mom was already frantically at work on dinner when Julianna arrived at eleven. An array of cold cuts, breads, condiments, and pickles suitable for a dozen clogged the kitchen table.

"So glad to meet you, Mrs. Meyer," Julianna said when she entered the kitchen.

"Oh, my, such a beautiful girl!" Mom was right: Julianna looked terrific in her tight blue jeans and white cashmere sweater.

Intense curiosity lured Hermie from his lair to check out his brother's girlfriend. After a brief introduction, he slapped some roast beef between two slices of bread, slathered on a dollop of mustard, and returned to his room. On the way, he slammed his fist into my upper arm. "She's a fucking ten!" he muttered under his breath.

Julianna was masterful at small talk, showing interest in virtually every aspect of my mother and her kitchen. Mom and I were equally infatuated.

"Sit down, Julianna, have some lunch!" Though Dad was the nominal Jew in the house, Mom was the Jewish mother.

"Mom! It's barely eleven o'clock."

"Julianna's had a long drive," Mom said. "I'm sure she's starving!"

Julianna looked to me and smiled. "Don't mind if I do, Mrs. Meyer."

When I finally managed to extract Julianna from my mother's orbit, we usurped Dad's den (my former bedroom) to talk. A risky intrusion, but safe until Dad returned from work.

"Have you spoken with your father?" I asked her.

"Yes. He dropped into my room last night while Mom was out shopping."

"And?"

"Very awkward at first. He apologized, said it was a terrible, stupid mistake."

"And?"

"And asked me if I could ever forgive him."

"And?"

"I said it would take time."

"What about your Mom?"

"He said he'd tell her if I insisted, but thought it'd be devastating to her. Said he'd thought long and hard about it—"

"Poor choice of words," I said. Julianna chose to ignore my ill-advised quip.

"...and telling her would make things worse," she continued.

"What did you say to that?"

"I told him it was his decision ... that my choice was to say nothing to her, as it wasn't my place to do so. I told him that I wouldn't be his ally in any cover-up ... and if I changed my mind later and told her, he'd have no right to feel betrayed."

"Very good answer," I said. "Are you satisfied?"

"Hard to say. It gives him the opportunity to continue his

infidelity, I suppose, though he swears he's never done it before and won't do it again. Not sure if I believe him . . . but, like I said, that's his business."

"You're being incredibly grown-up about this. Don't know if I could be as rational under comparable circumstances." Of course, I could hardly imagine comparable circumstances.

"I had my bout with irrationality. You witnessed it. I was crushed. He's my Dad . . . I've always looked up to him. It's hard to accept that your father's an ordinary mortal with lustful desires." *Or a dripping dick.*

"So, you're okay?"

"Maybe a little older and wiser, but yes, I'm okay."

"I have lustful desires, too," I reminded her.

"We'll see what we can do about those later," she said with that disarmingly seductive look she'd perfected. "By the way, are you sure it's okay that I stay over tonight?"

"No problem," I fervently hoped.

Mom had apparently warned Dad of our dinner guest and that he'd need to be on his best behavior, a frightfully low standard where my father was concerned. I was apprehensive when I heard the front door open. He stepped inside, humming the National Anthem. When he entered the kitchen and spied Julianna, Dad did a double take. Like a Looney Tunes character, his eyes nearly popped from their sockets.

"Well, well, who have we here?" he bellowed in a very un-Dad-like fashion.

"This is Julianna, Dad."

"Pleased to meet you, Mr. Meyer," Julianna said, employing her most engaging smile and offering her hand to my father. He responded with the dumbass grin of a jack-o-lantern.

"You're as delightful as a tax refund!" Dad said, utilizing

droll accountants' humor to minimal effect.

"Dinner's nearly ready, Richard. Hang up your hat and coat and join us at the table." The show was about to begin.

Mom had gone all out for dinner. Instead of the usual bricks of meatloaf and Brussels sprouts boiled to the brink of annihilation, it was the second coming of Thanksgiving with breast of turkey, cranberry stuffing, green beans, and a mountain of Potato Buds swimming in a can of pasty Franco-American turkey gravy.

While Julianna chowed down in a manner befitting a woman intent on pleasing her boyfriend's mom, Dad was foraging for something stupid to say. He shocked even me.

"Are you two fucking?"

"Richard!" screamed my mortified Mom. Julianna spit out a wad of turkey while I nearly gagged on a mouthful of Potato Buds. Hermie just sat there enjoying the show.

Dad pressed on. "Because if you are, you should be using protection. Are you using protection?"

Julianna didn't know whether to laugh or cry. Mom cried.

"*If* we were sleeping together, Dad," I said after finally managing to swallow my Potato Buds, "we would most certainly use protection."

"What are you crying about, Lydia?" Dad asked my mother in exasperation, as if his outburst was no more controversial than discussing the weather. "The boy needs to understand the importance of being properly prepared for compilation."

"Copula . . ." I began to correct him, but abandoned the effort in frustration. Hermie was laughing hard enough to propel food from his nostrils.

"So, Mr. Meyer, Charlie tells me you're an accountant," Julianna said, deftly changing the subject.

Dad nodded. "Got a little practice right here in town," he boasted.

"Fascinating profession," she lied.

Encouraged by Julianna's feigned interest, Dad proceeded to discuss his latest audit, a profit statement he compiled, and a tax return quandary that few accountants would find interesting. At least he was no longer probing our sexual habits.

The balance of the meal was understandably anticlimactic.

After the carnage had ended, Julianna and I helped Mom pack up the leftovers. Exhausting her supply of plastic bags, she asked Hermie to retrieve a box from the pantry.

"Why not use some condoms instead?" Hermie quipped. Suddenly, Mom burst into an unprecedented fit of hysterical laughter, cracking everyone up.

Later, when we were alone in the living room, I apologized to Julianna for my father's impropriety.

"Well it certainly took me by surprise," Julianna admitted, "but by now it seems downright hilarious."

"Dad says what's on his mind. No filtering . . . no editing. Just blurts it the heck out."

"It's not an inherited trait, is it?"

"I surely hope not."

"So we're about even," Julianna said. "We've both exposed our dysfunctional home lives."

"Your Dad's exposure was a tad more literal, don't you think?" A nod and a smirk signified her agreement.

After she finished in the kitchen, Mom advised that she'd make up Dad's den for Julianna. Not wishing to revisit the are-they-or-aren't-they-fucking conundrum, I offered no objection.

"I'll meet you in there after they're all in bed," I told Julianna later.

"Sounds good. And don't forget to bring the condoms," she said. "It's the least we can do for your Dad, don't you think?"

CHAPTER FORTY-THREE

Sleeping for Money

To put it simply and with a maximum of alliteration, I needed to make a dent in my debt to Doris Darlington. She'd paid for Annie's abortion and had thus far rebuffed my efforts to begin to repay her. I was determined to meet my obligation, if only to assuage my conscience, but to do so required cash. A part-time job was one option. But a classified ad offered an alternative more suited to my slacker sensibility:

SUBJECTS AGED 18-50 SOUGHT FOR SLEEP STUDY
14 Consecutive Nights @ $50/nt.
Contact Dr. Steiger at Central New Hampshire Medical Center

I could sleep my way to riches! I decided to investigate.

The mousy, bespectacled receptionist at Dr. Steiger's office handed me a pen and a four-page questionnaire. The questions ("Have you ever been committed to a psychiatric facility?") were designed to weed out the nutjobs and psychopaths. Beyond that, if you knew your name and phone number, you were eminently qualified.

Although it was a dubious honor, I was accepted for the study and instructed to report for an orientation at the hospital's sleep lab. Six of us would participate in the first study group. I was the youngest and least deranged. The group included a pair of stoners in their late twenties, one a skinhead, the other sporting a two-foot pony tail; a massive young lady who smelled like the livestock she raised on a nearby commune; a divorced, middle-aged waitress with insomnia; and an unshaven, forty-something alcoholic who just needed a place to sleep.

Dr. Steiger was a cross between Einstein and Bigfoot. His unruly mantle of cottony white hair gave the impression he'd just stuck his finger into an electrical socket. The purpose of the study, he explained to his motley subjects in his thick German accent, was to examine the effects of varying sleep durations upon performance and alertness. For the first week of the study, subjects would sleep for as long as they were accustomed; in the second week, they'd be awakened two hours sooner. Oral, written, and physical tests would be administered to measure differentials in performance and alertness. Inquiries would be made about dreams to determine both dream activity and retention under varying circumstances. Sounded like a blast. When Dr. Steiger invited questions, he received only one: "When do we get paid?"

The sleep lab consisted of a central room and six satellite chambers where subjects were connected to electrodes and encouraged to sleep normally. For me, at least, sleeping while strung up like a Christmas tree was hardly normal.

The study began on a Tuesday evening. Two lab technicians were present, each assigned to prep, monitor, and test three subjects for the duration of the study. I, along with Livestock Girl and Alcohol Breath, was assigned to Clare Kelly, a pretty, twenty-four-year-old Irish-American from Boston with a charmingly freckled face, a degree in psychology, and six months' tenure at the lab.

A retractable curtain preserved my privacy as I changed into my preferred nightwear, a pair of boxer shorts freshly laundered for the occasion.

"We don't often get college kids in our studies," Clare said as she transformed my head into a minefield of electrodes affixed with generous dollops of gel and tape. "And you smell a good deal fresher than your cohorts," she added with a grin, having just completed the same tedious preparation with Livestock Girl and Alcohol Breath.

"That's not saying much," I said, greedily inhaling her own sweet fragrance. Clare was about five-foot-three, with small, pert breasts; emerald green eyes; and a thick, well-tamed mane of auburn hair. A wedding band graced the fourth finger of her left hand.

"What made you decide to join the study?" she asked me.

I owe a bundle to a kindly old lady who arranged for my girlfriend's abortion. "I'd like to say it was scientific curiosity, but it's really the money," I told her. Like Doris on my first day in Lenox, Clare educed from me the Reader's Digest version of my life story, edited for general consumption. She was bright and charming. Although lacking the drop-dead glamour of Annie or Julianna, she had a subtle allure that gripped me like an infectious melody. The wedding ring, however, tempered my enthusiasm.

By the time Clare had finished working her electronic magic, I looked like Frankenstein in a bathing cap. It took a while, but I finally fell asleep.

Clare administered a battery of tests the next morning. The results established a baseline against which to compare the second week's data. Overall, it was a surprisingly comfortable night's sleep and an easy fifty bucks.

In the morning following my second night in the lab, I

invited Clare to join me for breakfast in the hospital cafeteria. We'd developed a rapport, and since we were both famished (and she was obviously married), neither of us read any ulterior motive into the off-handed invitation.

Over scrambled eggs and toast, I told Clare about my summer at the Clark Institute and the Darlington estate. I mentioned Julianna on several occasions, even rousing Clare's hearty laughter when I described my father's impertinent inquiry at the dinner table several weeks back. But when I tried to steer the conversation back to her, Clare declared breakfast at an end and headed home. The parallels with Catherine were uncanny.

Just as I had with Catherine, I became obsessed with Clare's reticence, advancing and debunking a host of hypotheses. An abusive relationship? Unlikely, as there wasn't a mark anywhere on her creamy white, thickly freckled skin. Was she a Russian spy, with dyed hair and fraudulent freckles, funneling seditious subliminal messages into my brain through those pesky electrodes? Too stupid to even consider. But my curiosity was piqued.

Clare passed on breakfast the next morning and was off for the weekend. Her replacement was a dour, middle-aged nurse with a considerable gut and an inconsiderable sense of humor. I had nightmares both nights.

I was relieved and delighted when Clare returned for her Monday night shift. When our wide-ranging discussions threatened to deprive me of sleep, she agreed to continue our conversation over breakfast. This would be my chance.

"Clare," I said, treading gently as I pondered a pile of pecan pancakes, "you've scrupulously omitted any mention of your husband. Is there a reason?"

Caught off guard, she hesitated, as if weighing her alternatives. Plates clattered and silverware clinked at nearby tables.

"Okay," she said finally. "I see that I can't evade your curiosity much longer." She put down her fork, took a long sip from her coffee mug, and came clean. She told me about Dennis, how they'd graduated together from Boston University and married soon after. How he'd parlayed an ROTC scholarship into a commission as a Navy lieutenant. "He deployed to Vietnam twenty months ago," she explained. "Four months later, he was reported missing in action over North Vietnam. He was flying a nighttime reconnaissance mission and never returned." Her words were precise, her voice impassive.

I grasped her hand involuntarily. She retained her composure. "I was three months pregnant when he left," Clare said, taking another measured sip from her mug. "Hope's now fourteen months old," she added with a broadening smile, "and the light of my life."

What could I say? Condolences were inappropriate; so was pity. Wishing, perhaps, to stifle any reaction, she resumed her account.

"I was living in Boston when Dennis went missing and when Hope was born. Hope's been my refuge . . . I'd have fallen apart without her. I needed her as much as she needed me."

I wondered how she'd coped.

"My mother was an angel . . . friends and other family were supportive too. But after a while," she said, "I began to recoil from the pity I saw in their eyes. I was that poor young mother whose husband is M.I.A. It defined me."

"So you left and came here?"

"I had to escape. I wanted to start over. Someplace where I didn't have to wear that damn cloak of pity."

While her story was heartrending, I admired her strength. "How do you work night shifts and still care for Hope?"

"My Mom," Clare explained. "She sacrificed her life in Boston to live with us here."

"And your Dad?"

"Left me, my mother, and my two older sisters when we were kids."

"Do your friends and co-workers know about Dennis?"

"No one in the lab knows, except now for you. I tell folks merely that my husband's in Vietnam. A couple of my local friends know, but no one else. That's the way I want it to stay, at least for now, okay Charlie?"

"Absolutely," I said. "And I'm sorry I pressed you. I had no right—"

"It's fine," she insisted. "I'm glad you did. I didn't want to mislead you."

An awkward silence intruded while I searched for something meaningful to say. I stared at the lumpy, half-eaten pile of pancakes on my plate. "You know, these pecan pancakes taste like cow dung."

"Everything here does." She laughed, abandoning her untouched bowl of oatmeal with a flourish. "And thanks, Charlie," she said, "for understanding."

CHAPTER FORTY-FOUR

And Then There's Hope

Week One of the Great Sleep Experiment transpired without incident. I slept like a baby, in spite of the knot of wires oozing from my scalp like an upturned bowl of spaghetti. Clare's cheerful presence enlivened my waking hours in the lab, and the prospect of our morning debriefings and occasional breakfasts together rendered my nocturnal imprisonment an almost ambrosial experience. I didn't want it to end . . . until the onslaught of Week Two.

Unlike most of my fellow students, I'd never pulled an all-nighter. I routinely slept eight solid hours a night. On six hours of sleep, I was lethargic. On six hours of sleep for seven consecutive nights, I was dysfunctional. As the lost sleep accumulated, I lost my appetite—except for the pecan pancakes at the hospital cafeteria that, unaccountably, tasted better as the week progressed—and my memory increasingly failed me. On several occasions, I referred to Clare as Annie, Julianna, or Mildred. Who in God's name was Mildred? I forgot where I'd left things, including my underwear. Breakfasts with Clare degenerated. I became as interesting and animated as a habitual gambler at a slot machine with a cup full of quarters.

On the twelfth night, I was irritable, my head ached, and I was near exhaustion. I began to drift off to sleep even before

Clare finished the tiresome process of attaching my electrodes. I plunged through the phases of sleep like a skydiver without a chute.

I found myself suddenly adrift in a rowboat on a broad, shimmering lake with Annie, Julianna, and Clare. They wore delicate white dresses that billowed in the gentle wind while I was clad like a groom in a formal tuxedo crawling with tiny wires of red, green, and blue which snaked from my toes up my legs around my genitals up my torso and finally terminated in electrodes attached to the bathing cap I wore on my head. And the lake then dissolved into a gentle stream that ran along a lush bank. We rowed gently down the stream, merrily, merrily, merrily, until we reached New Liberty, miraculously relocated to the banks of what was now a broad river. Hermie waved to me, displaying a white placard bearing the figure "10" in his upraised right hand. "She's a ten!" he shouted to me three times followed by "attaboy, Charlie!" And I saw my parents, gesturing from the shoreline, and my Dad called out to me, "Are you fucking them?" "Yes, Dad," I cried in exasperation, "all of them!" "Don't forget to use a condom!" he commanded. And New Liberty gave way to row after row of elegant Scarsdale estates and in front of one stood Mr. Darlington, waving to Julianna. He was naked from the waist down and the buxom blonde beside him flashed a toothy grin while Julianna screamed "Dad!" over and over in horror. And then we all clutched oars and rowed our little boat past a playground on a hill. Two infants with identical swollen faces waved at Annie and me, acknowledging us with cries of "Mama" and "Dada." And in a flash they brandished semi-automatic rifles that they trained upon each other before simultaneously pulling the triggers yielding gruesome streams of blood the color of my pseudo-Rothkos. "My babies!" Annie shrieked, "My poor babies!" And the river swelled into an ocean as we rowed past a mammoth aircraft carrier. Clare waved to a handsome, young aviator as he entered the cockpit of an airplane and the aviator waved back before a giant slingshot launched him into the sky through a bank of gathering storm clouds. And the rat-a-tat-tat of machine guns filled the air and a plume of black smoke cascaded from the plane as it plunged downward, spiraling into the sea. "NO! NO!" Clare cried out. And then we found ourselves back on the river with perilous rapids looming before us. White foam rose from the water as our rowboat hurtled toward the rapids. And then an enormous being emerged from the water with legs like steel pillars and the torso of a Cyclops. "Tractor, is that you?" I called out, but he failed to respond and sprang from the water like Moby Dick, begetting a tidal wave that flipped our suddenly beleaguered rowboat ten feet into the air. And the four of us were thrown headlong into the torrents of water as our boat bobbed and rolled like a plank of driftwood. I sank before rising to the surface, gasping for air as I struggled frantically to drag myself to safety alongside the capsized boat. And I watched in horror as Annie, Julianna, and Clare flailed in the rushing waters as the rapids drew closer. I heard them screaming to me. "Save me!" they cried in unison. And as Tractor rose up again I beseeched him: "Get out of my damn nightmare, Tractor, you don't belong here!" "Save them, Charlie!" he shouted. "I can't save them all!" I cried in horror as I lunged out to reach them with one arm while clutching the edge of the overturned boat with the other as we entered the rapids, buffeted like fallen leaves in the white foam. "Choose one, now!" he implored me, "or you'll all perish!" And then I heard Izzy's voice summoning me from the shore. "Pick one, you asshole, before it's too late!" And I stretched out my arm once more and one of them clasped my hand and we clutched each other like desperate lovers as we crashed through the rushing waters and just as my head was about to slam into a jagged rock she yanked me clear and the current cradled us, carrying both of us safely to shore and I turned to her but I was suddenly blinded by the sun and I couldn't make out her face and I cried out in despair...

I awoke with a start as Clare burst into the room with alarm. I was nauseated and drenched in sweat.

"Charlie!" she shouted, "are you okay?" I hesitated, gathering my wits about me, slowly realizing that I'd emerged from a terrible nightmare, recognizing that I'd never know the identity of the girl who'd rescued me from oblivion. Clare's shouts nudged me further toward consciousness: "Your numbers are haywire! Your heart rate's unreal!"

Clare insisted that I quit the study right then and there, concerned that I would suffer some permanent damage or injury. The lost sleep made me too stubborn to surrender. "No way!" I protested. Like a marathon dancer, I persevered until the bitter end.

Clare called a cab on the final morning and accompanied me to the fraternity house. Fortunately, the driver knew where it was; I'd completely forgotten. Blake and Tractor carried me upstairs and deposited me into my bed in the empty bunk room. I think I kissed Clare on the lips when she said goodbye but I may have dreamed it, since I dreamed of her all week long.

It took me most of the subsequent week to recover. The money I earned was not nearly enough to compensate for what I'd endured. Never again, I swore to myself. Easy money is never easy. I deposited the funds and sent a check to Doris along with a long, newsy letter.

Clare had gone to great lengths to assure my well-being. I was determined to thank her in person. I found her address in the phone book, bought (through a cooperative intermediary) a decent bottle of wine, and biked across town to her modest garden apartment. Her mother answered the door. She eyed me suspiciously until Clare emerged from inside. A baby wailed in the background.

"I probably should have called," I said.

"No, no, Charlie, I'm glad to see you," Clare said. "You had me a bit worried."

"I know. I apologize."

"No need," she said. Clare introduced me to her mother and invited me in.

"I won't stay. I just wanted to thank you for looking out for me. It was above and beyond the call of duty." The bottle of wine I handed her seemed woefully inadequate.

"You didn't need to do that," Clare said, acknowledging the gift, "but thank you." Then she led me into the kitchen and introduced me to Hope. I couldn't have imagined a more cherubic and beautiful child. Blessed with her mother's auburn hair and freckled face, she was busily engaged stuffing small cubes of fruit into her greedy button mouth.

Contrary to my intentions, I spent the next hour with Clare, her mother, and Hope at the kitchen table, talking, laughing, and savoring that inadequate bottle of wine.

CHAPTER FORTY-FIVE

The Epistle from St. Augustine's

Aletter appeared in my mailbox at the end of January. I recognized the handwriting as Annie's. I carried it back to the House while I mustered the courage to open it.

Dear Charlie,

I'm so sorry it's taken me this long to write to you. I've sat down to write this letter at least a half-dozen times in the six months since I last saw you. Each time I try, I end up starved for the words necessary to express my feelings. This time I've sworn to sit here until I've finished.

I was horribly rude to you during our time in New York. You ministered to my every need and I just cast you aside as if you meant nothing to me. I'll never forgive myself for treating you that way. In my grief, you became the unwitting symbol of my pain and my guilt.

I suffered emotionally much more than I'd anticipated. And when Dr. Epstein informed me that we had terminated a twin pregnancy, my heart just went totally numb. I shut out everything for weeks, not the least of which was you.

Maria told me she saw you on the green at Roberts last fall. She conveyed your concern for me. She told me how much more she'd seen in your eyes than you'd expressed in your words. She sensed how much it hurt you to stay away, describing it as an act of sheer selflessness. That, of course, is the Charlie I know and love.

Yes, Charlie, I love you and I miss you. Despite the horrible consequences, our lovemaking was an epiphany for me. I knew then I had the capacity to love a man and that you were the man I loved. Sometimes I imagine that the pregnancy that resulted was a rebuke from God. But how could God, who scorns me for my attraction to women, punish me for loving a good man like you?

It took me the better part of the last six months to conquer the pain and the guilt that you witnessed at its peak after the abortion. For weeks, I couldn't even say the word or think it. Yet despite my depression, I still know we did the right thing. All of the options were awful but we chose the right one. I know it in my soul.

I would be selfish if I said I wanted to see you again. If I were as selfless as you, I would have never written this letter, for fear of entrapping you yet again. For your sake, I can only hope that you've moved on and can invest your love more wisely in someone less likely to hurt or disappoint you.

Take care, Charlie, and be happy.

All my love,
Annie

I knew full well that I still loved her. Nor was I as selfless as she seemed to believe. I had repressed my thoughts of Annie as much to preserve myself as to protect her. I knew she still cared for me, but now there was Julianna and I was finally happy again. My Blue Period had passed. Yet it heartened me to read her words, to bask in her love and admiration. Annie was right—she probably shouldn't have written. But I was very glad she did.

CHAPTER FORTY-SIX

The Queen of the Realm
and the Knight Very Errant

I decided to hold off in responding to Annie's letter, to let it percolate. Winter Carnival was quickly approaching and I looked forward to spending it with Julianna. But on the Thursday afternoon preceding the big weekend, Julianna called to tell me that her grandmother had taken ill. She and her parents would go to Lenox to visit Doris on Friday morning.

"I *have* to see her, Charlie," she told me on the phone. "I hope you'll forgive me for ruining your weekend plans at the last minute."

"How bad is it?"

"A minor stroke. She's doing well . . . the hospital expects to release her tomorrow. But at her age . . ."

"Of course," I said. I shared her distress. "Would it be presumptuous of me to borrow a car, drive down there tomorrow morning, and pick you up? We can drive out and see her together," I suggested, "unless you think I'd be intruding."

"She adores you," Julianna said. "My parents would be going out of their way to pick me up, so that would work better for everyone."

"I'll be there by ten."

"Okay. And Charlie," she said ominously, "there's something more . . . I'll tell you tomorrow."

So here I was, blowing off Carnival with a date to see my date's sick grandmother. It sounded bizarre. Yet my date and her grandmother meant the world to me.

Tractor lent me his truck for the journey over the river and through the woods to grandmother's house. He'd nicknamed it the Hogmobile. It was a '57 Chevy pickup right off the farm with a big front end and a generous rear, much like my high school girlfriend, Rachel. Julianna laughed out loud when I pulled up to her dorm in the gas-belching, pea green jalopy with flaking paint, a rusted front bumper and Kansas plates. With my beard, shaggy hair, and mode of transportation, I looked every bit the part of the rural redneck.

"It'll get us there," I said, anticipating some wisecrack about the Hogmobile.

"My parents will be impressed," she said as she climbed into the deep bench seat. "And speaking of my parents . . ."

"Yes?" I bit.

"The shit has finally hit the fan."

"Meaning?"

"You remember that bimbo we saw with my father on New Year's Eve?" How could I not? "Well, her husband caught her with her legs wrapped around the dishwasher repairman—"

"No way! Problem with her upper rack?"

Julianna sneered. "Anyway, the hubby extracted a detailed confession fingering a handful—"

"*Really* bad choice of words."

"You're such an *asshole*," she snapped back, a grin creeping across her face despite her best efforts to constrain it. "So, as I was saying, she revealed a long list of victims—*including* dear old Dad."

"Ouch!" I cringed. "So your mother knows?"

"Yup . . . and she's barely spoken a word to him since she found out a couple of days ago. Should be an interesting dynamic at Gram's place."

"You sure I should be there?"

"Why not?" she said glibly. "You were a fucking witness. Literally!"

Julianna's parents had already arrived at the Darlington Estate when we arrived. Luisa met us at the door and escorted us directly to Doris's bedroom. Julianna's parents were at Doris's bedside along with an earnest, middle-aged Jamaican lady whom the Darlingtons had engaged as a nurse. Doris sat up, her back propped up against a pillow. Her trademark look of determination couldn't fully mask her pallid and weary countenance.

"Rumors of my demise are greatly exaggerated!" she robustly declared, channeling Mark Twain.

"You scared us, Gram," Julianna said as she tenderly hugged her grandmother.

"It'll take more than a piddling stroke to put me in my grave, dear," Doris said defiantly. I noticed a slight tic that periodically contorted the left side of her face.

"And so nice to see you, Charlie! You've put on a few pounds of hair, I see." With some difficulty, she adjusted to a more upright position. "I've missed having you rummaging around my library."

"And I've missed both the rummaging and your company."

"Mrs. Darlington needs to get some rest now," the nurse

said in her lyrical island inflection, "so I'm going to ask you all to leave us for awhile."

We retired to the living room where the awkwardness began. Mrs. Darlington continued to enforce the silent treatment against her straying husband. In response, Mr. Darlington shuffled around the rambling house in an effort to keep his distance from just about everyone. Julianna tried her best to shield me from the tension. Sickbed or not, only Doris would be up to the challenge of forging a solution to this marital standoff. The scene inspired two stanzas that I wrote later that night for my English Poetry class:

> 'Twas the night before Carnival
> And through the estate,
> There were visions of loveliness
> And snarls of pure hate.

> The missus was silent,
> The mister contrite.
> Can Doris alleviate
> The Darlingtons' plight?

Over the next several hours, the Darlington estate would become the setting for the quintessence of medieval-style shuttle diplomacy. The roles were clear. So long as the spark of life continued to burn in her royal breast, Doris was the undisputed Queen of the Darlington Realm. Her only child, Donald, Jr., played the Knight Very Errant. His wife, Beverly, was the Damsel in Distress o'er the Knight Very Errant's Untoward Excess. And Julianna was easily cast as the beautiful, innocent Princess. My role, perhaps, would be that of the veteran envoy, prized for his relations within and without the Realm. I had, after all, had relations with Princess Julianna, Princess Brigitte of France and Annie, the White Queen of the Land of the Lesbians, to name just three. Luisa, the housekeeper, was a natural as the Palace Courtier.

The Palace Courtier started the ball rolling when she entered the Great Hall to summon Princess Julianna to the Queen's Chamber. The Princess was constitutionally incapable of withholding secrets from the Queen who, for her part, knew perfectly well that something was rotten in the State of Darlington. Bowing to the Queen's entreaties, the Princess spilled the magic beans, revealing the treachery of the Knight Very Errant and the Court Bimbo.

Next, the Palace Courtier beckoned the Knight Very Errant to the Regal Bedchamber. The Knight Very Errant was humbled as he bumbled before the Queen, pledging forevermore to keep his roving Royal Sword safely within its Royal Sheath, except within the bedchamber of the aggrieved Damsel.

Meeting later with the Damsel in Distress o'er the Knight Very Errant's Untoward Excess, the Queen proclaimed, in so many words, that she "should just get the heck over it, Beverly, for God's sake."

And finally it was my turn. I followed the Royal Courtier into the Royal Bedchamber where the Queen played a dual role, adopting also the mantle of the Chancellor of the Exchequer.

"I want you to take back this check you sent me for the abortion bill. You've suffered enough from that unfortunate event and, as you know, I'm loaded, so let's let bygones be bygones and keep the money," the Queen insisted. "You'll need it far more than I. And I don't want you sleeping for money anymore . . . it's too depraved."

I protested mildly but retrieved the check with gratitude.

"And tell me how Annie's coping. Your letters said you've had little contact with her since New York."

I conveyed the gist of the epistle I'd just received from the White Queen of the Land of the Lesbians, leaving out the parts pertinent to our love life. The Queen of the Darlington Realm pronounced herself satisfied with the well-being of the White Queen and, reading adroitly through the lines, offered one last piece of royal advice.

"I'm not unaware of your feelings for Annie. And I know how close you and Julianna have become. Of course that delights me. But you need to understand that your head, your heart, and even your penis will all have their separate agendas. In the end, Charlie, be sure to follow your heart."

And so ended the wise counsel of the Queen.

CHAPTER FORTY-SEVEN

Shall We Dance or Keep on Moping?

A highly satisfying night with Julianna loosened me up for the return trip on Saturday. She declined my offer to attend the last night of Carnival, assuring me that the Darlington Carnival was enough for one weekend. Doris, once again, was the master fixer: Mr. and Mrs. Darlington had cooed like lovebirds throughout the morning. Perhaps they, too, had enjoyed a night of unbridled sex.

Returning to campus dateless on the biggest evening of Winter Carnival was a letdown and a waste of a top-flight fraternity house band. On a whim, I telephoned Clare. My pitch was straightforward: I'd left my girlfriend after a family emergency and hated to waste a good band. The only prerequisite, I told her, was a desire to have fun. Much to my surprise, and despite some initial reluctance, Clare accepted my invitation.

She arrived precisely at eight. She wore a stylishly short black jumper over a white turtleneck and patterned red tights. An intriguing braid wrapped itself in and out of the luxuriant waves of hair that tumbled across her chest and came to rest upon her modest but shapely breasts. I'd seen her only in a pedestrian white lab coat or the uninspiring housedress she'd worn on the day of my unannounced visit. Tonight, she looked wonderful.

Izzy and Leah came by the House later in the evening, after Clare and I had danced to near exhaustion. I'd left town on Thursday before I could inform Izzy of my change in plans. He and Leah were jolted by the sight of me gyrating across the dance floor with a pretty, freckle-faced, russet-haired, Irish lass instead of Julianna. As they awaited the conclusion of the band's version of *Bernadette*, Izzy mouthed to me a clearly discernible "what the fuck?"

"Izzy, Leah, this is Clare Kelly," I said, breathless, as soon as the music had finished. They offered a confused and perfunctory greeting, particularly when Leah noticed Clare's wedding band. By the time I explained the situation, they'd already warmed to Clare.

"Clare's just a friend, guys," I assured them earnestly while Clare nodded in affirmation.

The night flew by as the four of us danced and chatted. Clare and I had agreed in advance on a simple story: we'd met at the sleep lab, Clare's husband was far away in Vietnam where he'd been for some time, and this was an innocuous way for each of us to have some wholesome fun in the absence of our paramours. While Izzy and Leah accepted the premise, I could sense that they harbored a feeling that Clare had no business at a fraternity party, that her place was by the fireside dutifully awaiting the return of her warrior-husband, and that I, too, was somewhat beyond the pale in luring a married woman off the straight-and-narrow. Clare and I discussed it when I walked her home after the party.

"I had a wonderful evening. I haven't danced like that since college. And your friends are very nice," Clare said before turning somber. "But I pay a price for a night like this." I asked her what she meant.

"My guilt and the disapproval of others—like your friends

Leah and Izzy." I didn't want to admit that I'd reached a similar conclusion.

"Isn't that what you moved here to avoid?"

"Sure ... but it's not simply a matter of wiping the slate clean. You get to choose your poison: guilt or self-pity. And they get to choose theirs: pity or disapproval." The moonlight reflected her look of resignation.

"A conundrum," I acknowledged. "You're basically screwed whatever you do."

"Welcome to my world."

Over the next several days, I thought about Clare's dilemma. She'd taken a quantum leap in attending the party. She'd had a blast. Clare had a right to a life, and I wanted to do my part to help her live it. In so many ways she reminded me of Catherine and her struggle to shake the tragedy of her past. I wasn't seeking a commitment and neither was Clare. She was four years older than I and had a child—not where I cared to be at this stage in my life. So, I wondered, what was the harm in seeing a movie together, or grabbing a pizza at Tony's? Couldn't we keep it that simple? I wanted to try.

I called her later that week, asking her to a movie—as friends, I stressed. Clare hesitated, settling for a raincheck. The baby was crying. She had to go.

Two days later, she called me back.

"Forgive my reticence about the movies," she said. "You'll have to bear with me as I work this through."

"Not a problem," I said. "So ... do we do that movie?"

"No, Charlie, I'd like to make you dinner instead. With Mom and Hope." Was Clare testing me? If I were looking for a romantic connection, she might have thought, I'd be dissuaded by the presence of a potentially judgmental mother and a needy child. But if it was just friendship I sought, the more the merrier. Besides, dinner at her apartment offered the freedom she sought from the scrutiny of others.

I enthusiastically accepted.

CHAPTER FORTY-EIGHT

The Bosom of Bedlam

The last time a girl invited me to her apartment for dinner, I unwittingly consumed a plateful of hashish-laced brownies, engaged in a threesome with two rambunctious lesbians, and exhausted a half-dozen condoms without remembering how. Dinner at Clare's, I hoped, would be more conventional. I had no interest in a two-generational threesome with a fifteen-month-old voyeur.

Clare's mom answered the door. Though pushing fifty, Grace O'Malley looked at least ten years younger. Her strawberry blond hair was secured in a bun, and she wore a mid-length dark blue dress connoting a formality well beyond that conveyed by my plaid shirt, corduroy pants, and scuffed Frye boots. Her tone was friendlier this time—she'd finally let her guard down.

We passed through the dining room en route to the kitchen. The table was set for three, with candles burning at both ends—a fitting metaphor, it occurred to me, for Clare's chaotic life. As Clare stood in the kitchen tossing salad, Hope sat in her high chair tossing food, her chubby cheeks smeared with a variety of unidentifiable ingredients originally destined for her mouth. "Uh oh!" she crowed repeatedly.

Clare was a beacon of calm in the bosom of bedlam. She

wore a fashionably short plaid wool skirt with a long-sleeved, yellow turtleneck and black tights. Her hair still featured the bewitching braid she'd debuted at the fraternity party.

I sensed a look of concern when I presented Clare two bottles of wine. The bottle I'd brought the last time disappeared too quickly, I thought, so two seemed appropriate, even if they were the fusty old favorites of the impecunious undergrad crowd: Blue Nun Liebfraumilch and Mateus Rosé (a too-sweet white and a not quite red).

Hope was still processing a mouthful with her half-dozen teeth when Grace announced dinner. I removed Hope's high chair to the dining room table, acquiring a handful of mashed peas for my trouble. The food-splattered high chair was a curious counterpoint to the otherwise formal table.

Dinner was a Clare-and-Grace adaptation of Julia Child's beef bourguignon. The savory aroma of slow-cooked beef, onions, and red wine was a welcome change from the pedestrian fare at The Douche. We drained the rosé and opened the liebfraumilch, its Blue Nun label conjuring thoughts of Annie.

We talked about Clare's childhood in Boston, her two older sisters (both married, one a nurse at Mass General and the other a stay-at-home mom rearing Grace's other two grandchildren), and my unremarkable upbringing in New Liberty. Dennis's name was invoked frequently, mostly by Grace, though Clare didn't shrink from discussing him—just as Grace didn't shy from mention of the ne'er-do-well husband who'd abandoned the family when Clare was ten. Hope, too, contributed her own colorful, though largely unintelligible, monologue.

After the main course, Clare liberated Hope from her high chair, depositing her on the floor where she spurned a mountain of toys in favor of a pot that she pounded into submission with a spoon. While Clare and I cleared the table for dessert, Grace polished off the liebfraumilch.

Then, as if by the flick of a switch, the domestic tranquility devolved into chaos. Grace, by now increasingly unsteady, delivered the dessert course much as Sharon Hettleman's mother had launched her tray of cookies and Cokes when she'd discovered my hand wedged in her daughter's crotch: by air mail. Balancing a steaming tray of cherry cobbler with hands sheathed in oven mitts, Grace stumbled, toppling headlong into the dining room table.

"Shit!" she muttered, as she witnessed the pan slide from her grasp. Like a drunken gymnast performing a face-plant, the dessert landed unceremoniously, top-down, in the middle of the dining room table.

"Uh oh!" piped Hope proudly.

"Mom!" cried Clare, horrified more by her mother's rapidly advancing state of inebriation than the disembodied dessert dissolving the finish of the dining room table.

"Looks like the scene of a Mafia hit," I said unhelpfully as Clare shoveled the goop back into the pan from whence it came. Having regained her balance if not her composure, Grace slumped into her chair. She buried her face in her oven mitts while emitting a chorus of sniffles and moans.

Meanwhile, on the floor beneath us, Hope supplemented her pot-pounding with a soliloquy of her own, screaming what sounded like "Poop" or "Pope" at the top of her lungs.

"Did she defecate or is she Catholic?" I asked.

"She's reciting her name," Clare informed me. "I need to put Hope down now," she added, words that seemed to imply an impending execution. Clare bent down and hoisted her daughter from the floor. "Do you think you can deal with Mom for a few minutes?"

"Why not?" I said dubiously.

By now, Grace had discarded her oven mitts. She hummed *Oh Danny Boy* while her eyeballs spun in their sockets like a slot machine. "So, Grace, you doing okay?" I asked, though the answer was obvious.

Slowly, however, she emerged from her stupor. "I'm sorry, what was I saying?"

"No idea, Grace."

"Oh, now I remember," she snorted, rallying. "What are your intentions . . . with my daughter?" Her question came out of the blue. Her tone was more of concern than complaint. "She's a . . . a married woman. You know that . . . right?"

"Clare and I are just friends," I assured her. "I've got a girlfriend; I'm not looking for another."

"Don't hurt her," she implored me. "She's been hurt . . . too many times." Grace's anxiety was legitimate. Clare had been abandoned by all of the men in her life, intentionally and otherwise. I promised I wouldn't.

Grace turned suddenly pallid. "I'm going," she casually announced, "to be sick." Before I could respond, she expelled much of her dinner onto the table where it blended with the remains of the cherry cobbler, creating a mixed-media composition reminiscent of Jackson Pollock.

I was still cringing when Clare returned from the baby's bedroom. "What the heck, Mom!" she cried. Clare helped Grace to her feet and dispatched her, too, immediately to bed. I rushed to the kitchen, commandeering some paper towels and a trash can to tackle the mess.

"I'll deal with that," Clare said as I dabbed unenthusiastically at the wreckage. I was no match for someone accustomed to cleaning the crap from a toddler's tush. She emerged from the kitchen with rubber gloves and a bottle of foul-smelling yellow liquid. A hazmat suit might have been more appropriate. I stood by helplessly as she scrubbed and seethed.

After finishing the unseemly cleanup, Clare flopped into the couch and sighed deeply. Pondering whether to laugh or to cry, she chose the former, breaking out into a convulsive laughter that proved instantly contagious.

"I don't know who's the bigger child, Mom or Hope," she said.

"Has this happened before?"

"I should have warned you not to bring the wine. She doesn't know when to stop, which is why I don't keep alcohol in the apartment anymore," she said, indirectly answering my question in the affirmative.

"I'm sorry. I didn't realize."

"My fault. I just didn't think to tell you. A bottle would have been perfectly okay, but two . . ." I felt awful. Clare sensed my dismay. She arose and gave me a respectful peck on the forehead. "Really, Charlie, it's not your fault."

We agreed to call it a night.

"Welcome to my dysfunctional life," Clare said wistfully as I got up to leave.

"Let's do it again soon," I quipped. She laughed. "But seriously," I said, "let's just meet somewhere else, for a meal . . . or a movie. Grace can babysit Hope while they refinish the dining room table."

CHAPTER FORTY-NINE

'Cause My Baby, She Wrote Me A Letter

D*ear Annie-*
Your letter warmed my heart even as it tore at my soul.
I shudder each time I recall our last moments together in New York, and the heartache of leaving you broken. I was helpless to console you.

I understood your need to distance yourself from your pain and guilt and that I was inextricably linked to it. I knew it wasn't me you were rejecting, though it didn't blunt my misery. But I've never blamed you, Annie. It was the only way you could heal.

Most of all, I'm happy that you've moved on, and that the pain and guilt have subsided.

Like you, I suffered a bout of depression after New York. I called it my "Blue Period," though its perversity surprised me. I'll spare you the embarrassing details except to say that it took a heroic effort by Izzy and Leah to bring me to my senses.

I have a girlfriend now. She's Julianna Darlington, Doris's granddaughter. I met her early last summer when she visited the Lenox estate for a couple of weeks, but our relationship only blossomed this fall after I emerged from my funk. She's a freshman at Mt. Holyoke. You'd like her.

I tell you about Julianna for two reasons. First, so you can be secure in the knowledge that, like you, I've survived our mutual anguish and am functional again. And second, so you'll understand my reluctance to see you now for fear that you'll nudge me from my equilibrium.

All of which begs the question of the feelings I still harbor for you. When I read your letter, I longed to take you in my arms and lose myself in you as I once did, before the unintended consequences of those moments of bliss tore us apart. And I know that if we were together right now, I wouldn't be able to restrain myself.

I fear it is me now who's being evasive. For two weeks, I put off writing this letter because I didn't know how it would end. And maybe it doesn't. I just don't know right now, Annie. I hope you'll forgive me.

Love always
Charlie

CHAPTER FIFTY

Intervention Redux

I continued to see Clare after the Great Dining Room Debacle. We'd meet for lunch, usually mid-week, for a pizza at Tony's or a sandwich at Moe's. It gave her a chance to converse with someone other than her erratic mother; a daughter whose vocabulary was limited to "uh oh," "Poop" and "Pope;" or the losers she attended to at the sleep lab. Meanwhile, I spent almost every other weekend with Julianna, at Roberts or Mt. Holyoke.

I made no secret of my lunches with Clare. But one Wednesday afternoon in late March, returning to SciFi after one of those lunches, I stumbled into an ambush. Tractor intercepted me at the front door.

"Upstairs, *now!*" he commanded, chasing me to our room as if pursuing an opposition halfback. Inside, on the bed in the corner of our room, beneath *Untitled (Red Square No. 1)*, sat Izzy.

"Don't tell me," I said, reading the stern look on Izzy's face. "Another goddamn intervention?"

"Saw you with your sleep lab honey at Tony's an hour ago," alleged Tractor, the lead witness for the prosecution in this kangaroo court.

"So?"

"So," Izzy said, "she's *married*, Charlie!" He stood up and looked me straight in the eye. "You've already got a white-hot girlfriend in Julianna. Aren't you a bit out of line?"

"Hell, no!" I said. "Clare and I are fucking friends, goddammit!"

"Fucking friends!" said Tractor. "That's the fucking problem!"

"Come on, guys, *you're* the ones out of line," I said, calming myself while launching into my own defense. "It's a platonic relationship . . . I swear it."

"Sure," Izzy muttered, challenging my credibility. "This poor girl has a kid . . . and a *husband* fighting in Vietnam as we speak. How do you think it looks, you having regular trysts with a married woman under those circumstances? How do you think it makes *her* look?"

"Get off your high horses! It's not what you think," I insisted. "And the very way you approach it is what makes her life so damn complicated."

"No decent guy has regular meetings with someone else's wife," said Tractor.

"*I* do, you fucking farm implement!" I was quickly losing patience again.

"I meant *other than* you, you dick." Tractor shook his head contemptuously. "This sure wouldn't fly back in Kansas."

"We're not in Kansas anymore, Toto!"

While I understood where my friends were coming from, they lacked an important detail that I was loath to reveal. Yet the further this inquisition proceeded, the more I felt compelled to supply the exonerating evidence.

I raised my hands in mock surrender. "Okay, guys," I said. "I need you to swear that you won't reveal what I'm about to tell you to anyone else."

"What, you're doing her mother too?" Izzy wisecracked.

"Promise me!" I said.

"Sure, sure, we swear, we swear," said Izzy, while Tractor nodded in assent.

"Clare's husband is M.I.A. in Nam. His plane went down over the North a year-and-a-half ago. Chances of his returning alive are slim to none."

"Oh . . . *damn*," said Tractor, while Izzy added his own brand of eloquence with a half-hearted *"Fuck."* With that, the prosecution withdrew its case.

"Look guys, I appreciate your concern," I said, pulling up a chair. "It's because I've got a girlfriend . . . an admittedly *white-hot* girlfriend . . . that I can see Clare as just a friend. She's a sweet, terrific lady. She needs someone to talk to once in a while, to be 'normal' with. She came here from Boston to get away from petty, judgmental people who wag their tongues at the activities of the poor mom who's married to the M.I.A."

"She's basically screwed, isn't she?" Tractor observed.

"That's the point, guys," I said. "She's damned whatever she does."

"But look, Charlie," said Izzy. "You're a damn romantic. What if you fall for her—despite your best intentions?"

"I'll cross that bridge *if* I come to it," I said. "But really, Izzy, if you were me, would you dump Julianna for Clare . . . or *anyone* else?"

"No, I guess not."

"Then this intervention is over."

CHAPTER FIFTY-ONE

Simon Says

I didn't have a jealous bone in my body. Or so I thought. Jealousy is a particularly nasty emotion born of the fear, whether rational or not, of losing something you value, like a white hot girlfriend.

In high school I had nothing to lose. I had a grand total of two girlfriends, Sharon Hettleman, the girl who sucked off her previous boyfriend in the back of a schoolbus, and Rachel Gunther, whose red Chevy Malibu interested me more than she did. Sharon appealed to my male classmates for her advanced oral skills but never bestowed them on me. I flamed out spectacularly with her just short of second base. So no loss there. As for Rachel, my attitude toward a potential rival (had there been one) would have been a modification of comedian Henny Youngman's famous one-liner: "take my girlfriend . . . please!"

At Roberts, I'd somehow transformed from a sad sack to a campus superhero. Annie was every guy's dream. Still, I had no cause to fear losing her to some bigger, smarter, better-looking guy because—with the curious exception of yours truly—she didn't do guys. And the equally desirable Julianna Darlington never gave me the least justification for insecurity: she was a good friend, ardent lover, and as infatuated with me as I with her. All that changed abruptly one Saturday in April.

I borrowed the Hogmobile to visit Julianna at Mt. Holyoke. Spurred by her protest debut on Homecoming weekend, she'd volunteered with an anti-war group headquartered in nearby Amherst known as the Western Massachusetts Anti-war Coalition—WMAC, for short. WMAC drew its participants from the Five College Consortium including Mt. Holyoke, Amherst, and three other local schools. Julianna wanted to introduce me to some of her activist colleagues before spending a relaxing evening together at Mount Holyoke.

Per her instructions, I met Julianna at the WMAC office in a previously abandoned storefront on a sketchy side street in downtown Amherst. Tractor's broken-down pickup looked right at home in front of the ramshackle building. I found Julianna inside, coaxing an ancient mimeograph to churn out flyers promoting an upcoming peace march in Springfield.

"Print!" Julianna screamed at the recalcitrant old clunker. "Print, you old piece of shit!"

"I see you've made a friend," I kidded her, gazing at the sputtering machine.

"A medieval scribe could produce these flyers faster than this broken-down piece of crap!" Finally, she surrendered, shut down the balky contraption and kissed me hello. "I want you to meet some of my friends," she said, leading me to the rear of the dingy edifice where a collection of battered old desks lined the pockmarked back wall. A dozen or so student volunteers, evenly divided between men and women, were hard at work fomenting rebellion. Barking directions was a tall, ruggedly handsome dude with broad shoulders, well-chiseled features, a generous mane of wavy brown hair, and a well-trimmed beard. The guy could have played Jesus in the movies. His steel grey eyes conveyed a confidence bordering on arrogance.

Julianna diverted his attention from a colleague and began the introductions. "Charlie, this is Simon Allison the Third." *The Third? Really?* I disliked him immediately.

"Hi, Simon. I'm Charlie Meyer," I said, offering my hand. Simon managed a barely perceptible nod before returning to his conversation. I clumsily withdrew my hand.

"Sorry, I guess this isn't a good time," Julianna said in a hasty effort to excuse Simon's rudeness. She introduced me to several other volunteers before circling back past Simon's desk on the way out; he was still preoccupied.

"I'm taking off now, Simon," she called out. "See you tomorrow night at the meeting."

Simon interrupted his conversation and turned his full attention to Julianna, placing his large hands on her shoulders more familiarly than I would have liked. "Thanks for your help, Jules," he said. "See you tomorrow." *Jules?* He smiled at her for what to me seemed an eternity before extricating himself from her orbit and rejoining his colleague.

"Simon has exciting plans for WMAC," Julianna told me as we drove toward Mt. Holyoke.

"Seems like a horse's ass to me." I figured that driving a Hogmobile made me an expert on animal anatomy.

"No, *really*, Charlie, he's a terrific guy, brilliant mind—he's a senior at Amherst, a major in psychology." She came to his defense a bit too enthusiastically.

"What's this 'the Third' bullshit?"

"Comes from a prominent family ... industrialists, I think."

"Kind of like the Darlingtons," I said a bit smugly. Fortunately, she didn't take offense.

"He's got interesting ideas."

"Such as?"

"Such as *non-violent aggression*."

"What the hell does that mean?"

"Being aggressive in marches and demonstrations—*verbally, but not physically*—to induce tactical errors that will erode opposition support."

This struck me as unduly provocative. "How do you know this 'non-violent aggression' won't backfire?" I was growing weary of this bullshit. "It didn't take much for someone to smack you in the face with a two-by-four last fall."

"Well, we're not making much progress with these fainthearted 'peaceful' marches now, are we?"

"I can't believe what I'm hearing!" I shot back. "Someone's going to get hurt—and it better not be you!"

Julianna was unfazed by my anger. "Simon says we've got to take reasonable risks to achieve real progress."

"And *he* decides what's reasonable?"

"No one has to do anything they don't want to."

"And where are you drawing the line, *personally*?" I asked her.

"Well, Simon says—"

"FUCK!" I screamed before she could get another word out. "When Simon says spread your legs, do you spread them?" *Oh . . . shit! Did I really say that?*

"Fuck you!" Julianna shrieked. "I'm doing this shit to keep poor bastards like you out of Vietnam! I'm not the asshole with the low lottery number!"

"Julianna, I'm sorry . . . I shouldn't have said that."

"You think I'm sleeping with him, don't you?"

"Of course not," I protested, though I can't deny that the thought crossed my twisted mind.

"You jealous prick!"

"Come on, Julianna . . . I said I was sorry. The way he looked at you . . . called you 'Jules' . . . pawed at you . . . it really *bugged* me."

"Fuck off!"

She stared out the window for the balance of the ride, saying nothing. "Let's call it a night," she said coolly when we arrived at her dorm. "I'm not in the mood."

"Julianna," I pleaded. "Come on."

"Not tonight, Charlie," she snipped. "Talk soon." She hopped from the pickup, slammed the door, and marched away in a huff.

CHAPTER FIFTY-TWO

Washington or Bust

Yes, I was an asshole. I had no justification for my appalling display of jealousy. What's worse, I made my ill-advised comment to a girl still smarting from her own father's infidelity.

I tried calling Julianna more than a dozen times over the next two days. She wouldn't take my calls. I'd planned, during my truncated Saturday visit, to invite her to Roberts' spring concert weekend, but an invitation following my "spread your legs" wisecrack would have been as futile as an effort to convert the Pope to Islam.

So I resorted to the old flowers and poetry ploy that had worked so well with Annie. A dozen red roses were dispatched to Julianna's dorm room accompanied by the following ditty:

> *I said something stupid,*
> *Alarmingly crass*
> *And made of myself*
> *A complete fucking ass.*
>
> *Forgive me, my darling,*
> *My lover, my friend*
> *And join me for Roberts'*
> *Spring concert Weekend.*

No response. My calls continued unanswered. Several days later, I got a terse note in the mail: *Memo to the schmuck in the truck re the weekend: get fucked!*

I took that as a "no." At least she took the time to rhyme it.

As it turned out, the effort was all for naught. On Monday, May 4, 1970, four days prior to the spring concert weekend, the infamous Kent State Massacre took place. During what began as a largely peaceful student protest, Ohio National Guardsmen fired 67 rounds at unarmed anti-war protesters, killing four students and wounding nine others. It was an outrage.

Two days later, I met Clare for our now customary Wednesday afternoon lunch at Tony's Pizza.

"Appalling," she said as she took a bite of her vegetarian pizza.

"We should have ordered the pepperoni," I quipped, fully aware she was talking about the tragedy at Kent State. Clare gave me a look that branded me an asshole. "It's no joking matter, Charlie."

"I know, Clare... I'm sorry," I said, cognizant of how often recently I'd put my foot in my mouth and been obliged to utter those two words as penance. "I guess I just can't wrap my head around it. But at least it's jump-starting the resistance," I observed. "Campuses—including Roberts—are suspending classes and a huge march is planned for this weekend in Washington."

"Why don't you go?" she asked.

"Why don't you come with me?"

Clare put down her slice and took a sip of her coke. Then she surprised me completely.

"I've sat on my ass for the year and a half since Dennis went missing," she said. "Maybe it's time I do something."

"Clare, I would have thought this would be unusually difficult for you."

"Just because it's difficult doesn't mean I shouldn't do it." She brushed an errant strand of hair from her eyes. "It's time for me to stop the moping and do something meaningful, don't you think?"

"What about Hope?"

"I'll ask Mom if she'll hold the fort with Hope for the weekend. If she agrees, we could drive down in my VW on Saturday morning when I'm done with my shift."

Clare finished her shift at the sleep lab at eight on Saturday morning. She changed into a tee shirt and denim shorts before picking me up at the House. By nine we were blitzing down Route 91 en route to D.C. We weren't alone: hundreds of cars, trucks, and vans were on the same pilgrimage. Signs abounded. My personal favorite was the old van whose side three windows displayed, from front to back, a longhair in a tricorn hat, a coed flashing her breasts, and a sign reading "Washington or Bust."

Eight hours with Clare in a VW bug was both amiable and revealing. We probed ever more deeply into our personal histories. My home life, which I'd dismissed as dysfunctional, was staid in comparison with Clare's early years. She described a father who had physically abused her mother on numerous occasions before shacking up with a girl fifteen years his junior. She chronicled her mother's on-and-off struggles with alcohol. She talked of her marriage to Dennis, a man whose own jealousies often got the better of him. It was the first time she'd talked extensively about her husband. She transformed him in my mind from a symbol of her grief to a multifaceted individual with both virtues and warts. I sheepishly admitted my own recent foolishness with Julianna and how it may have cost me my relationship. Clare's perspective was valuable—even if it further cemented my status as an idiot.

It was blistering hot when we reached the outskirts of Washington around dinnertime. Parking anywhere near the National Mall was impossible, so we deposited the bug across the Potomac in Arlington, grabbed a bite at a local diner, and took a bus as far as the crowds allowed. The gathering was already monumental; perhaps as many as a hundred thousand, mostly college students, would congregate by the protest's peak on Sunday. The atmosphere was a curious mix of solemnity and celebration. While there was no doubting the weekend's somber agenda, the protesters found creative ways to cut the tension.

Clare and I absorbed the spectacle. We walked from the vicinity of the White House—within which an embattled President Nixon had virtually barricaded himself—westward to the Lincoln Memorial. The melodious toots of a makeshift kazoo band drew crowds near the Washington Monument. Guitar-toting hippies functioned as wandering minstrels along the Mall. The splashing of water and the din of genial merriment greeted us as we passed the Reflecting Pool, now a gargantuan wading pool where thousands had sought refuge from the intense heat. One guy carried an American flag triumphantly as he paraded around the pool stark naked.

As night fell, we scouted for a few square feet of turf to accommodate our sleeping bags, winding up near the Lincoln Memorial. We mingled with protesters from Maine to California. There was passion in everyone we met, and a collective sense that we were all part of something momentous.

Protest ballads serenaded us to sleep around midnight, but constant distractions made for a fitful sleep. A buzz arose near the Lincoln Memorial at about four in the morning. Rumors circulated that President Nixon was meeting there clandestinely with a delegation of protesters. It seemed so implausible that we went back to sleep, learning only later that the confab had indeed taken place, though to little avail.

Crowds swelled further on Sunday when speakers addressed the sweltering masses. They reflected a broad spectrum of political viewpoints, from garden-variety war opposition to chilling radicalism. A tedious address by prominent activist and babymeister Dr. Benjamin Spock was followed by a fiery denunciation of American policy from actress Jane Fonda.

As the speeches droned on, Clare and I meandered through the crowds. A prominent sign displayed on the north edge of the Mall caught my eye. It bore the acronym "WMAC," for Western Massachusetts Anti-war Coalition, Julianna's organization. Without explaining why, I diverted our path toward the placard. At a range of maybe twenty-five yards, I spotted Simon Allison the Turd huddled around Don't-Be-Jealous-of-Me Julianna. I shuddered. Along with fist-pumping, I observed butt-bumping, smooching, and goosing. What the fuck! A hundred thousand people on the Mall and I have to witness Simon Sez dry humping my girlfriend in public?

"What's wrong?" Clare asked when she noticed me clenching my teeth, fists, and ass.

"Movie Jesus over there is pawing my girlfriend," I said edgily.

"*That's* Julianna?" she said, gazing at the gorgeous girl being groped by the grubby guttersnipe.

"Maybe you're not as much of an ass as you thought," Clare

said sympathetically. "She *is* beautiful, though," she said, realizing that it wasn't much consolation at this juncture.

"Let's get the hell out of here."

CHAPTER FIFTY-THREE

Sleepless in Mianus

It was already mid-afternoon when we retrieved the car in Arlington and prepared for the long drive home. As she placed the key in the ignition, Clare turned to me.

"Would you mind terribly if we took a little detour?"

"What did you have in mind?"

"I'd like to stop at Arlington National Cemetery. It won't take long," she assured me.

We parked, obtained a cemetery map, and headed in the direction of the Tomb of the Unknowns. Clare remained eerily silent as I accompanied her along the path toward the memorial for unidentified victims of America's foreign wars. I deferred to her evident desire for solitude.

"Would you mind if I go forward alone?"

"Of course not." I dropped back respectfully as she walked ahead.

Others stood at the site paying their respects while a military guard paced back and forth with robotic precision. I could hear Clare's voice rising and trailing off, but her words were inaudible. At one point she began to sob softly, almost reverentially. Finally, after about ten minutes, she extracted a tissue from her pocket, dabbed her eyes, turned, and retraced her steps to where I stood. She remained mute until we reached the car. "Thanks," she said.

"For what?"

"For indulging me." Clare remained subdued until we left the cemetery grounds and merged onto the highway. "It was time for me to say goodbye," she whispered, her voice tinged with emotion.

I gently squeezed her right hand. Although her eyes were moist, I deduced from the set of her jaw that the matter was closed. Quickly, she shifted gears. "And how are you coping with your Julianna dilemma?"

"I'm basically screwed . . . I was obviously right from the beginning."

"Maybe, maybe not," Clare said. "Have you considered the possibility that your suspicion was unjustified? That your distrust gave her justification to pursue a relationship she'd resisted in deference to you?"

"Uh . . . no," I admitted. I liked myself better when I was cocksure that Julianna had been the transgressor. "Either way, it would seem that the horse is out of the barn."

"Wait it out," Clare said. "You might be pleasantly surprised."

It was after nine o'clock when we crossed into Connecticut. We'd shared the driving but were weary from our lack of sleep. Clare knew first-hand how poorly I functioned under such conditions. I suggested we stop at a motel for the night.

Clare concurred. "I'll call Mom after we check in to let her know."

We took the exit for Mianus, a town with a name as unfortunate as my initials. Off the ramp was a dated motel with a tacky Indian theme. A faux tee pee sprouted from the roof in the center of the complex. With the first three letters of its flickering neon sign burned out, it presented itself to travelers as the "Pee Motel." I had flashbacks of the Blue Pelican in Miami.

Against our better judgment, we parked Clare's VW and entered the motel office. Behind the desk stood the manager, a grizzled old man with the darting eyes of a serial killer. A cigarette dangled from his lip, his shirt pocket stuffed with a pack of reinforcements. At a small desk behind him sat a woman with the charm of a bag lady and half the normal allotment of teeth.

"Do you know your sign reads 'Pee Motel'?" I asked Smoking Man.

"Been busted since '65," he responded matter-of-factly. His voice cracked from his three-pack-a-day habit. "One room or two?"

Clare and I glanced at each other. We answered simultaneously. "Two," I said as she indicated "One." Then, just as quickly, we each reversed course.

"Come on, folks," Smoking Man growled. "We're all adults here. Save me the goddamn paperwork and share a damn room."

"Fine," I said definitively. "Please make that non-smoking."

"Yessir!" he said, mocking me while the Toothless Tramp stood behind him chuckling. He handed us a key.

The room was a dump. "No smoking" meant only that nothing in the room was currently smoldering. The place smelled like a mountain of old gym socks. The "free TV" transmitted snow on every channel. The pillows had the pliancy of sacks of potatoes. I offered to sleep on the floor in my sleeping bag while Clare could take the bed.

"Don't be ridiculous," she said. "You'd probably be eaten alive down there by whatever crawls out from under the bed."

I waited patiently while she closeted herself in the

bathroom to shower off the remnants of the hot Washington sun. She eventually emerged, wrapped in a towel. While Clare telephoned her mother to advise of our delay, I showered in turn and donned a clean pair of boxers.

Clare was already lying in bed when I joined her, the worn sheets pulled up against her shoulders. She had switched off the bedside lamp. Her face and hair were bathed in red from the flickering light of the neon sign outside. Her green eyes sparkled. Even in that tawdry neon glow, Clare was remarkably beautiful. She spoke first.

"I'd like you to do something for me."

"Anything," I said like an obedient puppy.

"I'd like you to kiss me."

"Clare . . . are you sure?"

"I'm sure."

So I did. It was a warm, long, soft kiss, the kind that generates goose bumps and makes you forget you're in a sleazy, no-star motel. The electricity of that kiss could have powered Mianus for a month. And then the threadbare sheets fell away, revealing her unexpected nakedness.

The growing bulge in my shorts gave new meaning to the name Tee Pee Motel. As my fingers grazed the curvature of her waist and hips, my brain shifted into overdrive. "We need protection," I said, sounding like my father.

"We're good," she replied. "I'm using a diaphragm."

"So this is not as spontaneous as it seems?" I was both surprised and flattered.

"I came prepared, but I didn't necessarily expect it. This trip was a rite of passage for me," Clare revealed, her breasts rhythmically illuminated by the pulsating light. "I can't be that pathetic girl with her eyes trained on the front door, expecting her husband to stroll back into her life at any minute . . . or the girl eternally mourning his probable demise." There was no hesitation in her voice; she had turned the page willingly. "It's time to move on," she said. "And, if you'll forgive me the premeditation," she added, leaning forward to bestow a gentle kiss, "I had rather hoped to share this part of my reawakening with you." And when she finished that brief soliloquy, she drew me into her like a hungry guest at a Thanksgiving feast.

I was glad to be the beneficiary of Clare's torrential release from two years of sexual repression. She was anything but rusty. She was lovely, sensuous, and passionate, not to mention voracious, irrepressible, even gluttonous. I imagined her moans of pleasure penetrating the six sets of paper-thin walls separating our room from the grimy motel office, inciting the Smoking Man and the Toothless Tramp to their own steamy session of sexual rapture.

Despite our best intentions, we got precious little sleep at the Tee Pee Motel. Clare was clearly captivated by my curious crookedness (and patently pleased by its potency). But really, what the heck was going on? I could feel that all-too-familiar shroud of confusion rolling in like the morning fog. Was I just the right guy in the right place at the right time or did our passionate night portend something more? Was Julianna a lost cause? And what about Annie? Was it time to reconnect with Annie?

If only Dad had an axiom for all this.

CHAPTER FIFTY-FOUR

The Nun Redone?

A phone message from Annie greeted me upon my return to campus on Monday morning. Though my mind and my dick were still numb from my night at the Tee Pee, I needed only a finger to return Annie's call. I longed to hear her voice again.

It had been nearly six weeks since I'd written her. Of course that was before I'd shoved my foot in my mouth with Julianna and slept with Clare.

"So how's my favorite lesbian?"

"I'm good, really good, at last." I was truly happy to hear that.

Annie cut to the chase. "I appreciated your letter and I get where you're coming from," she said. "You've got something good happening with Julianna, which probably makes this request inappropriate. But I thought, as you might say, 'what the fuck?'" I never thought I'd hear those words from the Nun. "So, Charlie, I called to ask if you'd be willing to chance another Spring Fling—next weekend—under whatever ground rules you lay down. But *only* if it wouldn't compromise your relationship with Julianna."

"Uh . . ." I sputtered as my wheels spun.

Either Annie was again desperate for a male cover for her

school's annual decidedly non-lesbian social event, or she was ready to throw caution to the wind in a longshot effort to rekindle our flagging relationship. While Julianna was surely out of the picture, either short-term or forever, there was the matter of my relationship with Clare which, at the moment, defied explanation.

Annie would have to have been an idiot not to pick up on my equivocation. When I didn't answer, she quickly backtracked: "I'm sorry. I shouldn't have—"

"No, no, Annie," I interrupted. "I'm glad you called. It's just that things have very recently changed for me and I need to think it through. Can I take a page from your book and sleep on it tonight? Call you tomorrow?"

"Of course," she said. "Talk to you then."

Considering this logically, which was nearly impossible, I ticked off the pros and cons:

The Pros:
1. Julianna had been the main reason I'd put off reestablishing any kind of relationship with Annie, and Julianna was now, at least for the time being, out of the picture.
2. My relationship with Clare was a complete muddle to me. The truth is, I had no idea if it was a one-night stand or the beginning of something even more messed up than that. Whatever else she was, she was too old for me, still married, and had a kid.
3. I still had very strong feelings for Annie.

<u>Cons</u>:

1. Annie messed me up before I messed her up. Did I want to go there again?

2. I hadn't seen or even spoken to Annie for nearly nine months. Those nine months had been like a drug rehabilitation program as I struggled to rid myself of my Annie-addiction. I was virtually off the juice. Did I want to risk a relapse?

3. Annie's still a lesbian and I'm still a guy.

The House had a keg on tap so I invited Izzy over to offer some objective advice. First, I filled him in on the latest developments. His reactions were predictable:

"You said *what* to Julianna? Were you frickin' nuts?"

"Probably."

"You did *what* with Clare? Were you frickin' nuts?"

"Possibly."

"You seriously need professional help. But on the other hand, Annie is Annie and she's nothing to sneeze at either."

"So?"

"So you're totally fucked up already. What have you got to lose?"

"My sanity?"

"That's long gone, Charlie."

He was probably right. I called Annie the next day and accepted her invitation. It couldn't be any worse than the damage I'd done at the last St. Augustine's Spring Fling. This time, at least, I'd bring condoms.

CHAPTER FIFTY-FIVE

Pepperoni and Sausage

Clare and I had studiously avoided any discussion of the previous night's exploits during our ride home on Monday morning. The subject was impossible to avoid by the time our Wednesday lunch came around.

"What in the world did we do Sunday night?" I asked her while debating the relative merits of pepperoni or sausage on our pizza.

"We had a special moment," Clare said matter-of-factly. She countered with mushrooms.

"It was more than a moment. It was the whole damn night."

"I guess it was. Pretty good time, I thought," she said with a grin, evading my obvious effort to get to the bottom of our encounter.

"Come on, Clare. What was it all about? I'd like to have some idea where we stand and how this changes things. This isn't just about sharing a weekly pizza anymore . . . is it?"

"They also have salads, grinders, pasta . . ." She clearly enjoyed taunting me.

"Clare!"

"Okay, Charlie," she said, finally relenting. "I had an emotional weekend. I turned some corners. I let myself go—at the cemetery and at the Tee Pee . . . I tried to let Dennis go."

"Was I just the guy in the right place at the right time?"

"You were the *right* guy in the right place at the right time. That's an important distinction."

"So now we're friends who fuck?"

"Is that such a bad thing?" she said almost flippantly. "Listen, Charlie. I turned a corner . . . but my life's still a mess." She shook her head. "Look at me . . . I'm still a wife or a widow with a young child . . . and you're just a screwed-up college junior, for God's sake! What more can there possibly be for us right now?"

I hesitated, grasping for an appropriate rejoinder.

"Don't look so wounded!" Clare said, prompted by my sad-puppy-dog face. "I adore you! But I don't want to hurt you, so you need to be the judge of what you can or can't handle. Like you told me when you invited me to your houseparty: no commitment required. And for the record, your friendship is much more important to me than the sex," she said, lowering her voice to a whisper, "even though I adore that crooked cock of yours."

"Okay," I said. "I'll see you the friendship . . . and raise you the sex!"

"I'm all in."

"So I guess we're going with the sausage."

"Eeew!" she said, wrinkling her nose before smiling.

CHAPTER FIFTY-SIX

Double-Bagging It

While I harbored more than a few misgivings about seeing Annie again, she enchanted me the moment I laid eyes on her. She met me at the bus station clad in a sleeveless button-down blouse and flared jeans that caressed her hips and celebrated her world-class derriere. She wore her hair in a smart bob haircut that softly brushed her shoulders and framed her porcelain face. Her countenance was so much brighter than I'd remembered from New York. Time had rinsed the weariness from her eyes, the veil of sadness was gone, and that familiar, radiant smile once again fit her as comfortably as an old pair of jeans. Any lingering resistance dissolved when she embraced me enthusiastically and planted a kiss on my lips that revealed that, like Clare, she was "all in."

"It feels like it's been forever, Annie," I said as we exited the bus station. "You look terrific, as always."

"I'm sure you say that to all of your girls," she teased.

"Perhaps, but I've never said it to the same girl for three years running."

"I'm honored," she said with a smile as we crossed the street for the short walk to the St. Augustine Inn. Unlike Roberts, Annie's college actively enforced its medieval ban on male visitors to women's dorm rooms. If the dorm monitor detected a violation, the Pope was immediately notified. So, despite its eerie association with our supernatural fecundity, the room at the inn was a necessity.

"You know, I honestly didn't think you'd come."

"Why wouldn't I?"

"I can think of many good reasons."

We walked past the restaurant where Annie and I had met to discuss the discoveries that had so shocked me during our eventful Homecoming weekend more than two years earlier. "I guess I just grew to miss my unhealthy obsession with you. Like an addict, I needed a fix." I was unnerved by the stark accuracy of that statement.

Annie smiled, then grasped my hand. "I'm so ashamed of the way I behaved in New York, the way I—"

"Forget it, Annie. It was a nightmare for both of us. I've already told you I didn't take it personally; I never loved you any less for it." She squeezed my hand tightly. "And by the way, 'love' isn't a word I use with my 'other girls'." *At least not yet.*

"Nor I with my girls." *A little lesbian humor.*

"You look so much happier."

"We've both been through the wringer since New York," Annie said. "But you look pretty good yourself, especially for one who's apparently lost a girlfriend recently. What happened with Julianna?"

"Rather not go into it. Too embarrassing. Suffice it to say I made an assumption that may or may not have been justified and said something I had no business saying. In short, I messed up."

"I'm sorry," she said sympathetically, "but I do take some comfort in knowing that she's no longer an impediment to my seeing you."

"Annie, I've never *not* wanted to see you . . . it's just that you fuck me up sometimes."

Last year's Spring Fling had been an exercise in frustration—frustration that had turned to ecstasy with tragic consequences. This year's edition was a radical departure. No longer masquerading as lovers to preserve the pretense of Annie's heterosexuality, we were just a couple of college kids into each other and having a blast.

Annie and I held hands as we strolled the few short blocks to the inn after the dance. Our spirits were high and our intentions were clear. There wasn't a kernel of doubt that we'd spend the night together. I was well supplied with condoms. So was she. Nothing was going to ruin this night now or a couple of months from now. This was our do-over. We deserved it.

Sitting beside each other on the edge of the bed in the low lamplight, we consumed each other's eyes in silence. I placed my hands softly behind her temples and drew her mouth to mine. Our kiss was deep, long, and passionate.

I thought about our last night together one year ago in this very place. Our lovemaking that night had been an unanticipated banquet of emotion. Annie had taken control that evening, sacrificing herself on the altar of my torment. This night, however, would be different. Our desires and expectations were parallel, our agendas aligned. But as we embraced, Annie's eyes flashed a sign of warning.

"I know, Annie," I said, reading her mind. I rose from the bed and fumbled through my overnight bag for my condoms. She, likewise, ransacked her purse.

"I've got one!" I announced as if I'd drawn a winning lottery ticket.

"Me too!" she said, laughing. "Maybe you should double-bag it," she suggested, half-jokingly, "just to be sure." So I did.

And though it felt as if I'd encased it in a ten-gallon garbage bag, my mangled member performed its magic. And when we finished and held each other close, there were no feelings of regret, confusion, uncertainty, shock, or anxiety to catalogue or analyze. In the morning, we could simply smile knowingly and lovingly at one another, free of the burden of explanation. I couldn't have been happier.

CHAPTER FIFTY-SEVEN

Glamour in the Slammer

It was an otherwise ordinary weekday night in the SciFi Tube Room. Tractor, Benny, and I were casually shooting the breeze while the television (which had been replaced, at Tractor's expense, following his screen-shattering outburst on draft lottery night) droned on in the background. Sue, the House mongrel, was dry humping Tractor's leg, a favorite pastime for Sue and a constant source of irritation for Tractor. No one but Sue could fathom why the flea-bitten canine treated Tractor's meaty limb as his personal bitch.

Benny happened to glance at a news report describing a violent encounter between police and anti-war protesters in Springfield, Massachusetts. A police officer had been seriously injured when a Molotov cocktail exploded during a fracas with members of the Western Massachusetts Anti-war Coalition. Film showed a group of demonstrators verbally attacking a police brigade armed with clubs and shields.

"Shit, Charlie, isn't that your babe?" Benny asked. I instantly focused my attention on the TV.

"Where?" As I spoke, another clip appeared in which several protesters were being dragged into police vans by billy-club-wielding cops. I recognized at once the imposing figure of Simon Allison The Turd. And beside him . . .

"Oh, my God!" I shouted. "That's Julianna!"

"Jesus," Tractor said, "she's feistier than a sow in heat."

I was beside myself, brewing a cauldron of emotions ranging from concern for Julianna's well-being to rage at the sanctimonious prick who lured her into this fix like a perverted pied piper. I bolted from the couch to the House phone, plunked in a few quarters, and dialed Julianna's dorm. Her roommate, Joanne, told me that she'd heard of the arrest through the grapevine but that Julianna had yet to return to her room. I asked her to contact me if she learned anything more.

Moments after replacing the receiver, I received a phone call. It was Doris.

"Julianna called me from the police station in Springfield a few minutes ago," she said in an unusually solemn voice. "Apparently she's been arrested in connection with an anti-war disturbance." Doris was clearly distressed.

"I just saw the report on the news. I'm not surprised she approached you first; I assumed she'd be hesitant to call her parents."

"Well, she probably called me because she knew I'd bail her out now and save the questions for later." Doris's displeasure with Julianna was unmistakable. "So, Charlie, I'm wondering if you'd be willing to drive down there and get my granddaughter the hell out of jail. I'll wire you the funds through Western Union."

"I'm on my way."

"Here are my keys," Tractor said. "Take the Hogmobile."

I followed Doris's instructions, retrieved $5,000 in cash, and drove to the Springfield Jail. The dingy old building was rife with reporters hoping to score interviews with the arrested protesters upon their release on bail. I forced my way through the boisterous crowd. Once inside, it took almost three hours to wade through the red tape necessary to secure Julianna's release. I was not permitted to see her and she had no way to know I was there.

It was nearly midnight when Julianna finally emerged from the bowels of the stark, antiquated facility. She stopped in her tracks when she saw me. Her expression was more one of embarrassment than anger. While she struggled to manifest a brave front, I could see the tears welling up in her eyes as she approached me. She sported a nasty bruise on her cheek and a bandage on her left hand. I put a protective arm around her shoulder and ushered her forcefully through the commotion. "There are dozens of reporters outside. Keep your head down . . . don't say anything or even look at them . . . just keep walking." She complied wordlessly.

When we had cleared the gauntlet, I grasped her arm and turned her toward me. She'd still not uttered a word. Her eyes were trained on the ground.

"Are you all right?"

Julianna looked up at me, working harder now to restrain the tears. A two-by-four to the chin had barely thrown her off stride. But now she was trembling and lost. I swore to myself I would not be judgmental. When she met my gaze, she saw a look of sympathy and concern rather than anger. She reacted accordingly, embracing me tightly while the tears flowed more liberally.

"Everything's gonna be all right," I said to her repeatedly, though I had no particular justification for my optimism. Word in the jail was that the injured policeman was in serious condition at a local hospital. Much would depend on his prospects for recovery.

I refrained from questioning her regarding the events of the day. It was clear she didn't care to discuss it.

"Please don't take me back to the dorm," she said. "I can't deal with it tonight."

"Okay, we can get a room at one of the motels near school. I need to call your grandmother and your roommate to let them know you're safe."

She nodded feebly, confirming the plan by default.

I booked us a room at a Holiday Inn. I called Doris and Joanne while Julianna showered. After cleaning up, she claimed one of the two double beds, delivered a perfunctory "good night," climbed under the covers, and fell quickly to sleep.

It had been a long and disturbing day. I'd seen a side of Julianna that I'd never seen before. Her feisty independence had unraveled, revealing a shattered, suddenly fragile young woman whose world had spun out of control. I looked at her wistfully from the other bed before I, too, dropped off to sleep.

When I awoke the next morning, Julianna was propped up against her pillow, staring at me. Her eyes were swollen and red. I sat down beside her, putting my arm around her tentatively, still uncertain of her feelings toward me. She offered no resistance. When she spoke, it was apparent she'd begun to recapture some of that old trademark spunk.

"And I thought you were the fuck-up," she said.

"Welcome to the Fuck Up Club."

"Thanks for last night," she said. "I certainly didn't expect to see you at the jailhouse."

"You have Doris to thank, mostly. She wired the money to spring you. But I've gotta tell you . . . she wasn't too thrilled about it."

"You know, they really do allow only one call. Gram was the

only one I had the courage to contact."

"What happened out there yesterday?"

"Goddamn Simon," she began, leaving no doubt about her bitterness toward him. "He egged us on . . . goaded us into confronting the cops with . . . you know, that 'non-violent aggression' crap of his . . . until one of them begins swinging his club at us." She exhaled deeply. "Then I'm looking over and I see Simon yanking something from his bag, lighting it and tossing it at the cop. Damn him!" Julianna rubbed her hands back and forth across her temples. "When it exploded, everyone ran. The cops chased those of us closest to the action . . . I couldn't get away quickly enough."

I pointed to her wounds. "How'd you get those?"

"A club grazed my face—it could have been much worse. The cut on my hand . . . probably some glass from the Molotov cocktail." She examined her hand carefully. "I wasn't even aware of it until I saw the blood dripping from the back of my hand. A paramedic treated it when we reached the jailhouse."

She looked at me. "I know what you're wondering. And no, I had no idea that Simon planned to do something as stupid as that . . . I wouldn't've had any part of it."

"I know that, J. D."

"And now for the hard part," she said, unconsciously fumbling with her bandages. "You were wrong . . . and right."

"Meaning?"

"Wrong to suggest that I was sleeping with Simon when you made that horrid comment to me." She paused as I winced. "Right to think I was attracted to him."

"That didn't give me the right to say what I said. I'll never forgive myself for that."

"Now for the really hard part." I steeled myself for what I knew was coming. "A few days after our disagreement, I slept with Simon. Only once . . . if it matters. It was the night before the March on Washington."

So Clare had been right. It *was* partly my fault. Julianna studied my eyes for signs of anger, disappointment, or hurt. It stung me, but I refused to show it.

"I went to the march, Julianna. I saw you there on Sunday, on the edge of the Mall, with the WMAC delegation. The asshole was pawing you mercilessly."

"Shit! I'm so sorry. I'm so embarrassed to have been manipulated like that. I feel like a high school freshman."

"You're young enough to make mistakes . . . and learn from them. And even though I was right about what an unmitigated asshole Simon is, I can't be the jealous asshole I was. I'm sorry, too." It felt good to clear the air. "So what happens now?"

"I'll go back to school. The term's almost over. Hopefully, Mt. Holyoke won't take any punitive action." She rubbed her eyes. "I have to tell my parents . . . Gram gave me a deadline on that. And I assume Dad or Gram will find me a good lawyer. And I hope to heaven that the poor cop recovers. Regardless of what happens legally, I'd find it tough to handle it if he doesn't come through this okay."

We dressed and checked out of the hotel. Julianna smiled at the Hogmobile in the hotel parking lot. I stopped the pickup in front of her dorm. She slid over the bench seat to kiss my cheek before hopping out. "I'll call you soon. And thanks, Charlie."

CHAPTER FIFTY-EIGHT

All Come to Look for America

It's been said that you can't have too much of a good thing. Dad, in his inimitable manner, would have turned that aphorism on its head: "Too much of a good thing will surely fuck you up." Call it Axiom No. 6.

On the romantic ledger, I had three pretty good things going. My long-smoldering love affair with Annie, dormant since last summer, had suddenly reignited into a three-alarm blaze. Another flame, the lately felonious Julianna, showed signs of rekindling following a dousing with jealousy. And then there was the steady flare of Clare, my Wednesday lunch buddy and occasional coital companion. Annie knew about Julianna, but assumed her out of the picture. Julianna knew little, if anything, about Annie, though her grandmother knew entirely too much. Clare knew something about both Annie and Julianna, though neither had an inkling of Clare. All of which, I feared, harbored a wealth of incendiary potential.

More than once, when I bemoaned my conundrum to Izzy while shooting the breeze in his dorm room, he'd stroll over to his bookshelf, flip through his albums, and extract *Do You Believe in Magic,* the debut album of the Lovin' Spoonful. He'd play for me a song written by John Sebastian that he considered particularly relevant. The lyrics of *Did You Ever*

Have to Make Up Your Mind included these quatrains:

Sometimes there's one with deep blue eyes, cute as a bunny
With hair down to here and plenty of money
And just when you think she's that one in the world
Your heart gets stolen by some mousy little girl

And then you know you better make up your mind
And pick up on one and leave the other behind
It's not often easy and not often kind
Did you ever have to make up your mind?

Sometimes you really dig a girl the moment you kiss her
And then you get distracted by her older sister
When in walks her father and takes you in line
And says, "Better go home, son, and make up your mind."

I often felt that Izzy had the wisdom that my parents sorely lacked. Though his platitudes and unsolicited advice could be annoying at times, he always had my back. And while I found it hard to argue with the logic of those lyrics, I found it harder still to make up my mind.

Junior year was virtually over. I could hear the fat lady singing. It was time to take stock: senior year was just around the corner. What then? If there's a corollary to Axiom 6, it's that too many bad things will also fuck you up. The comfortable refuge of the ivory tower would dissolve with graduation, and my low draft lottery status guaranteed me an unwelcome choice among four disagreeable alternatives: an all-expenses-paid trip to Vietnam; enlistment in some service or branch that might reduce, though probably not eliminate, the likelihood of a journey to the jungle; a lifetime exile in Canada; or a sabbatical in the slammer. Julianna and I would make a fine felon couple.

So, on the cusp of my last summer as an irresponsible college brat, I decided that there was only one thing left for me to do: ROAD TRIP!

Why not? I would simply hit the road "to look for America," as Paul Simon phrased it, finding myself and resolving my dilemmas, perhaps, somewhere along the way. Except for my spring break frolic in Ft. Lauderdale, I'd never transcended the boundaries of the northeast corridor, never experienced life beyond suburbia and academia. This would be my chance.

I had no itinerary, no one in particular to visit. I would just stick out my thumb and hitchhike across America. The thought exhilarated me. I'd let the spirit move me. I'd float across the highways like a leaf buffeted by the summer breeze. I bought myself a commodious backpack and some stuff to put in or carry on it: a poncho, sunglasses, sunscreen, bug spray, first-aid kit, canteen, sleeping bag, a handful of roadmaps, and as many clothes as I could manage. And just to be sure, I made a pilgrimage to Alice's for a box of condoms.

Well, perhaps I wasn't quite that cavalier. I discussed my skimpy plan with Tractor a week before the end of the term. He was driving the Hogmobile back home to Kansas for the summer. He invited me to come along. "You can meet my folks, see our spread, and have a home-cooked pork dinner," he said. "You're not too Jewish for that, right? And I'll introduce you to the hogs," he said with a smile, though I knew he really meant it.

"Oink, oink," I muttered, signifying my assent.

CHAPTER FIFTY-NINE

Like a Pig in Slop

Tractor and I loaded our stuff into the Hogmobile and hit
the road. The first day's plan was to drive to Indianapolis
where Tractor had an uncle in ghetto real estate. I didn't know
the "ghetto" part until we got there. Uncle Jerome had
promised Tractor a furnished dwelling unit for the night in a
garden apartment complex he owned somewhere on the north
side of the city.

You learn a lot about a guy when you sit beside him in a pickup
for fourteen straight hours. Even though Tractor had been my
roommate at SciFi, our paths rarely crossed. He studied most
often at a Christian Students' Center near the House and we slept
in the Bunk Room, so most of our interaction came in the Tube
Room, on the SciFi roof, or during my celebrated interventions.
We talked about all of the important topics: religion (he accused
me of being "a fucking heathen"; I branded him a "blind follower
of fairy tale dogma"; I proclaimed religion "the root of all of the
world's evil" and he allowed that my agnosticism was not my
own fault but the unavoidable consequence of my being a
"Jewcaholic," his colorful term for the product of a marriage
between a Jew and a Catholic); football (a game he considered
"the ultimate test of human strategy and strength" and that I
panned as a game for "shitheads so stupid to begin with that each

incremental concussion boosts their IQs a point or two"); and women ("I worship the ground my little Mary walks on," he said of his longtime girlfriend, adding that "she's also one heckuva a good lay" while he described me as a guy "whose dick has been in more holes than a golf ball"). He waxed philosophic about pig farming, telling me that "raising hogs is like playing football: you roll around in the trenches and get muddy, and the bigger you get the better you'll be."

"You get to know your hogs, you nurture them ... they become almost part of the family," he said.

"Part of the family? *Really*, Tractor?" I said. "Would you slaughter your sister and turn her into sausages?"

"Only if she were fat enough."

To Tractor, family (pigs excluded) was the most important thing. He was the youngest of six children, with four sisters and an older brother. His brother, he told me, was destined to take over the family farm that had been originally established by his "Great Granddaddy" Ludwig Herzog when he emigrated from Germany before the turn of the century.

I asked him why he didn't choose to attend the University of Kansas or some other big Midwestern school where he could take courses more relevant to agriculture. "You can't major in hog raising at Roberts," I reminded him.

"That's just the point, Charlie," Tractor said. "I was the first one in my family to ever even *attend* college. I got better grades in school than my brother or sisters, and my Daddy already had my brother ready to handle the farm. My parents had this crazy idea that I was somehow 'too smart' to be a farmer ... that I deserved something better. Figured a scholarship to some fancy eastern school like Roberts would open my eyes to a shitload of other possibilities ... that I'd find something I liked better than farming."

"And have you?"

"Nah, not really. I suppose I could go into oil exploration or something like that," he said. "But truth be told, I might just marry good ol' Mary and take over her family's farm in Ohio." He scratched at his unshaven beard. "They grow soybeans and corn, mostly, but I've got a hankering to add some big ol' hogs to the mix. Her Daddy's gettin' too old to handle it himself . . . and he hasn't got a son to pass it on to."

Tractor, it seemed, had a plan—which put him light years ahead of me.

It was about ten o'clock when we pulled into Indianapolis. As Tractor navigated his way toward the address his uncle had given him, I became increasingly squeamish. Calling this a "developing neighborhood" was like describing Linda Lovelace as a film ingénue. We knocked at the door of the designated address (the buzzer wasn't functional) and were met by a sturdy old woman with an impenetrable Polish accent. She stepped out the door, triple-locked her apartment, and led us to another unit further back in the same "garden" apartment complex. This was a garden apartment in the same sense that New Jersey is the Garden State. Most of the porch lights were burned out or smashed, and broken glass was scattered liberally along the darkened route to our refuge for the evening. Our guide to the netherworld instructed us incomprehensibly in the methodology for working our way through the sequence of locks required to permit entry into our unit. Then, in response to my halting inquiry about neighborhood safety, she assured us (as best I could tell) that it had to be safe because Tractor's uncle employed an armed guard to cruise the area "every so often." The security system offered far less solace than the comforting presence of a 275-pound defensive lineman.

Our apartment unit dated from the Thirties. It was

equipped with the furniture discarded by our parents a generation ago. The air conditioner was jerry-rigged in a manner reminiscent of a Rube Goldberg contraption and produced as much cooling as a melting ice cube.

While it was a long, hot, mostly sleepless night for me, Tractor slept like a pig in slop.

CHAPTER SIXTY

American Gothic

I t was already hot and sticky when we escaped Indianapolis early the next morning. The city smelled like a slaughterhouse. Our discussion topic for the day was the draft lottery. Or, more properly, what the fuck we were going to do in response to our perilously low draft numbers. Although the data remained fluid, I told Tractor of my growing impression that enlistment in the reserves substantially reduced the chances of going to Nam.

"The only other viable alternative I can come up with is to hightail it to Canada," I said.

"You'll freeze your ass off," Tractor said. "And you won't even be able to visit your parents without risking jail time."

"Visiting my parents *is* jail time."

"So I gather."

"Anyway, I think I'll cross the border later this summer, just to see what it's like."

"You should go up in the dead of winter. Then you'll *know* what it's like."

"So what's your plan?" I asked Tractor.

"I'll probably enlist in the Army," he said to my astonishment as I recalled the destruction he wrought in the SciFi Tube Room on the night of the draft lottery.

"Why the hell would you do that?"

"Because both my Daddy and Granddad served in the Army. You know, *every citizen's moral duty* . . . and all that happy horseshit." Tractor floored it to scurry past an eighteen-wheeler. "So, in the end it's really pretty simple," he said. "I can't disrespect my Daddy's expectations." Disrespecting my father's expectations was my reason for living.

In stark contrast to the sparkling new interstate highways that carried us from Indianapolis, our last hundred or so miles were on monotonous, two-lane Kansas highways that bored me silly. Tractor, however, was right at home. He relished revving up the Hogmobile to eighty-five to pass the long-haul truckers whose mammoth rigs dominated the otherwise sparsely trafficked roads. Long stretches of endless and (to me) unremarkable farmland predominated. From time to time a lonely grain elevator, feed store, or gas station would herald our passage through an anonymous and largely unpopulated town. Tractor's hometown of Wegner announced its presence with a generous dose of methane.

The odor of cow manure, in fact, permeated the entire community. It lingered as we drove through the two-block, late nineteenth century town center, and it persisted as Tractor steered the mighty Hogmobile onto the half-mile-long driveway to his ancestral home on the Kansas prairie. Though we'd arrived at dusk, I marveled at the rambling farmhouse begun by his great grandfather during the early Twenties and expanded, with a dormer here and an el there, over succeeding generations of Herzogs like a binge-eater's waistline. A profusion of barns, pens, trucks, and tractors gave testimony to the host of crop and livestock activities conducted by the Herzog family on their four hundred acres.

When she heard the Hogmobile pull up to the house, Tractor's mother burst out the front door to greet her long-absent son. As I might have anticipated, Carrie Herzog was an ample woman, more broad than fat, with Teutonic blond hair and blue eyes, a generous bosom, and legs like fenceposts. She was cordial and accommodating when her son introduced me, welcoming me inside and offering me a seat of honor in their commodious living room. I felt as if I'd been transported into a Grant Wood painting. Tractor's Dad, I imagined, would be a supersized version of the pitchfork-wielding farmer in *American Gothic.* Every clapboard, every dormer, every stick of furniture fit my romantic image of the classic Midwestern farmhouse. Hollywood designers would be hard pressed to concoct a more suitable set.

Carrie Herzog's fresh homemade lemonade was more refreshing on that sweltering June day than a cold Bud from the SciFi tap. Tractor's father and brother returned from the fields shortly after our arrival, predictably clad in sweat-drenched denim overalls. Max, his dad, was a broad-shouldered mule of a man in his mid-fifties with piercing blue eyes, sandy blond hair (thinning at the temples) and an exuberant blond moustache. Although his brother, Christian, looked very much like Tractor, he packed at least fifty pounds of excess fat around his prodigious waist. Christian's hands were easily twice the size of mine and his handshake was bruising.

We were too late for a tour of the farm but just in time for dinner. Though there were just five of us, there was food enough for a dozen. The entrée was pork tenderloin, easily the most luscious meat I'd ever tasted. Fresh homemade bread and butter accompanied a legion of wholesome side dishes. We washed it all down with bottomless steins of Muehlebach

Lager, a dark, German-style beer from Kansas City.

"This is one fine hog," Tractor said to his father as he savored the tender pork.

"Freda," his father said. "Fresh today. Your brother did the honors."

Suburban boy nearly gagged. You breed them, you raise them (maybe even bond with them), and then you slaughter them, cook them, and eat them. What could be more natural? So why was I gagging?

"You okay there, Charlie?" Tractor asked, rather enjoying the discomfort bred by my obvious barnyard naïveté.

"Just fine," I lied, washing down the bloody meat with a gigantic swig of Muehlebach.

Mrs. Herzog continued to refill my plate until I could no longer breathe. At the same time, she and each of the Herzog men consumed at least four times what entered my gullet. There was, it occurred to me, an eerie similarity between the care and feeding of a defensive lineman and the fattening of Freda the hog.

A good night's sleep, a breakfast of fresh eggs, biscuits, and home-cured bacon, a quick tour of the farm, a round of thank-yous, and I was primed to resume my journey through America.

CHAPTER SIXTY-ONE

Eye-High to a Horse's Ass

Nowhere was the cycle of life more evident to me than in the slice of rural America I'd experienced during my visit to Tractor's farm. There was a profound order to the endless rows of seedlings destined for human and animal consumption; the livestock conceived, fed, and slaughtered to serve the needs of man; and the generations of farm families who prospered from these classic rhythms of life. If only it smelled better.

Tractor dropped me off at the nearest highway. It happened to run north and south. I chose south.

Thirty minutes later I was still thumbing in the same spot. The chance of a bearded longhair with a backpack catching a ride on a lightly trafficked road in the conservative bastion of central Kansas was like that of a surfer catching a wave in a bathtub.

Finally, a large, battered white pickup bearing Texas plates and towing a horse trailer pulled to the side of the road ahead of me. I ran ahead, as best one can while toting a thirty-pound backpack, to where it stopped.

"Where ya headin' young feller?" a grizzled old coot croaked from behind the wheel. Good question.

"Anywhere south, maybe Texas?" I said.

"Well hop on in, then," he said, "'cause that's where we're headin'."

Though he looked sketchy, he sounded suitably welcoming, so I threw caution to the wind and my backpack into the rear of the truck and climbed aboard.

"You one of them hippies?" he asked me pointedly. But before I could respond, he launched into a soliloquy that would continue for miles.

"I say live and let live. Don't care if you don't wash, get all promiscuous," which he pronounced with the accent on the third syllable, "or plunge your circumscribed pecker into broken-down mares like the ol' girl in the trailer back there, 'cause you're all God's children." I'd never before thought of my pecker as "circumscribed," much less prone to bestiality.

"You some college brat?" Before I could say a word, he was off onto yet another interminable philosophical tangent. "You college kids think you're the cat's meow, even though you ain't got no experience livin'. You got it soft. Think you got all the answers. My daddy put me to work on a horse farm when I was eye-high to a horse's ass. No college vacation for me. No, sir! Bet I knew more about life on God's sweet earth by fifteen than you college brats will learn by the time you're seventy."

The trip proceeded pretty much along these lines for the next several hours. Amid the pontificating, I learned that my driver's name was William ("just call me Billy") Clapp. A widower, he was en route to a little town called Zephyr in central Texas where he lived on a small horse farm with his unmarried daughter, Fern, and his granddaughter, Aleece. He purchased the old mare in the van from a farmer not far from where Tractor lived.

"Why would you drive so far for an old horse like that?" I asked him.

"Got my reasons," was all my otherwise long-winded travelling companion would say.

Nearly six hours into our travels, which took us through endless vistas of flat, semi-arid prairie and past countless farms and silos, it began to rain. Soon, the rain was torrential, punctuated by fierce blasts of lightning and the rumble of thunder. The old truck's windshield wipers strained to slough off the onslaught. Yet old Billy just kept plowing along, even as darkness descended over the barren landscape. I knew we were approaching Billy's destination and that I'd need to find a place to sleep for the night. Against my better judgment, I asked his advice.

"Any idea where I might be able to spend the night in these here parts?" I'd always wanted to say "in these here parts" like the cowboys in the old TV series *Gunsmoke* and *Rawhide*.

"Don't rightly know, but if you don't mind sleepin' on the livin' room couch, I'm sure Fern and Aleece would be delighted to have the company of a fine lookin' young feller like you." His comment would prove prophetic.

It was still raining and blustery when we sloshed past the three or four mostly dilapidated old brick buildings that marked the center of Zephyr. The town's name, which refers to a soft, gentle wind, is cruelly ironic. According to Billy, the survey party that first plotted the town had been stranded there in 1850 by a massive "Blue Norther," a Texas-sized cold front accompanied by heavy winds and rain, and the town had been virtually destroyed by a devastating tornado in 1909. What were my chances of emerging unscathed?

Billy pulled off the road onto the muddy, unpaved track leading to the Clapp homestead. My heart sank when his headlights illuminated the bleak facade of his meager dwelling. A crumbling, unpainted porch hung from the front of the house like a dangling preposition. The exterior was sheathed in rows of rotting clapboards punctuated by a pair of double-hung windows. A rusting corrugated metal roof provided dubious shelter from the elements.

Billy and I jumped from the pickup and splashed through the puddles of mud that passed for a front yard. Tractor's hogs would have loved it. I retrieved my waterlogged backpack from the rear of the pickup. The sound of the rain pounding against the metal roof was deafening.

"'Bout time you're back, Billy!" came an accusatory voice from somewhere on the leaky porch.

"Got us a visitor, Fern!" Billy said. "This is ... what's your name again, young feller?"

"Charlie," I reminded him.

"This here's Charlie, Fern. Why don't you show the young man in ... while I move this old girl to the shed," he shouted above the din of the raindrops, referring presumably to the mare in the trailer.

What the fuck, old man? read the look on his daughter's weathered face. Fern was not dressed for company. Barefoot, clad in a threadbare cotton nightshirt and (quite obviously) no bra, she grudgingly led me inside. I removed my mud-caked shoes before entering a cramped, plywood-paneled living room furnished like a yard sale display. Two unmatched couches of cheap, badly scratched Naugahyde formed an "L" around a stained and splintered coffee table. A TV table, sans TV, stood in one corner of the room, piled high with old magazines, horseshoes, and an old kitchen blender. A tower of old clothes and yellowing newspapers occupied the other corner with a tall mirror secured to the wall in between. Crosses and other religious paraphernalia hung asymmetrically on either side of the mirror. The stale odor of cigarette smoke permeated the little room.

"I'm sorry, uh, your name is . . . ?"

"Charlie."

"Right . . . Charlie. Well I'm sorry if it looks as if we weren't expecting you . . . 'cause we weren't. And what's it again that brings you into our living room?" Fern asked.

"I'm sorry to barge in on you like this," I said. "Your dad was kind enough to give me a lift from Kansas where I'd been visiting a friend. I needed a place to sleep so he kindly offered me a spot on your couch . . . if it's not too much trouble, of course."

"Good ol' Billy," Fern said with a sigh of resignation. "Well, then, if he promised you the couch, then you'll have the couch." She lit a cigarette. "Where you headed to?"

"Uh . . . not entirely sure, Fern . . . okay if I call you Fern?" She nodded. "I'm hitching my way across country . . . looking to see America." I recognized how ridiculous that sounded the moment it left my mouth. I'm intruding on an impoverished family to indulge my adolescent fantasies of discovering an idyllic America while the real America was right there under my nose.

"Hmm." Fern was clearly unimpressed. "You a Kansas boy?"

"No, actually I live in New Jersey."

"I see." She did but didn't much care.

Just then Billy flung open the front door, dripping liberally onto the bare living room floor. "Still raining like an incontinent old mare," he said. "Glad to see you're gettin' acquainted." Billy peeled off his wet slicker and hung it on a nail protruding from the wall beside the front door. "Charlie here's a college boy, Fern. Goes to some high falutin' school back east." It was all code for *look at this spoiled little rich hippie boy I brought home for your amusement, Fern,* but Fern was obviously not yet amused. "Looks kinda scrawny . . . but I bet he has a horse dick," he added, guffawing, as I grew increasingly uneasy.

"Saved you some stew for dinner, Pops. Reckon I can scrounge up some more for Mr. Horse Dick."

My hunger outstripped my pride and I jumped at the offer. I followed them into the crowded kitchen. A blue wooden table with three chairs filled most of the available space in the center of the tiny room. Despite the high mileage on the principal appliances, the kitchen was adequately, albeit modestly, equipped. An old pot simmered on the even older range. Fern stirred the potion while unconsciously seasoning it with ashes from the cigarette dangling from her broad lips.

"Sit down, take a load off," Billy directed as he grabbed himself a chair. Fern ladled out two bowls of stew.

"Thank you kindly, Fern," I said, only vaguely aware of my appropriation of the local dialect. "I really appreciate this," I told her, hoping to assuage her irritation at my presence. Despite the ashes, the stew was remarkably flavorful, though I was unable to detect its principal ingredient. "This is delicious," I said, resuming my groveling.

"Horsemeat," Billy said flatly.

"Horsemeat?" I hoped that I'd misheard him or he was just mocking me.

"Don't reckon they serve that too often back in New Jersey," Fern needled me while I struggled to keep from gagging. "You didn't think that old mare Pops brought home with you was a thoroughbred racer, did you?"

"Uh, no, of course not," I stammered. I suppose it could have been worse: the meat could have been yesterday's hitchhiker.

My dining reverie was interrupted by the sound of a truck and the glare of headlights through the living room window. A door slammed and a young woman's voice shouted an authoritative "Fuck you, Donnie!" to the vehicle's driver. Donnie shifted loudly into reverse, then back into drive, before plowing on back to the road. Mud splattered against the front windows as he tore away. The young woman, whom I took to be Billy's granddaughter, jerked open the front door and made a raucous entrance. "Never wanna lay eyes on that bastard again!" she shouted.

"Aleece, we've got a guest," her grandfather calmly informed her.

"Oh . . ." she said when she spied me at the kitchen table. Aleece was a tall, long-legged reed of a girl, perhaps sixteen or seventeen, with long, tangled blond hair, blue eyes, and a generous mouth with thick, heavily adorned lips. Her cheeks were stained by streaks of mascara, compliments of the rain. In her pleasingly wet tank top and skimpy cut-off denim shorts she reminded me of Elly Mae Clampett, the fetching backwoods beauty on *The Beverly Hillbillies*.

"Aleece, this is Charlie . . . a hitchhiker your granddad picked up in Kansas this morning. Goes to some fancy college back east, but he's out these parts slummin' it for the summer." I couldn't have fashioned a more accurate though less appealing description.

"Problem with your boyfriend again?" Billy asked.

"Ain't gonna talk about it, Granddad," Aleece said, bringing the conversation to an immediate halt. She gave me a long, curious look, like a child peering at an exotic beast in a zoo, before heading to the bedroom she shared with her mother.

It was after ten o'clock when we finished the horsemeat goulash. Although they continued to fling sarcastic and marginally insulting zingers my way, Billy and Fern showed me what hospitality they could in light of their compromised living circumstances. Though it wasn't warm and fuzzy (at least not yet), it was just accommodating enough to ease my fears of becoming the next day's stew.

"Fern, go fetch some of that special hooch for our guest," Billy said as I began to rise from the table. Fern smiled conspiratorially. As she reached into an upper cabinet, she revealed a generous portion of her lower buttocks, a vista considerably more pleasing than much of the barren landscape that I'd witnessed from the front seat of Billy's pickup. She returned with a dark, unlabeled bottle and three shot glasses. Fern deposited her derriere on a kitchen chair while I reluctantly settled back into mine. Meanwhile, Billy expertly distributed the dark, soupy liquid among the three glasses. Though I would have preferred to abstain, I sensed it would offend my hosts, so I braced myself for the coming contest of stamina, one I knew I would lose. I watched as Billy lifted his shot glass and deftly tossed its contents down his gullet. A groan of satisfaction. Fern repeated the process, grimacing as the nectar rolled down her throat. Haltingly, I did the same. "Aaarrrgh!" I shrieked. The elixir singed my tongue, melted my tonsils, and plowed the lining of my throat before burning through my esophagus and exploding into my stomach. Humongous tears rolled from my bulging eyes as my face contorted like the image in a funhouse mirror. Billy and Fern convulsed with laughter as they watched their effete college-boy visitor squirm.

"Do him once more, Fern," Billy instructed, ignoring my protests. I'll admit, the second and third shots went down easier, and by the fourth it was old hat. The conversation became livelier and raunchier as the alcohol content in my bloodstream rose precipitously. I thought I noticed Fern downshift a button or two on her nightshirt to titillate me with another helping of cleavage. It was the last thing I remember before my head slammed onto the table and everything went black.

CHAPTER SIXTY-TWO

Lipstick on My Dipstick

I drifted slowly toward consciousness, my head still spinning from the moonshine and pounding from the incessant splatter of the rain on the metal roof. I lay on my back on the larger of the two living room couches, though I had no memory of how I got there. The room was only dimly lit. I heard two voices, whispering, arguing.

"You do it."

"No, you go first."

"We'll take turns."

"It's fucking *crooked!*"

"Gross!"

As my pupils adjusted to the darkness and my senses gradually revived, it became painfully obvious to me that I was stark naked from the waist down. The wet, furry sensation I felt between my legs was not normal. "What the . . . ?"

"Quiet!" one of the disembodied voices commanded, one that sounded a lot like Fern. "Just lay back and enjoy it, college boy!"

I can't quite explain my languid response to the Clapp Family mother-daughter weenie-roast taking place in my crotch. That I wasn't thinking clearly was as plain as the fate of the old mare in the shed. The lingering effects of the hooch had thoroughly disabled my mental faculties while seemingly enhancing the functionality of my rapidly swelling phallus. I was powerless to resist, unable to raise even the feeblest defense. The rotating pairs of lips on my dick had me utterly convinced that it had grown to truly equine proportions as Billy had jokingly suggested the previous evening. My prick had declared its independence and threatened revolt if I made the slightest effort to reclaim control from my cranial cockpit.

Was I truly conscious when Aleese mounted and rode me like a cowboy on a rodeo bull, shouting rapturous obscenities while tugging at my vestigial nipples like a demon? Or when, as I was on the verge of exploding, she dismounted and handed the reins to her mother, who then pounded me into near oblivion, panting and groaning like a car that wouldn't start, her breasts flapping like the wings of a flightless bird? Where were the condoms I'd so carefully packed? Did I not think, even for a second, that the family name of Clapp might portend some nasty contagion by that or any other name that would cause my crooked dick to seize up and crumble a few short weeks from now? Was I not more than a boy toy?

Despite repeated orgasms on the part of all involved, the Naughty Naugahyde Rodeo was an uninspiring ordeal and a hefty price to pay for a night of lodging. I'd been mocked, drugged, and plied with horsemeat, but the ravishing went beyond the pale. When the tag-team had finally had its fill, I rolled over listlessly and returned to sleep.

I awoke with a start when the early morning sun poured like molten lava through the uncurtained living room windows. I found myself covered in a plaid blanket. Peeking under the covers, I discovered my crooked dick in its proper place and apparently none the worse for the wear. My pants and underwear were neatly folded on the coffee table. Like me, the room had been stripped of nearly all evidence of my harsh treatment. But the lipstick stains on my dick confirmed to me that the episode was more than just a soggy dream.

Bacon (or whatever horsemeat product passes for bacon) was cooking in the kitchen. I quickly dressed. Fern was at the stove, inhaling a cigarette, while Billy sat at the kitchen table, his hands wrapped around a warm cup of coffee. Both exuded the innocence of choirboys.

"Some coffee?" Fern asked nonchalantly.

"No, thanks . . . I, uh . . . I'd like to get an early start," I said, *before you fuckers commandeer my dick again or turn me into stew.* Since Aleece was apparently still sleeping off the effects of last evening's bronco busting workout, I asked for and received permission to use the lone bathroom. I showered off the lipstick and any other residue of my ravishers' dastardly deeds.

Ten minutes later, I was out the front door hauling my waterlogged backpack down the muddy path toward the main road. Although the pack seemed strangely heavy, I attributed it to water absorbed during the storm. When I opened it moments later to retrieve a roadmap, I found a peace offering from my hosts: a fifth of moonshine. When I screwed the cap open, I was promptly accosted by the now familiar stinging medicinal blast of Clapp family hooch. Despite all I'd endured at the Clapp Family Lodge, I couldn't help but smile.

CHAPTER SIXTY-THREE

Turn On, Tune In, Drop Out

What the heck, I figured. I'd made it as far as Texas. How much further could it be to San Francisco? Well, about 1,650 miles. But, to paraphrase Lesley Gore, *it's my roadtrip and I'll go where I want to.*

I'd long harbored an inexplicable yearning to *turn on, tune in, and drop out*, although I hadn't a clue what any of that actually entailed. But I knew enough to realize that I wouldn't be doing those things on Fisherman's Wharf. Haight-Ashbury was the place to be.

The Haight-Ashbury district in San Francisco had been billed as the mecca of the hippie counterculture and the birthplace of psychedelic rock. It was where Jefferson Airplane, the Grateful Dead, the Steve Miller Band, and Janis Joplin rose to prominence. So I resolved, if and when I finally reached San Francisco, to go straight to The Haight.

It took eight rides and about thirty hours to hitchhike from Zephyr to the City by the Bay. The slowest part of the journey was the hundred or so miles I endured on a plodding cattle trailer from Sweetwater to Lubbock, just south of the Texas Panhandle. En route to a slaughterhouse with a shitload (quite literally) of dim-witted cattle, it smelled like the rest room at a chili cook-off. The methane assault on my nasal passages left me gasping. Then there was the four-hundred-mile swath of interstate beginning somewhere west of Albuquerque and ending in Kingman, Arizona, which I traversed in a 1967 Porsche 911 convertible, top-down, at speeds reaching 100 miles per hour. The driver, a high-stakes gambler heading to Las Vegas, amused himself by watching my eyes roll back into my head while I turned as green as a leprechaun. He had to peel me out of my seat and pry my heart from my mouth when he mercifully released me near Kingman following our death-defying, dual-state joy ride.

The last leg of my trip began just east of Oakland. Steve, a congenial student from San Francisco State, picked me up in his blue Corvair. When I asked if he'd drop me off at the famous corner of Haight and Ashbury, he offered me two valuable tips. The first was a warning: The Haight, he advised me, was not what it used to be. I was at least two years too late. The energy was waning and the streets were filled with meth freaks, pushers, Hell's Angels, narcs, and pimply-faced teenaged runaways. His second contribution was his cousin Cindy's address. She was a resident and a veteran of the scene, Steve told me, and if I presented her the brief note of introduction he'd scribbled out for me on a torn piece of paper, he was sure she'd allow me to crash at her pad for the evening.

Steve released me at the famous corner like a captive deer into the wild. It was nothing like I'd imagined. Sure, the hippie freaks were in evidence, but so were the toughs, the derelicts, the homeless. Ashen-faced boys and girls, many not past their mid-teens, careened aimlessly about the streets. It was a circus of unbridled dissipation.

I temporarily joined the march of the walking dead along Haight Street. I found a desperately needed laundromat on Clayton and sated my hunger with a couple of slices of oily pizza from a ramshackle storefront on Ashbury while I waited for my clothes to dry. It was past five when I retrieved my wardrobe and sought out the address on Page Street that Steve had given me.

The number corresponded to a shabby Victorian sandwiched uncomfortably between two younger buildings like a straphanger on a crowded subway car. A pretty, rosy-cheeked blonde answered the doorbell. She left me to wait in the foyer while she summoned Cindy. A doughy, pale-skinned girl in her mid-twenties eventually appeared. After consulting the note her cousin had given me, Cindy invited me in. The house was a rabbit warren consisting of countless rooms in various sizes and states of disrepair, each the makeshift domain of one or two youthful residents. A mélange of unidentifiable aromas from the communal kitchen mingled uneasily with the fragrance of incense and the pungent odor of marijuana.

"You can drop your pack in my room," Cindy said. She was slightly, but not unpleasantly, plump, about my height, and wore an embroidered white blouse and a long, flowing print dress from India. Her long, frizzy black hair was brushed to one side. She had an angular chin and animated eyes the color of dark chocolate. Puffy cheeks and pouty lips framed an engaging, gap-toothed smile.

Cindy's large, sun-drenched room was perched on the top floor of the once proud Victorian, up three flights of creaky stairs. Her roommate, Layla, the pretty girl who'd answered the doorbell, sat cross-legged on her bed, her head sandwiched between a pair of headphones. She couldn't have been more than seventeen. "This is Charlie, a friend of my cousin. He's gonna crash here for the night," Cindy informed her, treating the matter as a *fait accompli.*

I followed Cindy back downstairs and into the kitchen, where she offered me an unappetizing concoction she called *Macroshit*. She rattled off the ingredients: tofu, carrots, daikon, dandelion roots, lotus root, parsnip, and radish, all staples of her newly fashionable macrobiotic diet. It made me long for Mom's Potato Buds. I graciously declined, still gorged on my greasy pizza.

I followed as Cindy carried her bowl of *Macroshit* back to her room. I asked what had brought her to Haight-Ashbury.

"The music and the alternative lifestyle . . . those were the big attractions when I came here back in '65," she said between forkfuls of her foul macrobiotic feast. "The great bands—The Dead, Airplane, Janis, Steve Miller, Creedence, Santana—played The Fillmore and The Avalon." Her face lit up with a wistful smile. "It was rock heaven . . . and the hippie subculture was still fresh," she recalled. "But now . . ."

The setting sun was pouring through the bedroom window. Cindy got up to pull down a shade. "People used to come to Haight-Ashbury to find themselves," she said mournfully, "now, they lose themselves here."

"Why stay?"

"Because I've invested my heart and soul in this community." She told me that she volunteered at a homeless shelter and was studying toward a degree in social work. "Maybe I can help some of these poor kids pull themselves out of this maelstrom," she said.

Cindy eyed me curiously as she swept the last remnants of *Macroshit* into her mouth. "What about you, Charlie? Why are you here? What are you looking for?"

I described the tightly circumscribed parameters of my own background. "I wanted a glimpse of life beyond that," I told her. But her last question was one that I hadn't yet answered for myself. "As for what I'm seeking . . . I honestly don't know," I said. "Maybe an epiphany . . . or maybe just an escape."

While Layla remained conveniently glued to her headphones, I asked Cindy about her roommate.

"Typical runaway," she said. "Came here from L.A. almost two years ago . . . to get away from an abusive stepfather. Her mother sends her money regularly . . . out of guilt. I took her in partly to help her . . . and partly to pay the rent."

Our conversation was interrupted by a knock on the door. Cindy opened it to a lanky young man with a long, unkempt beard. He wore torn jeans and a flowered shirt while a string of beads hung loosely from his neck. Layla snapped to attention when he walked in, discarding her headphones and vaulting into his embrace. Cindy introduced me to Winston, Layla's boyfriend.

Winston extracted a small, glassine envelope from his pocket and waved it in the air triumphantly. "Anyone care to trip?"

So here's where I succumbed to peer pressure over common sense. Left to my own devices, I would've likely demurred. But Cindy was game, as was Layla, and I, under the circumstances, was a sitting duck. *When in The Haight, do as the Haitians?*

"First timer?" Cindy picked up easily on my initial reluctance.

"Pretty obvious, huh."

"Don't feel obligated, Charlie," she said, "but if you're willing to try, I'll be here to guide you." She smiled at me reassuringly. "I think you'll find it eye-opening."

The drug, referred to generally as LSD or just *acid*, was delivered in diffused form on a tiny scrap of paper or *blotter*. "Hold it under your tongue for about ten minutes," Cindy directed.

"I don't feel a thing," I said after the allotted time had passed.

"Too soon, Charlie." She laughed.

Winston stacked some records on the stereo. It wasn't long before the music exploded with a resonance I'd never experienced. The earthy, gravelly voice of Janis Joplin in *Piece of My Heart* blew me away.

Then came the light show. Multicolored haloes sprouted from light bulbs and tracers flared from moving objects like rocket exhaust. And slowly but surely the colors in the room grew richer and deeper, splitting and reforming into endless combinations, creating a kaleidoscope of intense, shimmering color. Cindy grinned at my wide-eyed, childlike wonderment.

I found myself drawn in multiple directions at once, yet firmly grounded by my keen awareness of all that transpired around me. The effect was unlike that of alcohol, which dulled the senses; on the contrary, my senses were profoundly enhanced—I could see like a deaf man; hear, smell and feel like a blind man. Even my sense of taste was affected. When Cindy opened a bag of M&M's and placed one playfully on my tongue, my mouth erupted in an explosion of flavor.

The effects of my first (and, incidentally, my last) acid trip intensified with time, although time itself seemed to expand well beyond its familiar boundaries. Everything was slower, more nuanced.

Like other rookie trippers, I periodically let loose with a play-by-play description. I regaled Cindy with the miracle of the melting walls and twisting ceiling. When I ran my fingers along her skirt, I could feel every thread, every ripple of the fabric.

"Touch my breasts," she said casually while sitting cross-legged in front of me, as if she were simply offering me another M&M.

"Really?"

"Sure!" She slipped off her blouse and unhooked her bra. I dutifully followed her instruction. *When in The Haight...*

"Oh God!" I cried out as she giggled. The warmth and texture of her skin made me shudder; the firmness and subtle plasticity of her breasts were astonishing. My fingers had become vessels of pure emotion. Inexplicably, I began to weep, but my tears were tears of elation. As I continued to whimper, Cindy caressed my cheek and kissed me. And then, preposterously, I laughed for what seemed like an eternity.

CHAPTER SIXTY-FOUR

Rendezvous With Catherine

I awakened under the covers of Cindy's bed, a few feet and a looming question mark from the sleeping bag unfurled on the bedroom floor. I was alone in the room. The time appearing on her clock radio, 1:45 P.M., probably explained my solitude.

I'd survived, even reveled, in my acid trip, but now I craved a modicum of normalcy—as well as a bite to eat. So I showered, dressed, and descended three flights of stairs in search of sustenance.

Cindy greeted me like an adventurer lately returned from some faraway jungle. "Welcome back!" she gushed as I entered the kitchen. Her smile was indecipherable. "I've got *Macroshit* or flax seed granola. Pick your poison." What I would have given for a bowl of Cheerios.

I reluctantly chose the birdseed. I itched to ask Cindy how I'd wound up in her bed, but reconsidered as the words were about to form on my lips. Better I don't know.

"What's on your agenda for this lovely Saturday afternoon?"

"I'd like to look up an old friend," I said, spooning the granola haltingly into my wary mouth. I asked for a phone and a phone book; she pointed me toward an alcove in a corner of the kitchen.

I hesitated, questioning the wisdom of what I was about to do. It'd been two-and-a-half years since I'd received the painful farewell letter Catherine had written from San Francisco. There was no assurance she was even still here.

There were two Catherine O'Mearas in the directory. I dialed the first; a man answered.

"Uh . . . hi . . . could I please speak with Catherine?" My heart was racing in anticipation.

"Who's calling?" the voice inquired.

"Tell her it's Charlie Meyer." I heard footsteps and chatter in the background. The wait seemed eternal.

"So it's 'Charlie' now?" Catherine said with evident pleasure. "Is that really you?" My heart leapt at the sound of her voice. "Where are you?"

"Right here in San Francisco. Wondered if I could stop by and say hello."

"Hold on a sec, Charlie." She conferred with her mystery man while I fiddled with the phone cord. "Could you meet me in an hour at the coffee shop on the southwest corner of Union and Columbus, just across from Washington Square Park? I can't stay long, but I'd love to see you!"

Of course I'd meet her. Anywhere, anytime.

Until this moment, I hadn't actually asked myself why I'd had the sudden urge to see Catherine again. Was I still infatuated with her? Was it the desire of a grateful pupil to salute the tutor who'd ushered him from clumsy boyhood into manhood? Maybe I longed to reveal the older, wiser version of the Charles Meyer she remembered. Or was it assurance I sought—assurance that she'd finally found the serenity and happiness that had eluded her for so long?

Cindy nodded, smiling mischievously, when I asked if I might stay one more night. I refused to even think about what that meant.

Catherine was already at the coffee shop when I arrived, sitting alone with a cup of coffee at an outdoor table. The shop was perched on a sunny corner, well ventilated by gentle ocean breezes drifting in from the Embarcadero. Coit Tower loomed up behind us.

She was as beautiful as I had remembered. Her blond hair was much shorter now and her precisely clipped bangs obscured the scar on her forehead. Her delft blue eyes were still spellbinding. She wore a pleasingly short, form-fitting, black dress that confirmed she had plans for the evening.

She didn't recognize me until I walked up to greet her. Her smile was radiant. She stood up and we embraced warmly.

"You've put on some hair since I last saw you." She laughed. "But you look great." She motioned me to sit down. "What brings you to San Francisco?"

I filled her in on my roadtrip, my narrative punctuated every so often by the rumble of a passing bus or motorcycle. "I couldn't pass up the chance to see you." I flagged down the waiter to order a coffee.

I asked how she'd been. She lifted her cup to her lips, took a sip, and replaced it in her saucer. "Terrific," she said. "I've got a great job downtown in hospital administration and, as you might have inferred from our phone call, a boyfriend." George was a divorced lawyer she'd met on a blind date the previous fall. "He has two great kids, a boy, 11 and a girl, 8, who live with his ex. We moved in together three months ago. You'd like him."

"So you're happy?"

"I haven't been this happy for a very long time." I savored those words.

Catherine drew admiring glances from the male passersby. Justifiably so. The slightly more pronounced crow's feet around the corners of her eyes, which imparted an endearing air of distinction, were the only signs of the passage of time.

"And how about you, Charles?" She caught herself. "Sorry—it's 'Charlie' now, right?"

"It always was 'Charlie'," I admitted sheepishly. "I figured that 'Charles' sounded a little more . . . sophisticated."

"I knew that," she said, laughing. "The Roths had always called you Charlie—said everybody did. So I played along . . . I didn't want to embarrass you." I couldn't help but smile.

"Well, to answer your question," I began, pausing briefly as the waiter delivered my coffee, "I've gone from that bumbling idiot . . . you remember, the jerk who vomited all over his girlfriend's breasts . . . to a guy with three wonderful women in my life."

"I hope you're not going to blame me for *that*!" She laughed again.

"Nah . . . but my dilemma would hardly have been plausible without you."

I couldn't begin to count the number of times I'd replayed in my mind the precious details of that last evening we'd spent together. I was well aware of the transformative effect it had on me, yet I often puzzled over the genesis of that night.

"Catherine," I said, cautiously sipping the steaming hot liquid, "there's something I've often wondered about . . . regarding that night." I hesitated, searching for the proper way to phrase the delicate question I wanted to ask. "Why—"

"—did I choose to take you into my bed?" She'd read my mind.

"Yes." I exhaled deeply. Catherine pursed her lips as she prepared to address my long-simmering question.

"After I'd invited you for dinner, I thought long and hard about how to repay you for all you'd done for me." She took another sip of her coffee, then gently patted her lips with her napkin. "I knew you were probably infatuated with me, but your concern for me . . . your love and caring . . ." Her voice crackled with emotion. "I *adored* you," she said. "But at the same time, Charlie, you were a *very* confused eighteen-year-old struggling mightily with your sexuality and your place in the world."

I shuddered to recall my naïveté.

"Sex was your Achilles heel," she said. "It sabotaged all your relationships." She glanced down at her cup, then back up at me. "I wanted to help you conquer your fears and insecurities . . . give you the knowledge and confidence you'd need to tackle the romantic possibilities that college would offer." She turned silent for a moment. "But I was *petrified* . . ."

"Of what?"

"That what I was contemplating could be misconstrued . . . or backfire. The prospect of sleeping with an impressionable young man half my age was daunting. New Liberty's a small town—and if anyone found out . . ." Catherine looked at me with those mesmerizing eyes. "Yet I knew . . . in my heart . . . you'd be discreet . . . that you wouldn't perceive me as a predator—or a conquest." She looked at me tenderly. "But at the same time, I didn't want to lead you on and hurt you."

She inhaled deeply. "I wanted so badly to give you something meaningful before we parted—something as meaningful and heartfelt as the gift you'd given me." She pierced my soul with those eyes. "I owed you more than that, Charlie, but I gave you that night . . . it was all I had to offer."

I struggled to contain the tears welling up in my eyes. I realized now what a risk she'd taken, and how much she'd cared for me. I reached across the table and squeezed her hand. "That night was the turning point in my life, and I loved you for it—I'll always love you for it."

Catherine's eyes grew moist, but she managed to tame her emotions. We spent a few more minutes catching up while finishing our coffees. She beamed as I described, however briefly, the women in my life. I knew she was happy for me.

"You have a big heart, Charlie. Trust it and you'll find your way." It was the same advice that Doris had given me.

"I hope you're not upset with me for tracking you down," I said with a hint of embarrassment. "You were pretty clear in your letter that you preferred I stay away."

"Not at all," she said. "The situation was different then, and you were in a much different place. I'm delighted to see what a fine young man you've become—though I do think you'd benefit from a shave and a haircut," she said with a grin.

"I'll take that under advisement."

"I wish I had more time, but George and I have a function to attend this evening. Are you staying in town for a while?"

"I'm heading back east in the morning."

"Well . . . good luck, then. And thanks so much for coming. You'll always be extraordinarily special to me."

We both stood up. We hugged again, more tightly this time. I think I detected a tear in her eye as she kissed my cheek. Mine streamed down copiously as I turned and walked away.

CHAPTER SIXTY-FIVE

A Letter to My Lovers

*D*ear Annie, Julianna & Clare-
    This is exceptional weed I'm smoking. Best ever! Arnie, the hippie freak who picked me up just east of Reno, calls it Iowa Gold. He grows this shit on a commune where he lives with a bunch of his freak-buddies someplace along the Iowa River. That's where we're heading in his big, old Dodge van. Iowa Gold is his cash crop. The commune runs on the profit he makes by selling the shit in Reno. Capitalism at work!

We're somewhere in Wyoming now. Or maybe Nebraska. Might as well be on the moon for all the desolation around us. And the sky is so BIG! These massive cumulus clouds just float over the barren landscape—like the smoke I'm puffing from this reefer. They're like lily pads on the surface of a calm lake, only I'm the frog peering up at them from below. Far out! Did I really write 'far out'?

Sent you all postcards before leaving San Fran. The usual crap: "Having a great time, wish you were here, Charlie." What did you expect me to write? I wasn't high at the time, so I'd the good sense to tell you nothing. I mean, really, how can you expect me to tell you about the fucked-up family in Nowheresville, Texas who got me plastered on moonshine so a mother-and-daughter tag team could hijack my dick in the middle of the night and ride me like a pony on a merry-go-round? Or the rather sweet, plump girl who put me up in her bedroom for two nights in Haight-Ashbury and took me on an acid trip? Woke up in her bed one morning and still don't remember how. I could tell you all about my adventures, but it would take more than the back of a postcard.

But now I want to come home. Yeah, it's been an incredible journey, but I miss each and every one of you. I'd endure a week or two of the circus at my house in New Liberty just to be able to swing by to see you, Annie, to hold you in my arms and taste your sweet lesbian lips again. And Julianna, I'd pop up to Scarsdale to visit you, if you're not already in the slammer, to catch up on what I've missed for too long now—your curvaceous body beside me, that sweet and sassy disposition. Then, on Wednesday, I'd hightail it up to New Hampshire, dear Clare, for our weekly lunch. We could order that sausage pizza, then replay the highlights of our night at the Tee Pee.

Fuck! Who am I kidding? I love you all, goddammit, and it's tearing me apart! Izzy tells me I'm nuts, that I've got to make up my mind. I'm in love with Annie the Lesbian, Julianna the Jailbird and Clare, the hot married lady with the adorable little kid and the boozing mom. The jukebox of my mind keeps repeating the lyrics from that damn song Izzy keeps playing for me:

> Then you bet you'd better finally decide
> And say yes to one and let the other one ride
> There's so many changes and tears you must hide
> Did you ever have to finally decide?

That day of reckoning is coming soon, I know, but the thought of choosing one of you, if you'd all still have me, is like having to choose which limbs to lop off (for the record, the pecker doesn't count as a limb—just saying).

I embarked on this odyssey, in part, to escape my predicament for a while. If I'm not near you, I don't have to juggle or choose. But out of sight is hardly out of mind. I told Cindy (she's the one I must have laid at least once, judging from the impish grin on her face that morning—courtesy, I suspect, of that beautifully bent boner of mine) that I hoped I'd find an epiphany of sorts—some profound moment of perfect wisdom in which the solution to my convoluted romantic dilemma would be revealed. Well, I'm still seeking that epiphany.

Between Arnie and me, we've been driving almost eighteen straight hours now. Haven't slept (you know what that's like, don't you Clare?) and this weed is keeping me up. You know, of course, I won't send this letter to any of you, let alone all three. But it's served its purpose—allowing me to slice through the fog in my brain, vacuuming the dust bunnies from the corners of my mind.

Be home soon. Love to you all.

Charlie

CHAPTER SIXTY-SIX

The Eggplant Chronicles

Arnie steered the old van down the pockmarked country lane and onto the muddy driveway that led to the farmhouse. Fresh puddles bore witness to a recent downpour. We were in rural Iowa, about fifty miles west of Cedar Rapids, totally off the grid. No neighbors for miles. One could hardly imagine a more perfect place to grow weed.

The farmhouse was an early twentieth century relic. It was a big, inviting home with a massive hip roof cleaved by a wide central dormer, like a Cyclops with an eyebrow. A covered porch hugged three sides of the building. Green shutters flanked the windows. It was elegant in its simplicity. About a hundred yards to the west, the Iowa River flowed lazily by while mature apple trees and fields of assorted fruits and vegetables held sway in random patches around the dwelling.

The storm clouds had receded into the distance revealing a bright, late afternoon sun. Arnie's housemates were picking vegetables on the east side of the house when our van pulled up.

Arnie had warned me in advance: a few of his housemates might berate him for entrusting me with knowledge of their marijuana operation. He'd been cavalier about his "sixth sense" when it came to judging people like me. He urged me to take their indifference with a grain of salt. They'd come around, he assured me.

Our arrival drew an audience.

"Guys, this is Charlie, a college kid from back east," Arnie announced as we stepped from the van. "Picked him up hitchhiking near Reno." I greeted them warily before they introduced themselves.

"Charlie shared the driving," Arnie told his housemates. "So I said he could stay the night." Two of them, introduced to me as David and Mike, cast icy stares.

After an awkward silence, David spoke up. "Sure, man, no problem." He looked in the direction of a seriously pregnant brunette in a peasant dress. "Faith, why don't you show Charlie around and set him up in the guest room."

David and Mike drew Arnie aside for his inevitable dressing down. "How do you know he's not a narc?" I overheard David protest as I shadowed Faith up the porch steps and into the house.

I counted eight participants in the commune, five males and three females, all in their twenties or early thirties. The house was as unpretentious inside as it was out. After a quick tour, Faith led me to a small guest bedroom at the rear of the first floor.

She urged me to make myself comfortable and join the "Family," as she called them, for dinner in half an hour. I couldn't help but notice the difficulty with which she carried her prodigious prenatal payload.

"When are you due?" I asked. It's a question I'd normally avoid for fear of misinterpreting the significance of ponderous poundage, but there was no mistaking Faith's condition.

"Tomorrow," she grunted. "It's tomorrow or bust."

Arnie wore a chastened look upon rejoining the Family in the dining room for dinner. Despite the awkwardness, I was overjoyed by the prospect of a home-cooked meal and a private bed in pleasant and comfortable surroundings.

Dinner was a sweeping take on a common theme. Eggplant ragu was served along with stuffed roasted eggplant and eggplant fries. The meal was a collaboration of the women, one of whom, poor pregnant Faith, was a veritable eggplant herself. "Bet you can't guess what we picked today," quipped one of my hosts.

While the women cleaned up in the kitchen after dinner, I excused myself to retrieve my backpack. I sifted through my dirty clothes for the liquor bottle. I'd decided to use it as a peace offering to counter the ambivalence to my presence at the farm.

"Anyone care for a shot of genuine moonshine?" I asked, returning to the dining room with the Clapp Family hooch. Interest abounded. "It was a going-away present from a family of Texas rednecks. It knocked me on my ass, so fair warning."

"I'll get some glasses," Mike said, scurrying into the kitchen. He returned with six shot glasses, each of which I filled.

"Remember, it's lethal . . ."

David took a gulp, winced, then broke out in a broad grin. "*Shee—it!*"

"First one bites you," I laughed, "but the next one goes down easier."

"God *damn!*" cried Arnie, grimacing while the others cackled.

The bottle barely lasted three rounds. But by then, the six of us were bosom buddies, sharing war stories and relating sexual exploits like drunken frat boys. Arnie's sins were forgiven, and I was no longer the unwelcome guest.

CHAPTER SIXTY-SEVEN

The Neat Feat in the Backseat

When I awakened the next morning, the house and grounds were deserted but for Faith, Mike, and me. Faith was at work in the kitchen while Mike had begun the strawberry harvest on a patch immediately behind the farmhouse. Faith explained the regular Tuesday regimen: the housemates awaken early, divide into two teams, load the Dodge van and a small pickup with excess fruits and vegetables, and embark on their weekly circuit of local groceries and farmers' markets to sell produce and stock up on provisions for the coming week. Faith was in no condition to participate, and Mike remained behind to keep an eye on Faith.

After a bowl of Faith's house granola (containing, to my relief, no eggplant), I approached Mike and offered to pitch in on the harvest in exchange for another night of lodging. My offer was enthusiastically accepted.

Mike was a bright, bookish guy with sandy hair and wire-rimmed spectacles. He'd been an English major at Purdue before becoming disaffected by politics, the war, and his prospects in academia.

"I needed a good long break," he said as he flipped a handful of berries into a wood-splint basket. He described how he'd met David at Purdue and become enamored of his self-sustaining, earth-based philosophy of life. David dropped out when his grandfather died and left him the farm, Mike explained. "Arnie and the others connected by various means, and the eight of us have been together here now for three years."

I marveled at Mike's strawberry-picking technique. He grasped the stem just above the berry between his thumbnail and forefinger, yanked gently with a slight twisting motion, let the berry roll into his palm, and then repeated the process with both hands until several berries had accumulated in each of his palms.

I asked Mike how the Family came into the drug trade.

"At first, we couldn't make ends meet," he told me. "Then Arnie suggested we grow some weed on the side. He'd raised and dealt some pot in a past life. After a bit of soul-searching, we decided to give it a try."

"And . . ."

"And it solved our money problems—and then some. We've even deposited a slug of our excess profits into a trust fund for Faith's child."

"Speaking of which, who's the lucky father?"

"We all are," Mike said. I gave him a quizzical look.

"We've got a very liberal sexual policy here. Family members are free to do as they please—but with no expectation of exclusivity," Mike explained as I butchered his berry-picking technique. "Family membership is a commitment. So the reality is that while any of the five of us *could* be the biological father, it doesn't matter whose particular sperm penetrated the egg. Faith's welfare and the child's welfare are the Family's responsibility and its collective good fortune."

"What if David decides one day to evict you?"

"Not an issue. He's already transferred the property into an irrevocable trust for the benefit of the eight of us and any of our offspring."

I diverted a plump berry into my mouth. "And what if the drug operation gets shut down?"

"What if the river floods us or a tornado destroys us? We'll take it as it comes," Mike said. "Life offers no guarantees, here or anywhere else."

Mike and I returned to the fields after a quick lunch prepared by Faith. Shortly afterward, an ear-piercing shriek rang out from the house. We made a beeline through the back door and into the kitchen where we'd left Faith just minutes earlier. She was clutching a kitchen chair in terror, a puddle of water at her feet.

"My water broke!"

"I'll get your bag," Mike said. "Charlie, help Faith to the front door while I bring the car around."

I helped Faith down the porch steps to where Mike had parked his old Chevy sedan. I made her as comfortable as I could in the back seat and sat beside her, grasping her hand. "Everything's gonna be fine," I assured her, "you're right on schedule." When the car door closed, Mike floored it.

"Take it easy, Mike," I urged as the car bounded over the gullies and potholes along the driveway.

"Uh, guys?" Faith whispered, "I'm having contractions . . ."

"How far apart?" I asked reflexively. I had no idea what significance her answer might have.

"I don't know," Faith whined. "Maybe two or three minutes?"

"How far to the hospital?" I asked Mike.

"Forty minutes."

"Are you kidding me?"

"Oh, SHIT!" Faith cried. "This is a fucking big one!" She winced, clutching her abdomen in obvious discomfort. "It won't fucking end!"

"Damn, Faith," Mike said. "I've never heard you utter a curse word in the three years I've known you!"

"I haven't been in the back seat of a fucking car forty fucking minutes from a fucking hospital having fucking contractions before, goddammit!"

"Breathe!" I said.

"What the fuck do you think I'm doing? Can't you drive this heap any faster, Mike?" A minute or so later, Faith grimaced in agony. "Oooow! Damn! God! Another one!"

"You had one about a minute ago," I said.

"No shit, Sherlock!" she shot back.

"That can't be good," Mike chimed in from the front seat as we careened down the snaking two-lane highway.

"Watch the road!" Faith said. "DAMN! Another one! Oh, my God! Feels like an elephant pouncing on my bladder!"

"Oh, shit," Mike moaned.

We were barely halfway to the hospital by this point. "Mike," I said, "I think we need to do something. I'm not sure we're gonna make it in time."

"What the heck do you know about delivering babies?" Mike was screaming now. "You can barely pick fucking strawberries!"

Faith went into moan overdrive. "I think it wants out, NOW!"

"Pull over, Mike!" I said. Then I looked Faith in the eyes. "This can't be that hard, Faith. Let's just take it easy and let it happen the way it's supposed to."

"It's supposed to happen in the fucking... oooooh!... hospital, goddammit!" Tears of pain and terror welled in the corners of her eyes. "Mike, Charlie's right. I think... ooooowwwww!... I think we need to do this now!"

Mike pulled the car to the side of the road. "Got any towels in the car?" I asked him.

"What do you think this is, a goddamn linen closet?"

"How about a blanket?"

"Might be one in the trunk. I'll look."

Mike got out of the car and searched the trunk.

"Can I pull off your underwear?" I asked Faith as sensitively as possible, recognizing how foolish it sounded.

"I'm not sure this is the best time to get frisky," she said, injecting a modicum of levity amid the pandemonium. "Do it!" she yelled while contorted in pain over the next contraction.

This was not going to be pretty, I thought, as I removed her underwear, still soaked from the breaking of her water.

"Here's the blanket," Mike said, showing little disposition to delve more deeply into the bedlam of backseat birthing.

It was too dark in the back of the car to see what I was doing. "Do you have a flashlight?" I asked him.

"Are you kidding me?"

"I've got to see what the hell I'm doing, Mike! Get me a fucking flashlight already!" I said. "Do you have any soap, water or alcohol of any kind in the car?"

"No!" Mike said in a growing panic.

"How about windshield washer fluid?"

"There's some in the trunk. What the heck for?"

"It's mostly alcohol. I've gotta clean my hands for this as best I can." Mike returned from the trunk with the washer fluid and poured it over my outstretched hands. The back seat was never going to be the same.

Faith was now yelping and moaning incessantly. "How are you holding up?" I asked, more calmly now. Some unrecognizable force was kicking in from deep inside me. I suddenly felt in control; the panic was dissipating. "Breathe," I implored her. "Are you comfortable?"

"You try giving birth in the back seat of the car and see how comfortable *you* are, dammit!"

"Try lying down. Put your head on that seat cushion there and get into the most comfortable position you can. Stay calm, Faith. We're gonna do this."

Mike was staring at us rigidly from the front seat, fear in his eyes. "Mike," I said, "why don't you try flagging down a passing driver. Maybe we'll get lucky and find someone who either knows what he's doing or can get to a phone to call an ambulance. But stay within earshot in case I need you."

I lifted Faith's skirt and focused the flashlight between her legs. I thought I detected a blood-tinged patch of hairy skin beginning to poke its way through. This was not what I normally hoped to see in this region of a woman's anatomy.

"I can't hold back any more," Faith said. "I'm going to push! Ooooowwww!"

"That's good," I said. "Push. That's it. Keep going. Breathe. You're doing great. I think I see the baby's head!"

I could hear voices out on the road. Mike had flagged down a local who, as best I could tell, drove off to seek help.

Faith pushed between her rapid contractions. I watched intently as the baby's head poked all the way through. Instinctively, I cradled the baby's head and let Faith's contractions push the little bugger further and further until *he* ("It's a boy!" I cried out in utter exhilaration) slid into my waiting hands like a center's snap to his quarterback. Faith let out an enormous sigh of relief and euphoria as the reality of her son's birth set in. She was physically and emotionally spent. Tears of joy were flowing like rivers from her bloodshot eyes.

And here I was, holding this slimy, slippery, incredibly precious little child in my hands. I was stunned, elated, and clueless as to what to do next. I wrapped the baby in the blanket, careful not to tangle his umbilical cord, and handed him gently to Faith. She promptly drew him to her chest and cuddled him. The baby began to cry, softly at first and then with more vigor. We both assumed this was a good thing, and it was.

"Welcome to the world, James," Faith said, smiling broadly at her newborn son. "You're beautiful!"

Just when I thought we were done, a mass of bloody matter slithered out of Faith's busy vagina. This was not pretty and yet another reason why Mike's back seat will never be the same.

"Eeeuwww!" I said, involuntarily. "What the fuck?"

"It's the placenta," Faith said calmly as she gently stroked little James. "It's normal, Charlie. Breathe!" she said, laughing.

We heard the sound of an approaching siren. An ambulance screeched to a halt directly behind us. Two paramedics hustled over. I stepped out of the car to let them attend to mother and newborn son. It was only then that I was struck dumb by the enormity of what had occurred. I thought also at that moment of the fate of the twins I'd created with Annie. I considered the fact that I, too, was the product of an unplanned and unwelcome pregnancy. My emotions were muddled and contradictory. I shuddered, laughed, then started to cry, whimpering in harmony with the baby I'd just delivered.

CHAPTER SIXTY-EIGHT

Couch Potato

While the ambulance carried Faith and James to the hospital, Mike and I followed in his birth-ravaged Chevy. Mother and child were doing just fine, but the doctors wanted to observe them for a day or two as a precaution. Mike called the house to spread the news. Before long there were ten of us, including James, plus a tower of eggplant pizzas, crowding Faith's tiny hospital room.

At the Family's invitation, I stayed another two nights at the farmhouse, helping in the fields during the day and enjoying the Family's camaraderie at night. I was accorded hero status that first day. Faith wasn't there to counter the hyperbole with which Mike and I described my primeval delivery techniques. When Faith and James came home the next day, James took over as the main attraction.

I'd experienced a lifetime's worth of implausible and outlandish adventures during my remarkable cross-country odyssey. But now I longed for a return to familiar faces, old haunts, the comfort of my own bed. I was already halfway home. I'd spent little for lodging on my journey, so with the money I'd saved, I splurged on a bus ticket from Cedar Rapids to New York. Though wary of bus rides since my sojourn with the Spirit of the Smelly Bus, this offered the prospect of rest and reflection, free of the anxieties of flagging down the next ride or securing a safe place to crash for the night. Arnie gave me a ride to the Cedar Rapids bus station and, as a parting gift, a generous supply of Iowa Gold.

The bus ride was mind-numbing—nearly twenty-four hours, with stops in Indianapolis and Pittsburgh. I slept fitfully. As I gazed from my window at the smoke-belching factories of the Rust Belt, I realized how much I already missed the vast and spectacular vistas of the West. The majesty of the mountains, the spaciousness of the prairies, and the enormity of the bright blue skies had been a revelation.

My mind wandered. I thought of the diverse individuals whose lives I had touched and whose lives had touched mine. Truck drivers, farmers, hippies, dropouts, and even peddlers of horsemeat earned my admiration, empathy, and respect. And yet everything paled in comparison with the transcendent feeling of cradling a newborn child in my trembling hands.

When the bus at long last approached the outskirts of New York City, I drifted back to the personal concerns I had so willfully neglected as I hitchhiked across America: the choice of a career, a Vietnam strategy, a surfeit of lovers. As I'd learned in the back seat of that Chevy, life has an uncanny knack of finding its own way, like rain trickling into a stream, in spite of the obstacles in its path. I'd tackle some of these challenges head-on in the months to come. Others would sort themselves out in ways I could have never imagined.

My bus pulled into the Port Authority Bus Terminal at 42nd Street in New York City in the late afternoon. I retrieved my backpack and caught the connecting bus to New Liberty.

I was surprised at how happy I was to see Mom, Hermie, and even Dad. Mom wanted to know absolutely everything about my journey. She'd never been outside the Northeast and longed to share my experiences vicariously. So I regaled her with a highly whitewashed version. I substituted phantom buses for the rides I'd thumbed and chaste lodging descriptions for the X-rated ones. My acid trip became a quiet night on Fisherman's Wharf. Dad, I suspect, had an inkling that the truth was edgier but probably preferred, at least this once, to leave well enough alone. I saved the baby delivery episode for last. Mom was awestruck.

"I'm so proud of you, dear!"

Dad, naturally, was less impressed. "It's bad enough to be Mister Prissy Art History Major," he groused, "but now you're moonlighting as the Merry Midwestern Midwife!"   .

Hermie was incredulous when I shared with him the unexpurgated versions of the tales I'd laundered for parental consumption.

I spent the first week following my return lying on the living room couch, basking in the glow of the brand new color TV set that Dad had recently purchased. I craved the mindless time without an agenda. I'd have stripped to my underwear and smoked a joint, but that would have been an affront to my mother.

I rarely arose before noon. At around two, Mom would repeat the same question: "Charlie, are you gonna sit in front of the TV all day again today?"

"Yup," I'd respond, buying myself a few more hours of lethargy without interruption or guilt.

After a week of unadulterated sloth, I was thoroughly refreshed and ready to resume my life. I began with a visit to Annie.

Annie had been spending several days a week in New York City on advertising shoots, modeling for ads targeted to women. "Maria's got a friend who works for a modeling agency," she explained. "She passed on my photo and I got a call."

I certainly understood the appeal. Annie was a natural for any product promoting that wholesome, girl-next-door image. "I'll buy whatever you're selling," I said.

"Right, Charlie. You never know when you'll need a tampon."

But I couldn't, or perhaps didn't want to, see Annie living what I imagined as the rarefied life of a model. "Do you actually like it?"

"It's not easy work," she admitted. "You sit around for hours in make-up . . . then pose under hot, bright lights. But the girls are nice, the pay's fantastic, and it's all so glamorous."

My brain was doing somersaults. *The girls are nice, she said!* If it were Julianna, I'd be scared to death that she'd be hit on by some lothario lurking behind the bright lights, ready to pounce at the first opportunity. But this was Annie, so I worried instead that a drop-dead gorgeous *female* model would sweep her off her lovely lesbian feet.

"And on top of it all," Annie said, "they comp you on the products you advertise. I've got cartons of Ivory Soap . . . and enough Kotex to last until menopause."

When we got around to my roadtrip, I offered up another sanitized rendition of Charlie's Cross-Country Chronicles. But I hesitated when the narrative reached Iowa. How would Annie react to The Neat Feat in the Backseat? Recalling my own contradictory emotions, I chose not to chance it.

No sooner had I returned from my reunion with Annie, than I dialed Julianna in Scarsdale.

"What the fuck, Charlie?" stood in for hello. "Weeks on the lam and all I get is a stupid 'having a great time, wish you were here' postcard of the Golden Gate Bridge?"

"They didn't have one for my bordello."

"You couldn't drop a dime for a call?"

"It would have been long distance, requiring vast quantities of change. And I didn't have the number for your cellblock in Springfield."

"Hah! Funny," she said sarcastically. "So how was it?"

"Let's see, I was ravished by a mother and daughter in the house of a horsemeat trader in Texas, took an LSD trip in Haight-Ashbury, and delivered a baby in the back seat of a Chevy outside a pot-growing commune in Iowa."

She laughed. "No, really."

"I actually did deliver that baby," I told her proudly.

"Gimme a break."

Though she'd eventually acknowledge the likely veracity of my LSD narrative and the Neat Feat in the Back Seat, I let the tall tale of Texas succumb to its own implausibility.

Living at home while visiting girlfriends in similar circumstances severely cramped my style. So, while I spent quality time over the next few weeks with both Annie and Julianna, it was all conversation and, as Dad might have said, no "compilation." The allure of New Liberty was fading; I had to get away.

Though classes were still a month off, I decided to return to SciFi. I'd check in with Clare, then complement my cross-country idyll with a voyage north. I'd never been to Canada, and as I'd yet to dismiss the Canadian solution to my Vietnam quandary, some reconnaissance was surely in order.

CHAPTER SIXTY-NINE

The Arsonist

Clare was more than willing to forgo lunch at Tony's for a tryst in my room at SciFi. It was the nourishment both of us needed. She looked great in her white babydoll top and faded jeans. She looked even better without them. We talked during halftime of our exuberant, two-condom afternoon.

"Is this why you returned to school a month early?" Clare asked me as she lay on my little twin bed beneath *Untitled (Red Square No. 1)*. She wore nothing but a seductive grin. Her question answered itself.

"So tell me about your cross-country trek. Your droll San Francisco postcard didn't cut it."

"I get that," I said before launching into my account. The beauty of this telling was that it was the truth, the whole truth, and nothing but. Unsurprisingly, Clare didn't believe a word of it either. So I changed the subject.

"I've got a proposition for you," I said, twisting to face her under the disheveled bed sheets. "There's a rock concert called Strawberry Fields in about ten days near Toronto. I thought I'd check out our great northern neighbor ... on the outside chance I'd spend the rest of my life there evading the draft. Care to accompany me?"

"First of all," she chided me, "living in Canada for the rest of your life is not the same as attending a summer rock concert. And secondly, I really can't go," she said definitively. "I'm not comfortable leaving Hope with Mom for an entire weekend."

"Is she drinking again?"

"Yes."

"Sorry to hear that."

"Me too."

"I'll give you a raincheck on the roadtrip. But you can make it up to me now," I said, directing her attention to my growing, albeit contorted, erection. And so the second half began.

I was determined to attend Strawberry Fields. If Clare couldn't go, I'd ask Julianna. "Can't, Charlie, but have a good time," she said. I knew it wasn't Annie's thing, but I endured her rejection as well. Then I had a brainstorm: why not ask the one person in Canada I actually knew, sweet and petite Brigitte, my sexy French soufflé from Montreal?

I dialed the number she'd given me when we parted a year earlier in Williamstown. A male voice answered, in French.

"Brigitte, uh, s'il vous plaît?" I stammered with guidance from an English-French dictionary I'd borrowed from one of my brothers. I had no idea what he said in response, but a few seconds later, a familiar voice came on the line.

"C'est Brigitte."

"Brigitte, it's Charlie Meyer. From last summer at the Clark?"

"Charlie!" She seemed as pleased to hear my voice as I was to hear hers. "How could I possibly forget you?" she said in her still heavily accented but deliciously provocative English. "You're the guy with the crooked cock, no?"

"And I didn't think the French had a sense of humor."

We exchanged pleasantries for a few minutes during which

I established two critical facts: the male voice was her brother's, and her boyfriend Marcel was now her ex-boyfriend Marcel. So I invited her to join me at Strawberry Fields.

"Oui, oui!" she chirped. "I would love it to join you!" It was as simple as that. I love the French. "We will have fun, no?"

"Oui, oui," I parroted. She agreed to contribute her brother's pup tent and gave me her address in Montreal.

No sooner had I hung up than I began to feel guilty, like I was cheating on someone. The referee had just thrown the yellow flag. What was that all about? It wasn't Clare I'd be cheating on. With Clare there were no egos to bruise, no pretense of exclusivity or commitment. *Win one for the Gipper!* she'd urge me.

It wasn't Annie, either. While I apparently occupied an exclusive position within the select category of Annie's male lovers, she had never foreclosed her pursuit of lesbian liaisons. She'd never demanded any commitment from me nor I of her.

Then there was Julianna. The assumptions of nonexclusivity applicable to Clare and Annie didn't apply to Julianna. By default, the 'normal rules' applied. Where was the rulebook? Where was Moses when you needed him? Although neither Julianna nor I had ever even intimated that our relationship was exclusive, I'd amply demonstrated my jealous disdain for competition by my Neanderthal reaction to Simon Allison the Turd. Did that render any dalliance with Brigitte (or, for that matter, the continuation of my intimate relationships with Annie or Clare) a rules infraction as to Julianna? *Fifteen yards for illegal intercourse? Illegal use of the penis—half the distance to the goal line?* Did the 'normal rules' require disclosure? I wasn't stupid enough to risk alienating Julianna by telling her I was sleeping with three other women. I came by each of those relationships honestly, or so it seemed to me.

It appeared that I had three choices: don't sleep with Brigitte, Annie or Clare; tell Julianna I was fucking them all and obtain her blessing; or just deal with my fucking guilt. This was a no-brainer: I'd deal with the guilt. I knew I was playing with fire. But was I an innocent bystander or a crazed arsonist?

CHAPTER SEVENTY

The Gendarme and the Baguette

It was almost too easy. I made it all the way to the Vermont/Quebec border in just two rides, the latter from an attractive pair of female, thirty-something, French-Canadian schoolteachers returning from a rambunctious vacation in the Big Apple. And while I imagined they were entertaining thoughts of the authentic French-Canadian *ménage a trois* we might enjoy together that evening, I was adamant it wasn't going to happen. Any other time, maybe. But not this time—I figured that Brigitte alone would provide me more excitement that night than an entire busload of horny schoolteachers.

The benefit of travelling with a couple of wholesome-looking young ladies in a car bearing Quebec plates became clear at the border. A VW van bearing New Hampshire plates and adorned with painted peace symbols was stopped ahead of us. While its scruffy, longhaired occupants were grilled and searched for contraband, the admiring guard waved my lovely hostesses right on through. That was particularly fortunate, since I'd stashed a well-stuffed pouch of Iowa Gold in my briefs.

Montreal was a much larger, more vibrant city than I had imagined. Glistening skyscrapers dominated the skyline.

French signage tyrannized its English counterparts like schoolyard bullies. The city had shimmering nightclubs, classy restaurants, and even its own home-grown terrorist organization, le Front de Libération du Québec, a leftist paramilitary group hoping to bomb its way to an independent French Quebec. What more could an American draft dodger conceivably want?

When we reached my destination, my hostesses pleaded with me to reconsider my plans for the evening. I suspected that they'd misinterpreted the import of the bulge in my briefs. I demurred, thanking them for their hospitality and assuring them that if it weren't for the fact that I planned to fuck my brains out with Brigitte, I'd have been happy to do the same with them. They left their phone numbers in case I changed my mind and bade me a fond adieu.

Brigitte and her brother, Philippe, lived on the top floor of a stone triplex on St. Antoine Street in the tony Westmount neighborhood northwest of downtown Montreal. Brigitte welcomed me into her stylish apartment with a charming smile and an enthusiastic hug. Her dark brown hair was perhaps a little longer than I remembered, but the sight of her thrilled me now as much as it had in my little room at Wilson Manor in Williamstown. She was as tempting as a chocolate éclair in her shimmering deep purple blouse and tight blue jeans.

"Come in, Charlie! I am hardly recognizing you!" she said, gesturing at my long hair and brushing her hand playfully over my beard. I still adored her train-wreck English.

"Saving a bundle on barbers and razor blades," I joked.

"I want for you to meet my brother, Philippe," she said, motioning toward a stocky, dour Frenchman with pencil-thin lips, a long square chin, and Brigitte's dark hair and eyes. Substantially older than Brigitte, he sported an off-putting smirk in counterpoint to Brigitte's delightfully contagious smile. Philippe ignored my outstretched hand and managed but a half-hearted nod.

After her surly brother sauntered off to his room, Brigitte and I caught up. She detailed her breakup with Marcel. She described him as an overly possessive brute who also happened to be Philippe's best friend. Perhaps that explained Philippe's hasty dismissal of me as a substitute suitor for his little sister. Brigitte asked me about Annie. "It's complicated," I said. And when I related my cross-country adventures to her she devoured them with rapt attention, especially the Neat Feat in the Back Seat.

"A *bebe*!" she said. "You are amazing, *mon chéri!*" She was the first to accept my elaborate tale as fact rather than fiction.

"The night, she is young!" Brigitte declared. "Let us go dancing!"

When it came to her work, Brigitte was deadly serious. A nuclear blast couldn't distract her. But when it came to play, she was a mischievous vixen. After a quick bite at a local café, we danced into the early morning hours to a raucous live band at Le Cercle, a local nightclub. Brigitte looked sexy when blowing her nose, so watching her prance and shimmy across the dance floor was a feast. She tantalized half the club, rebuffing at least a dozen guys over the course of the evening. It was all I could do to keep from mounting her on the spot.

When we'd exhausted ourselves, we walked back to her apartment. Despite the late hour, the streets were boisterous. Couples sat on stoops smoking or smooching, teens congregated on street corners in animated conversation, and music poured from open windows.

Much to my surprise and dismay, Philippe was there at two in the morning to greet us like an irate parent. He exchanged a flurry of angry French words with Brigitte. Then he turned to me. "Here!" he said, scowling, throwing a pillow and blanket on the living room sofa, making it crystal clear he wouldn't brook any shenanigans involving his little sister. "This is where you sleep," he said. I could hardly believe it—my dick was the size of a French baguette and this self-proclaimed *gendarme* was detouring all traffic from Brigitte's hungry vagina! I felt like a kid denied cake on his birthday.

Brigitte watched all of this with curious amusement. After the *gendarme* left the room, she explained that her brother was a tad overprotective. *A tad?* He was a one-man chastity police force! Did he think she was a virgin? Or worse, did he know she was a borderline nymphomaniac? Although my drooping chin and flashing eyes telegraphed my agitation, Brigitte calmly urged me to accept my fate. "I promise, Charlie, tomorrow I shall make you forget tonight, okay?" I thought about the possible *ménage a trois* I'd sacrificed to sleep alone on Brigitte's couch. But then I considered the possibilities of the following evening and decided that my crooked baguette and I could defer our gratification for one more lonely night.

CHAPTER SEVENTY-ONE

The Garden of Earthly Delights

On Friday morning, Brigitte and I stuffed a pup tent, a couple of sleeping bags, a blanket, several gallon jugs of water, a box of fruit and sandwiches, some clothes, and an economy-sized box of condoms into the tiny trunk and back seat of her brother's '67 BMW 1600 and headed to the site of the Strawberry Fields Festival in Bowmanville, Ontario, about five hours southwest of Montreal. She never revealed how she managed to negotiate the use of Philippe's car, but I suspect it was part of his penance for acting like a first-class dick the previous night. We arrived at about six, an hour or two before the concert was slated to begin. Tens of thousands preceded us, making it difficult to stake out a spot where we could park the car and set up our tent. We ultimately settled for a small patch of grass near a hillside, along the back edge of a broad valley, amidst a sea of cars, vans, and tents. The stage, surrounded by a horde of humanity, rose up in the distance before us. A marijuana-laced haze hovered over the proceedings like a dense coastal fog.

We decided to pitch the tent first, before the onslaught of dusk. We were about to provide the definitive answer to the eternal question of how many art history majors it takes to pitch a pup tent. We began by smoothing out the ground beneath which the tent would theoretically rise. We neglected to bring a hammer, so I used a rock not only to pound stakes through the various tent loops but also to pummel the bejesus out of my left thumb and index finger. "Merde!" I screamed, in deference to Brigitte. Meanwhile, Brigitte struggled mightily in her attempt to screw the tent poles together. These were obviously not the type of tent poles she most enjoyed screwing. After I helped her get the right tips into the right receptacles, we shoved them into the proper holes at the peaks of the front and back of the tent and stood them upright. It was all way too suggestive, given my frustrations of the previous evening. I then turned to my personal specialty, the guy wires dangling from the peaks of the tent. Guy wires have a tendency to attack my privates, so I was particularly careful to stretch them out in a manner calculated to do the least possible bodily harm. As I pounded a stake into the bottom end of the front guy wire, the tent pole audibly strained, then suddenly snapped, propelling the bottom third of the pole into my crotch like a magnet. "Fucking shit!" I cried, abandoning all efforts at French and reaching between my legs to confirm the survival of my gonads while Brigitte doubled over with laughter. At least a half-dozen neighbors in our little tent city shared Brigitte's amusement.

"Guess we won't need the condoms after all," she said, giggling.

"Maybe this will straighten the damn thing out," I grunted, cradling my balls as I struggled to catch my breath.

At this point, Brigitte did her best damsel-in-distress impression, gesturing to the shirtless master of the elaborate two-person tent that rose up like a mansion beside us. The smug, bare-chested tent-snob proceeded to secure a hammer and some duct tape and, in about four minutes flat, completed the erection of our pup tent. So the answer, apparently, is that it takes two art history majors to erect a pup tent: one to beat himself to shit in a vain attempt to pitch it and one to summon help to complete the job.

By the time the tent was pitched, it was dusk. We could hear the musicians warming up in the distance. Brigitte snared a blanket, I grabbed my weed, and we headed toward the stage, picking our way through the mass of humanity like mice in a maze. We secured a square yard of space to the left of the stage about halfway back into the crowd, spread the blanket, and settled in for the show. The sounds were amazing, especially when filtered through the prism of a pipeful of Iowa Gold. Procol Harum did a killer rendition of *A Whiter Shade of Pale* while the delicate notes emitted by Jethro Tull's flute danced over the throng like a stone skipping across a lake.

Navigating our way back to the tent later that night was a challenge. We dodged thousands of bodies, some awake, some asleep, some stoned beyond belief, as we poked our way through the dark haze. It took us forty-five minutes to reclaim the pup tent that had nearly claimed my manhood. Brigitte and I were spaced out and running on fumes. She was asleep in her sleeping bag before I could even slip into mine. Racked by exhaustion and still recovering from the blow to my privates, I resigned myself to yet another night of chastity.

We awakened on Saturday morning to the earthy sounds and smells of an outsized community picnic. Hordes of young people milled about in various states of undress and the air was thick with the sweet aroma of bacon and eggs simmering over open campfires. Enterprising concertgoers offered fruits, juices, and sandwiches for sale or trade. *Will Trade Food for*

Weed or Smack read a sign on the back of one van; *Chicks Wanted to Ball* recited another. There were few inhibitions in this overnight tent city: men and women shed garments like they were sloughing off mosquitoes, women paraded about topless as if prancing about their own bedrooms.

"Take off your tee-shirt and let's go for a walk," I said to Brigitte with a wry grin.

Brigitte had shapely breasts but was self-conscious about their small size. "I cannot compete," she said, brandishing a mock frown.

"Then wear your shirt and bare your delightful *derriere*," I teased. Again she declined.

We inhaled incense, marijuana, and the lighthearted atmosphere as we strolled randomly through the valley and surrounding hills comprising the festival's three-hundred-acre site. A Ferris wheel inexplicably plopped in the midst of the valley epitomized the carnival aura. Trailers furnished free food and tanker trucks normally used for dairy transport were repurposed to dispense fresh water. The concert's promoters provided portable lavatories as well as medical tents and hundreds of barrels for trash. The festival was largely devoid of the problems that had plagued Woodstock the previous year, and the mood was universally positive.

It was, however, searingly hot. Brigitte and I joined a caravan of sweltering concertgoers on a quest to cool off at the pond at Tyrone Mill, just a few miles south. There we found scores of our compatriots frolicking in the nude like water nymphs. A crowd of local residents bore witness, charmed by the spirit and titillated by the skinny-dipping that had transformed their local swimming hole into a nudist colony.

"Take off your clothes, Charlie. Jump in the water. I dare you to go skivvy dicking!" Brigitte challenged me, employing her marvelously mutilated mastery of the vernacular.

"That's skinny-dipping, Brigitte," I said. "And I'll go if you'll go."

She wasn't bluffing. Brigitte took off her tee shirt, stripped off her shorts and panties, and plunged in. It was the first time I'd seen her naked since Williamstown. I quickly stripped and followed her into the water, jealously guarding her sensational *derriere* against any and all interlopers.

By the time we emerged from the pond it was teeming with naked bodies like *The Garden of Earthly Delights* by Hieronymus Bosch. It seemed for a while that we'd remain naked: the shoreline looked as if a tornado had swept through a laundromat, scattering clothing haphazardly along the narrow banks and on the rocks and branches that lined the water. Like many others, we eventually gave up the search for the clothes we'd arrived in, settling instead for whatever we could find that would serve the purpose. Brigitte looked ridiculous in an oversized peasant blouse and a pair of shorts at least two sizes too big. I wound up in a garish orange tank top with jeans I had to roll up three inches. We both drew the line at donning other people's underwear. I suspected that many others would draw the same line and that when the weekend had ended, the shoreline would resemble the aftermath of an explosion in a lingerie factory.

We hitched back to the festival in time for The Youngbloods' opening act. Later, Jose Feliciano sang his version of *Hey Jude!* and Alice Cooper unleashed a manic performance employing everything from screen doors to rubber chickens. The frenzied light show accompanying his performance illuminated the entire valley, turning the smoky haze into a crimson red ring of hellfire punctuated by the writhing gyrations of dancing figures, a scene that probably frightened the crap out of the stoners and trippers in the crowd. Brigitte waited in vain for the advertised appearance of Montreal's cherished songwriter and poet, Leonard Cohen. To her great consternation, Izzy's favorite crooner failed to make an appearance.

As I danced with Brigitte on our little patch of festival grass, I swore that I would not go to sleep unsatisfied another night. Despite the profusion of exposed body parts on display at the millpond, the sight of her *derriere* was indelibly etched into my mind. "Let's go back to the pup tent and fuck our brains out!" I screamed to her (and everyone else nearby) above the din. She smiled, picked up the blanket, and followed my tortuous route back to the tent.

I zipped the tent and we quickly undressed, both of us thrilled to shed our ill-fitting clothes. The tent was pitch black and cramped, but we knew what to do. Her touch was electric. And even the dip in the pond failed to obliterate the intoxicating scent of her fine French perfume. By now, Mountain, the final act of the night, had begun its set. We ground to the soft rhythms of *For Yasgur's Farm*, the song they had debuted at Woodstock, and then climaxed to the cowbells and mighty guitar riffs of *Mississippi Queen*. It was well worth the wait.

CHAPTER SEVENTY-TWO

Boom-shakka-lakka-lakka

By Sunday, Strawberry Fields had grown to a swarming city of 75,000 or more. It had also become the drug capital of Canada. Marijuana, hash, hallucinogens, and a range of stronger offerings were openly traded throughout the weekend. My dwindling supply of Iowa Gold would prove more than adequate for our purposes.

The posters for the festival promoted it as "3 Days of Love, Sun & Sound." Sunday was our day to make up for any deficiencies in the Love department. We spent most of the morning in our tent making a significant dent in my condom supply. When she got going, Brigitte was insatiable, pushing me to my anatomical limits while taking full advantage of the unique benefits conferred by my crooked cock. If Friday had been a tease and Saturday mere foreplay, Sunday was the main event.

By the time we emerged from the tent that afternoon, we could barely walk. My balls were so swollen it felt as if a twenty-pound turkey was swinging from my crotch. I was ripe for a diversion. A raucous crowd near one of the water trucks drew our attention and we shuffled over for a closer look.

We'd come upon the Mud People, a mostly naked assemblage of revelers who congregated along the rivulets of mud generated in the wake of the tanker trucks dispensing water at the festival. A handful of teens and twenty-somethings descended upon the site, plunging into the viscous quagmire, writhing and wrestling in the muck like the pigs on Tractor's farm, making "mud angels" and otherwise wallowing in the slime with abandon, their bodies layered in thick, brown mud from head to toe. Others soon joined in. As the legion of Mud People expanded, so did the crowd of rapt spectators. The Mud People teased the onlookers, slinging heaping handfuls of sludge in our direction.

The festival's final night did not disappoint. I traded some of my Iowa Gold for a premium spot close to the stage. Brigitte and I got sky high on the balance. We grooved to the sounds of Grand Funk Railroad, featuring an elaborate drum solo that reverberated through the valley like artillery.

We retreated to the pup tent at around four in the morning, just as Sly and The Family Stone took the stage. Though tired, wasted, and still aching from our multitudinous carnal encounters, we knew this might be our last chance to get it on before packing up and heading home. Besides, there were still a few condoms remaining. So we zipped up the tent, zipped down our shorts, and rocked our hips to the beat of *Dance to the Music* and *I Want to Take You Higher*. And higher we went, catching a second wind that was a veritable nor'easter. "Boom-shakka-lakka-lakka . . . Boom-shakka-lakka-lakka," chanted the chorus. "Oooh, aahh, oooh, aahh," countered Brigitte. "Ooh, la, la! Ooh, la, la!" I muttered. Brigitte's moaning and my muttering elicited cries of "Down, girl!" and "You'll strip your gears!" from our envious tent-city neighbors, but we plowed on, as Tractor might have said, undeterred. Brigitte came violently in the middle of Sly's last reprise of "Boom-shakka-lakka-lakkas," shrieking and flailing so violently that she kicked loose the duct-taped front tent-pole just as I was soaring toward my own climax. And as I let go, the entire tent collapsed on top of us.

It was dawn when Sly and The Family Stone finished their set, concluding the festival. Brigitte and I cuddled for several more hours under the toppled tent, our bodies providing each other just enough warmth to combat the chilly Canadian morning.

We arose about noon and assembled our belongings for the journey back to Montreal. Brigitte and I were among the final stragglers. The once-teeming throngs had ebbed like a receding tide. All that remained in their wake were overflowing trashcans, discarded blankets, and the flotsam and jetsam associated with the delightful irresponsibility of youth. I didn't want to go home, but the party was over. School would resume in a few weeks and I'd begin the stretch run to full-fledged adulthood. The free ride would end as surely as the festival.

CHAPTER SEVENTY-THREE

The Dude with the Indefatigable Dick

My best friend Izzy Matz had come a long way since our days as immature freshmen. He'd methodically pursued a degree in engineering and transformed himself from a socially backward nerd into a confident senior with a clear understanding of where he was going in life. So it came as no surprise when he revealed to me during the first week of our senior year that he was engaged to marry Leah, the sweet, earthy girl he'd met at our first freshman mixer.

"That's terrific news!" I said. "You're made for each other. I couldn't be happier for you."

"Thanks," he said smugly. "And what about you?"

"What do you mean what about me?" I was pretty sure I knew where this was going.

"Is it still a weekend here with beautiful Annie, a weekend there with voluptuous Julianna, and a mid-week quickie every now and then with the pulchritudinous *Mrs.* Kelly?"

"Why are you on my case again?"

"Because, Charlie, if you keep on dicking around with your fucking harem you're going to lose that *one true love of your life.*"

"So who, pray tell, is that *one true love of my life?*" My tone became more caustic as my patience waned.

"Figure it out," he said, matter-of-factly.

"What the fuck, Izzy!" I said. "If it were that easy I would have done it ages ago."

"You know you're playing with fire, don't you?" he said, curiously invoking the very same metaphor I'd employed just a few weeks earlier when I'd made my plans with Brigitte. I figured that this was not a good time to tell him that Brigitte and I had screwed each other's brains out at Strawberry Fields.

"So what makes you the fucking font of wisdom on my love life?"

"I know what makes you tick," he said, annoying the hell out of me. "You're addicted to love, Charlie. You love the idea of *being* in love."

"And you don't? Is Leah just a fuck-buddy?"

"Of *course* I love Leah," he said. "But I'm not out there trying to go all Mormon on her by collecting a flock of sister-wives."

The best thing about my friendship with Izzy is that we could say anything to each other. And the worst thing is that we sometimes did.

"Fuck you, Izzy," I said. "I can handle my love life," I lied to us both.

And so I proceeded to ignore Izzy's admonitions by inviting Annie down for a weekend at Roberts. But then Julianna called to invite me to visit her at Mt. Holyoke for the same weekend. So I made up some excuse about needing the weekend to get my shit together for the start of classes on Monday and invited her to Roberts for the following weekend instead. To my relief, she accepted both my excuse and my invitation. Then I got a call from the petite Miss Brigitte inviting me to visit her in Montreal. Philippe was back in France and we'd have her apartment all to ourselves, she assured me. Like the addict Izzy pegged me for, I accepted her overture and tabbed the weekend after Julianna's visit for my second roadtrip to Canada. Three girls, three consecutive weekends.

And of course I'd be remiss if I failed to acknowledge the routine Wednesday nooners with Clare. We no longer suffered the pretense of meeting for lunch. Instead, Clare would pick up a pizza at Tony's on her way to the House and we'd consume it along with each other in my red- and blue-splotched room.

Tractor and Mary were astounded by the diversity of my love life. Mary would see me with Annie one weekend and Julianna the next. I suspect Tractor would complete the picture for her by casually suggesting that I was banging two others. My brothers dubbed me "Charlie, the Dude with the Indefatigable Dick" or "Indy" for short. Izzy had already begun calling me the "Arsonist."

"It's all under control," I told the guy I saw when I looked in the mirror. My hair was shorter now and my beard was history. "It's all under control."

CHAPTER SEVENTY-FOUR

The Revenge of the Turds

The desperation in Clare's voice on the other end of the line was palpable.

"I can't believe I'm calling to ask you this but I don't know where else to turn."

"What's up, Clare?"

"I have a doctor's appointment this afternoon that I can't postpone, Mom's back in Boston for a week, and my babysitter just called in sick. I've tried five neighborhood moms and I still can't find anyone to watch Hope," she said. "I hate myself for asking but is there any chance you could step up for a couple of hours?"

No fucking way is what I thought. "No problem!" is what I said.

"You're a life saver! Can you come by around two?"

"I'll be there," I said. *I'm totally fucked,* I thought.

The Clare I pictured lying naked on my bed with that sexy, come-hither look was not the Clare I encountered at her apartment that afternoon. This surrogate Clare was a frazzled imitation, scurrying around in search of her missing car keys, dragging me through the kitchen to show me where her daughter's milk and food were tucked into the refrigerator, and whisking me into Hope's clown-infested bedroom where the changing table, diapers, and diaper pail were situated.

"You *do* know how to change a diaper," she said as if she were stating the obvious.

"Of course," I said. *No way*, I thought, *I've never changed a diaper in my life!*

"Thank you! Thank you! Thank you!" Clare blathered as she reached for the knob of the front door, having finally located those elusive car keys.

"No problem, Clare," I called after her. "Hope and I will be fine." *Sure we will.*

Now what? I looked over at sweet, innocent-looking Hope. She had been playing quietly in a corner of the kitchen while her mother was doing her best impression of Daffy Duck. Hope glanced up at me, then scrutinized the kitchen for signs of her mother. *What the fuck,* she probably thought (or the toddler equivalent thereof), *Mom abandons me with this asshole?* Hope's lips began to quiver. The tears then flowed like a water main break. "Mommy! Mommy!" she cried in her most pathetic toddler voice.

So I did my clown interpretation. Consisting solely of making stupid faces, it only confirmed Hope's initial impression that she was saddled with a total asshole until her Mommy returned. Her bawling continued. Clueless, I reached into the refrigerator, retrieving baby food for Hope and a beer for me. No wonder Clare's mom had a drinking problem.

I tried to lift Hope into her high chair. She kicked and wriggled violently. As I prepared to lower her into her seat, she unleashed a powerful kick that struck me square in the upper lip. Blood poured down my chin and onto my sweatshirt like candy from a burst piñata.

I finally secured Hope into her high chair and scurried to

the sink for a paper towel to stanch the bleeding. Hope's mood turned on a dime. The spectacle of my bleeding seemed to amuse her. She suddenly decided to stop crying and start eating. I opened a container of peas. She shook her head. I closed the peas. I opened a container of sliced carrots. She shook her head. I closed the carrots.

"Fuck, Hope," I said in exasperation. "All I've got left is peaches."

When she heard the word 'peaches' she became animated. It was peaches she'd wanted all along. How was I supposed to know? The peaches had been chopped into small cubes. For every cube she ate, she chucked another across the room, smiling broadly at her ingenuity. At least she wasn't screaming.

When she was hurling three out of every four peach cubes onto the floor, I decided we'd both had enough. Her cherubic face was almost as much of a mess as the kitchen floor and my swelling upper lip. I briefly considered spraying her with the hose from the sink but thought better of it, toweling her off instead as best I could. Once out of her high chair, she motored out of the kitchen like a wind-up toy and into the living room where the entire inventory of Toys "R" Us was neatly piled in a corner.

Fortunately, Hope was more pleasant now. Convinced that I wasn't going to starve or abandon her, she pegged me as a worthy playmate. So for the next hour, Hope and I played contentedly with blocks, dolls, and assorted stuffed animals. We read *The Cat in the Hat* and *Horton Hears a Who!* Her verbal skills impressed me: she was particularly adept at mimicking almost anything I'd say. I found it rather amusing. "Fuck," I said, just to see what would happen. "Fuck!" she repeated proudly. Maybe that wasn't such a good idea.

All had been going well when Hope suddenly stopped what she was doing and exhibited what even I recognized immediately as a classic "poop face." I heard a small explosion followed by the rat-a-tat-tat of gunfire and, finally, the unmistakable odor of death.

"Oh, crap," I muttered to myself involuntarily.

"Oh, crap," Hope repeated.

I gave her a few minutes to conclude her business. She used the time to stand up and sit down repeatedly to assure even distribution of her feces throughout her diaper and beyond.

By this time, my babysitting sentence had gone on for two hours. I kept glancing at the front door in the desperate hope that Clare would return just in time to change Hope's diaper. When it became more onerous to endure the odor than to change the diaper, I reluctantly took charge.

Hope smelled like certain spots I remembered passing by on the New Jersey Turnpike. I lifted her onto the changing table. She acted as if this was no big thing, like she produced foul-smelling loads like this on a regular basis and was rather proud of it. With some difficulty, I unbuttoned her outfit and peeled down her pants. She was oozing with shit. I unfastened her diaper and nearly retched. She reminded me of the Mud People from Strawberry Fields, only much more rancid. I removed the diaper and lifted it over to the diaper pail like I was transporting a dead squirrel. Before long, the bloodstains on my sweatshirt were covered in excrement. I was creating a Jackson Pollock on my chest employing a colorful variety of body fluids. 'Mixed media' they called it. I smelled like I'd dropped through the seat of an outhouse. The more I struggled with her diaper, the more it amused Hope. While still on her back, she kicked playfully, laughing as she spread droplets of toddler dung onto the adjacent wall.

It took me the better part of twenty minutes to eliminate all visible signs of shit from Hope's diminutive anatomy. My initial diapering effort left much to be desired. Within seconds of standing her up, Hope's new diaper slid to her ankles like the New Year's ball at Times Square. My second effort was only marginally more artistic but proved more serviceable. Hope's clothes were soiled, to put it discreetly, so I rolled them into a noxious ball and found Hope a substitute outfit.

Just then, after the most repulsive half hour of my life, Clare strolled jauntily in through the front door.

"I'm home!" she pronounced cheerfully. I then heard a hushed "What the..." as she surveyed the peach residue blanketing the kitchen floor. When she screamed "Charlie!" I knew she'd spied the splotches of blood.

"Back here, in Hope's room," I called out in the calmest voice I could muster. When she burst into the room and saw Hope cooing in my arms and the forced grin on my face, she dismissed a multitude of worst-case scenarios and broke into a tentative smile.

"You've never done this before, have you, Charlie," she said, less a question than an observation.

"Not really, Clare," I said. "But we survived. Barely."

"What happened to your lip?"

"You didn't warn me that Hope had taken kick-boxing lessons."

"When I saw the blood..."

"I know. It all looks much worse than it is," I assured her. "Though I've got to say Hope shits like an exploding septic tank." All of us broke out in laughter, including Hope. Relieved, Clare lifted Hope into her arms and kissed her.

"How's my little girl?" purred Clare.

"Fuck!" said Hope.

CHAPTER SEVENTY-FIVE

A Grand Farewell

"**G**ram is gone."

Those three simple words shattered the serenity of a snowy December morning like a sonic boom.

"She passed away early this morning," Julianna said when she phoned me just after daybreak. She spoke calmly, but her grief was palpable.

"How?"

"A massive stroke . . . quick . . . painless."

"Just how she'd want it," I said. "I'm so sorry, Julianna. I know how much Doris meant to you." And how much she'd meant to me in the short time I'd known her. She was not only my great friend and confidante but also my mentor, guru, champion, and protector. I was devastated.

"She loved you," Julianna said.

"I know . . . and the feeling was mutual." I could no longer hold back the tears. "I'm so sorry," I said, whimpering.

"I know," she said softly. "I know." And then her own brave front gave way like a floodgate, and we both sobbed unabashedly through the telephone wires.

Tractor once again kindly donated the Hogmobile for my pilgrimage with Julianna to Doris's funeral in Lenox. What began as a teary embrace when I picked her up at Mt. Holyoke turned heartwarming as Julianna savored memories of her grandmother: how she'd given Julianna a little red tricycle for her third birthday, taught her to swim in the pool at the Lenox estate when she was five, read *Little Women* with her at seven, and encouraged her to appreciate the arts with trips to local museums and summer performances at the Tanglewood Music Festival in Lenox.

"She gave me a talk on the birds and the bees when I was thirteen and starting to date," Julianna said wistfully. "My parents never got around to it." I considered revealing my father's Five Axioms of Sexual Wisdom, but this wasn't the time.

"I lost my virginity at fifteen," she said as we drove west on the Massachusetts Turnpike, "to a boy I'd been dating since freshman year of high school. He kept urging me to go all the way, but I resisted. When he threatened to dump me, I foolishly gave in. A week later, I caught him making out in the school parking lot with a cheerleader. It was my first heartbreak." Julianna stared out the windshield, her moist eyes glistening like the snowdrifts along the highway. "Gram sensed my hurt and made me tell her the whole story. I would *never* have told my parents. Gram comforted me while I cried on her shoulder. I wanted to crawl into a hole and die, but she would *never, ever* stand for self-pity or surrender." Julianna wiped away a tear. "'*Believe in yourself, always,*' Gram said to me, '*and embrace life with a passion.*' That was her hallmark, Charlie. She always embraced life with a passion."

"I'll spare you the story of my first time," I said, stirring up my own happy memories of Catherine. "But I can assure you I was older than fifteen."

"I wasn't your first?"

"Forty-eighth, I think."

"You're so full of shit, Charlie," she said, flashing that patented Darlington smile and the concomitant Darlington dimple.

I pictured Doris the last time I'd seen her, after her mini-stroke in January. Despite the blow, she was propped up in her bed like a medieval queen, an indomitable force hard at work mending the broken relationship of her errant son and wounded daughter-in-law. Her will was compelling and her advice always sage.

The garish maroon Lincoln Continental driven by Julianna's parents was the only vehicle present as Julianna and I pulled up the long driveway that led to the Darlington Estate. The layer of fresh snow gave the big house an aura of almost supernatural stillness. A teary-eyed Luisa, Doris's longtime live-in housekeeper, greeted us as we entered through the massive wooden front door. Julianna rushed into the equally teary embrace of her father, and then her mother. Both welcomed me warmly as I offered my condolences. The house seemed eerily vacant without Doris's outsized presence.

Doris had even orchestrated her own goodbye. Her funeral would take place in two days at the historic Trinity Episcopal Church in Lenox, and a grand reception would follow at the estate. Luisa had a long list of Doris's friends and was able, with our help, to contact an extraordinary number of them in time for the service. As always, Luisa would manage the reception with the assistance of an army of the finest caterers in the Berkshires.

Julianna's father was Doris's only child, just as Julianna was her parents' sole offspring. But while there was little family to mourn Doris's passing, the number of friends and other admirers was astounding. The beautiful Gothic Revival stone church that hosted the funeral was filled with mourners, from the handful of her surviving contemporaries, many from her days in New York City, to assorted dignitaries from the worlds of art, business, and politics whom Doris had come to know through her philanthropic and art-related activities. Fellow art connoisseur and sitting Republican Governor of New York Nelson Rockefeller and his wife, Happy, attended the service. Even more exciting to me were the artists and their spouses whom Doris had befriended in the process of acquiring their work. Willem and Elaine de Kooning; Roy and Dorothy Lichtenstein; Andrew and Betsy Wyeth; Helen Farr Sloan, wife of the late John Sloan; Jasper Johns and Robert Rauschenberg were among the most recognizable names in attendance. The service, as Doris had directed, was short and sweet, devoid of most of the trappings of religion. Doris couldn't abide what I remembered her referring to as "pious claptrap."

The reception at the estate was a warm and loving testament to a remarkable woman. With Julianna by my side, I was privileged to meet and talk with many of Doris's art world friends. A large contingent from the Clark Institute attended, including Brigitte's nemesis, Myron Wheems.

I stole away from Julianna for a few minutes to pay my respects to Dr. and Mrs. Longworthy, the generous Park Avenue couple who had helped us through the trauma of Annie's abortion. They asked of Annie, of course, and I was happy to report she was fine. There was an awkward moment when I noticed Julianna heading in our direction. I extricated myself as quickly as possible from my conversation with the Longworthys in hopes of avoiding any lingering discussion of

Annie or her abortion in Julianna's presence. Izzy's admonition about 'playing with fire' simmered in my gut.

Julianna was a gracious hostess, making every effort to greet those she knew and introduce herself, along with me, to those she didn't. At one point she noticed a dignified, elderly gentleman with a cane sitting alone on a sofa, brooding. Luisa happened by at that moment, allowing Julianna to inquire about the individual in question and his connection with her grandmother. "Why don't you ask him?" Luisa said. "You'll be surprised by his answer."

And so she did. The soft-spoken gentleman introduced himself as Remington Davidson—Remy for short—from nearby Stockbridge. He was tall and ruggedly handsome, despite his advanced years. Generous eyebrows surmounted his steel-gray eyes. Tufts of silvery hair sprouted like cotton above his weathered brow.

"How did you know my grandmother?" Julianna asked him.

"Until she passed away, your grandmother and I were lovers," Remy said, his voice cracking with emotion. Julianna's jaw dropped.

"Excuse me?" I said, nearly spilling my glass of chardonnay.

"It's a long story," Remy said, but we prevailed upon him to share it. He nodded solemnly, beckoning us to join him on the sofa.

"I met Doris at Luna Park on Coney Island in the summer of '16. She was a blind date—a friend of a friend of my sister. I thought she was the most beautiful woman I'd ever seen," he said, smiling. "She was fresh, bright, sassy—a very independent woman. I fell hard for her." Remy's long, bony fingers danced across the silver handle of his cane like a daddy longlegs.

"But then came the Great War." Remy's words became more deliberate. "My unit was hit hard by German artillery fire ... it was June of '18 ... northern France. A piece of shrapnel lodged in my chest ... right here," he said, pointing to a spot on his left side, opposite his heart. "It was a miracle I survived. My convalescence lasted the better part of a year.

"For months, Doris wrote me almost every day, but ..." Remy paused to gently dab his eyes with a handkerchief. "But later, her letters became less frequent." He took Julianna's hand and looked directly into her eyes. "You see, by then she had met your grandfather, Donald. And by the time I got back to the States ..." His voice, now tinged with regret, trailed off. "My heart was broken," he said. He paused one last time to collect himself.

"Well, I married, too," Remy said, his mood suddenly more upbeat. "My wife, Gladys, was a wonderful woman. We had three lovely children, and I had a successful career. When the time came, we retired to Stockbridge," he said, eyeing Julianna wistfully. "One day, we were attending a concert at Tanglewood—it was about seven or eight years ago. And this tall, handsome, and strangely familiar woman approaches me. 'You're Remy Davidson,' she says. And then it dawns on me. 'Doris!' I shout, and we hug. I introduced her to Gladys and we caught up on almost fifty years of our separate lives. By then, your grandfather had passed away." Julianna and I sat there, transfixed.

"Gladys and I saw Doris socially from time to time in the ensuing years ... until Gladys passed away—a year ago this spring," Remy said. "When I felt the time was right, I called Doris and invited her to join me for dinner. She told me it was too hard for her to get out, but asked me instead to dine with her here. And before we knew it," he grinned, "we were lovers all over again." Remy fell silent, then he began to choke up. "Old loves never die," he said, tears flowing unimpeded down his wrinkled cheeks, "but, unfortunately, people do."

By this point, all three of us were weeping. Julianna sidled over and embraced Remy. "What a beautiful story, Mr. Davidson," she said through a veil of tears.

"Remy," he insisted. "I already miss her incredibly," he said. And then he looked pointedly at Julianna. "You wouldn't believe how much you look like your grandmother when I first met her. You are every bit as lovely as she was."

With that, Julianna broke down completely, politely but urgently excusing herself to seek refuge upstairs. I followed quickly behind her. There, we shared the deep, cathartic, soul-wrenching cry that we needed to move on.

CHAPTER SEVENTY-SIX

A Rich Piece of Ass

Julianna and I talked frequently in the weeks following her grandmother's funeral, though I didn't see her again until her family's annual New Year's Eve party. I was justifiably hesitant to attend. The vision of her father, his dick dribbling over the trophy wife he'd just banged in the swimming pool changing room, still haunted me. But Julianna begged me to chance it, promising to lock the changing room door if necessary. I relented.

To escape the chaos inflicted by the armies of caterers, florists, and liquor merchants upstairs, Julianna and I spent a quiet afternoon by the indoor pool. Her mocha-colored, two-piece bathing suit was the same one she so alluringly wore on the occasion of our poolside introduction at Doris's estate just eighteen months earlier. It beguiled me as much now as it did then. I would have ravished her in the changing room right then and there were it not for the unfortunate connotations associated with that venue.

The pool area was remarkably peaceful. The water, like a warm bath, provided a welcome respite from the frigid temperatures outside. The soothing humidity cloaked the windows with a thick layer of condensation while the sound of rippling water added to the comforting, womb-like ambience.

Despite the serenity, I could tell that Julianna had something on her mind.

"You seem distracted," I observed as she raised herself gracefully from the water and lay down on a towel she'd spread neatly across a lounge chair. I sat on the edge of the pool in front of her, dangling my feet in the tepid water.

"I am," she said. "I've been debating whether to tell you this . . . but I don't like the idea of keeping secrets from you." A pang of guilt pierced me like a bayonet. "My parents and I met with Gram's lawyers yesterday for a reading of her will." She leaned forward in the lounge chair as an uneasy look spread across her face. "She made generous bequests to the Clark and several of her favorite charities . . . left the big house to my father . . . established a trust for me."

"No surprises there."

"But Charlie," she said, pausing for a few seconds. "The amount she left me is *staggering.*"

"You meant everything to her."

"You don't understand. I knew, of course, she'd provide for me . . . but I never imagined anything of this magnitude. It's daunting!"

Julianna was no stranger to wealth, so the reason for her discomfort was not immediately apparent to me. I hesitated in asking the obvious question, for fear of sounding crass or out of place, but I couldn't restrain myself. "Would I be out of line to ask what 'magnitude' you're talking about? Two, three million?"

"Try fifteen to twenty."

"Jesus!"

"No shit. It's in trust for me until my twenty-fifth birthday when I can draw up to half. The rest when I'm thirty."

"I don't know what to say. That's a shitload of money."

"How am I supposed to handle that?"

While I certainly understood Julianna's apprehension, I was confident that Doris knew exactly what she was doing. "Doris trusted you . . . and she understood you," I said. "She wouldn't have done this unless she thought you were capable of handling it. And she's wisely given you some time to consider the obligations and possibilities in advance."

"It's still overwhelming," Julianna said. She reached out and touched my arm. "I wasn't sure if I wanted to share this with you . . . for fear that you'd see me differently . . . consciously or unconsciously. I don't want this to change me—or us." Her quandary was real. All I could offer was a pep talk.

"I understand your fears. But I suspect your grandmother knew you better than you know yourself. You're going to honor the Darlington legacy . . . and you're not going to sacrifice who you are in the process. I'm absolutely certain of it."

"I hope you're right."

"I know I am. But all seriousness aside . . . can I borrow fifty grand for a sports car? A girl of your means shouldn't be riding around in a pig farm pickup anymore. Don't you agree?"

"Charlie, you're an asshole," she said, grinning.

"And you're one hot, rich piece of ass."

Julianna's revelation was indeed a bombshell. Almost everything that took place on New Year's Eve around the Darlingtons' pool was explosive, it seemed. I couldn't help but wonder whether, despite my best intentions, I *would* see Julianna in a different light, just as she feared. I swore to myself I wouldn't, but could I really be sure?

"Oh . . . I almost forgot," Julianna said. "She left something to you."

My mind began to race.

"It seems she talked to you some time ago about *Subterranean Spring*—a piece of sculpture, if that's what you can call it—that she received many years ago from an artist . . . Marcel . . . something or other . . ."

"Duchamp!"

"Right. And it's—if I've got this right—a bidet? *Seriously?*"

"My God!" I exclaimed. "That is *so cool!*" I went on to relate the story Doris had told me about her encounter with Duchamp, his famous urinal, and the bidet he turned into a signed, 'ready-made' sculpture to amuse her. "Your grandmother was one amazing lady. I'll treasure it!" I couldn't begin to imagine how I'd explain it to my mother and father when I carted a bidet home for safekeeping.

I would learn a few weeks later, when it was sent to me by her estate's attorney, that Doris had also left me a heartfelt and highly complimentary letter of recommendation to be used in securing a position in the art world after my graduation. She'd thought of everything.

After Julianna's revelation, the party was anticlimactic. The changing room remained locked and, as best we could determine, not a single trophy wife was violated during the course of the evening.

CHAPTER SEVENTY-SEVEN

Gaping Crotch and a Red Paint Blotch

I was three weeks into my last semester at Roberts. In spite of my chronic romantic distractions, I'd managed to maintain a respectable grade point average. I had taken the tough courses earlier in my college career—the required allotment of math, science, and language courses, saving the dessert for last. In addition to a couple of 'gut' survey courses, I was just a passable poem or two (Creative Writing Workshop in Poetry) and a clever performance piece (Seminar in Avant-Garde Art) from my coveted degree. And, barring some decisive action on my part, I'd also qualify for a special graduation bonus: an all-expenses-paid ticket to Vietnam.

It was for creative challenges like this that I had retained a healthy wad of Iowa Gold. This, I decided, would be my weekend of genius. I'd light up on Friday afternoon and let the creative juices flow like lava until my typewriter had spewed forth pure artistry—hopefully no later than Sunday night. I considered importing one of my muses for inspiration, but then I'd wind up with a batch of sappy love poems or worse, dirty limericks ("there once was a lass from Nantucket...").

I elected to begin with the poetry. Armed with all the acuity a joint could bestow, I made my way to The Douche for Friday dinner. I scanned the dining room for inspiration—a suitably voluptuous weekend date, perhaps, preferably one with cleavage you could hike through. What I found was almost more than I could handle, both literally and poetically. Processing the sordid images during my meal gave me indigestion. But back in my room, I let the weed move me:

Friday Night Frights

Tremendous drooping ORBS of
BULBOUS flesh
Seeking the table-top
Like overzealous
Divining rods, blasting
Nearby eyeballs from their sockets
And generally
Ruining a tolerable meal.

My exercise in free-form poetry completed, I turned to classic rhyme with meter, a much more challenging assignment. The Iowa Gold had me in a zone, cooking with gas, shooting the rapids, flat on my ass. I could have written about beautiful Annie, sultry Julianna, lithe Clare, or petite Brigitte. Or I could compose an ode to a pair of old blue jeans:

Ode to an Old Pair of Pants

It's hard to believe that it's ended
Like this: in a heap, gashes unmended,
Bottomless pockets, gaping crotch,
Old grass stains, a red paint blotch,
Seams aburst, (please turn the page)

And noble blues turned white with age
Nevermore to rise resurgent
Bathed with love and cheap detergent.

Alas, it's come to elegy,
My ass laments the days to be
When pairs of choking underwear
Will cease to find your solace there.

You served me very well, my friend,
And now as you approach your end
I pledge that your remains will be
Degraded biologically.

There were other poems, of course, but most of them were wisely discarded when I descended from my high on Sunday afternoon.

Meanwhile, I needed an angle for my seminar in Avant-Garde Art. Of course, it would've been helpful to know what Avant-Garde Art actually was. I was partial to my father's definition: "sucky, stupid, and incomprehensible bullshit." I could work with that.

The concept took several hours to jell. I decided to go with a form of performance art. I'd produce a guided tour on film of the Roberts Art Gallery. But not just your ordinary tour. This tour would go where no tour had ever gone before. I began composing my cannabis-induced screenplay on Saturday night and finished late Sunday morning. This, too, survived the onset of sobriety.

A TOUR OF THE SPECIAL ROOMS AT THE
ROBERTS ART GALLERY

Setting: In front of the Roberts Art Gallery in Trumbull, New Hampshire. Camera trains on Charlie Meyer who is impeccably dressed in a dark suit with a Rothko-red tie.

CM: Good afternoon. My name is Charlie Meyer. I'm a senior art history major at Roberts College and it will be my pleasure today to take you on a very unique tour into the special rooms at the Roberts Art Gallery, known by those who love it as the RAG. We won't be focusing today on the stodgy old portraits or murky landscapes encountered on conventional museum tours, but will instead explore those often overlooked rooms without which no first-class art gallery can prosper. If you would kindly follow me up the steps behind me, we will enter the RAG, perhaps the finest collegiate art gallery in the country, and if not the finest, easily among the top five hundred.

[Camera follows Mr. Meyer as he gallops awkwardly up the stairs and through the front door of the RAG.]

CM: We're here in the entryway, officially now "on the RAG," as we like to say. Just behind me to your left is the first of the special rooms I'd like to show you today.

[Camera follows Mr. Meyer as he strolls, self-importantly, into the first room.]

CM: Welcome to the "Cloak Room," a rotating exhibition of fine textiles. If you look up behind the counter to my right, you will see several interesting items on display, including a fine example of a Red Sox baseball cap, an exquisite French beret, and a knit cap with an uncertain provenance. Fine examples of foreign and domestic outerwear are similarly displayed on the racks beneath. This is an unusual exhibit in that it changes from day to day, even moment to moment, although the foam rubber finger sculpture you see off to the right has been here for several years now, I'm told. Visitors are encouraged to contribute their fine textiles for exhibition, if even for a day, in consideration of which they receive small numbered tokens acknowledging their donations. Should they change their minds after their visit, they may retrieve their donations simply by returning the corresponding tokens. Let's take a moment to speak with the curator of the Cloak Room, Mr. Charles Davis.

[Camera focuses on Mr. Davis, a young man with drooping shoulders and an apathetic mien.]

CM: I see that today's display of textiles is unusually small.

CD: Yeah. Warm day today.

CM: How long have you been in charge of the Cloak Room?

CD: About twenty minutes.

CM: [Laughs] You're too modest, I'm sure, Mr. Davis. Can you tell me, Mr. Davis, for whom the Cloak Room is named?

CD: Are you serious?

CM: Deadly serious, Mr. Davis.

CD: It's for coats, that's why it's called a Cloak Room.

CM: I'm sorry, Mr. Davis, but if that were the case don't you think it would be called the Coat Room? [Chuckles] So, then, Mr. Davis, who was Mr. or Miss Cloak and why is this fascinating display named for him or her?

[CD rolls eyes and walks away disgustedly]

CM: Well, I'm afraid our Cloak Room Curator has more pressing obligations, so let's continue just around the corner here to our next special venue.

[CM points, camera follows as he shuffles around corner]

CM: Welcome to the second of our special museum rooms, the Men's Room. I'll just push open this door and you can follow me right on in.

[CM and camera proceed into Men's Room. One young man scurries from a urinal as the camera enters while an older gentleman continues urinating]

CM: Many of you may recall the avant garde French artist Marcel Duchamp who, about fifty years ago, shocked the art world by signing an ordinary urinal and declaring it art. Well, the Men's Room, as you can see, is obviously an homage to Mr. Duchamp, as this wall of urinals can attest. Let's say hello to this gentleman here. Hello, sir, I can tell by your posture that you are particularly fascinated by this wall-mounted artwork.

Man: Jeez, I'm just trying to take a piss!

CM: Is that a form of protest art?

[Man zips fly, flushes, and walks away]

CM: Artists are indeed sensitive creatures. If you'll look to my right, you'll see that the RAG had the foresight to provide, behind each of these metal doors, an individual seat from which a visitor can contemplate, with the door open, one or more of the Duchampian urinals or, by simply closing and latching the door, can consult his favorite art catalogue, newspaper, or even a novel. Let's step over to this stall here.

[Camera follows CM to a closed stall with two legs visible at the bottom. CM knocks at the stall door]

CM: Sir? I wonder if you'd like to share with our audience your thoughts about this fabulous Men's Room exhibition at the RAG.

Man in Stall: Go away!

CM: And can you tell us what you might be contemplating back there right now?

Man in Stall: Get out of here, you pervert!

CM: I guess it's just not a good time. OK, then, let's move on, shall we? Oh, I almost forgot. I just wanted to show our audience a fine example of graffiti art by one of our own local graffiti artists, an individual who signs his work "F.U."

[CM walks over to a corner of the Men's Room as camera focuses on a primitive drawing of a penis and a kneeling female figure]

CM: We're privileged to have this edgy work by F.U. on display here on the wall in the Roberts Art Gallery Men's Room. I've noticed that works of this nature tend to be ephemeral, so this is indeed an exciting moment. I believe this work is a riff on modern sexual mores, sexual identity, and circumcision. Note the flat planes and classic triangular lines of composition. Incredible. Well, then, let's move on to our third special room.

[Camera follows CM across main hall to a door marked "Women's Room," then follows CM inside. Women are heard screaming]

CM: We're honored now to show you the gallery known as the Women's Room. As I'm sure you're all aware, feminist art has reached new heights over the past few years and the dedication of a gallery specifically to the productions of women is a major coup for the RAG. It appears that the young ladies who were enjoying this gallery a few moments ago have departed, so I'll do my best to describe the current installation here in the Women's Room. As you can see, we have on one wall a perfectly symmetric line of porcelain artworks in the shape of common sinks. Note the minimalist ethic evident in the constancy of the line and the relation of each wall-mounted work to its neighbor. On the other wall we have what looks, at first glance, very much like the contemplation stalls we saw in the Men's Room exhibition across the hall. Here, though, you'll notice, as I push back the door (which, I think, is meant to heighten the anticipation before revealing the sculpture behind it), you'll see another work in porcelain, this time with gentle curves and ovals reminiscent, perhaps, of a woman's derriere. Note also the inclusion in this sculpture of a water feature. I'm advised that a flick of the little stainless steel handle on the left unleashes a motion not unlike that of a classic whirlpool. So clever! This indeed is a room that truly honors each and every Woman's Movement!

[Camera moves to position outside the Women's Room where a line of ladies has formed. The women in line look unusually perturbed]

CM: The fourth and final room on today's special tour is downstairs. If you'll just follow me . . .

[Camera follows CM down an unadorned concrete staircase past a furnace and through a door into a room filled with trash barrels. A man wearing a janitor's uniform sits on a crate in the center of the room]

CM: Our last destination today is a room with no name. But as you can all plainly see, this is the purview of the RAG's artist-in-residence, Mr. Amos Smith. Let's have a word with our resident genius.

[Camera pans to a bewildered Mr. Smith as CM approaches]

CM: Hello there, Mr. Smith. We're honored to meet you. Judging from the preponderance of trash barrels and other detritus in this room, I take it you work with so-called "found objects"?

AS: Uh. Yeah. I collect the trash.

CM: And what is the next step in your creative process, if you don't mind sharing with us your artistic secrets?

AS: I put it all in one of them blue barrels there.

[Camera pans to the blue trash barrels to which Mr. Smith points, then back to CM]

CM: And, by combining various types of objects, discarded papers, and other debris, you wind up with something very special indeed, I'm sure.

AS: Well, I hardly think it's that special.

CM: You are modest indeed, Mr. Smith. Thank you so much for talking with us today. We'll let you get back to your work and look forward to your next creation.

[Mr. Smith nods uncomprehendingly]

CM: Well, this concludes our tour. I thank each and every one of you for joining me today as we visited the special places that make the RAG so, well, special. Until next time, I'm Charlie Meyer wishing you an artsy day!

I handed in my assignments on Monday morning, before I could entertain second thoughts. Now that I'd done the heavy lifting, I could coast to graduation. But I hadn't anticipated the bump in the road.

CHAPTER SEVENTY-EIGHT

Requiem for an Old Schwinn

It was an otherwise typical Friday morning. It was cold, but less so than usual for late January, and not enough to turn the early morning rain into sleet or snow. But an arctic front had followed in the wake of the rain, and patches of ice were spreading like ugly rumors across the roadways. As was my custom, I hopped onto my ratty old Schwinn bicycle and headed off to my poetry seminar on the far side of campus.

As I pedaled along Main Street, daydreaming about Annie, Julianna, Clare, or maybe even Brigitte, a red Ford pickup backed precipitously into my path from a diagonal parking space near Lou's Diner. "Shit!" I screamed, my vocabulary shrinking dramatically in the face of abject terror. I reacted instinctively, swerving to avoid impact with the Ford's looming rear end. Thus redirected, my creaky Schwinn promptly skidded like a bar of soap across a patch of black ice. The ice, in turn, diverted my front wheel into a yawning pothole, freshly gouged by the elusive pothole gremlins that feast on Trumbull's roadways in winter. As it plunged into the gremlins' handiwork, my front wheel assembly buckled like a broken crutch, hurling me acrobatically over the handlebars like a gymnast over a vaulting horse. But alas, after an Olympic-quality somersault, I failed to stick the landing. The landing stuck me. As I rotated helplessly through the ether (one and a half times rather than an infinitely more felicitous whole number of rotations), a wedge of blue sky gave way to the gloomy gray of the rapidly approaching asphalt. Then came the sickening THWACK! heralding the convergence of skull and pavement. And if that were not sufficient cause for concern, horrified witnesses reported that my awkward descent was further distinguished by the unsavory collision of my gonads with the crumpled carcass of my expired Schwinn.

CHAPTER SEVENTY-NINE

I Could Have Been a V8!

*W*here am I?
Who's there?
Why can't anyone hear me?
Who turned the lights out?

These were just the first of a torrent of questions that would roil through my badly battered brain over the hours to come. I tried in vain to make sense of the various shards of information floating through my consciousness—if indeed it was consciousness. I recalled the sensation of being airborne, but couldn't recall why or when. And now, wherever I was—*if I was*—I felt strangely disembodied, adrift in an as yet unfathomable sea, ghoulishly disassociated from my anatomy.

I hear your muffled voices. Who are you? Where are you? I could swear I was speaking but my voice was mute. It occurred to me that I might be dead. I felt no pain. That was not a good sign. Pain was evidence of life. This wasn't hell, I reasoned, as I was in no apparent distress. *Am I in some kind of limbo? And what is that infernal beeping sound I keep hearing?* Perhaps I was merely dreaming, a far more hopeful prospect. *Am I dreaming? Why won't someone answer me?* But then, as if someone were tuning in a distant radio station, came a glint of recognition, a soothing and familiar voice.

"Can he hear us?" my mother asked.

A woman's voice responded. "Possibly, though there's no way to know for sure."

"Can I speak to him anyway?" Mom pleaded, her speech dripping with emotion.

"Of course," the woman replied, "it could be beneficial."

Beneficial to what? Hey, Mom, I hear you! Why can't you hear me?

"He looks just awful, Richard," Mom said. Those words disheartened me. Mom began to weep.

Why are you crying, Mom?

"Calm down, Lydia, your crying won't help." That characteristic lack of sympathy could only come from Dad.

Hey, Dad! Where are you guys? What the fuck? I can hear you but everything is black. Are you sure you can't hear me? I detected the sound of approaching footsteps. Another voice, this one male.

"Any change? Signs stable?" A doctor?

"No change. He seems comfortable." A nurse?

Am I in a hospital? Someone please answer me, goddammit!

"Dr. Wilcox, these are the patient's parents, Richard and Lydia Meyer," the nurse said.

"Pleased to meet you. Your son here is lucky to be alive . . ."

I'm alive! Slap me five!

". . . but I'm afraid he's incurred a serious head injury."

Shit!

"Charlie has suffered a subdural hematoma as well as a concussion resulting from the severe blow to his head from the biking accident. He has bleeding in the region between the skull and the brain. The resultant swelling has put him into a comatose state."

"Jesus Christ!" My father.

Jesus Christ! Me. Mom graduated from weeping to wailing.

"There must be something you can do for him," my father implored the doctor.

"His brain activity is good, he's breathing on his own, and he's stable, so we'll watch him very carefully over the next twenty-four to forty-eight hours. If the bleeding and swelling subside, he has a good chance to recover. If they worsen, we may have to take some action to relieve the pressure."

Fucking A!

"What action?" my father asked. *Good question, Dad.*

"We can drill small holes in his skull."

What! Am I some voodoo doll?

"What are the odds of recovery, and how complete might it be?" my father inquired as if conducting an audit.

"I can't lie to you, Mr. Meyer. He took a heck of a beating . . . but he's young and strong. I think his chances are good, though I can't guarantee there won't be lingering symptoms even in the best of outcomes. I'm hopeful. Now, if you'll excuse me, I have other patients to see. I'll check in every few hours and Nurse Edwards here will monitor your son around the clock."

I wondered what Nurse Edwards looked like. My mind was suddenly accosted by the image of a big-bosomed blonde bursting from her nurse's uniform in a steamy porn movie.

"Shit!" Dad muttered, reacting either to the doctor's prognosis or my pornographic imagery. "What's a *good chance*, fifty percent? Sixty? What the fuck does *good* mean?" Dad was thoroughly unaccustomed to the uncertainty associated with professions other than accounting.

Be cool, Dad. I felt like Ebenezer Scrooge embarking on his sojourn with the ghosts of Christmas. *I'm pretty sure I'm here but why the hell can't anyone hear me?*

I must have fallen asleep for a bit, though how the fuck do

you fall asleep if you're already in a coma? Because next thing I remembered ... was the sultry voice of Julianna at my bedside. By now I'd become wise to the protocol of my personal brand of comatose consciousness (again, if indeed I wasn't dead or dreaming), so I held my tongue (which, of course, was redundant under the circumstances).

"Charlie," she said, convinced that I had the awareness of a log. "What the *fuck* have you done? You're coming through this in one piece, you bastard. Promise me!" December had been an incredibly bad month for her. January wasn't looking much better.

If it's any consolation, this sucks for me too, J. D. She'd given me a creditable pep talk. Maybe not "win one for the Gipper," but still pretty good. I always admired her determination. Like her grandmother, Julianna was truly a pistol. If only I could hold her. *Won't someone plug my brain back into my body? Anyone?*

I heard someone enter the room. I shuddered. Was it Doc Wilcox?

No, Doc, put down the drills! I've already got enough holes in my head!

"Hello." Another familiar feminine voice. Annie?

Oh my God! Julianna was about to meet Annie! *The shit's about to hit the fan!* I imagined them wrestling to the floor, claws bared. My money was on Julianna. And I'm lying here comatose in my first row seat!

"Hi, I'm Julianna."

"Julianna! Charlie wrote me about you. I'm Annie."

"Annie?"

"Charlie's friend from back home, in New Liberty?"

"Oh," Julianna muttered, momentarily uncomprehending.

It wouldn't take long for Julianna to put together the pieces.

But if there had been any doubt up to that point, there was little left when Izzy sauntered in. My hospital room was now laden with more land mines than Vietnam.

"Izzy!" barked Julianna and Annie in unison. I wanted to hide. But I was already hiding in plain sight.

Oh, fuck! Julianna's no dummy. Annie's no mere pen pal, she'd probably surmised—she *had* to be a frequent campus visitor to be so well acquainted with Izzy!

Izzy greeted both my women warmly, making no effort to obscure his connections to each. "Any progress?" he asked them.

"The nurse says he's holding his own," Julianna stammered, her faltering voice betraying her growing discomfort.

"Hey, Charlie," said Izzy breezily, addressing the vegetable in the room. "You sure had it figured out, you old bastard . . ." *I'm a fucking vegetable and everybody's calling me a bastard! What's up with that?* "Congratulations. You fashioned yourself a foolproof strategy to evade Vietnam. I knew you were resourceful . . . but isn't this a bit extreme? Anyway, you've got your 4-F medical deferment wrapped up in a bow!"

Fuck yes! I hadn't even thought of that. But, to be honest, if I don't snap out of this soon, my draft board will classify me V8, for "medically disqualified on account of being a fucking Vegetable!"

Heavy footsteps tramped into the room. If that was Nurse Edwards, my porno fantasy was shattered. But alas, it was Tractor, who would definitely look like shit in that low-cut nurse's uniform.

"Hey, Annie. Hey, Julianna."

Oh, fuck. I could only imagine the expression on Julianna's face. No way Annie's just an old friend, she had to be thinking. And she's model-gorgeous to boot. I suddenly entertained the incongruous fear that Annie might fall madly in love with Julianna. Instead of a wrestling match, they'd be writhing in ecstasy on the floor within seconds.

I'm a dead man. I was already uncomfortably close. Now I wondered if I shouldn't just wrap it up and call it a life. But the fireworks had only just begun because yet another female had apparently entered the room. *Let me guess. Clare, you work in this fucking hospital! Is that you, Clare?*

Clare greeted Tractor and Izzy, then introduced herself to Annie and (I could only assume) a dumbfounded Julianna.

She's just my Wednesday afternoon fuck-buddy, J.D. Nothing more! Good thing Julianna couldn't hear me. I pictured Clare in her own sexy hospital outfit. There were two foxy nurses in that porno, if I recall.

"Are you a nurse here?" asked Julianna, hoping to establish a connection without devastating connotations.

"I work in the experimental sleep lab upstairs," Clare said. "That's where I met Charlie."

I'm so fucked! So fucked! At this juncture, I somehow lost a chunk of time. Maybe that was a good thing: I didn't really need to hear the screeching sounds of clenching brakes as the oncoming trains hurtled toward their inevitable collision. When I tuned back in to the conversation moments—or perhaps hours—later, another voice—a multilingual voice—had joined my deathwatch.

"*Mon Dieu!*" Brigitte exclaimed. "You look *horrible, mon chéri,* all bladdered and bruis-ed," she moaned, pummeling the language as she pounded yet another nail into my coffin.

"How . . . ?" I heard Julianna whimper. By now, she'd met three girls, each as stunning as the next, and each with an unstated but easily inferred tie to the corpse in the room, and probably to the crooked cock which, with any luck, was still attached to the corpse. I couldn't imagine anything more humiliating.

And speaking of that crooked cock, a funny thing happened. Though up to this point I'd felt no tangible connection to any part of my mangled body, I had suddenly begun to notice that faint sensation of engorgement frequently associated with a morning boner. *Is my mind playing tricks?* I had no way of checking. But *they* did.

"Do you guys see what I'm seeing?" Tractor whispered, just loud enough for all to hear.

"Tent-pole city!" shrieked Izzy. "This has *got* to be a good omen!"

"It's a fucking Sequoia!" Tractor belted out.

"*Oui*, but it is straight, no? As a yard of stick!" warbled petite Brigitte.

"It sure is!" Clare cackled.

"My God, a miracle!" Annie declared.

"*No, ce est une tragédie!*" Brigitte groaned, likely contemplating the potential diminution of my pecker's peculiar powers to impart prodigious pleasure.

Julianna, though understandably mute, couldn't have failed to notice the same thing. And worse, it was obvious that the three other women were intimately aware of the dubious rectitude of my dick, and more than intrigued at its curious transformation from chronically crooked to skyscraper-straight.

I'm not in control of this! My dick has a mind of its own! Though I was far more intrigued by this turn of events than anyone else in the room, I was becoming increasingly alarmed by Julianna's silence. The glee exuded by the others must have been directly proportional to the devastation heaped upon her.

Julianna! Forgive me, Julianna. I LOVE YOU MOST OF ALL! There, I said it! I finally said it! I was talking only to myself, so I couldn't possibly be lying, right? I loved all of these magnificent women, I really did, but I could live without Annie, Clare, and Brigitte, if I survived this ordeal and whatever indignities Julianna could choose to inflict upon me. But I couldn't abide the thought of losing Julianna again. *Izzy! I KNOW WHO SHE IS! THE ONE TRUE LOVE OF MY LIFE! It was Julianna all along! Forgive me, Julianna. Oh, please forgive me!* I was crying. Or at least I thought I was crying. In my disembodied state, I couldn't conceivably know.

"Look!" said Annie. "Are those tears?"

"Nurse Edwards!" Julianna blurted out, her voice vacillating between hope and anger. And from the waning sound of that voice, I could tell she was leaving the room. After summoning Nurse Edwards, I had no way of knowing whether Julianna would return or continue walking—right out of my life.

I continued to sob. *Julianna! Come back, Julianna! OH, GOD, PLEASE COME BACK!*

"He's moving!" Izzy squealed with delight.

"JULIANNA! PLEASE, PLEASE, JULIANNA! I LOVE YOU MOST OF ALL! PLEASE COME BACK!" I pleaded, this time audibly, or so it seemed judging from the gasps of the startled observers at my bedside. I felt my eyes opening. The light was blinding at first. I felt a sudden burst of pain in my *bladdered* and *bruis-ed* limbs. And my head throbbed like a motherfucker.

Julianna hadn't returned. Annie had also departed. *I awake from a life-threatening coma and everyone flees like humans retreating from invading aliens in a Grade B science fiction movie!* Clare and Brigitte, at least, rushed to embrace me, ever so delicately, while Tractor and Izzy, considering themselves above such displays of affection, looked on smiling and high-fiving.

But the commotion just outside my room was equally intense. Annie placed her arm on Julianna's shoulder. I could see them hazily through the doorway as my eyes adjusted to the light. Julianna was wailing, her shoulders heaving, as Annie struggled to comfort her. J.D.'s anger was palpable. While those at my bedside celebrated my renaissance, my eyes were fixed on Annie and Julianna. Moments later, both re-entered the room. Her eyes still filled with tears, Julianna strode purposefully to my side.

"First of all, Charlie, you are a piece of shit!" she bellowed. "I thought I was your only lover and now I find you've been juggling four! FOUR!"

"But—"

"Shut the fuck up, asshole! And you had the nerve to get all pissy over Simon!"

"Julianna, I—"

"I'm not finished, you pile of pig manure! I'm back in this room for one reason, you shitbag. I fucking *love* you! I've loved you from the first day I met you. And as hurt and humiliated as I am at this very moment, I won't give up on your sorry ass!"

Annie, Clare, Brigitte, Izzy, Tractor, and even Nurse Edwards (who was quite a looker after all) and Dr. Wilcox (who'd crashed the party upon word of my revival) joined in an unrestrained round of applause that filled the room.

"I love when you talk dirty, J.D.," I muttered, tears streaming gratefully from my bloodshot eyes.

CHAPTER EIGHTY

Papa's Got a Brand New Bag

My recovery was as long and hard as my realigned penis. The month I spent in the hospital seemed like an eternity. I'd broken both arms and badly bruised a kneecap; my face had looked like a rotten pumpkin. My concussion symptoms—dizziness, occasional double vision, and recurrent headaches—gradually diminished. After my discharge, I spent hours in grueling outpatient rehabilitation sessions while struggling to catch up on my studies. My physical therapist was a hottie, but I was a reformed man. I'd miraculously survived and had every reason to believe I would fully recover.

Julianna was alternately my crutch and my drill sergeant. She visited every weekend. She refused to let me slough off academically or physically. With patience, care, and understanding, she nursed me back to sexual health as well. It isn't easy to make love with two broken arms and a battered kneecap. And while the collision between my mangled bike and genitalia had left me sore for weeks, the serendipitous straightening of my dick was a wholly unanticipated dividend (or consequence, depending upon your viewpoint). James Brown's lyrics were prophetic:

Come here mama and dig this crazy scene
He's not too fancy but his line is pretty clean
He ain't no drag
Papa's got a brand new bag

Julianna's devotion and wit were the balm that assured my recovery. I'd made the right choice and was exceedingly grateful for her forgiveness, support, comfort, and most of all, her unqualified love. I didn't deserve that love, but I swore to myself I'd do everything in my power to preserve and enhance it.

She, too, finally got some good news when the grand jury refused to indict her or her fellow protesters in connection with the Molotov cocktail incident in Springfield the previous spring. There was no credible evidence that any of them had knowledge of, much less conspired with, Simon the Turd. The full recovery of the injured officer was a welcome bonus. The Turd, on the other hand, would spend some quality time in the slammer. Good riddance. And, in the months after her arrest, while the fusty, tweed-jacketed administrators at Mt. Holyoke College debated possible punitive actions against her, Julianna's twelve-gauge lawyer threatened to sue the crap out of them. The administrators proved conveniently spineless and no sanctions were imposed.

On a lazy Saturday afternoon in April, Julianna and I made delicate love beneath the fading blue Rothko-esque splotch on the wall above the bed in my room. Lounging together in post-coital bliss, Julianna wondered aloud why I'd never pressed her for details on her epochal conversation with Annie outside my hospital room on the night I awoke from my coma.

"I didn't want to rock the boat," I told her. "Whatever she

said to you, it motivated you to come in and blow me away with your expletive-laden proclamation of love. It saved me. Why risk reopening the wounds I'd inflicted upon you?"

"Well, now I think you should know," she said and proceeded to enlighten me. "Annie told me of your tortured history together, about the complications of her lesbianism, the bombshell of her pregnancy. She described the emotional distress of her abortion and its aftermath. At that point I was reeling."

I was surprised that Annie would choose to reveal so much to Julianna. "That's a lot to process, especially after what you'd just endured," I said.

"No shit. And if that weren't enough, she just totally blew me away by informing me that Gram had arranged the abortion! Jesus Christ, Charlie! But it was when she spoke so reverentially of Gram's wisdom and support that I completely lost it."

"Annie and I were struggling with her pregnancy. Doris helped us sort it all out."

"I understand that now," she said, and then continued. "Annie then told me about the letter you wrote her when she sought to resume your relationship several months after the abortion, if I remember correctly. She told me that you had proclaimed your love for me 'in no uncertain terms,' as she put it . . . and how the two of you resumed your relationship only after that silly flap over Simon." Julianna trained her deep brown eyes on mine. "But the most important thing . . . was that she told me she loved you enough to step aside for us. She said she was uncertain when, or if, she could give you her full commitment, but that if I could, she wouldn't stand in our way. She swore to me that you were worth it—that my embarrassment and anger at that moment would soon pass, and that I shouldn't let it foreclose our chance for a future together. I found that astonishing."

My admiration for Annie and her selflessness rendered me speechless.

"I can see why you loved her so much," Julianna said.

"But you still could have run," I said. "Why didn't you? What possessed you to come tearing back into my room with pistols drawn and firing like Faye Dunaway in *Bonnie and Clyde*?"

"It happened so fast. I thought my head was going to explode. But in the end, I think it had a lot to do with Annie's mention of Gram. I stayed with Gram for a week last summer while you were gallivanting across America delivering back-seat babies. I knew she was gradually failing. It seemed as if she wanted to impart some last pearls of wisdom before leaving us. She often spoke of you . . . with real affection . . . but she never revealed to me any of what Annie had told me that night at the hospital." Julianna pressed my hand between both of hers. "Out of the blue at dinner one night, Gram made a comment that didn't resonate with me at the time: '*The ones you love will inevitably disappoint you. When they do, you need to love them even more,*' she said. I assumed then that she was talking about my father's dalliance, but as I stood there listening to Annie, it occurred to me that she may well have been referring to you."

Doris, bless your soul.

"And I suddenly understood also that she knew all about your foibles. She knew about your troubles with Annie. And I suspect she might have even known about your dalliance with that little French sexpot Brigitte! Yet she'd vetted you long ago. If she thought you were wrong for me, she would have told me, but instead she urged me not to run—even if you hurt me."

"I guess the rumors of your grandmother's demise are indeed exaggerated."

"And that's why I'm here beside you stroking that magic penis that got you into trouble to begin with. The one that is now *exclusively* mine. Right, Charlie?"

"Ouch!" I howled when she inadvertently touched my crippled knee. At least I thought it was inadvertent. "Right!" I eagerly but painfully affirmed.

"Shut up, you wimp," she snapped back as she deftly lifted her smooth, warm body over mine, slipped my surprisingly straight dick between her legs, and began to rock.

CHAPTER EIGHTY-ONE

Eight Balls

Julianna and Annie became friends. To Julianna, Annie was the older sister she never had. And free of the sexual tension, confusion, and longing that had characterized our relationship for so long, my own friendship with Annie became even more poignant. So it was gratifying to me when Annie appeared, unannounced, to witness my graduation together with Julianna, Mom, Dad, and Hermie.

Graduation day was unbearably hot, the speeches unbearably long and trite. Diplomas were dispatched in assembly-line fashion, the rigor interrupted only by the spectacular header involuntarily performed by one of my classmates as he ascended the stage in advance of his feet. The spontaneous yelps of the crowd marked the afternoon's lone highlight. Julianna and Annie clapped and hooted like high school cheerleaders when I hobbled up to claim the Latin-inscribed scrap of parchment that I would bury in a drawer, long forgotten, for decades to come.

Although she hadn't attended the ceremony, Clare threw me an informal graduation party afterward. Hope, more mobile and vocal than ever, lit up when I strolled into Clare's apartment, greeting me with a hearty "Fuck!" which, much to the mutual dismay of both Clare and me, had become in little

Hope's mind a term of endearment. Izzy, Leah, Tractor, and Mary all made appearances. Much to my relief, Dad behaved admirably, somehow restraining himself from asking all of the obvious questions posed by my presence in the home of a young, attractive woman with an absent husband and a child. Although Clare and I still managed to enjoy an occasional lunch, often with Julianna if she was in town, our libidinous Wednesday nooners were a thing of the past. If she lamented their passing, she never let on.

Dad splurged for dinner that night for Julianna and the immediate family at Caruso's, a long-time Trumbull institution that boasted of the fact that it hadn't changed its menu in thirty years. I hardly considered that worth crowing about. The tacky faux Roman décor, complete with sappy murals depicting gondoliers with faces obscured by thirty years of grease and grime, was as hackneyed as the afternoon's oratory. Julianna utilized the occasion to present me part of my graduation gift, the part she could display in public. It was one of those ubiquitous, black plastic Magic 8 Balls, the kind every kid acquires at some time or another in his or her life. Ask a question, shake the ball, get a pithy answer. This, Julianna felt, was a metaphor for my future. I'd been too focused on my rehabilitation to apply for a job, though I was confident that Doris's letter of recommendation would open doors for me when the time was more propitious.

Our meal, if nothing else, was bountiful. The stuffy, black-uniformed waiters eventually cleared the carnage and reset the table for the dessert course. My father cleared his throat like he was starting a lawn mower, calling attention to the dangerous fact that he was about to speak.

"Charlie," he enunciated in that unnaturally deep voice he used as a harbinger to what he considered impending profundity. "You made it, kid. You graduated. Your Mom and I weren't so sure back in January. We're proud of you, right Lydia?" But before Mom could open her mouth, Dad had already resumed his speech. He paused briefly to consult a tattered scrap of paper he'd excavated from the pocket of his sports jacket. "In case you're wondering, it cost your family a grand total of $29,357.19 to put you through college. May your children some day return the favor," he said, chuckling, though the humor largely escaped me.

And then Dad looked earnestly at Julianna. "Young lady, I have a question for you." He inhaled deeply, preparing to launch. I clenched my teeth, expecting another highly indelicate inquiry into our sex lives. "Are you in it for the long haul with our new college graduate, Miss Julianna Darlington?"

"Come on, Dad, that's not fair!" I protested, secretly relieved that he hadn't chosen a more objectionable line of inquiry. Mom was embarrassed. Hermie snickered. Julianna, momentarily nonplussed, reached for my Magic 8-Ball, shook it, flipped it over, and announced the result.

"Signs point to yes," she said with a luminous smile.

-The End-

About the Author

ARTHUR D. HITTNER is the author of four critically acclaimed books: **Artist, Soldier, Lover, Muse** (Apple Ridge Press, 2017), a novel about an emerging young artist in New York City during the late Depression and prelude to World War II; **Four-Finger Singer and His Late Wife, Kate: A Novel of Life, Death & Baseball** (Apple Ridge Press, 2019), a dark, romantic comedy that transcends mortal boundaries; **The Caroline Paintings** (Apple Ridge Press, 2020), an art-sleuthing novel inspired by the saga of Andrew Wyeth's 'Helga Pictures'; and **Honus Wagner: The Life of Baseball's Flying Dutchman** (McFarland Publishing, 1996), recipient of the 1997 Seymour Medal awarded by the Society for American Baseball Research for the best work of baseball biography or history published during the preceding year. He has also written or co-written several art catalogues, a biography and catalogue raisonne on the artist Harold J. Rabinovitz, and articles on American art and artists for national publications including *Fine Art Connoisseur*, *Antiques & Fine Art* and *Maine Antique Digest*.

A retired attorney, Hittner spent nearly thirty-four years with the national law firm now known as Nixon Peabody LLP, resident in the firm's Boston office. He served as a trustee of Danforth Art (formerly the Danforth Museum of Art) in Framingham, Massachusetts and the Tucson Museum of Art in Tucson, Arizona. He was also a co-owner of the Lowell Spinners, a minor league professional baseball team affiliated with his beloved Boston Red Sox.

Married with two children and four grandchildren, Hittner currently divides his time between Oro Valley, Arizona and

Natick, Massachusetts. He is a graduate of Dartmouth College and Harvard Law School.

For additional information about the author's other books, please visit www.hittnerbooks.com.

Made in the USA
Middletown, DE
08 September 2020

17670442R10265